KARMA

Balancing the Scales, Book One

RJ BLAIN

Pen & Page Publishing

KARMA

BALANCING THE SCALES, BOOK ONE

Karma Johnson has spent her entire adult life working to become a member of FBI's Child Abduction Rapid Deployment team. She's earned her transfer to CARD, but when she's caught up in the kidnapping of an infant from a festival, she learns what it's like to be the victim. Pretending she's a teen keeps her alive while trying to get herself and the baby to safety.

But the kidnapping only scratches at the surface of a far more nefarious ' scheme, one that will test Karma's skills, her patience, her sanity, and her beliefs.

Chapter One

I KEPT a death grip on my purse and my duffel bag so the movers wouldn't run off with them when they did their last sweep of what used to be my home. It hadn't taken them long to remove what little I owned; it was noon and the maids had already arrived to make the place shine.

The only thing left to do was hand over the keys to the new owners, who were ten seconds from finding out I preferred talking to people I didn't like with my feet and hands rather than my mouth. Words, like secrets, were best kept close to the heart, especially when it came to business.

Unable to delay the inevitable, I hoisted my bag onto my shoulder, spun on a heel, and left home. The young couple waited at the bottom of the stairs, looking up at me as I eased my way down the rickety metal grate staircase. I hated the way I could see the ground ten feet below, and I hated the way the damned thing swayed just enough to make me think it was going to collapse.

If the young couple wanted the death trap, they were

welcome to it, and I'd gladly take the fifty grand in profits my obsessive restorations had earned me despite having only lived there for four years.

As long as I lived, I would never again own a home with a rickety metal staircase.

"Miss Johnson." Mrs. Avery, the proud wife of Mr. Avery the Third, pulled her hair up into a tight bun. "I hope we didn't interrupt anything."

"Just supervising the maid service, Mrs. Avery. They should be finished within the hour if you're ready to move in." I faked a smile.

After wrinkling her nose and giving a dainty little sniffle, Mrs. Avery replied, "It'll do. Thank you kindly for bringing them in."

Why did the buyer for my house have to be such a snoot? It's not like the couple was buying a mansion on the outskirts of the city. Baltimore had a lot of beautiful homes, especially tucked in the more picturesque parts of the city, but mine wasn't one of them. The townhouse was a little too close to the rougher parts of the city for my comfort.

Given a week, the riffraff would figure out there wasn't someone associated with the FBI living on the street. I had no idea what would happen without the FBI-marked cars prowling around the neighborhood, but it wasn't my problem.

I was moving on to different waters, finally advancing my career after five tough years combatting violent crimes in Baltimore.

"It's only polite." I located my keys, unclipping my personal keys to my home and offered them to the woman. "That's the last set. You have the rest from the closing. Little key is for the storage in the back, big one is for the primary front door, and the one with the red wrap is for the wall safe. Yellow is for the back door."

Mr. Avery the Third grabbed the keys from me. "Thanks, darlin'. Give your parents our regards. Seems right rotten for a little thing like you to have to deal with all the paperwork of sellin' a property."

At five one, I was little. To make matters worse, despite being twenty-nine, I looked more like I was sixteen, which was great for working with kids but not so good for getting their parents to take me seriously.

I made up for my weaknesses in other ways, including my ability to keep my cool despite wanting to drop kick the smug man in front of me. An assault charge would ruin my career, my life, and everything I had worked hard to build.

Sometimes life wasn't fair.

Smiling hurt, and so did saying, "Sure thing."

They weren't worth getting angry over. I flicked them a two finger salute, resisted the urge to flick a rude gesture at the pair, and headed for my car. Behind me, Mrs. Avery cleared her throat, a delicate sound. I came to a stop, sighed, and turned. "Something you need, ma'am?"

"You need to either cut that or dye it again."

Choices, choices: job and career or the assault charge that went with the satisfaction of smacking the woman to the concrete.

I lifted my hand to my hair, spun a lock around my finger, and kept on smiling. It wasn't *my* fault the ends faded to snow white after a while, ensuring my black hair was often tipped with white.

"Right. Have yourselves a nice day. Watch those steps." I stepped off the curb, circled my car, and unlocked it before sliding behind the wheel. I shifted into gear and pulled out of my spot so neither one of them could stop me from making my escape.

I needed to relax before my kickboxing match, else I'd run the risk of killing someone in the ring. While I competed in all three kickboxing divisions, full-contact was more my speed, and after the past few weeks, I needed to blow off some steam.

The Federal Hill Jazz and Blues festival would do. Good music was medicine for the soul, and the festival never disappointed.

WITH THE DAY so nice and the festival so popular, I had to park over a mile away. With my trunk loaded, I didn't have enough space for my bag or purse. I sighed and hefted them over my shoulder. They'd annoy me, but I wouldn't care so much once I found a place to sit down, relax, and listen to the tunes.

I wasn't about to leave my things on the back seat to entice thieves.

For mid-June, the weather was hotter than I liked, and I had broken a sweat by the time I made it to the fringe of the festival. I smiled at the sound of music in the air accompanied by the hum of laughter and conversation. It was as though a switch went off, and my agitation with the Averys vanished in a puff of smoke.

It wasn't rock and roll, but the music soothed my soul.

To complete my relaxation assignment, I needed a funnel cake and a snow cone, stat. I was convinced half of Baltimore showed up for the funnel cakes and stayed because of the snow cones, and I was as much a sucker for them as everyone else in the snaking line. I claimed a spot behind a black woman with a herd of six children, the youngest a baby in her arms, the eldest a disinterested teen determined to pretend she wasn't with the rest of them.

The girl caught a glimpse of my bag, and her dark eyes focused on the kickboxing patches I had sloppily sewn to it. "Nice."

"Thanks." I shifted the bag on my shoulder.

"Been kickboxing long?"

"A few years," I evaded. I'd been doing it since I was six. My adoptive parents had been determined to find an outlet for my incessant energy. I didn't like Pop's karate and I *really* didn't like Ma's yoga. Kickboxing had given me an outlet in a form I enjoyed, which was enough to make everyone happy, me included. "You?"

"Last year."

I grinned at meeting another sister of the ring. "Like it?"

"It's fun."

As soon as the two words left the teen's mouth, her mother turned and noticed me and my bag. A brilliant smile illuminated her face. "You're into sports, missy?"

"Sure. I'm competing tonight."

The teen's eyes widened. "You compete?"

Nothing trapped me in a conversation faster than an enthusiastic teen with a mother desperate for her kid to be interested in something—anything. Two different pairs of hopeful eyes watched me for two totally different reasons.

The mother's brows were also furrowed, probably from worry. Moms always worried when their little girls took an interest in something like kickboxing.

It was a rule.

"Full-contact, Super Flyweight," I reported. "Barely. I was Flyweight last year, but I put on some more muscle."

"Organized?" the girl blurted, her eyes fixed on my patches. I turned my body so she could get a better look at my bag.

"I'm pretty casual, but there's a WAKO event tonight. I qualified, so I'm going to step in the ring and see how it goes."

"No shit!"

"No shit," I agreed, grinning at her. "Name's Karma, but call me Kit Kat. You?"

"Kit Kat? That's badass."

"Thanks. It's what I go by in the ring. Most of the other competitors don't know my real name. The jokes. Ye God, the jokes."

The girl laughed. "Right. I'm Chloe."

"Nice to meet you, Chloe. Have you settled into a division yet?"

Chloe shook her head. "Too new, but I spar with the lightweights."

"We might be tiny, but we're fierce," I warned her, winking.

"But isn't it dangerous?" Chloe's mother asked, her tone worried.

"Not really. Bruises heal, and it's pretty uncommon to sustain a bad injury when learning. Instructors are pretty careful. The risk does tend to go up during serious competitions, though." I flashed the woman a grin. "We don't want to hurt each other during a spar."

"Still seems dangerous."

I dumped my bag on the ground, set my purse between

my feet, and unzipped the duffle, pulling out my gloves. "We wear protective gear. Put one on, ma'am."

Taking the baby out of her mother's arms, Chloe watched me, her eyes bugging out as though I were the Messiah returned to Earth. Chloe's mom took one of my gloves, sliding her hand into it. I helped her velcro it into place.

I held my hand to her, palm up. "Go ahead. Punch my hand with that glove on."

"Really?"

"Yeah. Punch me." The woman hit like a kitten, and it took all of my willpower not to burst out laughing. "As hard as you can."

"You sure about that, sweetie?"

"Yep."

Underneath the kitten was a lion, and she hit my palm hard enough I slid back a step. Laughing, I shook out my hand. "Hurt you any?"

"No."

"In beginner sparring, we start out nice and gentle. Lots of padding, lots of protection. Once she's more experienced, she'll be able to protect herself on the streets, too. Kickboxing is good for that. It's a martial art, after all. Maybe not your traditional style, but that's okay." I helped the woman out of my glove and stuffed it back in my bag. "Every little bit helps a young woman nowadays."

"You think so?"

"Know so."

"Huh." Chloe's mother crossed her arms over her chest and looked down her nose at me. "How long to be useful?"

If Chloe didn't start breathing soon, she'd probably faint. I understood protective parents; my job was to help worried parents find their missing children. What I didn't understand was when parents resisted giving their kids a way to protect themselves.

"Pretty quick. If she's fit, she'll start kicking and punches fast. Every move can be used against an opponent. She'll learn to take hits. Defend herself." I shrugged. "It's helped me. When you're small like me, you need all the help you can get. Won't help against a gun, but close up? It'll make a huge difference."

"Huh."

The younger children milling around the woman's feet chose that moment to burst into activity, squealing at each other and running in tight circles, bouncing against the others in line.

Festivals were never boring. I grinned.

With a low cry, Chloe's mom dove into the fray while Chloe stared with wide eyes. "Shit." The girl looked like she wanted to help, but her hands were filled with her infant sibling.

"I can hold the baby if you'd like," I offered.

A second later, I had both arms full of squirming baby, who stared up at me with huge brown eyes, cooing and stretching up her little arms. A girl, if the pink onesie she wore was any indication. Chloe followed her mother, grabbing hold of a toddler and yanking him to her side.

As always, when trouble showed up, so did an audience.

The kid Chloe wrangled struggled and opened his mouth, probably to shriek like a banshee. I winced in anticipation, but Chloe clapped her hand over half his face before he made a sound, hissing something that put the fear of a trip straight to hell into him.

Containing her brother with one hand, Chloe made a grab for the next one, a little older and a lot slyer than his sibling. He dodged, sticking out his tongue and blowing raspberries.

All in all, holding the quiet baby was the better end of the child wrangling deal. I shifted the girl in my arms, and she cooed at me again.

"Who is a cute baby?" I murmured, adjusting my hold on her so I could wiggle my fingers for her to play with. She reached for me, her pudgy fingers closing around one of mine. "Yes, you are."

As fast as the chaos had begun, Chloe and her mother reined it in. Both heaved sighs of relief, and Chloe's mother turned to me. "Always surprisin' how much trouble six kids and one funnel cake stand can be."

I nodded my agreement. Ma and Pop had always had their hands full with a house full of fosters; I'd been an infant when they had taken me in. I'd been the lucky one, the one they had actually adopted instead of being a part of the constant stream of kids seeking a forever home.

"You've been around babies before." Chloe's mother grinned at me. "She's fussy, my Annabelle, but she's taken a right likin' to ya."

"I like kids." I grinned down at Annabelle. "She's really cute."

Babies always seemed to come in two types; adorable or horrific. Annabelle scored full points in the precious angel department with her big eyes, her smooth, rounded cheeks, and her friendly smile.

"You here on your own?"

I nodded. "Figured I'd enjoy the music before the competition tonight."

"Will the competition be violent?"

Lying didn't help anyone, and it wasn't a secret kickboxing could get rough. I shrugged. "It's a martial art. They're always a bit violent. Full contact is rough, but they're also running light contact stuff tonight, too. I can probably swing some tickets for you and your kids if you want in."

"Chloe? You want to go?"

Chloe's eyes widened so much I worried they'd pop right out of her head. "You mean it?"

"Sure, baby. We don't got nothin' goin' on tonight. Where's the competition?"

I told her where the sports center was located, gave her details on when the matches would start, and how she could get tickets.

To my surprise, Chloe's mother pulled out a cell from her pocket. It took me several moments to realize she was buying tickets online. "I'll print 'em when I get home."

"Nice. Don't know how late you're staying, but if I'm able to get away from the match, I'll try to find you and say hello." I meant it, too.

A little kindness went a long way, and Chloe seemed like the sort of girl who needed a subtle nudge in the right direction to stay out of trouble. At least with kickboxing, if she got into trouble, she'd be able to defend herself. The thought of any one of the family becoming a victim made me shiver.

"We'd like that. I'll probably leave the littles with their pa; only sport he likes is football."

In Baltimore, there were two types of sports enthusiasts: baseball and football. Anything else was on the fringe. That would be a battle Chloe would have to fight on her own. I chuckled. "Well, if Chloe decides to pursue kickboxing, if she ever decides to hit the field, she'll be a force to be reckoned with. Kickboxing chicks are tough."

"Your pa would like that."

The line shuffled forward, and I gave my purse a shove in the right direction so I wouldn't disturb Annabelle. Chloe grabbed my bag and carried it to the next stop. I smiled my thanks. "The gear's not too bad, either. Compared to other sports, that is."

"The class has loaner equipment I use," Chloe admitted.

"I got a spare set of gloves you can have. I think they'll fit." The spares were brand new, but I could replace them easily enough. I nudged my bag with my toe. "Hope you don't mind red. I've got extra wraps you're welcome to, too."

Chloe's mouth dropped open. The gleam of unshed tears made her eyes glisten. "No shit?"

"No shit, Chloe. I'm not using them. Always glad to help out a fellow kickboxing chick. Sure, we can be mean, but we stick together."

"You're—" Chloe's gaze snapped to a point behind me, and her mother gasped. My entire body tensed. With a baby in my arms, I didn't dare spin and kick like I wanted; I couldn't risk hurting Annabelle.

The cold ring of a gun barrel pressed to my temple.

"Keep quiet and calm and nobody gets hurt. Got it?"

I adjusted my hold on Annabelle. The instant a chance presented itself, I'd take it. My first priority was the baby's safety.

My world narrowed to the feel of steel on my skin and the presence of someone tall behind me. I glanced at the angle of his weapon arm. Not tall, average. White male. Tanned and muscular enough to be a real problem if I had to fight him. His arm flexed, and the gun dug into me.

If I moved, I'd probably end up with a hole in my head.

Out of the corner of my eye, steel glinted. A second

gunman, a white male with his face covered by a ski mask, had his weapon aimed at Chloe and her family. "Back up."

Chloe stared, her mouth hanging open. Her dark skin had a grayish pallor.

"Do it, Chloe," I whispered. If the girl acted, we'd both end up dead.

She swallowed and eased her way back several steps, as did her mother. They kept the other kids behind them.

"That's right. Nice and easy," the man behind me said. His arm curled around my throat, and strong fingers dug into my shoulder. If he wanted to put me in a sleeper hold, he had me in the perfect position to do so without breaking a sweat. "Everybody just stay calm and nobody gets hurt."

I clenched my teeth, forcing myself to take slow, deep breaths. I scanned the crowd; there were a lot of witnesses, and most of them had phones out. Some were taking pictures or videos. Others had their phones half-lifted to their ears as though uncertain whether or not to place that all-important call to the police.

Every second mattered.

"Okay, little girl. Back up slow and easy and you'll walk out of this alive," my captor ordered.

With all my identification in my purse, including my FBI badge, pretending to be a teen was likely my best bet; an adult woman was a lot bigger risk to a kidnapper than a cooperative teen. I slid my foot backwards until the back of my heel bumped against his toe. Step by step, he forced me back, gun still held to my head.

One wrong move, and I'd end up with a bullet in my skull. As long as I stayed alive, I could do *something*.

Corpses couldn't help anyone.

Chapter Two

I LOCATED three gunmen in the crowd by the time my kidnapper had dragged me through the festival to the street. Uniformed officers watched, but with at least three weapons pointed at me and Annabelle, they kept their distance.

Their caution saved my life. I knew it, the cops knew it, and my captors knew it. It saved Annabelle's life, too.

Hostage negotiation was a perilous line of work. One wrong word could get someone killed. I'd been there too many times, standing where the police were standing, watching and waiting for the perfect moment to save a life.

Sometimes it worked. Too often, it didn't.

Remaining calm and cooperating would keep me alive longer. If I put up a fight, it was entirely possible one of the gunmen would take the shot. Violence would escalate. If Annabelle wasn't killed in the opening volley, the police reacting to the crack-bang of a gun discharging would elevate her risk of death substantially.

Worse, someone in the crowd might get shot, too.

The cops knew what they were doing. They worked their way between the civilians, moving with quiet urgency, ordering people to back away. There were a few panicked screams, but the gunmen kept moving, keeping their weapons trained on me.

I had no idea who they were, but they were professionals. They were dressed in clothing that gave away their gender and race, but the relevant details were hidden behind ski masks and shades. They had to be sweltering in the baggy clothing, which also helped them hide their physical builds and weights.

As an FBI field agent with a history in violent crimes, I had enemies; it came with the job. Until I knew who the target was, I didn't dare do anything. If I was the target, Annabelle's life would likely end the instant my captors were clear of the festival grounds. If she was the target, my life was likely forfeit the instant I was no longer useful.

If I was the target, I might be able to sell my cooperation for her life. I could talk them into leaving her on the street to be found. There were options.

Step by step, I was guided backwards through the parting crowd to the road. A car door opened behind me. Without easing his hold on me, my captor dragged me inside. Annabelle whimpered, which I recognized as a precursor to crying.

The instant my feet were in the car, a dark SUV, one of the accomplices slammed the door shut and dove into the front passenger seat. Tires squealed and the vehicle shot away. I winced at the thump of wheels bouncing over the curb.

Annabelle wailed. My entire body tensed.

Instead of shooting, my captor kept his gun aimed at

my head. "Buckle up, little girl. If you cooperate, you go home alive. Got it? Make yourself useful and keep the kid quiet."

I swallowed, jerked my head in a nod, and adjusted how I held Annabelle. Grabbing my seatbelt, I pulled it over my body and buckled it.

I held Annabelle close to my chest, resting her tiny chin on my shoulder. I patted her back, rocking a little in my effort to soothe her, whispering, "Come on, baby girl. Be quiet."

Little hands clutched at me, and I supported the back of her head. Her wails quieted, although she still whimpered. Shivering as the reality of my situation crashed down on me, I stared out the window, watching for landmarks, signs, and anything else I could use to chart my path.

I leaned towards the window to glimpse at the side mirror. Two black SUVs tailed the car, and dread cramped my stomach.

By using multiple vehicles, all the same make and model with their windows tinted so dark it was impossible for anyone to tell who was inside, splitting up and spreading law enforcement resources would be easy. When a third dark SUV joined the lineup, I clenched my teeth.

Someone had gone through a lot of trouble to pull off a very public kidnapping. The driver floored the gas, tearing through intersection after intersection. I flinched at every red light, especially when the driver swerved to avoid collisions.

The four cars hit the exit for I-95 fast. Instead of merging, the vehicles kept to the shoulder until a gap opened. At midday, traffic was lighter than I liked, giving them ample room to swerve across lanes. The speed they were going would ensure a quick death if we hit anything. I fought my instinct to close my eyes and wait for the inevitable.

"We split at the interchange for the Beltway," my captor ordered.

"Roger," the driver replied. A moment later, I heard him relay the orders over a radio. Even if someone from the police or FBI tapped into their radio frequency, the orders were relayed in such a way any listeners would only know something would happen at the interchange.

With four SUVs to chase, pursuit would be difficult. With so many dark-colored SUVs on the road, finding the right one would be like looking for a needle in a haystack, especially if the drivers dropped to the speed limit and hid among other cars.

Annabelle whimpered again, and I cooed at her. The driver began relaying distances to the interchange, which puzzled me. No one else spoke on the radio, which dashed my hope of rescue.

Silence kept anyone from learning their plans, including me.

It didn't take long to reach the Beltway. One car kept going, one headed for the Beltway backtracking towards Washington, while the car I was in headed for the stretch circling north of Baltimore tailed by the fourth SUV. As soon as we hit the Beltway, at least three more dark SUVs joined the chaos and scattered into traffic.

I wanted to whimper like the baby I held. Four cars was bad enough, but with at least seven playing a game of cat and mouse with the police, our chances of being recovered plummeted.

The vehicles all slowed to the speed limit. No matter how

many times I checked the side mirror, I saw no sign of flashing lights to indicate we were being pursued.

"We split again at I-70."

"Yes, sir."

Sir? I risked a look at my captor. He still held his gun pointed at me. The way the barrel faced, if he pulled the trigger, he ran a high risk of hitting Annabelle. Eliminating wrestling him for the weapon as an option, I took in my situation detail by detail. Three men in the car with me, all likely armed with at least one gun each. The fact so many vehicles were involved warned me it was a group, as professional as they got. Their accomplices were likely armed.

The odds were not in my favor.

I-70 headed west; while it continued east, it came to an end and wouldn't give my kidnappers a viable route of escape. By going west, it was possible to either skip north into central Pennsylvania or continue to western Pennsylvania. If they took I-68 to I-79, they'd reach West Virginia. Either route gave them a lot of options.

The instant we crossed state lines, the FBI would be all over the case, bringing in a Child Abduction Rapid Deployment team specialized in tracking down kids, and I had no doubt they'd be assigned to Annabelle's kidnapping. CARD lived and breathed to rescue kids, and I was no different.

If I lived long enough, I'd be a member of CARD myself; technically, I already was a part of the team. I'd completed training, I had my assignment, and I was already on call.

My phone was probably ringing in my purse, since the FBI knew I was in Baltimore and could start work immediately. The irony made me sigh. If I hadn't been kidnapped with Annabelle, I'd be working with the local police, doing something productive. Instead, I was seated beside my kidnapper playing a frightened teen.

I wasn't often grateful for my youthful appearance.

It was time for me to get my head out of my ass and do something useful. I'd be taking a risk, but if I could develop some form of relationship with my captors, professionals or not, they might hesitate to pull the trigger.

I drew several deep breaths to steady my nerves. No matter what, I had to keep my voice quiet, act like I was frightened, and cooperate. Pushing the limits would only increase the chance of dying before I could either escape or be rescued.

Whispering worked. Whispering didn't alarm people; it conveyed fear. Swallowing, I asked, "What do you want with us?"

"You're just a bonus, sweetheart. Behave yourself and you'll walk away safe and sound. Understood?"

"Yes, sir," I mumbled.

"Good. You have a job. You do it well, you'll walk away."

I had to give him credit; he was a good liar. Instead of spitting in his face for feeding me his bullshit like I wanted to, I replied, "Okay."

"You take care of the baby. That's it. You take care of the baby, keep her nice and quiet as you can, and do what you're told. That's your job."

"Okay."

"Good girl. Your name?"

"Kat." Two could play at the lying game, and I had a feeling if I told him my name was Karma he'd think I was lying.

"Alright, kitten. You just sit tight and behave yourself."

I jerked my head in a nod, scooting towards the door. The

fear response would be what he expected. While he didn't lower his gun, he relaxed. My new position gave me a better view of the side mirror.

The lack of pursuit disappointed me, but I wasn't surprised, either. Tracking one car was child's play. With so many accomplices, it'd take a miracle for the police or FBI to find us. The cold, professional side of me appreciated their skill.

It was a nightmare scenario, the type of job no one in CARD wanted to face. Any kidnapping was bad, but when the perps had resources, ambition, and strategy, the chances of recovery were slim.

The CARD team assigned to Annabelle's case would try, but without divine intervention, they'd fail. If I believed in statistics, and I did, Annabelle and I were already dead. We just didn't know it yet.

I REALLY WANTED MY GUN. With my gun, I'd feel a lot more secure and a lot less like a victim. I was in the business of helping victims, not walking around in their shoes. Instead of the constant rush of battling time, I had to wait.

There was a lot of waiting in a crisis situation, but with the FBI, the wait was filled with work. There was always *something* to do. Leads had to be checked. Information had to be reviewed. Evidence had to be logged. Decisions had to be made.

As the victim, I waited with nothing but my own thoughts for company. The silence between the kidnappers offered me hope. I knew nothing about them. As long as that continued, they could afford to release me.

If they assumed I was a teen, they likely believed there was nothing useful I could tell investigators about their operations. What I had gleaned from their methods wasn't much since their use of multiple cars had been exposed from the start. However, the fact they had called in extra cars at exits along the Beltway would help the FBI in the future. If I kept my mouth shut, my kidnappers wouldn't have a clue I knew anything.

My initial impression of my captors matched their behavior; they thought I was a teen. Teens probably counted like kids to them, and they didn't seem eager to splatter my brains all over the leather interior of the SUV.

That was something at least.

Time lost meaning to me; without my phone or watch, I drifted from moment to moment. Distance became my benchmark. After merging onto I-70, my kidnappers opted for I-68 and a run for West Virginia. Had the cops already called the FBI?

If they had gone through my purse for my identification, they probably had. My badge was clipped to my wallet. As long as they checked through my things, they'd know I had been taken.

In the chaos, would the regular police remember—or care? With a mother who had watched her baby be stolen right out from under her nose, they were probably distracted. Once CARD was involved, my purse would become evidence. They'd find my badge. If the cops were smart, they'd assume I was a suspect.

With an agent involved as a victim, how would the FBI react?

My training hadn't included the improbable case of being kidnapped along with an innocent.

We were somewhere in the wilds of West Virginia when Annabelle started to cry, and no matter what I did, she wouldn't quiet. I had my suspicions her problem involved a messy diaper and a serious case of hungry.

Infants had limited modes of operation, and unless they weren't feeling well, they were easy enough to understand.

I felt my captor's gaze on me, questioning me without words.

"She needs something to eat and a diaper change," I whispered although I wanted to scream.

"Pull over," he ordered. "Get the bag out of the back. This is how this is going to work, sweetheart. You're going to take care of the baby. Try to run, try to do anything other than take care of her, and I'll put a bullet between your pretty eyes. Understood, kitten?"

"Yes, sir."

"Good girl. Keep cooperating. I'm a man of my word. You do what you're told. If you do, you go home." The man kept watching me, and I had the unnerving feeling he was grinning behind his mask. "You do have really pretty eyes, too. Would be a shame if we had to rob the world of a girl with amber eyes."

I shuddered and was grateful when my side door opened. A blue baby bag was dropped on the floorboard at my feet. Adjusting my hold on Annabelle so I could unbuckle my seatbelt, I considered the chances of making a run for the woods.

The twenty feet may as well have been miles. Bullets traveled fast, and with at least two guns pointed at me, I had no chance of making it. Sighing, I slid out of the SUV and went to work.

The kidnappers had come prepared for an infant,

confirming Annabelle had been their original target. In addition to diapers and the basic necessities, there were bottles with formula premixed, and a collection of toys, and pacifiers. The supplies offered me hope they intended to keep her alive for a while. Once I had her cleaned and changed, I sifted through the bag to get an idea of how long they meant to keep her.

"Looking for something, kitten?"

"Baby oil," I improvised, lifting the tiny bottle, which I had already put to good use. "Not a lot here. Not a lot of powder, either. No thermometer." I bit my lip, wondering what else I could add to my list. "She'll need shampoo, a little brush, a comb, and a light blanket. She'll smother if she stays in this onesie all the time."

"Get back in the car."

I packed everything back into the bag, shoved it to the side, and got back in, holding Annabelle so I could feed her. When done, I cradled her against my shoulder with a towel under her so I could burp her. Compared to the babies my parents had coming in and out of their house, Annabelle was a dream. Once she was burped, she dropped right to sleep, and I envied her.

When—if—she grew up, she wouldn't have any memories of the day gunmen stole her from her mother and siblings. Her mother would remember, Chloe would remember, but Annabelle wouldn't understand the terror. At most, it'd be a hazy recollection, more like a dream than reality. If she was anything like me, Annabelle wouldn't recall anything before the age of four or five.

It'd be a mercy.

I made myself as comfortable as I could with a gun pointed at my head, watched the road signs, and tried to guess where we were going. West was the most I could deduce. My captors hadn't said a word about directions, roads, or anything of use since we had merged onto I-70 outside of Baltimore.

I settled into a waiting pattern, forcing myself to relax and let my body rest when I wasn't taking care of Annabelle. If a chance presented itself, I would be ready.

Chapter Three

I HATED SMART KIDNAPPERS. I especially hated kidnappers who understood the limitations of the human body, particularly mine. They pushed me to the edge of my endurance, and when I was too damned exhausted to do more than keep my eyes open, they finally stopped for a much-needed break at a large travel center somewhere deep in either West Virginia or Kentucky. I wasn't sure which way was up anymore, let alone which highway we were on.

Dehydration had my throat burning for water. My steps were unsteady. All three of my kidnappers removed their ski masks, which guaranteed I wouldn't be leaving their custody alive. I knew what they looked like.

"This is how this is going to work, kitten. You're going to go into the ladies' room. I'll be waiting for you. No funny business. I'll have the baby here. You don't want her hurt, do you?"

I shook my head.

"Good, kitten. You go wash your face, smile like a good

girl, and come right back out. If anyone asks who you're with, just say your Uncle Phil is waiting for you. Behave. You'll get a nice hot meal into you, and everything will go nice and easy. Understood?"

"Yes, sir."

"Good. Move it. No detours, and don't even think about asking to borrow a phone. I'll pop you in the head so fast you won't know what hit you before you're dead."

"I got it, I got it," I hissed.

My annoyance made 'Uncle Phil' grin. True to his word, he stalked me all the way to the bathroom, which was empty of any possible help. I took my time, leaning against the bathroom sink with my forehead against the mirror. All I wanted was to sleep, but fear and anxiety crawled under my skin.

If I slept, would they get rid of me when I had no chance of defending myself? Groaning, I grudgingly took my captor's advice to wash my face. My pale complexion had turned stark white, and no amount of scrubbing brought any color back to my face, not even a hint of red.

My eyes, at least, remained clear.

Stifling a yawn, I staggered out of the bathroom. Phil waited, Annabelle sleeping quietly in his arms. Handing her over, he grunted and tilted his head in the direction of the food court. His two accomplices met us halfway there, carrying several large paper bags.

They found a booth tucked in a corner, crammed me against the wall, and fed me tasteless burgers and fries until I couldn't force another bite. When I stared at the leftovers without seeing them, I was aware of the men moving.

"The kitten ready to go?" the driver asked.

Something about his question reminded me I had a job to

do. I needed to profile him so I could remember his face if I did somehow survive. I stared at him, careful to keep my expression blank and uncomprehending.

All things considered, it was pretty easy to let exhaustion keep me looking as numb as I felt.

The man had dark eyes, dark hair, tanned complexion. High cheek bones. Probable Hispanic background with a healthy mix of American Caucasian. Once I had him categorized, I did the same to the other man, who was probably a relative.

Phil chuckled. "She'll do. Let's get back on the road before someone notices us."

Once I slid out of the booth, I was given Annabelle, who remained sound asleep despite having been moved around so much. I followed after Phil and was flanked by his two accomplices.

Every other stop, usually to change and feed the baby, I had sat in the back on the passenger's side of the car. Before I could climb in with Annabelle, Phil took her out of my arms. I tensed, my eyes widening.

"You know how to drive, kitten?"

"I do," I whispered.

"Good. You're driving."

I gaped at him. What sort of idiot made the hostage drive? Being the driver opened a world of possibilities for me, assuming they didn't shoot me the instant I deviated from their plan. What sort of idiot made the *exhausted* hostage drive? "Are you nuts?"

Laughter answered me. The car keys were thrust into my hand. "It's only until we cross the Kentucky border, kitten. If they have a road block, you're going to talk us through it. Got it? After that, you can get some sleep."

I hung my head, sighed, and admitted defeat. "Yes, sir."

The SUV wasn't much different from the ones the FBI used. I swallowed a yawn, started the car, and gripped the wheel so hard my knuckles whitened. "Where am I going?"

"Westbound. I'll tell you when we need to turn if necessary. Keep it between the lines and try not to fall asleep behind the wheel. No car seat, you know. Wouldn't want to hurt the baby, right?"

"Right." I put the car in reverse, backed out of the spot, and navigated through the travel center maze to the onramp for the highway. I kept my speed just below the speed limit, activating the cruise control so I could keep my foot hovering over the brake.

Phil grunted, which I took to be approval because I couldn't handle the thought of him being angry at my driving skills. "Parents are probably missing you by now, kitten."

I wondered about that; had the FBI notified them? It was likely. They were my emergency contacts. "Probably."

"Tell me about them."

I was too tired to feel much satisfaction at the man's questioning. I had to remind myself to form the relationship. The more he knew about me, the less likely it was he'd pull the trigger. A moment of hesitation could save my life.

If I became more than just a victim, I had a chance to get out alive.

If I survived, I might be able to save Annabelle, too.

"Sure. Pop's an accountant. Ma's a fashion designer. They live in Vermont. Used to live in Georgia. I moved to Baltimore for school."

"School?"

"College." FBI training counted. It was a lot tougher than

any college I had been to, and I had several degrees chosen specifically to up my chances to join CARD. It had worked, too. "Graduated early."

"Good for you. What are you studying?"

Doubting criminal law would impress the criminal very much, I fell back on a pleasure minor I had taken to keep me busy. "English Lit."

"Not a very useful degree there, kitten. You should consider taking it as a minor."

What sort of kidnapper made college recommendations to their victim? Puzzled, I forced my attention to the road. "Sure. It's not set in stone yet, anyway."

"Not until after your second year, right?"

"Yeah. First two years are to fill up the electives and other required courses." I had spent seven years in college and university to build my resume so I could join the FBI at twenty-three, which was the youngest I could apply. The first two years I had spent doing just that, filling up on every single required course I could. "I've heard it before. English Lit's a dead end career, but it's a gatekeeper, too."

"Sure is, kitten. You can find a lot of work if you pick a good major to go on top of an English minor—even a lit one. A business degree with writing skills could take you pretty far. There's lots of room for a smart woman who can handle a legal document."

"You're weird," I muttered, shaking my head. Any other day, I would have been in the fast lane, blowing by the turtle in an SUV, but I was too tired to risk it. It took too much of my focus to keep the car between the lines. Night driving was tiring enough, and I was at my limit.

"Why do you think that, kitten?"

"Aren't you going to rape me, kill me, and toss my body in

a gully somewhere?" All three men burst into laughter. I scowled, clenching my teeth. "What's so funny?"

"I'm a man of my word. You cooperate, you go home, safe, sound, and untouched. I wasn't paid to kill or rape you. Wasn't paid to kill the baby, either. I will if I have to, but I'd rather not have to. Get me?"

I squeezed the wheel tighter. During my career with the FBI, I'd seen a lot of violent crimes; it was mandatory before acceptance into CARD. "Okay."

"Good. We're ten minutes from the Kentucky border. If there's a stop, you convince them we're family. Got it?"

"I don't have my license with me."

"Figure something out then."

I winced. The likelihood of there being a checkpoint into Kentucky was slim to none. I hadn't seen a single sign of pursuit. My kidnappers hadn't used the radio. They hadn't even made a single phone call. Even if the plate number, make, and model of the vehicle had been broadcasted in an Amber Alert, it was unlikely anyone would find us.

Thanks to the heavy crowds at the Federal Hill Jazz and Blues Festival, our pictures were probably in circulation. If there was a checkpoint, the cat would be out of the bag. I could work the conversation in my favor without tipping my kidnappers off.

If the officer was an FBI agent, I'd be golden. There would be a solid chance of rescue or escape.

Luck wasn't with me. A sign welcomed us to Kentucky, and the blockade I had been foolish enough to hope for wasn't there. I kept driving, biting my lip until it hurt to keep myself awake.

"Pull over," Phil ordered.

I obeyed, putting the SUV in park. I slumped over the wheel, resting my forehead against the leather.

"Don't you worry yourself a bit, kitten. Everything will be just fine for you." Phil paused and sounded far too cheerful when he added, "If you keep behaving, that is."

"I got it," I mumbled under my breath, unbuckled my seat belt, and opened the door. I had no recollection of them adding a car seat behind the driver's side. I ended up sitting between Annabelle and Phil with a good view of the center console so I could watch the minutes tick by one by one.

I WAS ASTOUNDED to learn it was possible to reach Denver, Colorado from Baltimore, Maryland within twenty-four hours by car. Instead of heading into the city, Phil drove into the mountains to a remote cabin. I hadn't learned the names of the other two men. Their care with their words impressed me.

It was as if they actually meant to keep me alive and were protecting me by refusing to give me any information of real substance.

Annabelle grew fussier and fussier with each hour, and I didn't blame her. I'd be fussy, too. Car seats couldn't be comfortable for the number of hours she had spent in one. I did my best to soothe her, but I was so tired I could barely see straight.

I carried her into the cabin, halting as I took in the rustic decor. A baby crib with monitor waited by the couch along with a traditional baby carrier and enough packs of diapers and bulk containers of formula to last through a siege.

I was both horrified and reassured by the preparations.

No one who intended to kill an infant would spend so much time or money on caring for one.

However, the amount of supplies warned me they were in for the long haul if necessary. Someone had spent a small fortune preparing for Annabelle's kidnapping. What I didn't understand was why. Chloe and her mother hadn't looked rich; kickboxing gloves weren't too expensive, and as far as sports went, the investment to participate was minimal, nonexistent if using loaned gear.

What did they have that the kidnappers wanted?

Targeting Annabelle made sense; Chloe or one of the younger kids would be harder to keep hidden. An infant wasn't hard to hide. Taking me was a factor I didn't understand either.

"Go on in, kitten. Why don't you feed the baby and get her ready for bed? Everything you need should be there."

At least Phil wasn't waving his gun in my face. The weapon was holstered at his side in easy reach. I carried Annabelle to the couch and went to work. I needed to wait until the three men were no longer on their guard. If I could get a gun away from them, escape was possible. If I could disable them, I'd be able to take Annabelle and make a run for it.

"What's going to happen now?" I whispered while I changed Annabelle's diaper and took my time wiping her down to make sure she didn't have a rash.

"We wait. When we get what we want, you and the baby will be left where you can be found. You go home, and that's it."

"And if you don't get what you want?"

Phil's silence was all I needed to know. If negotiations for ransom failed, the FBI would find my body along with Annabelle's. My gut told me there'd be no paid ransom.

What could Annabelle's parents have that a well-organized group of professional kidnappers would want? Mercenaries. I settled the baby in the crib, covered her with a lightweight blanket, and sat on the couch.

"You don't seem surprised."

"I watch television. I kinda have a few guesses on what will happen."

"Good. I won't have to explain it to you, then. Out of my hands, kitten. Behave yourself. It's the only chance you have."

He was probably right, but I had little to lose and a lot to gain, and I wasn't about to quit before I even had a chance to get started. The first thing I needed was sleep. Once I was fresh, I'd start looking for weaknesses in the trio's patterns. Once I established the break in their habit, I'd turn it to my advantage.

Unless there had been witnesses, the FBI would be challenged to locate us. The SUV's tinted windows would have kept the curious onlookers from catching a look at me, and they had been careful about all our stops. I couldn't count on CARD to locate us.

I yawned, watching my three captors move through the cabin, checking everything over. The first thing they did was slice through the phone cord. Ten minutes of work, and I'd have a functioning phone again. If they were truly smart, they'd damage the jack. I could fix a phone cord. Peeling back the wires and twisting the right wires together would give me a connection long enough to call the police.

Faking disappointment, I kept watching them. They gathered the knives and took them to the SUV.

I really hated smart kidnappers, especially the ones who made errors I couldn't capitalize on—at least yet.

Once they did a top to bottom search of the cabin, Phil made himself comfortable on the armchair while the other two men vanished into the bedrooms down the hall. "Looks like it's you and me, kitten. Get some sleep. You didn't get a whole lot in the car, did you?"

There was a blanket draped over the back of the couch, and I snatched it, wrapping up in it. If I wanted to escape, I needed to be fresh. I needed sleep.

I needed to wait.

Hating myself for my inability to act, I curled up on the couch, lying on my side so I could react if Annabelle needed me. It didn't take long for my exhaustion to pull me under.

Chapter Four

LIKE A WELL-OILED MACHINE, Phil and his associates rotated guard duty. There was always someone alert watching me and Annabelle. While the cabin had a television, Phil removed the batteries from the remote as a clear indication he didn't want me watching anything. He also removed my ability to determine time. Minutes, hours, and days melted into one another, the monotony only broken by the few times I managed to fall asleep and the rotation of my guards.

My kidnappers had cut themselves off from everyone, including their conspirators. The world went on without us. Our isolation prevented me from knowing what information had been released about the kidnapping.

In a way, the arrangement worked to my advantage. As long as the television remained off, there was no chance of them discovering I was an FBI agent unless someone told them. While they had cell phones, no one was contacting them.

It was smart. By avoiding phone communications, the

FBI couldn't track them. Without a name or number to work with, cell towers couldn't be used to pinpoint their location.

I really, really hated smart kidnappers.

Without any other options, I waited, taking care of Annabelle and playing with her. The thought such a happy, easy to care for baby might become yet another statistic infuriated me.

That I'd become one, too, didn't help matters any. My parents had adopted me a year after their baby had been kidnapped. I'd been abandoned, left with a tiny golden locket with my first name etched on the back.

Ma had viewed it as the universe paying them back for fostering so many kids. I was Karma, and the rules of karma were simple enough. All the good given out would pay itself back. I was supposed to be the good karma paid back for the little boy they had lost.

A CARD team had given my parents closure, finding their baby's body long after his death. I'd been six when they had come to the door. The team of four had all showed up. Watching four men break down and cry for the child they hadn't been able to save had stayed with me all the way through high school.

It had chased me through college, too. It had chased me right until I had showed up for my first day of FBI training, one of the rare candidates who wasn't selected through law enforcement positions of one form or another.

It kept me going through my first year when I found out just how violent crimes could get. Whenever I thought about quitting, I remembered the faces of four men who had fought for Ma and Pops's little boy and came back with a body to show for their years of work.

If I was going to go out, I wanted it to be because I had

fought that battle, wagering everything to make a difference. Ma and Pops would understand.

I was Karma, and I wanted to be that good bit of fortune for Annabelle, Chloe, her mother, and the rest of their family. Putting my life on the line was part of the job.

I just hadn't expected to be doing it so soon.

A phone rang, and I almost jumped out of my skin at the sound. Phil answered, "What do you got for me?" There was a long moment of silence, then the man turned his head and looked at me. "Come again?"

I tensed, my eyes widening at his scrutiny. The blood drained out of my face at the way he frowned.

Phil snorted. "The kitten I grabbed with our target might be sixteen or seventeen. She's declawed, too. Been doing a good job of taking care of the infant. She doesn't know our names. All she's got is a good look at our faces."

Good behavior paid off sometimes, and while I forced my eyes to remain wide, I relaxed a little. By defending his decision to keep me alive, Phil had crossed a line. I went from an easy kill to someone to hesitate over.

A real professional would finish the job if forced, but I might be able to buy myself some time. Was the caller telling Phil he had grabbed an FBI agent? Or was it a harmless inquiry on the unexpected extra?

I waited and held my breath.

"The current plan? I'll dump the kitten with the infant. The kitten seems smart enough to take care of things. I'll put her near a police station and let her figure it out. By the time she gets there, we'll be long gone."

Phil sighed. "I figured as much. Give it two days. Call me back with an update. If there's no progress, I'll take care of it."

Hanging up, the man returned his cell to his pocket. "You better start praying that little girl's parents decide to cooperate, kitten."

"Is this about money?" I whispered.

"No, sweetheart. It's not about money."

I clenched my teeth. "Kat. My name's Kat. If you're going to kill me, at least have the decency to call me by my name."

"Kitten's got teeth," he replied, amused. "Short for Katherine? I'd rather not, but business is business, little lady."

Business was business, and if I got a hold of his gun, I'd show him he wasn't the only one willing to kill during a job. "Yeah, it's short for Katherine," I lied. "How'd a nice guy like you get into something like this?"

Phil laughed. "Long story, Kat."

I rose from the couch and paced across the room and down the hall. Both bedroom doors were closed, and I heard at least one of the men snoring. I paced back to the front door, staring out into the mountain forest. "Not like I'm doing anything else. The baby's asleep."

Annabelle had been put down for her nap, and if my guess was right, she'd be quiet for another two hours. The car seat, which could double as a carrier, was beside the crib along with the bag.

If I could down Phil, I could be out the door in one to two minutes. They left the front door unlocked. I had no idea where the SUV keys were, which meant I'd be on foot, but if I could take him out quietly, I'd have some time.

Their first mistake had been their effort to keep me in good health. I was in good shape; I had to be to survive in the FBI as a special agent. Even loaded with an infant and her bag, I'd be able to run for a long time before I had to stop.

"The money, of course. Doesn't hurt I'm good at it. Once

we're done with this job, we'll disappear and no one will find us. Sorry, kitty cat. That's just the way it goes with this line of work."

Phil's position on the armchair would make downing him difficult. I stalked my way to the kitchen and sighed at the empty state of the coffee maker. Anything I could potentially use as a weapon was kept high up, even the tin of coffee.

"Can I have some coffee?" I hadn't asked for anything since I'd been grabbed.

"Sure, kitten."

I stepped out of the kitchen to let him by. The instant he passed me, I spun and kicked, smashing my foot against the back of his neck. Without waiting to see if that was enough to knock him out, I followed up with a punch to his head, cracking the side of my fist against his temple.

Phil crumpled to the floor, and I caught him under the arms as he fell to minimize the sound. I froze, listening.

All was quiet.

Dragging Phil into the kitchen, I searched him, confiscating his gun and phone. Like most phones, his was locked. To my relief, he hadn't disabled the emergency dial function, which I pressed. Unwilling to risk my voice waking Phil's accomplices, I ignored the operator's voice on the other end of the line.

It was time to make a run for it and hope the police responded to the silent call. If they did, they'd be right behind me. All I had to do was run with Annabelle and find someone from the police or FBI.

Easier said than done.

I slammed the butt of Phil's gun against the back of his head to make sure he wouldn't be getting up anytime soon before hurrying to Annabelle's crib.

The baby didn't wake as I loaded her into the carrier. I grabbed a container of formula, snatched the filled bottles I had in the fridge, and stuffed the basics into the bag before making a run for it.

IF I HAD KNOWN DOWNING Phil would be so easy, I would have done it the first time I had been alone with him on guard. My regrets hounded me no matter how many times I told myself it wasn't worth crying over spilled milk. I needed to get Annabelle somewhere safe. Nothing else mattered. I'd have plenty of time to beat myself up for my hesitancy to act later.

I had escaped, but now I needed to survive long enough for my flight to make a difference.

My fear of discovery drove me, whipping me into alternating between a run and a jog. When I was forced to slow to a walk to catch my breath, I checked over my shoulder, terrified of the possibility I had been followed.

The mountain air and high elevation made it difficult to breathe, slowing me down far too much. Most times I had to think things through, but the rare time my gut instinct told me I needed to run, there was a reason for it. Sometimes I never found out what that reason was, but my flight versus fight instinct rarely led me astray.

The forest was strewn with rocks and pine needles, which helped me mask my tracks. Locating a trail was part of my job in CARD, although we'd have access to people and dogs to help with searches. Checking for a trail in the woods was part of the job.

Criminals liked dumping bodies in the forest.

When I could, I hopped from rock to rock, which slowed my pace but let me move without leaving obvious footprints among the bed of needles. What I really needed was a shallow stream so I could walk through the water, make distance, and emerge where there was more rock than trees.

Annabelle wasn't too heavy, but it didn't take long for my arms to start burning from the effort of carrying her, the carrier, and the bag. I was tempted to dump the carrier.

With her life and safety depending on its protection, however, I didn't dare carry her in my arms. If necessary, I could set the carrier down and go for my gun.

The padding could make the difference between life or death for her.

The gun I had stolen would make the difference for me. I'd have hell to pay from my supervisors for stealing a weapon, but if I survived to endure the scolding and possible reprimands, I'd smile through the entire thing.

At least the mountain made it easy for me to keep from getting lost. I had one goal: down.

Down the mountain would take me somewhere. In search and rescue ops, standing around and waiting for help was the way to go, but I couldn't afford to wait for someone to save me. Once I found a road, I'd be able to get some-where. Roads always led to *somewhere.* If I followed the road downhill, I'd be certain to head away from Phil and his conspirators.

It was a terrible plan, but it beat doing nothing. The clock was ticking, and I had no idea when the hunt for me and Annabelle would begin.

※

I RAN until I couldn't take another step. Fighting my downward momentum so I wouldn't fall and drop Annabelle sapped me of strength. While the mountain was smoother than the jagged peaks I expected from Colorado, a fall would end in disaster.

Sinking to my knees, I set the carrier on the bed of needles beneath the tall pines, checking on the infant. Her dark eyes were open, and she stared at me, cooing and waving her little hands.

While she didn't touch me, my chest tightened at the thought of anyone wanting to hurt her. My breath caught in my throat. Tears stung my eyes as my frustration welled up.

"Let's get you fed, baby girl," I whispered, sliding the bag off my shoulder. "I can't warm it up properly for you. I'm sorry."

Annabelle didn't seem to care her milk wasn't warm. She drank, kicking her little feet and clutching at the bottle. When she was finished, I stashed the empty bottle in the bag, grabbed the towel, and burped her, watching the woods while I patted her back.

Everything seemed quiet, which unnerved me more than I thought possible. Shivering, I secured the baby in her carrier and staggered to my feet. Maybe I couldn't run, but I could walk.

If I had to walk all the way back to Baltimore, I would.

I lost track of time as I made my way down the mountain. The sun was still up, although it was steadily sinking towards the western horizon. I turned in a slow circle, stopping when I caught a glimpse of a shadow moving through the trees. Fear zapped through me, chilling me from the inside.

I slid my arm through the handle of the carrier and settled it in the crook of my elbow. Pulling out Phil's gun, I thumbed the safety off and lifted the weapon, careful to keep my finger away from the trigger.

I considered calling out, but instead, I backed away, scanning the trees for any sign of a potential threat. Checking my six revealed nothing, and I clenched my teeth in my anxiety.

I engaged the safety, but I kept my grip on the handgun.

"Animals," I muttered. Forests were supposed to have animals, although I didn't want to run into any of the predators lurking in the Rockies.

My training didn't handle how to take on a bear or a wolf or any other sort of man-eating beast that might come after me in the woods. I set Annabelle's carrier down long enough to do a full check of Phil's gun and count rounds.

Eight bullets wouldn't get me far. That the weapon wasn't fully loaded bothered me. Who had gotten into the man's sights already? I breathed until my sense of calm was restored, lifted Annabelle's carrier, and continued picking my way down the slope, checking my six so often my neck hurt from the effort.

Maybe I couldn't see anything in the woods, but the bad feeling refused to go away. I bit my lip.

It was just an animal. I could deal with an animal. Phil and his conspirators would probably shoot to kill and take Annabelle.

All the thought did was spur me into moving faster.

THE GENTLE SLOPE made way for jagged rocks and ravines leading into a valley. I gaped at the obstacles, wondering how I would get through or around them without getting myself or Annabelle killed.

I settled into breathing slow and deep to keep my heart rate slowed and maintain my calm. Screaming wouldn't help. Screaming would attract every human and animal on the mountain. Taking out Phil's gun and shooting pine cones off the trees, while satisfying, would waste bullets and notify everyone there was a crazed shooter around.

I had built a reputation on being short without having a short temper. I didn't lose my cool.

Breathing helped.

To help keep calm, I checked on Annabelle. The baby slept. It amazed me just how much she slept. Of all the babies my adoptive parents had fostered, none of them were so quiet.

It made me worry. Babies weren't supposed to be so quiet. They were supposed to fuss. They were supposed to cry the instant their perfect worlds were disturbed.

I couldn't even tell if there was something wrong with the infant, and a new fear stirred. I had been grateful for her quiet; it had kept us both alive—still kept us alive.

I crouched beside the carrier, tucking the thin blanket around the little girl. "At the rate my imagination is going, it'll be a yeti that eats us out here."

Sighing, I stood, stretched, and put my hands on my hips, staring down at the ravine below. A stream trickled through it, and the thought of water had me taking a tentative step forward to get a better look over the edge.

I had no idea how long I'd been on the move, but my throat burned with the need for water, and I was well aware dehydration would finish me off long before any animal or human. I still had two bottles for Annabelle, but when they were gone, I would need to find water to mix with her formula.

"Shit," I hissed through clenched teeth. The way straight down looked steep. Too steep. It was even worse than the wretched staircase at the house in Baltimore. If I took a single misstep, I wouldn't have to worry about anything ever again.

Fear shivered through me, and I backed away from the edge, my heart pounding at the thought of even trying to climb down the rocks.

I'd find a way to go around. No matter how long it took me, I'd go around. Still trembling, I grabbed the carrier and backed away from the edge, putting distance between me and a very painful death.

Chapter Five

THERE WERE WOLVES IN COLORADO, and one was stalking me through the forest.

With the sun nearing the horizon and casting long shadows over the mountain, I was running out of time to get rid of the beast before the darkness fell and left me and Annabelle easy prey for it. The ravine I followed opened to a valley, and the stream had grown into a river, something far too wide and deep for me to cross.

I could swim, but my attempts were more of a flail, and while I kept my head above water, asking anything else from me resulted in hysterical laughter. Fellow trainees and colleagues in the FBI had tried to fix me, but the end result was pathetic at best.

In dire need, I managed. Otherwise, I was hopeless, and everyone knew it.

It wasn't an accident that the nine partners I'd worked with in the FBI were all good swimmers. My first partner had been transferred elsewhere; I liked to believe I wasn't part of the reason he had transferred, but we hadn't liked each other all that much. His willingness to use me, no matter the cost, had left me with scars.

Some of them were even visible.

My next six partners hadn't lasted long. Apparently, I was too much of a stick in the mud to work well with others. I understood why; my tolerance for failure was low, second only to my intolerance for unnecessary risk.

I watched over my partners carefully, guarding their lives far better than my own. The men I had been partnered with hadn't handled that well, especially not when I was good at it; I somehow knew when shit was about to hit the fan and made certain I got there first and put an end to it before they got hurt.

The eighth had almost killed me. When I had woken up in the hospital after surgery, he had vanished.

Security cameras had captured his guilt on film, but I had never found out what had happened to him. There hadn't been a trial. I guessed he was still out there somewhere, but I'd never know for certain.

I tried not to think about him. It had taken years before the nightmares of him pulling the trigger had faded.

My last partner had been different, and I would have given just about anything to have Jake with me. My five foot one next to his six foot two made a lot of people stop, stare, and laugh. He cracked every short joke in the book, waiting until I was off guard to nail me with them.

The way he found humor in just about every situation was exactly what I needed, because being hunted by a damned wolf while carrying a baby after being kidnapped and carted halfway across the United States wasn't my idea of a good time. I was supposed to be the one who viewed everything with a calm and critical eye. I didn't snap under pressure, but my tolerance for the unexpected and stressful was crumbling to nothing.

Annabelle chose that moment to cry. While her wails were quieter than most babies, the sound had bumps racing along my skin. I echoed her, but instead of a wail, the noise I made was more like a strangled squeak. In the time it took to set the carrier down and try to soothe the infant, I lost track of the wolf in the woods.

I had two choices: hunt for the wolf while the baby cried, or deal with the baby and hope I could pinpoint the wolf's position afterwards. I chose taking care of Annabelle, but I was careful to thumb off the safety of Phil's gun, keeping it at hand in case the wild canine decided to come too close for my comfort.

A single whiff was all it took for me to identify the source of Annabelle's unhappiness. I changed her diaper, set the soiled one aside, and contemplated using it as a weapon. The smell was enough to make my eyes water. If I slapped a wolf across the nose with it, would it help?

Probably not. I'd probably just piss the damned thing off.

Frustration, anger, and helplessness conspired to bring the burn of tears to my eyes. I wasn't suppose to be a crier. The first time I had taken a round in the arm during a case gone south, I hadn't cried. Instead, the instant the all clear had been given, I had screamed curses at my first partner, who hadn't kept a watch on my six like he had promised he would. Watching my own back had prevented the shot from going through the back of my head instead of my arm.

It had taken three other agents to keep me from strangling the bastard for risking my life so he could look good for our supervisor. In the following six months, I'd been shot three more times. One of the FBI's psychologists had filed a request for my partner's transfer. My new partner hadn't been much better, although I had managed to avoid any injuries when he had flaked out on me.

Jake would've laughed at me, watched my six, and told me to put myself back together so I could go kick the wolf's ass, since kicking ass and taking names was my job, and I was supposed to be good at it.

My only regret was the fact the giant of a man was staying in Baltimore while I was moving on to CARD. HRT had snapped Jake up the instant he had started looking for other waters thanks to my taking the dive to join CARD.

If I got eaten by a wolf after being kidnapped along with an infant, Jake would never forgive me. He would probably hunt down my corpse and tear into me, fully expecting his lecture to reach the afterlife.

Breathing helped. Breathing always helped, and I clung to the thought while crouched beside Annabelle's carrier, determined to get my head back into the game. I could deal with a wolf.

Phil was more threatening than a wolf.

I had a gun, it had bullets, and I was a good shot. I didn't need to worry about a *wolf*. I could shoot it in the head and go about my business. Sure, I'd piss off the animal rights people, but if I had a choice between me or the wolf, the wolf was going to eat rounds.

I inhaled, held the breath to the count of twenty, and exhaled long and slow.

Maybe I was lost in the woods in Colorado, but I wasn't helpless. I could protect myself and Annabelle. Staying calm was the first step. When everyone else panicked, I was the one who kept cool.

It was a hell of a lot easier to keep cool when I had my partner nearby guarding my six. I shivered, checked over my shoulder, and came nose to nose with a wolf large enough to bite my head off without having to work at it.

The scream burst out of me before I could swallow it.

Shooting the animal in the head would have been smart, but as I twisted around and scrambled backwards, I struck it with my gun instead of firing. I hit it hard enough its head snapped to the side, although it stood its ground. It blinked at me.

I blinked back.

It bared its teeth in a wide canine grin.

I pistol whipped it again. In retrospect, I really should have used the soiled diaper.

Normal dogs probably would have either run or chewed my face off for hitting them. The wolf stared at me, and it didn't even growl. It did, to my relief, cover its big teeth. I scrambled backwards, bumping against Annabelle's carrier.

"Good… wolf?"

Did people have wolves as pets? Did wolves even come in such massive sizes? I'd seen mastiffs before, and the wolf was a match for the ones I had seen, although a great deal fluffier than the short-coated dogs I was accustomed to.

The wolf sat down, panted, and lifted its paw like it wanted to shake hands with me.

I should have shot the wolf, but instead, I turned the safety of my gun on, stowed it in the baby bag, and stood. I grabbed Annabelle's carrier, swallowed, and walked.

The wolf was obviously a figment of my imagination. Mastiff-sized wolves didn't exist. I was so stressed out I was hallucinating. Sometime after fleeing from Phil's hide out, I had snapped. I had snapped so hard I was convinced giant wolves existed and wanted to shake hands with me.

I blamed Jake. Jake always reminded me a bit of a wolf with his tall but lean body. He had the look of a predator, especially when we were on the track of a criminal.

I hummed thoughtfully. It made sense. If I couldn't have Jake watching my six, my stressed psyche had settled for a giant wolf to fill the position. Wolves belonged in the woods.

Was this what it was like to snap on the job? I sighed, shaking my head.

Plain and simple, I had lost my mind, and it had conjured up a big bad wolf to take care of me. Great.

Maybe if I walked long enough and fast enough, my psyche would give up on the idea of having a big bad wolf around.

Luck wasn't with me. The wolf followed me, heeling like a well-trained dog. I'd seen a lot of them during my time with the FBI, and most of them had been owned by the local police. I liked police dogs. They knew they had a job, and they did it well—often better than their handlers.

"This is a load of bullshit," I announced.

Annabelle cooed and waved her arms and kicked her feet. The wolf made a huffing sound, which reminded me a lot of Jake when he was fed up with something—usually me. I had no problem admitting I wasn't the easiest person to work with. I was a woman on a mission, and I didn't like people who got in the way of my mission. Usually, I responded with a cold, silent stare.

Cold, silent stares unnerved people, and it annoyed Jake whenever I leveled it at him. That was when he started huffing. Maybe I deliberately used it on him to keep him on his toes, but that was a different matter.

I wondered if my former partner knew I was missing. If Jake knew, he was probably huffing.

He did that when I got myself in trouble, and I was in a lot of trouble.

The wolf huffed and followed up with a long-suffering sigh.

"Not you, too," I hissed.

The wolf's golden eyes stared at me in silent reproach.

WHEN NIGHT FELL, clouds blocked out the light from the half-filled moon, leaving me in total darkness. When the rain started, I used the baby bag placed carefully over the handle of the carrier to keep the water off Annabelle. I cursed until my throat was so parched all I could do was sit in the mud, tilt my head up at the sky, and pretend the little bit of water I managed to catch in my mouth was enough to satisfy my thirst.

I was so, so tired. When the tears started, I couldn't make them stop, no matter how many times I wiped them away. The wolf sighed, flopped beside me, and rested its—his—big head on my leg. I'd figured that much out about the wolf since it had started following me around. The wolf was most definitely a male.

"Who the hell keeps a wolf as a pet, anyway?" My question came out as a sobbed croak. "Who the fuck loses their pet wolf in the woods?"

The wolf's answer was another long-suffering sigh, which I heard less frequently than his huff. I guessed the wolf was staring at me as he liked to do, though I couldn't really tell in the darkness. My vision had adapted enough I could make out shapes, but that was about it. The occasional flash of lightning overhead didn't help; every time I adjusted, the bright light ruined my sight and gave me a headache.

"I really shouldn't curse so much around a baby. Ma and Pop would murder me and hang me from their patio railing as a warning to the fosters. Watch Annabelle's first word be fuck, shit, or damn. Then they'll blame me for it."

The wolf sighed again, which I preferred over the huff. The huff led to all sorts of bad things. Once, I had made the mistake of ignoring Jake's huffing, resulting in him pistol whipping his unloaded gun across my ass. Both of us had landed in our supervisor's office as a result.

Jake had found the whole thing hilarious. I was still amazed we hadn't both been fired over it. Then again, our boss, when told of what had happened, had started laughing and hadn't been able to stop for almost twenty minutes.

I had no idea how long I sat in the mud while the cold rain fell, but when I could muster the energy to get up and get moving again, I did. With one bottle left for Annabelle, I was running out of time to find drinkable water or civilization. My sore, aching body protested the movement, but I gritted my teeth through the discomfort.

I shouldered the baby bag, grabbed hold of the carrier's handle, and trudged through the mud one painful step at a time. I had to find civilization eventually.

How large could the Colorado mountains be?

WALKING through the night wasn't good for my nerves, which were already rattled by the presence of a mastiff-sized wolf and a cranky baby. I didn't blame Annabelle at all; it wasn't her fault she was hungry, tired, and wet from the rain that had persisted until dawn. The rising sun burned the clouds away until their tattered remnants were all that remained of the storm.

All in all, I was rather proud of myself. I hadn't found civilization, but I *had* found my way to the bottom of the mountain. Unfortunately, that put me in the middle of a valley surrounded by even more mountains.

Fortunately, valleys had a tendency to have streams, rivers, and an assortment of other water sources, which was enough to keep me moving. If I found water, I'd test it first, wait a few hours, and if I didn't fall over and die from it, I'd use it to make a bottle for Annabelle. I hated the thought of leaving her hungry for that long, but I wasn't about to risk poisoning her.

With water, I'd be able to survive for weeks. I had enough formula to last a long time, too. Warming up the bottles and cleaning them would be a problem, but I'd figure something out.

Lifting my chin, I straightened my back and kept moving. Survival had been drilled into us during training. Dealing with violent crimes put us at risk. Lost in the woods wasn't quite the same as surviving a firefight with criminals hell-bent on killing us, but the basic principles remained the same.

We lived to fight another day to defend and serve. In that, the FBI was no different from the local police forces. In my department, we stepped up when the cops needed us to take it to the next level.

Working within CARD was no different. We couldn't protect or serve if we died. I had one job, and that was to get Annabelle safely home. I reminded myself of my duty with each step, especially when I really wanted to stop, lie down, and sleep.

I heard the water before I found it, and I tilted my head, holding my breath to listen. I picked up my pace, the rush of adrenaline bolstering me when I should have collapsed in an exhausted heap.

A waterfall cascaded from rocky heights, thundering into the clear waters of a river cutting through stone banks. While the area surrounding the waterfall was more of a gorge, the river calmed downstream and a gentle slope covered in pines and moss led to the shore.

Unlike Baltimore's Inner Harbor, the water *looked* clean. There was no sign of oil slicking the surface, nor was there yellowed froth floating where the water was so still there weren't even any ripples.

Unfortunately, the dark blue color warned me it was probably far deeper than I liked. I approached, setting Annabelle's carrier a safe distance from the shore before creeping towards it on my hands and knees.

The ground was slick and muddy, and I shuddered at the way it oozed between my fingers. When I found a spot where I could kneel without pitching face first into the river, I leaned forward and dipped my hands into the water.

My fingers went numb, and I yanked my hands back with a squeal. "Fuck that's cold."

Guiltily, I glanced over my shoulder to check on Annabelle. She was trying to eat her toes, which was a far cry better than her scolding me because she was hungry.

Of the wolf, there was no sign. Part of me was dismayed

he was gone, though I wasn't surprised. Like me and Annabelle, he was probably hungry.

I was grateful we weren't his first choice for a meal.

While I wanted to yell my complaints to the sky, I kept my voice quiet. "Mutt. At least you could have led me to your home. Fuck you. Hear that, wolf? Fuck you. Go home and enjoy your breakfast, asshole canine. Who keeps a damned wolf as a pet, anyway?"

I sighed, braced for the numbing cold of the water, and dunked my hands, scrubbing away the mud. Once my hands were tolerably clean, I backed away from the water, pulled Annabelle a little closer, and dug out the baby bottles.

Rinsing them would be a nightmare, but without any other viable options, I went to work. At least without the lid, one of the bottles made a good cup for me. Every instinct I had wanted me to guzzle water until my thirst faded, but I took cautious sips.

Throwing up cold water wouldn't help me at all.

I had no idea how long it took to clean the bottles to my satisfaction, but when I was finished, my hands and upper arms had paled and were splotched with red from the chill. I filled the bottles so they could warm enough I could mix in formula, capping them and setting them within the bag so they wouldn't get dirty.

Staggering to my feet, I stared downstream, rolling my stiff and aching shoulders. Following the river was likely my best bet. The river had to go somewhere. Once I found a road, I'd manage.

Annabelle wailed, and resigned to either a dirty diaper or a fit of hunger, I turned to face her.

Two facts asserted themselves. First, there was someone near Annabelle's carrier. Second, I didn't know him, nor was he in a uniform, instead wearing hiking clothes. I snarled a curse and adjusted my foot beneath me so I could charge across the distance between us.

My foot hit a slick patch of mud and moss and flew out from under me. My lower back cracked into a stone, driving the air out of my lungs. Gravity took hold, and before I could do more than shriek, I slipped head first into the water.

Chapter Six

MY HEAD SUBMERGED, and the cold stunned me. I didn't even struggle when my body slipped beneath the water. The river closed in around me, as suffocating as any coffin. I stiffened, remembered I had to move if I didn't want to drown, and flailed as I tried to figure out which end was up.

The little my instructors had managed to beat into me kicked in. Instead of sucking in a lungful of water, I blew out, forcing the water from my mouth before it could go down my throat.

Beneath the smooth waters, the river had a strong current, and it dragged me deeper. Without a full breath of air, I wouldn't last long.

I never did, even when I went into the water prepared. It usually took a push from Jake to get me in the pool, where I proceeded to thrash in a panic before realizing it was shallow enough I could stand up.

The river wasn't shallow enough for me to stand. While my eyes were open, the waters blurred my vision enough I failed to distinguish anything. I focused on a section brighter than the rest and struggled towards it.

Swimming with my lungs full of air was bad enough. The burning need to breathe set a fire in my chest, throat, and lungs. I knew what would happen if I gave into it.

I'd drown. I'd drown and die, just like I was convinced would happen every time some asshole, usually Jake, convinced me to go near a pool. I wouldn't die doing something useful. I'd die from slipping and falling into a river.

I found a rock with my foot, and determined to at least make some effort to survive before I washed downstream as a fresh corpse, I kicked. A blissful second later, my head emerged from the water, and I sucked in a breath.

After hundreds of hours in the pool, I had learned one trick. My doggy paddle was enough to make full-grown men cry, make my partner double over in hysterical laughter, and had earned me a reputation as a liability in any case involving water.

It kept my head above water in the pool. What more could anyone want from me?

The river was a different matter altogether. My clothes were determined to drag me down to the bottom, something I'd been warned about. On several occasions, my instructors had forced me to strip down to my bra and underwear after tossing me in fully kitted for a case.

Water-logged clothing drowned people, and since I was already a liability, they had taught me how to help the poor bastards saddled with dragging my skinny ass to shore.

I doggy paddled until I could draw in a deep breath. When my lungs were so full they ached, I gave up my pathetic attempts to swim, let the water pull me down, and went to work. The shoes went first. I always wore them a little loose so I could pop them on and off without tying them. Next, I shimmied my way out of my jeans, which eliminated a lot of the weight.

Maybe I couldn't swim worth a shit, but I could strip with the best of them. I fought my way back to the surface, spitting water and curses.

An arm slipped over my chest and shoulders. A mix of panic and relief at the realization someone was in the river with me took hold. The hours of training with Jake in the pool kicked in. Despite my instincts screaming at me to struggle, I forced my entire body to go limp, tilting my head back to keep my nose and mouth above the surface.

Floating in the water while someone else did the swimming was one thing I did well. It was usually safer for rescuers to wait for their victim to drown so they wouldn't end up a victim, too. I made up for my inability to swim by keeping my cool and playing dead once someone had a hold on me.

I closed my eyes. Closing my eyes helped me control my panic and focus on breathing. If I couldn't see what was going on, I couldn't react to it. I couldn't afford to panic.

The chill of the water sank into my bones the instant I stopped moving. My teeth chattered, and I shuddered from the cold. Concentrating on my breaths, I kept them slow, deep, and even.

I kept doing it until my world narrowed to the way my breaths slipped in and out of me. Pleasant numbness spread through me, something I should have been concerned about, but I filed it away as unimportant.

No matter what, I couldn't fight. If I fought, I'd drown and take my would-be rescuer with me. My head was above water. While the river lapped at my chin, I could breathe.

When my bare feet scraped against slimy rocks, I jerked. My awareness of my body returned at the feel of an arm sliding beneath my knees.

Someone was carrying me. A hot hand pressed to my throat to check my pulse. Had my heart rate slowed? I should have felt the rapid thudding of my heartbeat due to the surge of panic that always followed my submersion in water. I was aware of heat against my back, my side, and beneath my legs.

The murmur of voices dragged me back to reality, but my ears refused to distinguish individual words. Why did my ears always have to ring so much after I was in the water? It was like my entire head protested against submersion and crippled my ability to think, thus ensuring a far higher chance of drowning.

"Let me get her out of her shirt first."

Why did the first words I always comprehended after a bad experience in the water involve someone taking my clothes off? Why did Jake always have to sound so damned amused by it?

It wasn't fair.

Comprehension hit me. Why did *Jake* sound amused?

At the first tug on my shirt, I burst into motion, opening my eyes to stare into wide dark eyes while grabbing for my shirt. Dark brown eyes the shade of the world's best chocolate except better.

Yep, those were Jake's eyes all right. It should have been a crime for a man to have such pretty eyes.

"Don't you take my shirt off!" I shrieked, yanking the hem down. We tussled over it. He won, pulling it up and over my head. My traitorous hands shook too much for me to throttle him.

So much for being calm and cool.

"You'll die from hypothermia if you keep that on, stupid." Jake shook his head, and before I had a chance to tear into him, he wrapped a blanket around my shoulders. "Fancy meeting you here, partner."

I grabbed the blanket and held onto it, staring at Jake, a thousand questions banging about in my head. I blurted, "What the hell?"

Jake sighed, shook his head, and worked his hands beneath me, lifting me up without a single sign of exertion. Considering our differences in height and build, I probably didn't weigh much to him. "Did you hit your head?"

I bristled at the question. "You're supposed to be training for your new post."

"You're supposed to be in New York on route to your assignment," he bellowed back. "Or did you forget CARD members are supposed to be *rescuing* kidnapped kids instead of *being kidnapped?*"

Someone snorted on a laugh, and I jerked, turning my head. At the sight of at least ten FBI agents in their vests and full field gear, I felt my face burn as I blushed.

"Fuck, fuck, fuck. Fuck shit! *Fuck shit.*" I groaned and kicked my feet in the futile hope Jake would put me down. "Please put me down," I begged in a whisper.

"Not a chance. You know what happens if we let you walk around right after you go swimming. If you can call that flopping around swimming. You'll get dizzy from the water in your ears and faint."

"Why are you here? Where's Annabelle? Is she okay?"

"The baby's fine. Someone's running her down to the ambulance to have her checked over. You're the one I'm worried about."

I drew in a breath, held it, and sighed out my relief. "Why are you here?"

"Isn't it obvious?"

"Nope, pretty sure it's not obvious. Can you put me down now? I'm not going to faint."

Jake snorted and shook his head. "Not happening, so you may as well settle down. I'm going to carry you to the ambulance. You may as well just accept it."

"Bullshit! Fuck you. Put me down."

"Not happening."

"Why are you here, anyway?"

"Come on, midget. You're smarter than this. I know you better than anyone else in the FBI. Of course they called me in when you were kidnapped. I'm the only one who can predict what goes on in that crazy head of yours."

"Bullshit. Fucker. Put me down."

"I'm not putting you down, and it's not bullshit. You were kidnapped. You're one of us. Of course they assigned more than CARD to the case."

"Oh." While I had hoped that would be the case, the reality of it hadn't actually sank in. "You can put me down. Really. I can walk."

"On pine needles and jagged rocks with no shoes or pants? I'm not going in the river again to fish them out."

"It's not my fault I suck at swimming," I wailed.

"At least you remembered to get rid of the weight. You didn't try to drown me, either. You lasted long enough for someone to get to you. That's exactly what you're supposed to do. You did good."

My face burned from embarrassment, and my blush worked its way down my neck. "Damnit, Jake. Put me down."

He laughed and argued with me all the way to the

ambulance.

I HAD a vague memory of warning Jake I'd rip his intestines out of a hole I drilled in his big toe if he didn't put me down and let me walk. After that, everything was a big blank. The next time I blinked, I was somewhere else.

The white walls and the beeps of a machine clued me into the fact the somewhere was a hospital. I regarded the IV stuck in my arm with disdain. Did catheters always have to hurt so much? I contemplated yanking the damned thing out, which would hurt like hell and probably make me bleed all over the place.

"Don't you even dare," Jake warned through a yawn.

I stared at my ex-partner. He was still dressed in work clothes, including his bulletproof vest. "Did you leave your casual clothes in Baltimore?"

"No."

While I often used the cold, silent stare on him, Jake reserved his for when I had escalated a situation from huffing annoyance to beyond ready to pistol whip my ass. "What did I do wrong?"

"Nothing."

I blinked. "Then why are you looking at me like that?"

"No reason." He kept staring, and I could have sworn there was a yellow gleam in his rich brown eyes.

"Who the hell keeps a wolf as a pet?"

The corner of his mouth twitched upward. "Someone brave?"

"Don't you mean stupid?"

"Tibetan mastiff crossed with a Siberian husky. He's a

search and rescue dog. He was given your scent and set loose to track you down. His collar is rigged with a GPS transponder."

I felt my brows rise. "Someone bred a Tibetan mastiff with a Siberian husky and got a giant wolf?"

I didn't believe it for a second. I had seen enough pictures of wolves to recognize a wolf when I saw one. Sure, it had been about the size of a small horse, but it was all wolf from the tip of his wet nose to the end of his tail.

"So it seems."

"I didn't see a collar."

"From my understanding, it tends to get hidden under all that fur."

"Why wasn't his handler with him?"

"That dog runs fast, and once he picks up a trail, he runs. When he ran, we tracked him from the road."

"Shitty dog ran off," I muttered.

"Dog whistle. When we got close, his owner whistled for him."

"Isn't that sorta stupid?"

"No, he's trained to return to the spot he left when he was called. He's a really smart dog." Jake stretched out in his chair, propped his elbow on the side of the bed, and leaned towards me. "Unlike a certain FBI agent I know."

I reached with my left hand towards the catheter, arching a brow at my former partner in silent challenge.

"You were dehydrated and had hypothermia. Add in the fact you wouldn't wake up when you fainted, and they thought it was wise to keep you overnight for observation. If you yank that out, you'll bleed everywhere. I'm sure they won't be willing to release you." Jake made a show of checking his watch. "If I tell the nurse you're awake now, they might be able to slip you out today. You know how these hospitals get. Gotta release the prisoners during sane hours. I could make you stay here for another day."

I froze. "You wouldn't dare."

Jake smirked, got to his feet, and leaned over the bed to kiss my forehead. "I was certain we'd be dealing with a body. Good job getting yourself and that little girl out alive. You did good. I'll go let your keepers know you're awake so you can get discharged today."

"You're an asshole, you know," I called after him.

He waved at me, sticking his head out of the door to talk to someone before returning to my side. "I'm not an asshole. I'm your rescuer. I jumped in that cold water just for you."

"I was swimming just fine."

"You were under the water more than above it. That's not fine."

"I was working on my strip tease. You know I can't swim and strip at the same time. Come on, Jake. Don't be a dick about this."

"I still can't believe we've spent that much time with you in the pool for you to barely manage the dog paddle." Jake sighed, grabbed a newspaper from the floor, and sank down on the chair. "The nurse will be around in a few minutes, probably to yank that IV out."

"I could just yank it out myself."

"This again?"

"Hey, the nurses are busy. I'm trying to be considerate here."

Jake rolled his eyes, shook his head, and opened his paper. "This is my favorite headline: Who's the real target? Babe or Baby? WAKO kickboxing champion kidnapped with infant."

My mouth dropped open, and I felt the blood rush out of my face to pool in the vicinity of my feet. "What?"

"I could repeat this headline all day long. Who's the target? Babe or Baby? WAKO kickboxing champion kidnapped with infant. How is that pronounced? Whacko seems pretty accurate to me."

"I'm not a WAKO kickboxing champion," I spluttered. It was the truth, too. I hadn't won any belts under the WAKO umbrella.

"This pretty picture tells me otherwise." Jake turned the newspaper so I could get a good look at the front page. It was definitely me, and I was kicking the hell out of another chick's face. Below it, surrounded by text, was a picture of me accepting a belt for having progressed through the finals. "Nice outfit."

The outfit in question was barely there; the sports bra did a good job of keeping me covered and supported, and I had picked the shorts specifically to tweak Ma's nose. "I have no idea what you're talking about."

I thought it was pretty impressive I managed to speak with a neutral tone and expression when I wanted to die of embarrassment and run for the hills.

No one from the FBI was supposed to learn about my hobby.

Jake reached down and picked up another newspaper. "Infant Kidnapped with Four-time Kickboxing Champion." When he showed me the image, which was split between a picture of Annabelle and a picture of me kicking a different chick in the face, I wrinkled my nose and turned my cold and silent stare on him.

The next newspaper was even worse. The image was from before I had partnered with Jake. I had been on a mandatory one-month vacation to recover from an injury and hadn't dyed my hair, resulting in a lot of white-tipped hair. Jake cleared his throat and announced, "Baby kidnapped with Kit Kat the Vixen, Kickboxing Champion."

"That's a terrible nickname," I observed, although I was forced to admit my hair did look a little like a fox's tail when pulled into a ponytail. "Her hair is *so* much longer than mine."

"Uh huh."

"You're not buying it, are you?"

"Not for an instant."

Careful not to yank out the IV, I pointed at Jake. "Don't you talk shit about my hobby. You collect baseball cards. You giggle when you get a rare card, too. I've heard you. You *giggle*. You stalk baseball players to get your precious little cards signed, too. And you only have your duplicate cards signed so you can have a matched set with your mint originals."

Jake snorted, folded the three newspapers, and set them beside his chair. "It was better to go the kickboxing route than announce to the world an FBI agent was kidnapped. They'll be announcing the fact you're an FBI agent—"

"No fucking way. No. They can't. *No*." In my hurry to get up and put an end to anyone exposing my role in the FBI publicly, I yanked the catheter out. Pain blinded me, and I yelped, slapping my left hand over the bleeding wound. "Fuck!"

A nurse stepped into the room, took one look at me, and sighed. "You ripped the catheter out, didn't you?"

"She sure did," Jake said, shaking his head and pulling his phone out of his pocket to play with it so he wouldn't have to watch me bleed all over the hospital room.

Chapter Seven

DESPITE JAKE'S threats of keeping me at the hospital another day, they discharged me several hours later. The doctor checked me over, deemed me healthy, and kicked me out.

The hospital forced me to leave in a wheelchair, which I thought was ridiculous. "I can walk."

Jake snickered and kept pushing the chair, slapping my hands whenever I tried to wheel myself to the door. "But I'm having so much fun pushing you."

"Pushing my buttons!"

"Every last one of them."

"How the hell did I put up with you as a partner for so long?"

"Maybe I should get a transfer to CARD. I'm not sure they'll be able to handle you without help."

I contemplated if killing Jake would count as justifiable homicide. Instead of putting my kickboxing skills to good use, I jumped out of the chair and ran for the front doors. I caught sight of several FBI agents waiting in windbreakers a match for the one I was wearing. Someone—probably Jake—had found a pair of slacks and a dress shirt for me. I wore his jacket, and I didn't care that I swam in the damned thing.

"Agent Johnson," one of them greeted.

I checked the hospital for any sign of reporters, tense until I did a full circle without spotting a single camera. I focused on the blond-haired man who had greeted me. Were all male FBI agents giants? I pulled my hand out of my pocket and thrust it out. "Nice to meet you."

"I'm Mitch. This is Donny, Fred, and Paul. Seems we owe you a big thanks for your work."

I tilted my head to the side. "CARD?"

As one, they nodded.

Mitch cleared his throat. "What do you know about the case?"

I liked the direct approach, and I wasn't exactly surprised someone had shown up to grill me right away. "Two day time limit before they'd live up to a death threat. That's it. They were pretty close-mouthed. One gave a fake name, rest hardly said a word the entire time. Professionals." I sighed, running my hand through my hair. "Fuck. I need a bath."

"First you try to drown yourself. Now you want more water? Crazy woman," Jake muttered. "You were supposed to let me wheel you out the doors."

"Smart women run for freedom when the chance presents itself."

"Agent Thomas," Mitch greeted. "Thanks for coming out. Seems your predictions on what Agent Johnson would do were spot on."

"No problem at all. That's what partners are for."

"Former partners," I reminded him.

"You ain't in New York yet, Kit Kat."

"You're never going to stop calling me that, are you?"

"Nope."

"I hate you."

"No, you adore me. I jumped in that cold water for you."

"Okay. Get it out. Stroke your ego. We don't have all day. Praise yourself so I can smile, nod, and agree with you." I tapped my foot. "I'm waiting."

"Are you sure you folks want her?"

Mitch coughed. "I've heard her new partners are preening in New York. They didn't get the assignment because they're on vacation thanks to being one team member short."

"I hope they like to swim," Jake muttered.

I stomped on his foot. "So I guess I'm not fired or a suspect?"

Mitch shook his head. "You weren't a suspect for very long. The idiots in Baltimore delayed things, but once we were put on the case, it went along pretty quick. Let's get somewhere more private. I hope you don't mind some questions."

"Don't mind at all. Lead the way."

"I'm going to just tag along if you don't mind." I got the feeling Jake intended to come along even if they minded.

"That's a joke, right?" Mitch sighed. "Yes, you can come along. May as well. It'll save her from having to go through two questioning sessions. You'll represent your side of things, right? It's nice to do joint operations, but damned, it's a pain in the ass, too."

"No kidding. I'm transitioning, too, which only confuses things."

"HRT, right?"

"Yep."

"Tough job."

Jake gave Mitch a long look, the faintest of frowns in place. "I'd say your jobs are even tougher."

"Where's Annabelle?" I asked.

"Safe. She's on her way back to Baltimore. Her father flew in last night. They're in protective custody. We've got a car this way."

I wondered why people called SUVs cars, especially when they were about as big as a truck. At Mitch's gesture, I got the front passenger seat. I buckled up, stretched my legs out, and sighed. "I was supposed to meet with my new landlord. Shit."

"Taken care of," Mitch replied. "The New York headquarters handled things for you, so you won't have any unpleasant surprises waiting. Or, more accurately, the Johnsons handled everything after we notified them of your disappearance."

I grimaced. "Shit. I haven't called them."

Jake reached between the seats and offered me his cell. "Yours is still in evidence. You'll get all your stuff returned once we head back east."

"Thanks." I stared at the phone for a long moment before sighing. "Actually, I'll do this later. After questioning." I offered the phone back.

"Nope. Call them. Don't start acting like a chicken shit now."

"You are such an asshole, Jake."

Mitch cleared his throat, his mouth twitching as he fought to suppress a grin. "It's a twenty minute drive to the office. You have time."

"Fuck you all." I jabbed at Jake's phone, dialing Pops's number from memory. Apparently Jake had put his number in the phone under the label of Father of the Shrimp. "Really? Really? I hate you, Jake."

He laughed. "Saw the label?"

I flipped him my middle finger since the phone was ringing.

"Hello?" my pops answered.

"Hey, old man. It's me."

"Thank God, pumpkin."

I considered my options and decided it was best to toss the apology out first and wait out the storm. "Sorry."

"Whatever for, pumpkin?"

"Everything. Also, I'm not a pumpkin," I hissed.

"You'll always be my pumpkin."

"Why can't you call me a princess, an angel, or something nice? Must I always be an orange squash?"

The men in the back of the SUV choked on their laughter. Mitch stared at me, and when I glared at him, he held his hands up in surrender before starting the engine. I flipped him the bird.

"Afraid so, pumpkin. You okay?"

"Ripped out the IV trying to kill Jake. Other than that, fit as a fiddle."

Jake huffed.

At the rate I was using my middle finger, it was going to get stuck in the upright position.

"Why were you trying to kill that nice man?"

"It seemed like a good idea at the time. Is Ma around?"

"Sure is, pumpkin. I'll get her for you in a minute. Can you tell me what's going on?"

"No idea yet. I haven't been briefed or debriefed. All I know is that I had a gun to my head and was given the choice of cooperating or finding out what happens when shot in the temple at pointblank range."

"You did just fine, pumpkin. Sorry about the newspapers. They said they needed to manufacture a reason you might be a target."

"Manufacture? And here I thought I was so beautiful everyone wanted to grab me off the street at gunpoint."

"That you are. If you're done fishing for compliments, here's your ma."

Calling Pops an asshole was a fast way to get him to pay me a visit to kick my ass, so I kept my mouth shut. A moment later, Ma said, "Baby?"

"Hey, Ma. Sorry for worrying you."

"You okay?"

Ma wouldn't be too pleased if I told her about the IV, so I replied, "I'm all right. They kept me for observation, but they didn't have a whole lot to observe."

"Good to hear. When you coming home?"

"Good question. I'm not sure. I haven't been debriefed yet, so it might be a while."

"You want us to fly out there?"

"It's okay, Ma. I have no idea how long I'll be here. For all I know, I might end up being on a plane headed east in a couple of hours."

Several snorts from the back seat warned me I'd probably be stuck in Colorado for a lot longer than I liked.

"All right, baby. You just give us a ring if you change your mind or need us. We can be on the next flight out if you need us."

"Thanks, Ma."

"Of course. You sure you're okay?"

"I'm okay."

"The news said you were in stable condition in the hospital."

Shit. Unless I managed to distract Ma or convince her I was safe and sound, she'd never let it go. I bit my lip. "Okay, so there was a river. I fell in. Jake had to go fishing for me. That water was *cold*, Ma. I'm fine. Mild hypothermia at worst. They just wanted to keep an eye on me. They let me out and everything."

"You better thank that nice man properly, you hear me?"

"Yes, Ma."

"Good. Now, why don't you tell your ma how you let someone get the jump on you while you were holding a baby?"

I closed my eyes, slouched in my seat, and wished I could disappear. "Her sister, Chloe, was interested in my gym bag. Saw the kickboxing patches. She's just started, so I was chatting with her about it. I was distracted. It was a festival, Ma. I was *supposed* to be distracted. You're always telling me I need to relax. I was relaxing."

"Don't you give me any attitude, Karma Clarice Johnson."

"Sorry, Ma."

"Damn right you're sorry. You thank that nice man properly, you hear me?"

"Yes, Ma."

"Good. Now, I'll let you off the phone before you run up his phone bill. Give us a call when you know something, okay?"

"Okay."

"Be more careful, baby."

"I will, Ma."

We said our goodbyes, and I heaved a sigh of relief when I

heard the line disconnect. Another snort from the backseat heralded a fit of uncontrolled laughter.

"Hey, Mitch?"

"Yes?"

"I guess killing the fuckers in the back would get me kicked out of CARD, wouldn't it?"

"Probably."

"Well, shit."

ALTHOUGH I HAD SPENT at least half a day and a full night unconscious, I was stifling yawns by the time we arrived at Denver's FBI headquarters. To my dismay, there was a news van parked on the street, and where there was a news van, there was a reporter. I slid down in my seat until I couldn't see out the window.

"I hate reporters," I muttered.

"You're going to end up on the floor if you keep that up." Mitch sighed. "Don't worry yourself about the reporters. Secured parking is a wonderful thing. They aren't going to see you go into the building."

"Why is there a news van here? You didn't identify me as FBI, did you?"

"You were exposed," he confirmed. "Sorry. Wasn't our call. They didn't give specifics, just that you were a part of the FBI. They said you're a vacationing FBI employee who was caught up in a kidnapping case. Apparently, we can't buy publicity that good. It was pure luck you had such an interesting hobby on the side."

"I'm supposed to be a field agent, Mitch."

"And being ousted as FBI won't influence your ability to

work with CARD. Your new team made sure of that."

"My face has been all over the newspapers. That will influence my ability to work with CARD. Kidnappers will see me poking around and know trouble is coming."

"Give it a couple of weeks. No one is going to remember you."

Mitch parked the SUV. For a long time, all I could do was groan and cover my face with my hands, muttering about how my life had turned into a nightmare.

When I made no move to unbuckle my seatbelt and get out, Jake opened my door and poked me in the ribs. "It'll work out."

"Like hell it'll work out."

"You could always start kickboxing professionally."

I slapped my hand over the buckle to unfasten it, shoved the straps off, and glared at Jake, contemplating the ways I could inflict the most harm without an official reprimand. "You're pushing a bit hard, Jake."

If his huffs were his warning I was toeing lines, mine was the deathly calm way I spoke those six words.

"All right, all right. Let's get you through questioning. I'll feed you all the pizza you can eat and pay the bill."

"You can do better than pizza."

"I could, but you called me an asshole after I jumped in a river and saved you from drowning." Jake grinned at me and stepped out of my range. "If you're nice to me, I'll upgrade you from pizza to Italian."

I narrowed my eyes. "Pizza is Italian. I am not buying what you're selling, sir."

"It'll be really good pizza?"

"Does Denver have really good pizza?"

"If it does, I'll find it."

"All right. Let's get this over with."

"She seems like quite the handful," Donny said, arching a dark brow at me. "Big personality in a little package?"

"Only the best," I replied, lifting my chin. "They didn't hire me for my good looks *or* sparkling personality."

Jake chuckled. "They hired her because of her multiple degrees and utterly unflappable handling of cases that would make men like us cry. She blew through eight partners before they managed to convince her I was worth keeping around."

"No one convinced me of anything. You just refused to go away."

"At least you didn't compare me to herpes this time."

"That's your thanks for fishing me out of the river."

"I'm hurt, Karma."

I stared at him. "Is that even possible?"

"I'm absolutely devastated."

"I'm still not buying what you're selling."

"You're so cruel."

Mitch cleared his throat. "Sorry to interrupt, but shall we head upstairs so we can get this over with?"

I flipped my middle finger at Jake and followed after the other CARD members, shaking my head in amusement at Jake's shamelessness. When we passed through security, I was aware of people staring at me.

Without my badge to prove I was a member of the FBI, I fidgeted. Meeting new agents for the first time always went the same way. No one ever believed I was actually in the FBI. I either looked too young, was too short, or too feminine, or too *something* to be treated like I belonged. Sometimes agents changed their tunes after watching me work, but as often as not, no one believed.

I clenched my teeth. I didn't need anyone to believe, as long as they respected my badge and gun. Determined to keep my dignity and pride intact, I straightened my back and lifted my chin.

"Uh oh," Jake murmured, resting his hand on my shoulder. "They aren't the bad guys, partner. They're just curious."

"Curious? About what? The size of my tits? My other measurements? How about my gun handling skills?" At the rate my temper was fraying, I wouldn't make it to the elevators before I snapped. I knew it, and judging from the way Jake tightened his hold on my shoulder, he knew it, too. "I'm not in the mood."

"Of course you're not," he soothed. "You had a gun held to your head, you were dragged halfway across the country, and put in a situation none of us ever want to be in. They're staring because they're incapable of comprehending how so much awesome could be squeezed into such a tiny package."

"What do you want, Jake?"

"For once in my life, absolutely nothing."

"I'm really not buying what you're selling, Jake."

"That's because you're awesome *and* smart."

"Mitch? Can I borrow your gun?"

"No."

"I just want to whip him across the ass with it. Come on. It'll be good stress relief."

"I'm pretty sure that's assault and sexual harassment."

"Huh. Even if he deserves it?"

"I'm afraid so."

"That's really not fair."

There wasn't much point in taking an elevator to the third floor, but I was grateful I wouldn't have to climb so many steps. I blamed hunger and a dislike of hospital stays for my weariness. What I really needed was a cup of coffee. When had I last had coffee?

I couldn't remember, which was a bad sign.

"Coffee," I blurted.

"I was starting to wonder when you'd remember you haven't had any coffee yet."

"I will pistol whip you so hard you will wake up in next week," I grumbled.

"You're still mad about that?"

"Yes."

"What are you two bickering about?" Mitch asked, holding the elevator door open for everyone.

"He pistol whipped me in the ass a few months after we became partners. I annoyed him."

"He pistol whipped you."

"In the ass."

"What sort of partnership did you two have?"

I blinked, frowning at the man. "A good one?"

Jake jabbed me with his elbow. "That's not supposed to come out as a question. We're amazing together and you know it. Our case record was superb."

"That *did* influence my tolerance levels for you," I confessed. "Unlike those other eight idiots I had for partners, you actually understand the concept of watching my six."

Jake got a troubled expression on his face. "I better warn your new partners about that. I'll make a list. Better yet, I'll swing by New York and brief them. You'll eat them alive if I don't warn them."

"Are you sure I can't borrow your gun, Mitch? Please?"

"Positive."

"Well, shit."

Chapter Eight

COFFEE MADE life a whole lot better. The first sip soothed my nerves. The second had me slumped contentedly in my chair, and the third induced a coma-like state no one dared to interrupt for at least five minutes.

I had no idea what the delay was about, but I had a hard time forcing myself to care. I had coffee. Everything was better with coffee. As long as I had my hands wrapped around the coffee-warmed mug, everything would work out fine.

Jake prodded me under the conference table with his foot. "Damn, Karma. Don't fall out of your seat over there."

"The last time I had coffee was the night before a bunch of professional kidnappers dragged me into their SUV and drove me across the United States. Can't a girl enjoy her coffee?"

"Should we give you a few more minutes alone with your java?"

I tried to kick Jake, but I was too relaxed to do more than flop my foot on the floor. "Just get ready to fetch me more coffee. Need three or four more to function."

"I should have had the nurse add coffee to the IV."

Someone cleared his throat and clapped his hands together. "All right. Let's get to business, shall we?"

I cracked open an eye. While Jake and I had done an extensive amount of traveling around the east coast, I hadn't met the gray-haired man standing at the head of the table. He had a set of three scars stretching across one cheek, partnered with a stripe of white hair near his ear.

While I had been enjoying my coffee, someone had brought in a digital data board, which the man gestured to. I stifled a yawn and wiggled my way upright. I took another sip of coffee and tried to force my expression to something resembling interest.

Men, especially the older agents, expected good behavior from me. The good ones expected it from everyone, but the real assholes expected better from me than my male counterparts. It came with the territory, but it always left me with a bitter taste in my mouth and an urge to drag some bitchy chick into the ring.

Beating down the bitchy ones always satisfied me a hell of a lot more than making a run at the good girls learning to defend themselves. When I got in the ring with them, I had a habit of trying to teach them rather than releasing all the pent-up steam from a bad day at work.

The man pulled up a map of the United States with Federal Hill, Baltimore and a spot near Denver, Colorado flagged. Nothing connected the two points, so I offered, "South out of Federal Hill to I-95 to the Beltway heading north to I-70, cutting west on I-68 and onto I-79 into West Virginia before cutting south and west again into Kentucky. After that, things got a bit blurry, so I can't tell you the exact roads."

Everyone stared at me, and someone seated near the head of the table jotted down my directions. Without a word, the man tapped on the glass, magnifying the map so he could chart out the route my kidnappers had taken.

"Define blurry, please," the man said once he had marked the routes on the map.

"Barely conscious."

"Reason?"

"They grabbed me to take care of the baby, apparently. I was informed I would do that job, keep her quiet, or outlive my usefulness. I didn't exactly sleep during the trip. Whoever they were, they were professionals. Kentucky was about when I hit my limit, sir."

"So you have no idea of the route they took to Colorado?"

"It was pretty direct, sir. They stopped to change drivers. When they filled up, they were quick and used the credit card processors on the pumps. I didn't get a look at their cards. They were careful to make sure the only thing I saw was their faces. One gave me a fake name. They believed I was a teen, sir."

"No offense, Agent Johnson, but you look like one."

I shrugged and took a sip of my coffee so I wouldn't say something I'd later regret. "Worked in my favor this time, I'd say. If I looked like an adult, I'd probably be dead."

"Probably."

Great. I didn't need anyone telling me the guy was hard and cold as stone. I ran into similar agents all the time; they were only happy cuffing criminals, and anyone who got in their way ended up getting plowed over. Blaming him for being the product of his job wouldn't do anyone any good, so I kept my mouth shut.

There was one way to deal with a man like him, and it was to only speak when spoken to. That, at least, I had down to an art.

"Take it from the top, Agent Johnson. The morning of the day you were kidnapped with Annabelle, what were you doing?"

"Moving out of my house, sir."

"Why?"

Questioning sessions were all about getting as much information as possible. My job was to answer truthfully, no matter how stupid I thought the question was. Sometimes, the missing pieces of the puzzle were found in the most obscure places.

It didn't make me happy having to relate every detail to fellow agents, however.

"I had sold the property so I could move to New York City, sir."

"Why?"

"Post assignment change, sir. I am scheduled to begin working at the FBI headquarters in New York."

"What position?"

"I have been assigned to a CARD team stationed there, sir."

"Doesn't it seem rather suspicious a future CARD team member is involved in a high profile kidnapping?"

I blinked. "High profile? Sorry, sir. I have no idea what you're talking about."

"Really? You have no idea? Witnesses claim you spent a

substantial amount of time talking with the family before you took possession of the infant."

I stared at Jake across the table in open accusation, and he held his hands up in surrender. While I expected questioning, the tone was damning enough I didn't need a mirror to know 'suspect' was still jotted on my forehead. When I turned my glare to Mitch, he mirrored my partner's expression.

I sat straighter, set my coffee down hard enough I heard the mug crack, and leveled my coldest stare at the gray-haired gentlemen firing questions at me. "Chloe, the teenage girl of the family, noticed the kickboxing patches on my bag, sir. She had questions. I answered them for her. Chloe was holding the girl, Annabelle, when her siblings decided to make a scene. I offered to hold the baby so she could help her mother."

I had done substantial damage to the mug, but I ignored the coffee dripping onto my legs, forcing myself not to blink while I met the man's gaze. Keeping silent, I waited for the next question.

"Why were you in the line with the family?"

"I like funnel cake, sir."

"So, you want me to believe that after you sold your home and moved out in the morning, you went to a music festival to have funnel cake."

"I had actually sold the home several weeks prior. That morning was my move out date. Once the movers had finished loading the truck, I was supervising the cleaning company I had hired. The new owners, the Averys, met me there to take possession of the keys. I left the property and headed to Federal Hill to relax before my tournament, sir."

"Your tournament. Explain."

"Kickboxing tournament, sir." I considered shutting my mouth and forcing him to ask more questions, but I decided the route of least resistance would best serve me in the long run. "I didn't have room in the trunk of my car for my bag, so I took it to the festival with me. I was planning on staying the night at a hotel in Baltimore after the tournament before driving to New York the next morning."

"While I was aware of the cover story provided to aid our investigation, I was unaware this was a legitimate hobby."

I breathed so I wouldn't do something stupid like finish smashing the cracked mug slowly bleeding out its coffee all over the table and my legs. "I thought the photographs the Johnsons provided would have been sufficient evidence I am actually active in the kickboxing community, sir."

"Images can be doctored and created when necessary, as you are well aware from your work with the FBI."

"If I am considered a suspect or accomplice in this kidnapping case, I respectfully request a lawyer and invoke my rights to legal counsel." I shook, and I couldn't tell if it was a result of the coffee, my growing rage, or shock at the open hostility of the man standing at the head of the table.

"We're merely establishing all of the information for this case from your perspective, Agent Johnson."

I kept my mouth shut, clenching my teeth so hard my jaw ached. The silence stretched on, and chairs squeaked as the gathered FBI employees fidgeted and waited for one of us to crack.

The only thing I was cracking was my mug. The hot coffee on my leg hurt and was annoying, but I forced myself to sit still, chin lifted, back straight, and my gaze focused on the gray-haired man I wanted to kick in the face more than I wanted my next breath.

I had worked too hard and risked too much to have my efforts undermined by anyone.

"Oh, for fuck's sake. This is ridiculous. Someone get Agent Johnson a towel and a new cup of coffee," Mitch said, rising from his seat and slapping his hand to the table.

My adversary jumped, startled by the interruption. I remained still and quiet.

"No one asked you for your opinion, Agent Jeffreys."

"Agent Simons, she's invoked her right to counsel. We're stonewalled. Good job. Go ahead and question her. We can sit here all day and get nothing done as a result, thanks to you. Did you even bother reading the briefing report, or did you breeze over here from Washington chasing after some conspiracy theory?" Mitch circled the table and headed to the door.

"You weren't given permission to leave," Simons said.

"With all due respect, sir, you aren't my boss, nor are you my supervisor. You aren't even in my division. I have real work to do, and since we won't be getting any information out of this session, I'm going to put my skills to good use." Pausing long enough to fire a glare at Simons, Mitch left the conference room, slamming the door behind him. Clearing his throat, Donny rose from his seat, inclined his head, and excused himself. The other two CARD members followed in his wake.

"Where do you think you're going?"

"To work," Paul answered, hesitating long enough to tip me a two-fingered salute before leaving the room. "This case isn't closed yet."

Jake shrugged and rose, sliding his hands into his pockets. "This is sidelined until a good lawyer gets here. I recommend you send for the best. Agent Johnson won't accept anything less. She isn't going to say a word until legal council is provided. She won't move out of that chair, no matter how long she has to wait, no matter how much hot coffee has been spilled on her, and I really doubt she'll allow anyone to touch her until you're putting her in cuffs after reading her rights and declaring formal charges. I sure hope you get the lawyer here before you have to take her out on a stretcher. That's the type of agent she is, has been, and always will be. Good luck, gentlemen. You'll need it. When you're ready to proceed, I'll be down the hall."

Most agents would have been infuriated by their partner abandoning them, but I knew better. Jake wasn't my partner anymore, but by leaving, he was supporting me and demonstrating his trust in my decision. He spared himself from watching his prediction become reality, and I was grateful for that.

Jake was a lot of things, including an asshole, but he never abandoned his partner. He had my six, although I had no idea what he could do to help me.

I clasped my hands together on my lap, and I waited.

AGENT SIMONS DIDN'T ORDER a lawyer called, which didn't surprise me. Many agents didn't take me seriously. It was one of the most annoying parts of my job. The only way I could prove myself was to go through with my threat, and once I gave my word, I didn't go back on it.

The conference room had a phone, and it would have taken him all of five minutes to make the call to bring in an attorney. The two men with him didn't make a move, although the one who was supposed to be taking notes had tossed his pen onto the table and propped his feet up on the chair Donny had vacated.

"You're going to be difficult about this, aren't you?" Agent Simons muttered.

If he hadn't figured that out when I didn't move despite being soaked from the knee down in coffee, there was no helping him. I wielded silence as a weapon, wondering if they'd bother with bringing a lawyer in.

I had my doubts.

When I had applied to join the FBI, I had done my homework. I had investigated methods of gathering information. I had taken the time to learn what tactics worked. Interrogation was a hard job made simpler through psychological games and discomfort.

Agents of other organizations, particularly the CIA, were trained to withstand hard interrogations. I had been given the basics as a part of my training, but I had learned a lot more from books on the side.

I was tired of playing Agent Simons's game, and we were only an hour into it. The conference room clock was on the wall above the portable board, which had turned off from inactivity. I only checked the time when Agent Simons was pacing, his back facing me.

I was hungry, I was tired, I was thirsty, and most of my coffee had ended up on me rather than in me. If I moved an inch, I had the feeling my foot would become a very close acquaintance with Agent Simons's face. I amused myself with considering the best type of kick or punch I could use on the man.

Retreating into my thoughts, I strayed from my plans of violence to reviewing every word, step, and action I had taken since the moment Phil's gun had pressed against my temple. I wasn't even sure how many days had gone by since I'd been kidnapped. I hadn't thought to check the date on Jake's phone.

"You're really making this difficult for everyone," Simons announced. "We do not have time to waste on your childishness."

The door opened, and a man dressed in a crisp black suit and tie with white shirt stepped in. He had short-cropped brown hair that stuck up every which way, although it looked like he had made a futile effort to tame it. He took in the room, his gaze settling on me before shifting to Agent Simons. "I must have misheard that. Who is wasting time on childishness? I was unaware a federal agent defending her constitutional rights classified as childishness. Where is Agent Johnson's attorney?"

Agent Simons straightened, his mouth opened, but he didn't say a word.

"Agent Johnson, where is your attorney?"

Simons's note taker picked up his pen and spun it between his fingers. With the addition of a suit, probably someone higher up the chain than I ever hoped to be, my interest increased tenfold. "Agent Simons has not called for one."

The man was definitely trying to hide a smile; there was a playful look to his blue eyes. A lot of FBI agents had hard exteriors and odd senses of humor.

Once I was dried off and my legs stopped throbbing from their introduction to hot coffee, I'd probably find some humor in the situation.

"Agent Simons, you are off this case. Get out of my building. You'll be contacted later. Don't leave town."

I pinched myself so I wouldn't grimace at the order. I'd

been tossed off cases before, but in my time with the FBI, I had managed to avoid making such a disgrace of myself I had been sent home. Reassignments happened. Sometimes other agents couldn't handle working with someone small and feminine. Sometimes a case was close to wraps and we were needed elsewhere, but I had never been tossed for violating a basic constitutional right.

Agent Simons turned the shade of the newcomer's shirt. Some men who were tossed argued and tried to talk their way into staying. Simons swallowed, his Adam's apple bobbing. Nodding, he went to the door, opened it, and left, shutting it quietly behind him.

"Senior Special Agent Johnson, I am Assistant Director Henry Dunhaven. You're not a suspect, nor are you being charged with anything. You are, of course, welcome to legal counsel if you feel it is necessary."

I tensed at the emphasis on my rank as a senior special agent; Addressing someone as agent met the basic requirements of formality between peers. Everyone in the room was a special agent. Everyone who was a field agent was one.

To point out I had seniority made some point, but I couldn't tell what that point was, considering Simons's removal from the equation.

"That's all I needed to know, Assistant Director, sir."

"I apologize for Agent Simons's unbecoming behavior. Someone has a change of clothes for you in the hallway. If you have no objections, I'd like to move forward on this case as soon as possible."

I rose from my seat, wincing when both of my legs protested the movement. "Of course, sir."

"Thank you for your hard work, Agent Johnson. I would

ask you to not hold Agent Simons's distasteful behavior against our office."

If Assistant Director Dunhaven wanted to play nice, I'd play nice, too. "Of course not, sir."

I left my broken coffee mug for someone else to deal with. There were limits to how nice I'd play.

Chapter Nine

JAKE WAITED for me in the hall holding a pile of folded clothes in one arm. "I'm going to have to make sure your new team has your clothing sizes. Otherwise, you'll end up running around New York either naked or filthy."

"Seeing me naked should be classified as criminal," I agreed.

Sighing, my former partner handed me the pile. "Could you stop attracting trouble? It's terrible for my digestion."

"Just point me in the direction of the bathroom, Jake."

He pointed down the hall.

While someone had found me clothes that fit, I was dismayed to discover the skirt didn't even reach halfway to my knees. At least the underwear fit, and someone had the foresight to give me a pair of stockings to go with the skirt and blouse. The outfit was formal enough for a meeting with just about anyone.

At least the stockings hid the angry red on both my legs from exposure to my coffee.

A pair of heels rounded out the outfit, and I was sorely tempted to discover whether or not I could kick someone while wearing them.

I needed some time in the ring before I really did snap.

When I finally emerged from the bathroom, Jake was waiting for me, his arms crossed over his chest. "Took you long enough. What were you doing in there? Preening?"

"Never underestimate the struggle involved with wiggling into tights. I burned the shit out of my legs and was trying to decide if I needed them checked. I decided I would survive."

"How bad?"

"No blisters. I'm good to go."

"That Mitch fellow handled bringing in the management."

"Nice of him. Did you have to go into the kids' section to find clothes?"

"Pretty much."

"What's going on, Jake? Give it to me straight."

"Simons likes to think himself a top investigator who always gets the answers he needs for a case. I warned him you wouldn't respond to his typical methods. He's old school."

The old school type included men who didn't believe women had any business serving as special agents and often went out of their way to force female agents out of the Bureau. "Same old shit, different state."

"Pretty much."

"At least they can't throw me off a case I haven't been assigned to, right?" I sighed and ran my hand through my hair, grimacing as I got snagged in a tangle. "You can put me in nice clothes, but there's no masking this sort of mess, Jake."

"Despite appearances, I wasn't the one who picked the outfit. I supplied the measurements, that's all. It fits okay?"

"It'll do. I need coffee, Jake. I need coffee in a mug that is impervious to harm. I need it, and I need it now."

He laughed, placing his hand on the middle of my back and propelling me down the hall. "You need more than coffee. It's being taken care of."

"What was the deal with Simons, anyway? He was about as friendly as a pissed off cobra."

"You're a woman doing a man's job. What else?"

I snorted. "Of course. I should have known. Old school. Right."

"You really do need some coffee. Come on. Back to the conference room with you. With Simons off the case, I have a feeling things will go much smoother. Whoever promoted him needs to be fired. I'll pay up on the pizza as soon as we're done with questioning."

"I need a hotel, a bath, and some sleep."

"Didn't you sleep enough at the hospital?"

"I hate you, Jake."

"Admit it. You love me. I jumped into that cold, cold water for you."

I headed back to the conference room and let myself in. Someone had cleaned up the coffee and taken away the mug. In its place was a stainless steel travel mug with a screw-on lid. The four-member CARD team had returned to their seats, and Assistant Director Dunhaven had taken Agent Simons's place in front of the screen displaying the map of the United States.

"Sorry for the delay, gentlemen," I said, taking my seat after checking to make sure I wasn't about to sit in coffee.

Instead of taking the seat across from me, Jake flanked me. When he backed his chair up to prop his feet up on the table, I glared at him. "Don't you dare," I mouthed at him.

He frowned at me but kept his feet on the floor where they belonged.

"Let's start this from the beginning. Fill us in on what happened, beginning from the morning of your kidnapping, Agent Johnson."

While I expected questions and a lot of them, giving me the space to lay out the entire incident would give everyone at the table a chance to see the entire picture. While I talked, Assistant Direct Dunhaven manipulated the board, creating potential routes to the cabin in Colorado and marking potential stops. No one said a word until I described the cabin, the shifting rotation of guards, and the full descriptions of the three men, including a breakdown of their habits.

"We were wondering about the sequence of events leading up to the 9-1-1 call placed from where you were held hostage. How, exactly, did you acquire a cell phone?"

"One of the kidnappers had it. I waited until his accomplices were asleep. I had kept quiet until that point. They had put anything I could potentially use as a weapon out of reach. I asked for coffee, knowing the tin was stored too high for me to reach. He made the mistake of getting up and going to retrieve the tin. I kicked him in the back of his neck, followed up with a punch to the head, and then I hit him with his own gun, which I took into my possession prior to grabbing the baby and leaving."

"So you used your kickboxing skills to escape."

I pinched the bridge of my nose and focused on my breathing. "Yes, sir."

"Do you feel kickboxing is a good form of martial arts for female special agents?"

Not expecting that sort of question, I froze, staring at Dunhaven, wondering what his game was. "Any form of martial art is appropriate for all special agents, sir. There are situations where we may be disarmed. Having a fallback skill is critical. Gender doesn't matter."

"So you'd be a supporter of all special agents undergoing full martial arts training?"

"Sure. It's a good way to get fit and stay fit while having the benefit of adding another layer of protection. If I had not taken kickboxing, sir, I'd still be in that cabin awaiting a death sentence, as would Annabelle."

"No one is criticizing your actions."

"I didn't think you were, sir. I'm merely stating the facts."

"Please forgive the directness of this next question, but I was given orders to ask."

I tensed. "Sir?"

"Exactly how did you manage to hide the fact you were so involved in kickboxing during your career with the FBI?"

I coughed, covered my mouth, and fought the rising tide of giggles. I didn't giggle, not in front of anyone from the FBI. Laughing wasn't one of my behaviors either, but I fought to choke back my need to chortle at the question.

"I didn't feel it was relevant to anyone's interests, sir. It's a hobby. Lawful activities outside of work are encouraged. We work long hours."

"It's impressive you were discreet enough to manage keeping such an activity secret, Agent Johnson. Even your partner of four years had no idea you were involved with kickboxing. Initially, there was concern someone had stolen your identity for the kidnapping."

"That explains Simons's behavior a little," I admitted.

"No, it doesn't. We had fully verified you could, in actuality, have a rather successful career kickboxing if you decided to pursue it." Dunhaven chuckled, tapping on the board to pull up a file about me, which included a lot of photographs of me kickboxing. "We did want to verify a few facts with you."

"Sir?"

"Is it true you began training when you were five?"

"Six, but yes. It's true."

"Your championships?"

"Four of them, none affiliated with WAKO. The match I missed was supposed to be my first tourney with WAKO."

"How long would it take for someone to become proficient in kickboxing with lessons three times a week?"

"What level of proficiency are we discussing?"

"Able to defend themselves in real-life situations."

"Not long, sir. A few months for the basics? If the course is designed specifically for self-defense, it is all repetitions, muscle memory, and practice spars. It's no different from other martial arts. It varies from person to person. It's similar to how we go through firearms training and maintain our skills."

"Do you credit your skill in kickboxing with your success with this case?"

"I definitely wouldn't credit my swimming skills," I muttered.

Jake kicked my ankle. I kicked him back.

Someone across the table snickered and coughed to cover it.

"All right. I think we have what we need. If you think of any details, let us know. Do you have any issues with sharing a room with Agent Thomas?"

In normal circumstances, if a pair of single rooms wasn't available at the FBI's hotel of choice, paired agents ended up sharing a room with two beds. Maybe other female agents cared, but I had no issues with Jake in the room with me.

We were partners, and we couldn't do a good job of watching each other's back if we were in separate rooms, especially during a more dangerous case. We had come to that conclusion long ago, almost always sharing a room. "None, sir."

"Excellent. If you remember anything, let us know immediately."

Recognizing a dismissal when I heard it, I rose from my seat and headed for the door, pausing long enough to shake Dunhaven's hand before making my escape with Jake at my heels.

We sighed our relief in unison.

"How about that pizza, partner?"

"It better be good pizza," I warned him.

THE NEWS VAN was still hanging around the FBI office when we left, and I made a point of sliding as low in the seat of the loaner SUV as I could to avoid detection. "Damned reporters."

"They'll back off when they either get an interview or can't find you."

"How about we go the can't be found route. I like that option. I'm not paid enough to be interviewed on the news."

"You've dealt with reporters before."

"Not when the vic was *me*," I retorted.

"Well, there was that one time you got shot," he reminded me.

"We weren't partners then."

"Still counts. You were cornered by reporters then and did just fine."

"No comment repeated over and over again is hardly fine."

Jake chuckled and eased the vehicle around the news van. When he turned the corner, he said, "You should be clear."

"I'm comfortable," I lied.

"Bullshit. For the record, if you ever scare me like that again, I will hunt you down and pistol whip your ass."

Angry Jake huffed, but an infuriated Jake issued ultimatums, and I had no doubt he'd do as he threatened. "Maybe I was scared, too."

He spat curses. "Damn it, Karma. I'm sorry."

"It's not your fault. I let my guard down. I was off duty. I wasn't paying attention."

"I wasn't there to watch your back."

"Uh, hello? Training for HRT? No shit you weren't there to watch my back. You were doing what you were supposed to be doing, which was training."

"Technically still my partner until you reached New York."

"Technically not still my partner, Jake. We ceased being partners when we went off to different training branches."

"Bullshit. Once a partner, always a partner."

"Your new partner—or partners—won't like you cheating on them, Jake."

"They'll deal."

"Look, Jake. Stop being an ass about this. You knew the instant you partnered with me I was working to get into CARD just like you were working to get into HRT. Our partnership was a temporary arrangement from the start. Don't make this difficult."

"I'm not. You're the one being difficult. Accept it. A working pair like us doesn't come around every day. We're the showcase example of what a good partnership looks like, and you know it."

I sighed and slouched even more in my seat. If I went much farther, I'd end up out of my seatbelt and on the floorboard. "Yeah. We did good, Jake."

"We did better than good. We did great."

"You're going to be a hell of an HRT agent."

"Do you think I should send sympathy cards to your new team? Maybe flowers? They aren't going to know what hit them."

"You're really going to be an asshole about this, aren't you?"

"Yep."

"When do you head back to training?"

"I'm done training. Waiting for my official assignment. Part of the reason I was assigned to the case. The FBI may as well get what they're paying for, right?"

"I thought it was because you knew what went on in my crazy head."

"That, too."

"Did knowing what went on in my crazy head help?"

"I told them you'd find the largest body of water and fall in without fail. I was right."

"You did not."

"I did. It's true. Ask Mitch. He witnessed it. I warned

them all you'd find a way to try to drown yourself. It's like you're attracted to trouble *and* deep water. Sure enough, first time I see you, you're in the water trying to drown yourself. You scared the life out of me when you went under, by the way. I should have realized you were working your strip tease."

"You are such an asshole."

"No, a real asshole wouldn't have jumped into that water. Fuck, if I had known how cold it was, I probably would have waited for you to doggy paddle to shore and fished you out that way."

"Keep talking, Jake. I will suffocate you with your own pillow tonight."

"Are you ever going to ask about our end of the case?"

"I figured you'd get around to telling me eventually."

"Now you're just being mean. Ask me, Karma. Ask me. I want to give you every little detail like the shameless gossip I am."

"Maybe over pizza. If there were any actual drama for you to gossip about, you would have already spilled it."

"Aren't you even a little curious?"

"No."

"You're lying to me."

I snickered. "Would I do that?"

"Yes."

"Feed me pizza and I'll take pity on you and ask. Just to satisfy you. It can be thanks for having to go into that cold, cold water."

"You are such a bitch, Karma."

"Karma's a bitch," I agreed.

"You just punned me with your own name, didn't you? That's so wrong."

I grinned. "What can I say? It comes and goes."

"You did not just go there."

"Who, me?"

Jake groaned. "You win. You win. Just don't pun me any more. Please."

"That'll teach you for withholding information from me. I'm expecting every detail served with my pizza, sir."

"ALL RIGHT," I said around a mouthful of pepperoni pizza. "Spill it, Jake. I want every little detail you can give me without being drawn and quartered for talking about it."

"I'm pretty sure they stopped drawing and quartering people a long time ago."

"Semantics. Talk, Jake. Talk."

"So, there I was. I'm lounging about at home because you were supposed to be driving to New York, and I didn't have anyone else to bother. Sunday afternoon television is a real drag, by the way."

"Uh huh."

"Did I mention you were *supposed* to be driving to New York?"

"I think I heard something like that from somewhere. Stop delaying. Get to the point."

"Spoilsport. Fine. I got the call around five in the evening. The boss told me I needed to get my ass to the office yesterday. Considering I wasn't assigned anywhere, I figured something big was going on that was calling in off-duty agents. Anyway, I get there, I'm dragged into her office, and a printout of a photograph of you with a gun held to your head is slapped in front of me." Jake grabbed a piece of pizza and devoured half of it before sighing. "Boss asks if I know the person in the picture. I tell her, 'Sure, I know the bitch.'"

"I'm not buying what you're selling, Jake. Our boss would never do that. She'd show up at your house with the photograph, wave it in front of your face, and start screaming. Otherwise, she'd call you and clearly state the situation. Because it's you, she'd probably say an agent was missing and ask you to come in to help."

"You're ruining my fun again."

"Did you really expect me to believe that was what happened?"

"Yes."

"The truth this time, Jake."

"How'd you know she'd show up at my house with the photograph? She didn't scream, though. She did tell me to hurry up and get dressed. We went to the crime scene first to check in with the preliminary investigation, which was being handled by the local police department. They had called in CARD immediately, but no one had thought to identify the second victim—you—until an hour or two later. You were over CARD's normal age group, and the local police were too distracted by the fact an infant had gotten snatched to get their heads out of their asses and go through your purse."

"The boss must have been pissed about that."

"Definitely. We lost a lot of time thanks to their blunder."

"Okay. Did you lose them at the Beltway when the cars split?"

"Unfortunately. After that, we found nothing of use. Everything we got was a dead end, red herring, or otherwise useless. We didn't even get any calls saying someone had seen a girl like you at all. It was unbelievably frustrating. Then, we got word from Colorado that a 9-1-1 call had come in, dead air on the line, and a couple of thumps with the added bonus of an incoherent groan."

"I was hoping that'd turn into something productive."

"It did. So, the cops go over to investigate, see the black SUV, and preemptively call in backup. Good thing they did, too. Ten minutes there, there's a firefight, three dead perps, two injured cops, and a whole lot of leads. The mess of baby supplies confirmed it was probably the holding location, but when there was no sign of you or the baby, they called me in. I was on the next flight out."

"Why bring you in, though? That's what I don't get. Colorado is way outside of your general jurisdiction."

"Anyone who knows you at all knows how protective you get when there are kids involved. They wanted me around to talk you down if necessary. Of course, the SAR guy who reached the site first is apparently cut from the same cloth, because he immediately went to check on the baby. That's how you ended up in the river, right? You saw him, freaked, and fell in."

I sighed. "Right."

"Good thing I was there. They probably would have let you drown a little before jumping in to save your ass."

"Can someone drown a little? Isn't it an all or nothing deal? I'm pretty sure it's an all or nothing deal. Thanks for not letting me drown, Jake."

"Anytime."

Chapter Ten

WHEN I WOKE up around dawn, I watched the news, one of my few consistent morning habits. Sometimes the media got something right and dug up clues that the FBI had missed. The habit had led to a breakthrough in more than a few cases.

To my pleasure, I discovered the news station running a clip about the kidnapping. A representative from the FBI handled the press conference regarding Annabelle's safe recovery, sparing me from having to make a public appearance. Instead, they directed focus to a clip of the reunion, which showed the entire family in tears in an elegant living room. Annabelle's father was an older black gentleman with salt and peppered hair. His suit caught my attention, at odds with the rest of the family's casual attire.

When the report finished, I was counting my blessings they hadn't displayed my picture for the world to see—or given my real name. From what I saw of the newspapers Jake had stashed in the hotel room, the newest picture they had printed was about six years old. They used my kickboxing nickname in all the articles and on television.

It wasn't as obscure as I wanted, but I appreciated the chance to continue my life with some hope of maintaining a sense of privacy. My involvement in Annabelle's rescue was reduced to using martial arts to defend myself from our kidnappers and taking Annabelle to safety.

I'd have to be careful to keep the white tips of my hair dyed, but it was a small price to pay.

Jake chuckled. "Doesn't look like it'll be too bad for you, Kit Kat."

I had my doubts about that. "Someone will leak my real name. Just you wait and see."

"Probably, but it'll blow over fast. There are pictures of you on the internet from witnesses who either caught a video of the kidnapping or took stills, but we couldn't do anything about those. I warned them you'd flip your lid if your name was exposed."

"Thanks."

Jake's phone rang, and he grabbed the device from the nightstand positioned between the beds. "Thomas."

When he sighed, I echoed him. Jake sighing after answering the phone was a bit like his huff. A sigh usually led to a huff, and about ten seconds later, he lived up to my expectations.

"Understood. We'll be there." Jake hung up, clenching the device like he wanted to throw it across the room. "We need to go. Apparently, we've been booked for a flight back to Baltimore. It leaves in an hour and a half. Someone will be waiting for us at the airport to get us through security."

"How far away is the airport?"

"Thirty minutes. Move it. Get your skinny ass into your skirt."

I flipped my ex-partner my middle finger, dove for the bathroom, and took the quickest shower of my life before wiggling back into the black skirt and white top from yesterday. At least I hadn't had to worry about pajamas; Jake had my emergency travel bag from when we had been partners. In all honesty, I still had one for him, too. A few weeks after we had become partners, we had decided to keep duplicate bags of essentials for each other for when we had to travel and had no time to go home.

While I was getting dressed, Jake took a fast shower. He opted for black slacks, dress shirt, jacket and a tie. He wore his gun in a shoulder holster. At least I wouldn't have to go onto the plane feeling like I was the only one overdressed. I dug through his bag, found a second black tie, and wore it.

"Now we're twins," I said, double checking my appearance in the mirror before stuffing the rest of my things into my travel bag.

An FBI agent was waiting for us in the hallway, and he nodded to both of us. "I'll take care of checking you out."

I saluted him and marched as fast as my heels allowed. Jake lengthened his stride to stay ahead of me, guiding me to the SUV he had on loan from the Colorado office.

It was a good thing someone was waiting for us at the airport; the place was packed, and if we had had to navigate security without bypassing the lines, we would have missed the flight. The woman who met us handed me a black purse. It wasn't mine, but when I peeked inside, I found a passport, my badge, and my wallet.

In the bottom was a Glock, and I frowned at the presence of the weapon. "Interesting."

"You qualify to carry it on the flight," she replied, pulling out a clipboard. "Sign."

I recognized the forms to confirm I had received the weapon and my property, and I flipped through them, signing in the appropriate places. "Thanks."

"Have a safe trip."

She escorted us through security, directed us to the correct gate, and left.

Jake peeked in my purse. "Fancy. I have one of those, too. Not fair. Yours is new."

My years of imagining worst-case scenarios bit me in the ass. I contemplated the reasons the FBI would have sent someone to kit me with a new gun, my badge, and everything I'd need to do my job. "This doesn't actually comfort me at all. In fact, this worries me. They wouldn't send someone to issue this to me when they could have waited for me to get to Baltimore. I could have gotten one in Baltimore. Why did they give me one now?" I realized I was rambling, hated myself for doing it, but the words kept spilling until Jake clapped his hand over my mouth.

"I will gag you, Kit Kat."

I tried to bite his hand, but he cupped his palm to avoid my teeth.

"Behave. What is it with you, anyway? You can't swim, and the instant you get anywhere near a plane, your head goes right into the clouds. The plane isn't going to crash. Take a chill pill."

"But I don't have any chill pills. I'd take one if I had them." I really would, too. Some things never changed. I always got a case of the jitters before boarding. I also got a case of the talkies, too.

Jake was okay with the fidgeting, but once I started talking a mile a minute, he started huffing.

"In the unlikely event of trouble, you being drugged would not be in anyone's best interest."

"You really went there." I glared at him and tried to bite his hand again. The way he had his hand cupped over my mouth didn't do anything to muffle or impede my ability to speak, but it did draw attention from everyone else at the gate waiting to board. "People are looking at us."

"They're looking at you. Specifically, they're probably looking at your legs. Have I told you your legs are absolutely fantastic in that skirt?"

I stretched out a leg to check out my calf. The heels made the muscles more prominent. "You think so? Look at my calves, Jake. They're monstrous. I have yeti calves. Hairy and everything under the tights. How can you like yeti calves?"

"I stand by my claim. Your legs look absolutely fantastic in that skirt."

"I feel like I should tell the world there are men who don't mind yeti calves."

The boarding announcement for our flight played over the airport sound system. I dug through my purse for the boarding pass, but Jake uncovered my mouth, put his hand between my shoulders, and propelled me to the gate.

The attendant took one look at us, reached under her podium, and pulled out two boarding passes. "These are for you, ma'am, sir. Please take your seats."

Jake took them, nodded to the woman, and kept pushing me down the ramp to get on the big plane that'd take us home.

ONCE THE PLANE was in the air, I relaxed a little, staring out the windows at the clouds below. The clouds always made flying worth it, especially when the turbulence was so bad it felt like I was riding a persnickety bastard of a horse. I wasn't sure if the window seat was good or not. If the turbulence knocked the plane out of the sky, which seat was safer? Did it matter?

I contemplated the nature of plane crashes, making thoughtful noises in my throat. As though takeoff had flipped a switch in my head, my thoughts bounced from one another until I had a difficult time figuring out which end was up. I made so many noises Jake started huffing. Once the huffing started, I made noises to deliberately discover what sort of sounds I could lure from him.

The gentleman with the aisle seat kept staring at both of us like we had lost our minds. Three hours into the flight, I leaned forward, stared into the stranger's deep blue eyes, and said, "Statistically speaking, it's safer to fly than it is to drive, but for some reason, I rue and lament the—"

Jake clapped his hand over my mouth. "Please pardon her, sir."

I tried to bite him again, but he avoided my teeth.

Our seat mate waved his hand dismissively. "This has been the most entertaining flight I have ever been on. By all means, continue."

Jake joined me in staring at our seat mate. "Are you sure?"

"Very."

"Okay," my ex-partner replied, removing his hand from my mouth.

"I rue and lament the necessity of flight. It would have been far more fun to drive. Right? We could have taken a road trip. Now, of course, statistically speaking, you're far more likely to survive a car crash than a plane crash when at altitude, but that's a different matter."

"You just had a road trip."

"It wasn't a fun road trip. Come on. Why did we have to fly?"

"It's faster."

"So? I'm not a bird. If I were meant to fly, I'd have wings. They'd probably be attached to my arms or shoulders. I'd have tail feathers, too. Birds need their tail feathers to help control their flight paths. I do not have a tail nor do I have wings. I was not meant to fly. I rest my case. If I were meant to fly, I'd have wings."

"Do you have an off switch? Why is it every time I take you on a plane, you babble? English isn't going out of style. You don't have to bank words."

"It could be worse. She could be one of those panicky fliers. I've shared enough seats with those to last me several lifetimes," our seat mate contributed. "If they aren't screaming every time we hit turbulence, they're doing the heavy breathing thing. Babbling is far better than that. Talkative and fidgeting I can deal with. The screaming and gasping and whimpering at the slightest bump is enough to drive a man to drink."

"She's normally calm, cool, and collected, right up until she's in the air. Then her dignity oozes out of her ears, and she sticks her head in the clouds."

"We're above the clouds," I pointed out.

"You're like an emu, except noisier. The clouds are your sand."

"Ostrich. They don't actually stick their heads in sand to hide, either. That's just a myth," I informed my audience of two.

The captain announced we were making the approach to Baltimore-Washington International. Thanks to the incessant turbulence, I was still buckled in. I patted the seatbelt. "I'm ready. No crashing please, Mr. Pilot," I muttered.

"How old are you again?" Jake prodded me with his elbow. "I should demand hazard pay for this. Think the boss would let me get away with it?"

"In your dreams maybe," I retorted. "You're joking, right? I'm the one who should get hazard pay."

"Forgive me for asking a potentially offensive question, but how old are you, miss?"

"If I had a dollar for every time someone asked me that, I would have paid for my first degree without needing a student loan. Probably my second, too." I sighed my heaviest sigh. "Twenty-nine."

"I should take your badge away until you behave like you're twenty-nine."

"You're a cop?" our seat mate asked, his eyes widening.

"When she acts her age instead of her shoe size." Jake pointed at my heels. "Why do they make high heels in children's sizes, anyway?"

"What's your name?" I asked, sitting up and pressing my heel to the top of Jake's foot, pushing down until I heard him hiss through his teeth.

"Kennedy. You?"

"The giant is Jake. I'm Kat," I replied, thrusting my hand out. "Nice to meet you."

Kennedy stared at my hand for a long moment before shaking it. "Nice to meet you, too. I think. I confess, I'm having a very difficult time imagining you as a police officer, ma'am."

I had a difficult time imagining myself as a regular police office, too. "Don't worry about it. I'm not."

"Be glad there's only a few minutes until we're on the ground. Be very glad. I probably have to put up with her for the rest of the day."

Threatening Jake with bodily harm wasn't wise, and neither was announcing I was armed and dangerous while on a plane, FBI agent or not. Instead of vocalizing my annoyance, I dug my heel into Jake's foot. "Ignore him. He secretly loves me, but he's far too much of a man to admit it. He's afraid of commitment."

"Yeah, to an institution," Jake muttered.

We stared at one another before I cracked and snorted a laugh. "Tell anyone I laughed at that and I'll make you regret it, Jake."

"If you'll remove your heel from my foot, I will give you my oath I will not inform anyone you're capable of laughing."

I eased up with my heel. "Deal."

"From a man's perspective, Miss Kat, I would like to present evidence that most men are not, in actuality, afraid of commitment, but are rather afraid of rejection after announcing a desire to commit to a woman." Kennedy grinned and winked at me. "Then again, he might be onto something with the institution thing."

"So Jake's really just afraid of rejection?" I grinned. "I told him I was leaving him for greener pastures within five minutes of meeting him."

Jake sighed. "That was four or so years ago."

Kennedy nodded, and while his expression was serious, the corners of his mouth twitched. "Considerate of you, giving him advance warning. No room for misinterpretation, right?"

"Exactly. It prevents misunderstandings and inappropriate fraternization."

"Is there ever appropriate fraternization?" Kennedy rubbed his cleanly shaved chin. "That's an interesting subject."

I frowned. "Hey, Jake. When is fraternization appropriate, anyway?"

"It's detailed in the employee handbook. Go read it. Put those degrees of yours to good use."

"That's just mean, Jake."

"That's what you get for annoying me the entire flight."

"But you make it so easy."

We bickered until the plane touched down, and we kept bickering until we managed to get off the plane, following Kennedy, who halted at the end of the ramp to wait for us. "It was a pleasure to meet you both."

I nodded to him, smoothing my skirt, shifting the weight of my travel bag over my shoulder, and going through the motions of making sure I was presentable.

"Pleasure was all mine," Jake replied, shaking hands with the man. "Sorry if she bothered you during the flight."

"She wasn't a bother at all. You headed to the exit? We could walk together. Beats dealing with the lines alone."

"Kat?"

"Sure." I stretched my legs, wincing at the cramp in my calves.

Jake tapped my shoulder. "You okay?"

"A bit stiff."

"How is it you, the little thing you are, are the one who is stiff? I'm fine."

"You're a freak. Carry my bag," I demanded, holding it out for him. "What was I thinking wearing heels on a plane? Will they kick me out of I go barefoot?"

Jake took my bag and slung it over his shoulder. "Leave your shoes on. At least look like a professional."

"I'm on vacation, remember?"

"I was supposed to be on vacation until I had to slog halfway across the country."

While Kennedy looked curious about our exchange, he didn't ask any questions, and we walked across the airport towards freedom. Security was tighter than usual; twice the normal number of guards and airport personnel loitered in the terminal. I tensed, shifting my purse on my shoulder so I could reach for the Glock hidden within its depths.

Jake bent over and whispered in my ear, "I noticed."

The presence of extra security could have been nothing more than a precaution, but I had a difficult time believing the FBI would have made an arrangement for extra security at BWI when Denver's airport had been working under normal operations.

I checked our six, but saw nothing more unusual than a steady stream of passengers heading for the final departure gates. Tilting my head to the side, I headed for the wall, placing my back to it so I could watch the crowd. Jake joined me.

I wasn't sure if I liked the fact Kennedy followed along.

"Something wrong?"

Jake huffed, but before he could say anything, I bumped into him with my hip and shrugged. "Just a bit weirded out. Flights do that to me. I'll be okay in a minute. Just wanted to get out of the crowd. I'm not a fan of large crowds. Why is it so busy here this time of day? I just need some air."

Agoraphobia wasn't one of my problems, but it made a good fallback, and after my nervous chatter on the flight, I hoped Kennedy didn't think too much about my lie.

"Understandable. The first few times I flew, I was edgy for a while, too. Especially with all the changes they've made to security lately." Kennedy checked his watch. "I've got to get to a meeting, otherwise I'd stick around. Take care, you two. Try not to let the crowds bother you, ma'am."

"Have a safe trip," I replied, waving until Kennedy left.

Jake and I sighed our relief when he was gone.

"You realize we're both being a bit paranoid, right?" Jake unbuttoned his suit jacket, and I realized he was making his Glock accessible. "What's the plan?"

"Walk out and hope we're just imagining security is tighter than usual?"

"Hold on, let's at least make it look like we're stopped for a reason. Open my bag," I whispered. In order to reach my bag, I had to go up on my toes. While I hunted for an imaginary missing object, Jake stood still. I was aware of him scanning the crowd, searching for threats. To make my stop appear realistic, I shuffled things around in the bag, grumbling faked annoyance. "Damnit, I can't find it."

"It can be replaced," he replied, playing along with my game. In a softer voice, he reported, "The guards are watching the passengers, all right. One or two gave us a second look but ignored us after you started searching through your bag."

"If I act my shoe size instead of my real age, I'd walk backwards down the hall," I offered. "It's just a coincidence, right? They issued me a gun as a precaution, not because they were expecting trouble. Right?

Jake twisted around to stare at me, snorted, and cracked a smile. "You watch my six, I'll watch yours."

Our days as partners were supposed to be over, and we both knew it. All things came to an end, but I'd watch his six one last time.

The truth of the matter didn't stop me from saying, "Always."

Chapter Eleven

JAKE HELD my bag out of reach and guided me by dangling the duffel as if it were a carrot. I couldn't hop very high in my heels, which helped me pull off the immaturity of walking backwards in my effort to reclaim my property. While I made grabs for the bag, I scanned the crowd behind my partner.

We were drawing a lot of attention from passengers and security alike.

Passengers flowed around us in a hurry to leave the terminal. Most of them stared at me until they noticed me noticing them. Between mad grabs for my bag, I engaged in staring contests until I found a pair of men in suits who continued to watch us, averting their stares until they thought I had turned my attention elsewhere.

"Two men in suits are watching us," I whispered, making another jump for my bag.

"Agents?"

"Don't know."

"Sharp left; there's a set of restrooms down a hallway. I'll meet you out here in five." Jake lowered my bag enough I could yank it out of his grip, which I did.

Feigning annoyance, I spun and stormed to the women's washroom, plowing my way inside while Jake laughed and headed into the men's room. As he went, I caught a glimpse of him pulling out his cell phone.

I'd have to time five minutes in my head. I headed into a stall, locked it, and waited. I counted the seconds. Some agents could time themselves with near-perfect accuracy, but I wasn't one of them. I missed my watch and phone. My watch was long gone, and my phone hadn't been returned to me along with my badge and wallet. After a minute and a half, I flushed the toilet and left the stall, taking my time washing my hands and fussing with my hair. The layout of the restroom allowed me to watch the door through the mirror.

As women flowed in and out, I caught sight of both men waiting outside the door.

When I hit the five minute mark, I stepped through the door, my right hand thrust into my purse, my fingers wrapped around the Glock's grip. Someone sidled up to me, bent down and whispered, "They're from Homeland Security."

My heart took up residence in my throat. How could someone as big as Jake sneak up on me? "Fuck, Jake. Don't scare me like that." Shivering, I loosened my hold on my Glock and eased my hand out of my purse. In a whisper, I added, "I could have shot you."

Both of the agents nodded a greeting to me. Without a word, they fell in step with me and Jake.

"What the hell is going on?"

"Someone called in a bomb threat in the middle of the night, so they upped security," the taller of the two agents explained. "They thought it'd be wise to have someone meet you at the gates. You two left before we could intercept you."

"I might be cursed, Jake. You better run back to HRT where you belong."

Jake huffed. "The instant I'm home, I'm faxing CARD with a full list of the bullshit they will have to put up with."

"Wait. I didn't file my air carry request twenty-four hours in advance of flying." I blinked, peeking into my purse to confirm I was actually armed with a Glock. The gun was definitely in my purse. "Someone pulled strings."

"That took you three hours longer than I expected."

"It's been a long… week? What day is it, anyway?"

"It's been twelve days since you were grabbed. Today's Friday.

I gaped at Jake. "No shit. That long?"

"How long did you think it was?" Jake frowned. "We should have focused more on the time table, not that it made any difference on your end of things."

"I thought it was a couple of days at most."

"We'll deal with it once we're at the office."

I felt stupid for not having covered the basics. The two Homeland Security agents guided us through the airport to a pair of black SUVs waiting at the airport's loading zone. I slid into the back seat of the front car, and Jake followed me in. Both SUVs left at the same time and mixed in with traffic.

My former boss was in the front passenger seat. "Welcome home, Karma."

"Thanks."

"You hanging in there? You look a bit green."

"Twelve days?" I blurted.

"She didn't know?" she demanded.

Jake winced. "Apparently not. My fault. Things were hectic, and the team lead decided to be a dick during questioning."

"So I heard. Washington's pretty pissed he was tossed from the case."

"His fault for failing to call in an attorney when she invoked her right to counsel. She was justified. We'd be shit FBI agents if we didn't uphold the law." Jake clacked his teeth together. "They need to get rid of those relics before the Bureau loses good agents to bullshit."

"Speaking of the law, I didn't file my air carry papers, Boss," I said, tapping the back of her seat.

"It was filed on your behalf. Relax, Karma. It was a legal carry."

"But why?"

"Why don't you tell me why?"

I sat back in my seat, crossed my arms over my chest, and scowled. "I'm a target because I rescued Annabelle, aren't I?"

My boss clapped. "Well done."

"Okay. What about Monday? I'm supposed to report to CARD on Monday." I recognized the initial signs of panic looming on my mental horizon, and I slid into the habit of evening my breath to maintain my cool.

"There's someone ready to drive you to New York City later tonight. You're going to be the anchor for your team until this blows over."

Anchor was a nice way of saying I'd be sitting behind a desk and working as a relay between the other three field agents and the internal support members of the FBI. Normally, the anchor position was handled by someone from the support staff, and I bristled at the demotion. "That leaves them short in the field. How long?"

"However long it takes, though I can't imagine it taking more than a week or two to get the all clear. There's no point in arguing. You'll be working as the anchor unless your team needs you on the ground, so you won't be completely stuck in an office. You'll still deploy. You'll just be working out of the local police stations. Your new supervisor will have more details. I don't know the specifics."

I read between the lines; I was supposed to be grateful I wasn't being yanked off active duty altogether. "Yes, ma'am."

"What about me?" Jake leaned between the seats.

Our former boss lifted her elbow, pressed it to Jake's forehead, and shoved him back. "You're done. I should toss your tall ass out of my car and make you walk home. Be thankful we're dropping you off at your house."

I widened my eyes and sucked in a breath. "My car!"

"It was towed to one of our lots. Nothing seemed to be disturbed. You'll be driven to New York in one of our fleet vehicles. Your car'll be freighted to you next week."

"Oh."

"Anything else?"

"Was it really twelve days? It didn't seem that long."

"Considering your blood tests were positive for trace amounts of sedatives, we theorize your kidnappers had drugged you to skew your sense of time."

"Those motherfuckers," I grumbled. "I didn't even realize. Jake? Did you know about this?"

How had they managed to drug me without me even suspecting I had been drugged?

"No, I didn't know. I would have told you if I had. You hadn't counted the number of times the guards shifted. I thought it had been obvious they were trying to confuse your sense of time, so I assumed you were aware you had been hostage for a long time." Jake slumped in his seat and tilted his head back. "Sorry. It was a stupid oversight. I should have gone over the time tables more thoroughly."

"There's a reason we don't normally allow people close to the vic to be involved in the investigation. Vision is clouded and emotions run high."

I flinched at the reminder I had been a victim, turning my head to stare out the tinted window. "Am I that unpredictable?"

"There's a time and a place for thinking outside of the box," my boss replied, blunt as always. "It worked out this time."

I thought about everything I had done from the instant Phil's gun had touched my temple. Every step I had taken had had one goal: to get Annabelle out of the situation alive. The only unconventional move I had made was attacking Phil and incapacitating him so I could escape with Annabelle.

Instead of answering, I watched cars as the driver headed towards Jake's house, which was located on the outskirts of Baltimore. Thirty minutes after leaving the airport, we arrived. Melancholy smothered me.

I had been happy enough to ditch my other partners, but saying goodbye to Jake the first time around had been bad enough. When the driver pulled into his driveway, I held my fisted hand out, staring at his house with its immaculate lawn and flower beds with perfect blossoms.

"Watch your back," he said, bumping my fist with his.

Without another word, Jake walked out of my life for the second time.

TWELVE HOURS after arriving in Baltimore, I reached New York. Four hours had been lost answering questions. An hour into the interrogation, I had come to the conclusion no one was going to learn anything new from me, but I cooperated in the hopes we had missed something in Colorado.

We hadn't.

My new apartment, which was a ten minute walk from the FBI's NYC headquarters, was a disaster area of boxes. The driver helped me unload the rest of my things from the SUV and left me trying to turn chaos to order. Despite purging half of what I owned during the moving process, I had doubts I'd make everything fit.

I called my parents to let them know I had arrived safe and sound, convincing them they really didn't need to come to New York. Pops understood. Ma didn't, but ultimately I had my way.

If anyone else clung and hovered, I'd hit someone. I was tempted to find a kickboxing studio in the city, but until the aftermath of Annabelle's kidnapping blew over, I couldn't afford to make myself a target.

I spent the weekend unpacking, venturing out of my apartment long enough to get groceries and go to a salon to dye my hair. I normally matched my natural color, but I decided to go with red and had her give me a shorter, spiked cut.

It startled me how two changes could make such a dramatic difference in my appearance.

My last effort to prevent anyone from recognizing me was to buy color-changing contacts. Amber eyes drew attention, but when I tinted them to brown, I barely recognized myself in the mirror.

If I had known of the hell waiting for me at CARD, I would have quit before I started. My kidnapping had built me a reputation among my team, and despite what Mitch had said in Colorado, it wasn't a positive one.

My boss had been trying to warn me in Baltimore, but I hadn't read between the lines. All three of my partners were older, and the fact a woman had qualified to join CARD didn't sit well with them.

The worst was Andrew; his dark eyes narrowed whenever I entered the room. He was the oldest of the team, and he was cut from the same cloth as Simons. While Jerry was younger, he had at least ten years seniority on me, and he liked clucking his tongue whenever I deviated from their set game plan.

Silent and steady Brent had no use for me and liked to pretend I didn't exist.

Our first case as a team came three days after I joined them. While I went out with them as promised, my job as the team's anchor involved sitting in a police station in Albany monitoring the team's comms.

Anchor was a nice way of saying out to pasture. I knew it, the team knew it, and so did the cops. The ones who didn't toss pitying stares my direction ignored me.

Without being on the ground, without going over the evidence, without being truly involved, I couldn't truly contribute. I relayed information from the FBI's support staff to the other CARD members.

In the grand scheme, I was an over-glorified secretary with a gun.

There was one advantage to my post; I heard the results

of the internal data first. Michelle Gianni, age five, had been kidnapped from her school in Pennsylvania. The Amber Alert had made a positive hit in New York, providing us with a trail to Albany.

The vehicle involved in the kidnapping had been dumped on the outskirts of the city. Five hours after our arrival in Albany, while the CARD team was on the scene with the vehicle, I did my own investigating, digging through the information we had on our vic.

I found the kidnapper in her school transcripts, pulled his record, and relayed the information to the team lead. Andrew thanked me but pursued his leads first.

If I had been more aggressive, if I had been on the ground, if I had done a lot of things differently, Michelle Gianni might have survived.

Ten minutes had spelled the difference between life and death, and we had been on the wrong side of the line.

I said nothing, but I knew the truth. Our supervisor, gray-haired and colder than ice Ian Malone, knew the truth, but he accepted our failure without a word.

The only one to accept any blame for Michelle's death was me, and I carried the burden in silence. My doubts engulfed me, and Jake's last words haunted me.

I watched my own back because there was no one to watch it for me. I had never missed anyone so much in my life. The gym became my sanctuary.

In the dead of night when no one watched, I retreated to the still waters of the pool. Hundreds of hours of coaching hadn't helped me swim, but I doggy paddled my way around the shallow end until my world narrowed to my sore, aching muscles and bone-deep exhaustion.

It took me less than two weeks to recognize the truth.

While CARD teams were required to have a minimum of four members, I wasn't needed.

I'd been put out to pasture, belonging in name only. We were always on call, and my secure phone served as my shackles. My entire job could be done between my phone and laptop. Showing up at the office was an unnecessary formality unless I had paperwork to fill out.

Paperwork was the one thing I could count on.

Andrew dumped everything on my desk to maintain the illusion I was worth my paycheck. Once upon a time, I would have learned the names and faces of every agent in the building. Instead, I kept to myself and waited for the ax to fall.

Two months after reaching my dream of joining CARD and learning the truth was a bitter pill to swallow, Andrew tapped on the door of my office, carrying a file in his hand. I stared at him in the numb daze that always settled over my shoulders when the man came near me.

"We've been called in. Here's the brief." Andrew slapped the file onto my desk. "We leave in ten. Get the preliminary preps done."

I picked up the file, opened it, and stared into the smiling face of a young boy. According to the file, he was ten and had disappeared during the night. In silence, I read through the papers. Jacob Henry had been last seen at his home when his parents had put him to bed. The next morning, no one could find him.

There was nothing written on the circumstances of the disappearance. "Runaway?"

Andrew shrugged, turned, and left.

I picked up my landline, dialed the local police department in Johnstown, Pennsylvania, and began making arrangements to turn their station into our base of operations. When Andrew came back ten minutes later, I was still on the phone hammering out travel arrangements. Without looking up at the team lead, I picked up the forms they needed to transport their firearms on the short flight and held them out.

"Hotel arrangements?"

I waited for Andrew to take the first set of forms before grabbing the confirmations out of my printer and offering them along with the reservation for an unmarked car, which would be waiting in Johnstown at the airport with a driver provided by the police.

"Good." Flipping through the papers, Andrew halted in my doorway. "You've made a mistake."

"There's no mistake," I assured him, unholstering my gun and locking it in the drawer of my desk. It was tempting to lock my badge in there, too, but I resisted the urge, instead stuffing it in my purse.

"You don't have your air carry form in here."

"I'm not bringing my firearm." The Glock would sit and gather dust along with the rest of my skills. There was no point in bringing a weapon I wouldn't use.

There was no point when I was going to take them to the airport and leave them there to do their jobs. I didn't need to be in Johnstown to anchor. I could be anywhere. I could be nowhere.

No one would notice.

"What do you mean by that?"

"I have my qualification sheet should I require a firearm. I don't need a gun to anchor."

"Is there something you'd like to say to me, Agent Johnson?"

I grabbed my keys off my desk, turned off the lights, and left my office. If there wasn't a missing ten year old in Pennsylvania needing the team, I would have told the man where he could shove my gun and badge. "No, sir."

"You have a good eye for form detail. You don't miss anything on that front, do you?"

I stared at him with dead eyes, wondering what had driven the man to offer something that sounded suspiciously like a compliment. "Sir?"

"You should probably get your information fixed in the system. Your eyes are brown. Was requesting an exotic color on your identification card necessary?"

I reached up, lightly fingered the contact, and removed it. I repeated the process with the second contact, holding them on the tips of my index and middle fingers.

"I actually do have something to say to you, sir. I quit." While he gaped at me, I dropped the contacts to the floor, dug my badge out of my purse, and let it fall, too.

I left without looking back. They didn't need another desk monkey in the FBI wasting time and resources. Someone—anyone—could serve as their anchor. No one needed me.

Chapter Twelve

I LEFT my car parked in the FBI building's underground garage. Once word of my abandonment of duty spread, I was sure someone would impound it. I added it to my list of things I no longer cared a single fuck about.

Why had I spent so much effort and heartache on CARD? Why had I thought I'd make a difference? There was zero indication I needed to remain an anchor; I had long since dropped off the radar in the public eye, serving my duty to boost the FBI's reputation.

I already had the death of one child on my hands because I hadn't been good enough to be anything other than a complacent desk jockey. I could predict exactly what Andrew would do. He would head to Johnstown, he'd work his case, and Jacob Henry would either live or die. Unlike Michelle, Jacob would probably show up within the next twenty-four hours, safe and sound.

Most disappearances worked out that way. CARD's involvement didn't necessarily mean anything.

I made it two blocks before someone caught up with me. I heard the slap of his shiny oxfords on the concrete approaching me from behind.

"What the fuck do you think you're doing?" Andrew bellowed.

"Quitting. I thought it was obvious." I kept walking.

When he grabbed my arm and yanked me around, I dropped my bag, jerked free and adjusted my stance, pulling my fist back to rearrange his face. Brent approached, followed by Jerry and our supervisor. Before I could strike, Brent lifted his hand and caught my wrist.

"We need you to deploy," he said, his tone impassive. "Let's not turn this into a pissing contest on who can accumulate the highest number of assault charges."

Brent had a good point, although I'd rather choke than admit it. "Your supervisor is more than qualified to fill in as an anchoring desk jockey. You have your perfect team then, Andrew. One without a woman contaminating it."

Had I always spoken in such a dead monotone? The four men flinched, and Brent released my hand. I stooped, picked up my bag, and shouldered the strap.

I made it two steps before a hand fell on my shoulder. I dropped my things and tensed in preparation to fight.

"Wait," Brent ordered.

"You're going to miss your flight."

"We need you to deploy."

"Your supervisor is more than qualified to fill in as an anchoring desk jockey," I repeated. "You could probably pick anyone off the street with a high school diploma and basic literacy skills to handle the level of make-work you've tossed on my desk. I'm sure an entry-level secretary would be willing to help you out."

"CARD deploys in teams of four minimum," Brent reminded me.

I turned and pointed at the team supervisor. "Use him."

Ian Malone arched his gray brow. "Interesting solution, Agent Johnson."

"You are qualified, aren't you? Or are you just going to hide behind your showcase trio of male agents? The only thing this so-called pathetic excuse of a partnership is doing is getting kids killed. I didn't sign up for that. I signed up to save kids, not get them killed when I can't browbeat you old, set-in-your-ways desk ornaments into following viable leads, which resulted in the unnecessary death of a little girl. Take your precious male egos and go fuck yourselves."

Too infuriated to be bothered with anything anymore, I walked away, leaving my bag at their feet.

LEAVING my wallet and keys behind was only the start of my mistakes. Too angry to pay attention to where I was going was my second. Spending so much time trying to drown myself in the pool without supervision had resulted in more endurance than was healthy when infuriated to the point of tears.

By the time I had calmed enough for rational thought to sink in, I was so thoroughly lost I had no idea where I was or how long I had been walking. Allowing my embarrassment to keep me from asking was my third mistake.

After that, I stopped counting my acts of stupidity. I'm sure I had broken at least a few laws by quitting without warning. My career was over, and without it, I had nothing.

For as long as I could remember, I had been driven by one purpose.

When I stripped away the layers of my life that had revolved around reaching my goal, I was left with no real options. Abandoning my duties in the FBI would be a black mark against me, ensuring no sane company would want me.

I had washed out, and it had only taken two months.

There was a chill in the late August wind, carrying the promise of fall. It wouldn't be long until most schools were in session. There was always a surge in kidnappings and runaways near the start of the school season. In training, we had been warned about the phenomenon.

It should have been my time to shine, not crumble to pieces.

I had done my job. I had laid low to let the fallout blow by. I had given up kickboxing to keep under the radar and prevent anyone from discovering my whereabouts. Like everything else I had done in my life, I had done it to secure my position in CARD.

It had taken me less than fifteen minutes to throw it all away.

There were so many things I could have done. I could have requested a transfer to a different team. I could have requested to return to the violent crimes division I had left. I could have requested a transfer to just about any other division within the FBI.

Before I had burned bridges, I could have even applied to join an entirely different branch of law enforcement or a different agency.

Instead, I had trapped myself in the box of limited thinking. Instead of considering my options, all I had done was focus on what I had wanted and what I hadn't got.

Quitting was truly the first of my mistakes. I should have gone to Johnstown, endured, and tried to pretend everything was okay. I should have done my job—the job I had worked so hard to get.

But no, I had allowed my emotions to break out of their cage. I had allowed my calm, cool exterior to crack. There was no one to blame except myself.

I had expected so much more. I had expected to make a difference.

I hadn't expected to become an ornament and unnecessary addition to a team that didn't want me. In Colorado, I had been given hope I was actually wanted in New York. Why had Mitch planted the seed of hope?

Why couldn't my team have men like him in it?

Better yet, why couldn't my team have someone like Jake in it?

Jake had been right about a lot of things. Warning me to watch my back had only been the tip of the iceberg. No one would watch my back, not anymore.

The anger flowed out of me and left me cold, tired, and shaking in its wake. I slid out of the flow of pedestrians and leaned against a concrete-fronted building, staring up at the gray, darkening sky. A hint of red and orange promised a brilliant sunset to come.

I closed my eyes and breathed. The lung-burning fumes of the city seared through me. Parts of Baltimore smelled the same way, but it didn't take long to escape it and find green, wild spaces. Somewhere on the island was Central Park, but I had no idea where.

I hadn't had a chance to visit it or anything else in the city. I hadn't ventured far, sticking to the FBI headquarters, my apartment, the gym, and a few stores.

Two months, and I knew nothing about the place I was supposed to call home.

There was one place I could always go, but the thought of facing Pops and Ma and seeing the disappointment in their eyes kept me rooted to the pavement. The last place I could think of was the ring. I had let my hair grow out over the past two months, although I had kept dying it red to hide my real color.

A few minutes with a razor, and I wouldn't need to worry about my hair or its color. Some time in the ring would let me forget for a while. Without my identification, I couldn't get into most of the clubs. I still looked too young, and the studios valued their operational licenses too much to risk a random stranger coming in to fight.

My time in the FBI working violent crimes had exposed me to the reality of the world. In Baltimore, there were illegal fighting circuits, the type of places anyone could go, bet, and fight.

I no longer had anything to lose, and buried somewhere in New York was likely such a circuit—if I could find it. It was the exact sort of place I never would have gone to before. Not all people who went made it out alive.

It was violence glorified, and the deaths of fighters happened. It happened often enough the FBI worked to break the circuits.

They kept popping up, rebuilding as fast as they were dismantled.

A woman fighting among men would be a novelty, even for them. My hundred and fifteen or fewer pounds wouldn't impress anyone who fought there. The circuits attracted people from all walks of life, including former military men who had lost everything and looked for a place to keep fighting when they were no longer welcome in the government's many wars.

My understanding of their choices should have bothered me a lot more than it did.

Rejoining the crowds, I considered my options. It was possible the FBI had already put an alert out for me, especially if they decided to pursue an abandonment of duty charge, something they could do as I hadn't followed protocol. If they didn't, I had twenty-four hours minimum until they'd file a missing person report.

Twenty-four hours was a long time.

Twenty-four hours wasn't enough time.

I FOUND Central Park by accident. The sun was low on the horizon, casting the walkways meandering through the green lawns and trees in shadow. I wouldn't find an entry to a fighting circuit in the park, but there was something calming about the place, an escape from the city I hadn't known I had needed.

I breathed, and the scent of living things filled my lungs. The stench of the city was still there, but the deeper I walked into the park, the more it faded away. Twisting pathways cut through the trees, and sometime after night fell, I found an empty bench near a pond and sat, staring over the still waters.

The shore was close enough I could dip my toe in if I wanted.

When the clouds scattered and the moon reflected on the still waters, I waited for the world to go by and leave me behind.

The bench creaked and shifted under the weight of someone sitting beside me. A wise person would have scoped out anyone coming so close, but I couldn't bring myself to care enough. I dug my toe beneath a small stone and, with a jerk of my foot, launched it into the pond. The ripples erased the image of the moon.

"Wanna talk about it?'

I didn't recognize the man's voice. "Not particularly."

"I'm pretty sure most of us have quit at some point or another. It's considered a rite of passage in our office. If you haven't tried to quit at least once, you haven't found your limit. If you can't find your limit, you can't surpass it. If you don't know your limit, neither do we. If we don't know your limit, we can't cover your back."

I dug up another stone and sent it arcing into the pond. If he, whoever he was, was expecting an answer, he'd be waiting a long time.

My silence didn't seem to bother him too much.

"We don't have an easy job. Of course, most agents don't actually make it out of the office when their fuse blows. Then again, most of us don't have our integrity challenged so openly, either. There are some lines we try not to cross, and that's one of them. It never ceases to amaze me how the trigger often appears small and insignificant. For example, an implication about a lady's choice of eye color. Pulling out the contacts and dropping them on the floor was a nice touch, by the way."

The logical side of me recognized the FBI had hunted me down for a reason. The rest of me had a difficult time caring.

When I said nothing, the man chuckled. The reaction roused my curiosity, but I kept my gaze fixed on the pond. The ripples of my pair of stones had all but faded away.

"If you were wondering, your supervisor went to John-stown in your place until you're ready to work the case."

"They'll enjoy having a fourth man in the field with them." I regretted the bitter words the instant they left my mouth.

"He said, and I quote, 'If I find out I have performed a single duty outside of Senior Special Agent Johnson's normal operational scope, heads will roll.' Interesting choice of words, I think."

I shrugged.

"Did you know Central Park is one of the very first places we look when someone finally blows their lid and needs to take a walk? Something about the park draws people. It's a pretty calming place, isn't it? However, it's not exactly the safest place after dark. There's a nice cafe nearby. Let's go have a cup of coffee where it's warm."

With nothing to say, I settled for another shrug.

"You're a tough nut to crack, aren't you?"

I dug up another rock, worked my shoe beneath it, and launched it so far it landed on the opposite shore of the pond without hitting the water.

"A little girl died because I didn't do my job well enough. Because I couldn't get them to listen to me."

"Another little girl lived because of you. What happened in the Gianni case is not your fault."

"Great. Does everyone know about that case?"

"It's my job to know. I'm your supervisor's boss. Part of my job description. I've walked around in your shoes plenty of times. Under normal circumstances, Ian would be the one seated here talking to you, but I think we can both agree his method of handling your integration to the team was flawed."

"Well, shit." What was my supervisor's boss doing in Central Park talking to me? I didn't even know the man's name, but I didn't need any writing on the wall to figure out his presence was bad news for me in one way or another.

"You're into kickboxing, right?"

"I quit."

"Why?"

"Apparently, I valued my work with CARD too much." I shrugged and went on a hunt for another stone to pitch into the pond. "I quit because of the publicity."

"You didn't want to make yourself or your team a target, so you dropped off the radar."

There was no point in denying the truth. "Right."

"Make any friends outside of the office?"

"No."

"Why not?"

I shrugged. "We work a lot of hours. Not a whole lot of time to go making new friends."

Kickboxing had been my way of meeting new people.

"The majority of which you spend in your office avoiding every other agent in the building."

"So? I can anchor from anywhere. Office just makes it easier. I could anchor while swimming if I wanted."

"Difficult to do when you can't swim, Agent Johnson. That notation was underlined and highlighted to make certain we were aware of your inability to keep your head above water."

I sighed. "Right."

"Not to malign my gender too much, but us men can be pretty stupid sometimes. You have a record of taking very direct approaches. You have been shot in the line of duty several times. You take risks. You push the envelope. You have an interesting file. Think about it from your team's perspective. Their partner was killed in the line of duty, and his replacement is someone with a known record of putting herself in danger. Did it occur to you they are attempting to protect you?"

"So what? It got a little girl killed."

"You know it. I know it. They know it. You proved you know what you're doing during that case. That doesn't change the fact they've been letting you rot doing a desk job, but you also allowed them to let you rot."

I clenched my teeth. "I was given my orders, sir. I was not notified I was permitted to resume active field duty."

"I didn't introduce myself, did I?"

"No, sir."

"Kelvin Daniels."

Finding another rock with my foot, I launched it into the pond.

"I warned Ian taking too many precautions would cause trouble. Fine. I have a proposal for you."

"I'm listening."

"That's a positive first step. Good. I sometimes enjoy taking an unconventional approach with cases. I'd like to run an idea by you. It might be a bit dangerous."

"More dangerous than a high risk of paper cuts?"

"You won't be sitting at a desk all day."

"I'm listening."

"Can I convince you to listen over a cup of coffee? I don't know about you, but I'm freezing out here."

"Maybe if it's whisky flavored."

"There will be no drinking while on duty."

"I already quit, so I'm not on duty."

"Rejected."

"What?"

"Your proposal to quit has been rejected."

I wasn't sure what to make of that. Confused, I turned to face my supervisor's boss. While the darkness obscured his features, he didn't look very old to me. "If I agree to coffee, will you leave me alone?"

"Probably not."

"Why not?"

"Are you kidding me? Anyone who can withstand being stonewalled as an anchor for two months is far too valuable to let go. Remember, I get the performance reports. I've seen what you can do from a desk without seeing the crime scenes firsthand. I can't wait to see what you can do when you're back in the field where you belong. Now, get up and march. I'm going to take you for something to eat and a coffee, and I won't accept no for an answer."

Chapter Thirteen

KELVIN DANIELS'S idea of going for something to eat and a coffee was some upscale Italian restaurant on Fifth Avenue, the sort of place I couldn't afford even if I wanted to go, which I didn't. I was painfully aware of being underdressed compared to everyone in the establishment.

The waiter didn't seem to care what I wore, treating me no differently from everyone else, which startled me almost as much as the fact Daniels seemed to know everyone. The man, who couldn't possibly be older than thirty, waved cheerfully to the fifth person in the past ten minutes to swing by our table to say hello.

"What's your proposal?" I asked, pushing my pasta around my plate. Despite not having had anything to eat since breakfast, my appetite had abandoned me sometime after the opening course of salad.

"I will give you all the information for the Henry case and one of our unmarked cars. Run with it, see what you can dig up."

I lifted my brows, and my fork slipped out of my hand to clatter to the plate. Flushing, I snatched the utensil up. "I'm sorry. Did you just say you wanted me to run with it?"

"That's exactly what I said."

"Without a partner."

"Without a partner," he confirmed. "You'll be under strict orders to pull out and wait for backup if the situation becomes dangerous. You have a proven track record of good solo work."

"And you'll give me all current information on the case?"

"Yes. You'll be able to use the data that has already been gathered and processed."

"You're basically ordering me to act as a rogue agent?"

Daniels chuckled. "Something like that. I'm not above poking sticks in the spokes when an opportunity presents itself. If you leave after dinner, you can get to Johnstown sometime before dawn. You can hit a hotel halfway there if you get tired. It's a six hour drive. The team flew into Pittsburgh and drove to Johnstown from there. That said, the clues seem to indicate Jacob Henry is no longer in the area."

"Runaway or kidnapped?"

"The team has decided it is a probable runaway case."

I frowned at the slight change in Daniels's tone. "You don't think it's a runaway case."

"My personal opinion is not a factor in this investigation."

"Considering CARD typically isn't called in unless a child has crossed state lines, what are you not telling me?"

Daniels sipped at his espresso, watching me with eyes so dark they were almost black. "The child has affections for several relatives in New York. It is currently theorized he is trying to reach one of these relatives. However, the team has opted to do a thorough sweep of the area surrounding Johnstown, leaving a great deal of the investigative work to the local police department."

Spinning my fork in my pasta, I thought over his words, forcing myself to take a bite, chew, and swallow. Considering I barely tasted what I was eating, the restaurant felt like a waste. "Uh huh."

"There are some interesting items in Henry's file."

"So, let me get this straight. You have potential leads on this child's disappearance, and you're opting to turn it into a game?"

"I'm merely giving you the opportunity to examine the case with complete freedom to pursue any lead you want without being ordered off the trail. Of course, you can't quit if you want to see the file."

I stared at him, and he grinned at me and shrugged. "Rules are rules, and I couldn't in good faith break such important rules."

"I am not buying what you are selling. Sending me off solo is breaking the rules."

"But I'm signing off on it. If I sign off on it, it's not breaking the rules. By authorizing you, I'm the only one at any risk of reprimand. Don't tell me you haven't thought about running a case the way you wanted instead of completely by the book."

"You're insane."

"The unmarked car is a Corvette."

Setting my fork down so I wouldn't drop it, I took a sip of my water. The FBI had a fleet of unmarked cars ranging from vehicles that should have been scrapped decades ago to sports cars, but I had always ended up with mid-sized cars or standard SUVs.

"It's yellow. Yellow makes it faster."

"Right."

"It's a convertible."

My cheek twitched. "Are you trying to get me to handle the case or steal the car?"

"Let's make a wager, Agent Johnson." Daniels leaned towards me, and his slight smile unnerved me.

"I don't make bets. Not about work."

"So that means you're not actually quitting?"

I scowled. "I didn't say that."

"Hear me out before you say no."

"Fuck. Fine. I'm listening."

"We are going to work so well together."

"Not if I can help it," I muttered.

"We will treat this as a scenario, one your team is unaware you are participating in. You will be playing the role of a rogue agent who has decided that playing by the book is beneath you. Of course, for the sake of the scenario, there are certain rules I can't allow you to break, but you're the only one who will know that. You will work this operation under the assumption it is you versus the world. Your goal is to recover Jacob Henry and see him taken into safe custody. You may use whatever methods you see fit within the guidelines I give you."

Rogue FBI agents happened. Sometimes the restrictions of our jobs made agents snap. Most retired or quit. The few who went off the deep end became a risk to everyone.

"You could just order me to do that, sir. Assuming I don't actually quit, that is."

"It's more fun this way."

"You open your mouth and present information that should be restricted to the FBI, but then you continue talking, and I start severely doubting you're actually in the FBI."

Without hesitating, he pulled open his jacket and flashed me his badge. "You should have asked that an hour ago. I should give you a failing grade, but I'm taking your circumstances into consideration. I am really your supervisor's boss. Ask anyone in the office. They'll tell you where my office is and even show you up to the top floor."

I winced. "Right."

"As a rogue agent, your job will be to avoid detection from law enforcement while accomplishing your objective, which is to locate and protect Jacob Henry. There will be a team tasked with tracking you down. They will be aware you are running a scenario as the target of their training exercise. They will also serve the secondary role of backup should you require it."

"I have to evade an FBI team specifically tracking me down while working under a CARD team's nose?"

"Exactly."

"In a yellow convertible Corvette."

"I have faith in you."

"Right."

"Here's the wager. If you pull it off, you get to keep the Corvette as your official FBI car. If you fail, you aren't allowed to quit."

I opened my mouth, furrowed my brows, and clacked my teeth together. "So you're saying that either way, I can't quit."

"You weren't supposed to notice that."

"What if I say no?"

"Plan B involves handcuffs."

No matter what I said, I would lose. "I'm pretty sure this is coercion, sir."

"I can't just let the agency lose such a talented resource. In my years of management, I have found honey works better than threats. Today's variety of honey is a yellow convertible Corvette you get to use as your car. It'd be such a shame if I had to give it to someone else. I'm sure that Andrew fellow in your team would like it a lot."

I narrowed my eyes. "He likes the car, doesn't he?"

"He wants it with every bone in his body. Actually, there's only three or four people in the office who don't want it. If you win, it's yours. You get his dream car. To sweeten the deal, you get to prove, openly, you have earned your spot on the team and deserve to be in the field like every other agent in CARD."

"You're a tricky son of a bitch," I hissed.

"That's the nicest thing anyone has said to me all week."

"Just so we're clear on my opinion of you: I want to douse you in gasoline and light you on fire."

He laughed. "Finish your dinner, Agent Johnson. You have a long drive ahead of you."

THE CASE FILE for Jacob Henry was far thinner than I liked. I spread the pages out on my desk, standing while I flipped through the papers, cursing Kelvin Daniels under my breath. While I read, I made an appointment with a twenty-four hour hair salon to install extensions. When I told the woman I wanted to add at least a foot to my current length, more if possible, she made a strangled noise in her throat.

After several minutes of begging, pleading, and bribing, I convinced her to take the job. In three hours, I'd be a whole new woman.

Even the FBI tended to forget women could extend the length of their hair without the use of a wig. A wig would have made things easier—and cheaper—but FBI agents were trained to spot wigs, and few criminals got good wigs or knew how to wear them without being obvious about it.

I smiled and returned my attention to the file. At first glance, Jacob Henry looked like the perfect child. He had good grades, didn't get in trouble, and enjoyed sports, though the file didn't note any specifics on his after-school activities. He had two uncles and an aunt living in northern New York. His parents had twenty years of marriage behind them. The Henry family was wealthy enough to make them a target for a kidnapper.

What caught my attention, however, was the fact that Mr. Henry worked in the same branch of government Annabelle's father did. A chill ran down my spine. They didn't work together, and from what I could tell from the file, it was unlikely they ever had worked together.

Mr. Henry was an accountant, which indicated it was a coincidence. I drummed my nails on my desk, staring at the wall while I thought through the potential connection.

I grabbed my phone from its cradle and punched Daniels's extension. He picked up on the second ring. "You're not wimping out on me already, are you?"

"Did Annabelle's father ever work with Mr. Henry?"

"It didn't take you long to notice that. Good. No, we can confirm they have not worked directly together."

"Any potential connections within their employment?"

"It is something we are looking into."

"No ransom requests?"

"Unlike the Greenwich case, no ransom demands have been issued."

I jotted down notes so I wouldn't forget. "Thanks."

"You have your new phone with you?"

I glanced at the cell phone Daniels had given me. "I have the phone."

"You have earned a tidbit of intel. It's secure. As I find out relevant information, I will load the data to the phone. Now, listen carefully. This is important. If you get in trouble and need backup, break the phone. Hit it against something as hard as you can. That will trigger an emergency beacon. Make certain you keep the device charged at all times. Never turn it off. If you do so, the emergency beacon will activate."

Picking up the phone, I flipped it over in my hands. There was no brand on the device, although it had a similar build to an iPhone. "Okay. So, keep it charged and turned on. Break it or turn it off if I get into trouble. Why didn't you tell me this when you gave me the phone?"

"I wanted to see if you'd call me about the connection first. If you didn't, I figured you wouldn't need that function. Since you did, well, I foresee you running into trouble."

My instincts told me he knew a lot more than he was telling me, and his withholding information would land me in hot water. Something about his tone also made me think he was challenging me, daring me to prove something to him. What that something was, however, eluded me. "You really are an asshole, Mr. Daniels."

"I try. I try really, really hard. I'm so grateful you have noticed and appreciate the great lengths I have gone to transform myself into the ultimate asshole."

"If you want me to do this, you need to give me the keys to my Corvette, sir." I slammed the phone into its cradle.

Gathering up the file, I stuffed it into my briefcase. Unlocking my desk drawer, I retrieved my gun and methodically unassembled it, checked it over, and reassembled it before loading it. I took an extra pair of magazines and added them to my briefcase.

I was wiggling into my shoulder holster when Kelvin Daniels made his appearance in my doorway, attracting the attention of the few agents still in the office. They kept their distance, their expressions curious. Daniels jangled the keys.

Before he could change his mind about the car, I snatched them out of his hand. "Where's it parked?"

"Bottom level of the garage. I already told the guards you'd be leaving with it. I also told them to make sure your car isn't bothered while you're gone."

"My opinion of you hasn't changed."

"Will it change if I tell you I'm giving you a head start? I won't send the cavalry after you until noon tomorrow. I won't tell them what kind of car you're driving, either."

"No, it won't change my opinion."

"You can't douse me in gasoline and light me on fire. There would be witnesses."

The watching agents snickered.

"Why do I get the feeling they wouldn't care?" I hissed, pushing by him and heading to the elevator.

"Why can't you just admit you have fallen shamelessly in love with me?" he called after me.

"Not in this lifetime, Mr. Daniels. Not in any lifetime. If I'm not mistaken, you're also wearing a wedding ring, although I can't imagine why anyone would want you around."

"I'm hurt."

I halted at the elevator and stabbed the down button. "Are you ever going to leave me alone?"

"I wasn't planning on it."

To my disappointment, pressing the button over and over didn't summon the elevator faster.

I RETURNED to my apartment long enough to grab a nap before heading to the salon. Four hours and almost a thousand dollars later, the stylist had managed to give me thick red hair that fell halfway down my back. I had no idea how she managed to pull it off, but it involved a lot of layers and made my head weigh a ton.

My first act was to contain it in a messy bun piled on top of my head.

Armed with coffee, I hit the road.

With the CARD team prowling around Johnstown, Pennsylvania, it was the last place I wanted to go but the first place I needed to look. The devil was in the details, and if I wanted to get to the heart of Jacob Henry's disappearance, I needed to retrace the boy's movements.

The lack of evidence at the Henry house screamed runaway, but there were other options—options no one liked considering. Both of the boy's parents were accounted for, as were his close relatives. However, the possibility existed someone close to him had lured him out of his bed and out of the house, leaving him easy prey for a kidnapper.

"Where could you be, Jacob?"

Most runaways were found within a couple of days, returned to their families a little worse for wear but safe. Older teens tended to be gone longer. The fact Jacob, age ten, hadn't been found yet worried me.

Going by the book, CARD had no substantial reason to believe foul play was involved. Kids ran away from home all the time. CARD was only involved in a small fraction of runaway cases, which were typically handled by the local police departments.

If what I knew was accurate, CARD was involved because of the possibility Jacob crossed state lines to reach a relative's house. Which relative would Jacob go to?

More importantly, why?

After pulling over, I turned on my hazards, got out my new phone, and sent Daniels a text requesting phone records for the relatives living in New York.

My phone rang within a minute.

"Johnson," I answered.

"Why do you want the call records?"

"If you want me to like you, Mr. Daniels, you'll get me the records," I replied, forcing my voice to sound as sweet as possible. "Would it help if I said please? Pretty please? With a cherry on top?"

"But I'm curious."

"You're one of those mother hen supervisors, aren't you? I thought I didn't have to play by the book for this."

"I do need a legal reason to pull those records, Agent Johnson."

I sighed. "Fine, fine. Since *you* have to play by the rules, I'll tell you. Since there was no sign of forced entry, Jacob likely left his home on his own. So, I wanted to find out if any of his relatives had made a call to the Johnstown, Pennsylvania area in the days leading up to his disappearance."

"You're suggesting an arranged familial kidnapping?"

"I'm suggesting someone may have convinced Jacob to leave his home on his own, after which he may have either ran away with someone of his own free will or been kidnapped," I corrected.

"You have my undivided attention."

"Can I play devil's advocate? Wait, let me figure out how to make the phone work through the car speakers. I'll call you back in a minute."

"Okay." Daniels hung up.

It took me several minutes to figure out how to link the phone to the car, but I hit the road once I plugged the phone into the car's built-in USB charging port and called Daniels.

"Start talking," he ordered.

I gunned the engine and sped west. "I'm about to make a lot of crazy assumptions here, so bear with me."

"I can work with crazy if you explain the crazy to me. If it's just incoherent rambling, I'm not sure I can work with that."

"I'll talk slow and use small words so you can understand me, sir."

"Good. Continue."

"Assumption one: the Greenwich and Henry cases are linked. Assumption two: the group behind the Greenwich case has insider access to information."

"I follow."

"Crazy scenario one: The perps figure out Jacob has a close relationship with his uncles or aunt. They hold one of them hostage, force them to make contact with Jacob to lure him out of the house, and kidnap him."

"Please never become a criminal."

"Sir?"

"Just please promise me you'll never choose to become a criminal."

I ignored his request and said, "Crazy scenario two: The family isn't involved in the case at all. Instead, he does as kids do and made arrangements with other children his age.

Maybe they're playing a game. Despite the belief children never play outdoors, there's still a forbidden fruit quality to playing a game of hide and seek at night."

"That doesn't explain why Jacob would still be missing."

"Have you checked to see if there are any other children missing in the area?"

"I assumed the police would have notified us if…" Daniels coughed. "I'll find out and let you know when I know."

Discussing wild ideas was a part of the investigative process, but the idea I was about to toss out was crazier than my normal arsenal of conspiracy theories. I didn't like conspiracy theories. I liked facts.

I only started concocting theories when I didn't have enough facts to work with.

"Crazy scenario three: Mr. Henry is part of the group responsible for the Greenwich case, is the reason they knew to target someone like the Greenwich family, and had arranged for his own son to disappear to draw resources from the Greenwich case. That case is still open, isn't it?"

Daniels was silent for a long time. "It is still open. If Mr. Henry is involved in the case, why hasn't a ransom request been sent yet?"

"Avoiding pattern development. The group that kidnapped me and Annabelle were highly organized. They were a professional outfit. Patterns are how we often identify and catch criminals. The professional groups know this and work to avoid developing patterns. Ransoms are high risk. If they develop a pattern, then they run a higher risk of being caught."

"I follow."

"How big of a town is Johnstown?"

"It's small."

"If he works for the government, why is Henry living out there?"

"It used to be his summer home. According to the interviews we've had with the Henrys, they didn't want to uproot Jacob again, so they decided to enroll him in the public school system in Johnstown this year. It's speculated Henry's planning on retiring soon."

"Crazy scenario three sounds promising. As an accountant, wouldn't he have an idea of a project's importance from the flow of money in the varying departments? If he was overseeing the financials for that specific project, he would have been aware of heightened activity due to increased expenditure. So, what exactly was Mr. Greenwich working on?"

"Security software for military weapon systems."

"Does the CARD team know this, sir?"

"No one else has come up with a legitimate reason to link the Greenwich case to the Henry case. At this point, the circumstances of the Greenwich case were not relevant to the Henry case. I will look into the specifics of Mr. Henry's work and determine if the circumstances you've suggested are viable. If so, I'll kick the information to counterterrorism and Homeland Security. If that *is* the case, I'm not sure I can leave you flying solo even with the precautions I put into place. You ruined their plans by rescuing Greenwich's infant. It's entirely possible they'll target you."

"I'm aware, sir. That's why I was working as an anchor."

"A moving target *is* harder to hit, I suppose. And you're driving a very fast car."

"If this kidnapping has been done by the same group, you should check into the sales of all black-colored SUVs matching the make and model of the ones used in the Greenwich case. They had at least seven or eight vehicles on the route they took me. If we assume they used the same trick at the other splits, that's a lot of cars they had to get rid of."

"The investigators working on the Greenwich case have been looking for the vehicles used in the kidnapping."

"It might be worth asking if there have been a lot of the same type of car in the Johnstown area."

"You're not going to Johnstown?"

"That, sir, would be telling. If I told you, I wouldn't be doing a very good job as a rogue agent doing exactly what I want. Make sure you get me the information as soon as you can."

"I'll call you," he promised before hanging up.

I pulled over, checked my files, and set the GPS to guide me to the house of Jacob's favorite uncle to pursue the first of my crazy conspiracy theories.

Chapter Fourteen

ON MY WAY to the first uncle's house, I stopped at a Walmart and purchased new clothes, including a fake leather jacket suitable for concealing my gun. I went with a casual appearance, matching the shortest denim shorts I could find with a halter top.

Anyone who knew me from the FBI offices wouldn't expect me to wear something showing so much skin, especially when it revealed several of the bullet scars I had picked up over the years.

Not even Jake had seen me wearing anything so scandalous outside of a swimsuit or the sports bra and spandex shorts I wore when kickboxing.

A little after eight in the morning, I pulled into the driveway of a quaint two story house with an overgrown yard and a picket fence in dire need of repair. I parked the Corvette and slid out of the vehicle, keeping my sunglasses on to mask the color of my eyes. Pulling out a notepad and

pen from my briefcase, I shoved them into the back pocket
of my shorts.

Closing my briefcase, I locked it before engaging the
Corvette's car alarm. I took my time going up the walkway
and scoping out the property before stepping onto the small
porch. I discovered the doorbell didn't work, sighed, and
pounded on the door.

"Hold yer hosses," a man bellowed from deep within the
house. I heard a few thumps, a couple of curses, and had a lot
of doubts about the nature of Winston Henry.

The door opened to reveal a naked man in his middle
years, his body toned, covered in tattoos, and with a wide
grin revealing several missing teeth. "Well hello there,
darlin'."

"Are you Winston Henry?"

"Sure am, darlin'. What can I do ya for?"

I took my badge out of my pocket and discreetly flashed
it. "FBI. I have some questions to ask you. May I come in?"

Winston straightened, his expression turning serious. "Is
this about Jacob, ma'am?"

"It is."

"Of course. Please, come in."

Interesting. It was a rare man who could switch between
a southern drawl and a more formal northern accent so
flawlessly.

Like the exterior of the home, the interior was in dire
need of repair, although the place was mostly clean. I glanced
around, taking in the collection of family photographs
hanging on the walls. There was a landline sitting on a small
table near the front door. An unpainted section of new
plaster captured my attention.

I narrowed my eyes. Could the mark be for a wire tap or

a bug? While I wanted to linger and check the spot, I followed Winston into his kitchen, which was located at the back of the house.

I pitied whoever had to do the dishes, which had spilled out of the double sink and taken over the counters.

"Please, have a seat, ma'am." Winston gestured to the table, which was the only surface in the kitchen not covered in junk or dirtied dishes.

Sliding onto one of the old upholstered wooden seats, I tested it for its sturdiness before resting my full weight on it. "Has anyone spoke to you yet?"

Winston sat across the table from me and clasped his hands together on the table. "Not yet. I figured someone would be coming by. My brother called to ask me if I had seen Jacob yesterday morning."

"What time?"

"Six or seven? Not quite sure, ma'am. I was still asleep when he called."

"What did you think about the call, Mr. Henry?"

Winston sighed and shook his head. "It's right weird, ma'am. My brother isn't the most, well, talkative of fellows. You get me? So he calls, wakin' me up, soundin' more annoyed than anythin' else, sayin' how he can't find Jacob and demandin' if I had seen him. I hadn't. Don't get me wrong, I love my brother, flesh and blood and all, but we ain't real close. I ain't seen Jacob since he were three."

"Right." I pulled my notepad and pen from my pocket and jotted down some notes. "Why would he ask you, then?"

"That's what I don't get. I haven't seen Jacob in years. He's, what, nine or ten or eleven or some shit like that? Sometimes I talk to the kid when I talk to my brother."

"Would you say you've spoken to Jacob enough for him to recognize your voice on the phone?"

"Sure. He knows who I am right away when my brother gives him the phone."

Winston's tendency to switch between accents made my skin crawl, and I made notes about his odd vocals and to find out when he had been in the deep south. "How did your brother sound?"

"As I said, pretty annoyed. I'm not really close with my brother, but he gets snippy. He don't much like how we grew up and doesn't want it around that boy of his."

A lightbulb went off in my head. "You grew up south." I considered the southern states and tried to place his accent. "Tennessee?"

"Damn, darlin', that's either a right good guess, or you've been down home."

I chuckled. "Talk however makes you feel comfortable, Winston. So, you grew up in the south?"

"Sure did, darlin'. All of us did. When my brother went and got himself that fancy job with the government, he changed, yanno? We all moved up north so we wouldn't be so distant. We're all the family we've got. Ma died in New York when the towers collapsed, and Pa was killed in an accident. Got nobody else."

"Just you and him?"

"Nah, got us a sister and brother, too." Winston got up, went to the counter, opened a drawer, and pulled out an address book. He opened it to a page and slid it in front of me. "Here's how you can reach them, ma'am. I imagine you got my address from my brother. This should help you a bit."

"Thanks, Winston. Really appreciated." I took my time

copying down the sets of numbers and addresses. "When you talk to Jacob, what sort of conversations do you have?"

The man sighed and stared at his hands. "It ain't always pretty, ma'am. The talks we have, I mean."

Alarm bells went off in my head, and it took all my will to keep my posture calm and relaxed. Body language made a difference, and I couldn't afford to look tense. If I tensed, so would he.

If he became wary, I'd lose a chance for good information. "Raising a boy ain't easy, is it?"

Winston cracked a faint smile. "You got yourself a bit of the drawl there, darlin'."

"Good upbringin', right?"

"Damn right, darlin'."

"What wasn't so pretty about your talks with Jacob?"

Winston drew in a breath, held it for several long seconds, and then sighed. "He's been brought up pretty restricted, ma'am. His ma teaches him so my brother can move around with work. Jacob wants friends his own age, and he talks to me about it sometimes, ya know? So I listen sometimes. I listen real hard, and it ain't pretty, when a little boy just wants to have himself some friends."

"Do you think Jacob would run away?"

"Wouldn't doubt it for a second. He just wants to go to school proper like, where he can make himself some friends. Why, it was just a week or two ago he was cryin' because he didn't want to go back to Washington with my brother and his wife."

Winston's thoughts supported Jacob as a runaway risk, but the way the man described his brother bothered me. "You ever try to do anything about his schooling problem?"

"If I could, I would, darlin'. If I could, I would. Don't

reckon I know what I can do about it. Jacob's mother's a sweet lady, but she's prim and proper and don't really like us Henrys very much, though she took quite the fancy to her man. Prolly because he has the money she wants."

In the end, so many decisions in life came down to money, and I resisted the urge to sigh. "Your family has special circumstances, then. Do Amelia and Peter talk to Jacob?"

Snorting, the man shook his head. "Amelia ain't ever met the boy, ain't ever talked to 'im on the phone, either. My brother and sister don't right get along. He blames 'er for Ma's death. Peter's happy enough with his own boy, and don't need another, so he says."

"You talk to Amelia and Peter often?"

"Sure do. I keep 'em in the loop. Only seems right, being family and all."

"Do you have a number I can reach you at, Winston?"

"Sure do, darlin'." He gave me the number, which I wrote down. "Sorry I can't be of more use."

"You were very helpful, Mr. Henry. I appreciate your cooperation. I'll let you enjoy your morning. Don't be surprised if other law enforcement officers come to pay you a visit. We're trying to be as thorough as possible."

Winston thrust out his hand. "Thanks so much for takin' the time to talk to me, darlin'. If it helps find Jacob, I'll use my last breath answerin' whatever questions you folks have."

"No, thank you, Mr. Henry." I meant it, too. Despite Winston's lack of attire, he came across as the kind of man who would do anything for family.

Unfortunately, that made him a prime suspect, but I had other calls to make before CARD decided to come visiting the rest of the Henrys in New York.

I LEARNED nothing of use from Amelia, but Peter had a lot of opinions, and he wanted to share them with me. All of them.

Over the course of my career, I had met a lot of different people. I had questioned some of America's most hardened criminals, and I had grilled little old ladies who probably felt guilty if they accidentally killed a fly.

Over the years, I had never met someone who talked quite as much as Peter Henry.

He offered me a cup of coffee while he was on his second pot, guzzling the black fluid like he was afraid it would disappear. The more coffee he drank, the faster he spoke, until I had a difficult time translating his southern drawl.

"Mr. Henry, can you tell me anything about your brother's son, Jacob?"

It was my tenth attempt to turn the conversation back to the missing boy. I was keeping a tally of how many times the man went off on a tangent to keep myself from pulling my gun and shooting at his feet to make him dance to my tune.

Shooting innocent people was on my list of things I wasn't allowed to do during my rule-breaking binge.

"Winston's always complaining about that boy, saying I should do something about it. Like what am I supposed to do? I have a boy of my own to raise. I don't need the troubles of another one. Never really met the boy more than a time or two, and that was years ago. Don't really care to, either. No offense meant, ma'am, but how my brother raises his kid isn't my problem."

"Do you ever speak with Jacob on the phone?"

"Why would I? Not my kid, not my problem. It'd do the world a lot of good if other people stopped trying to raise another man's son. That's a big problem with how things are done today. I don't need anyone telling me how to raise my boy, and I sure as hell don't want to be telling anyone how to raise theirs. I get the whole family thing, but we're not his kind of people, and I don't want anything to do with his kind of people."

While Peter had gone on a rant about others trying to raise his son, who was with his mother in the back yard, he hadn't mentioned 'his kind of people' before. "What do you mean by his kind of people? Your brother's?"

"Yeah, his kind of people. The rich kind driving around in their fancy black and chrome SUVs thinking they're all that and a cup of coffee. I'll tell you something. They ain't worth even half a cup of this coffee. You should have a cup of coffee. It's real special."

I made a note about the reference to the SUVs and the type of people his brother associated with. "No thanks, too much coffee in the morning eats my stomach alive," I lied.

In all honesty, if I didn't get a cup of coffee soon, there'd be trouble for someone, but I wasn't about to accept a cup of coffee from someone who acted like he was higher than a kite on speed.

"Your loss."

"You ever meet these rich kind of people with their fancy SUVs?"

"Once. Never again, I tell you. I stopped going around his place after the first time I met them."

"When was that? Do you remember?"

"Sure do. Don't think I'll ever forget. Actually, wait a second. I have a picture."

I had to fight hard to mask my excitement. "I'd love to see this picture."

"I got a few. My lady loves her camera, and she takes pictures of everything. I got a whole album from that visit." Peter hurried out of the room, returning several minutes later with two large photo albums, which he set on the table in front of me. "Go on and have yourself a look. If you need them for evidence, by all means, take the albums. We got the originals on film. My lady's pretty upset about the whole thing. We might not be close to my brother's family, but we have a boy of our own. Anything to help."

"You don't mind if I take the albums?"

"Names and dates are written on the back of the pictures."

"This is really helpful," I replied, stacking the albums on top of each other. "I'll take you up on that offer. I'll have these returned to you as soon as I can. Can you confirm this number is good to reach you at?" I asked before reciting the number I had gotten from Winston.

"That's my fancy new cell number. Don't use it much, but I carry it around with me. That'll work. My regular phone's what I use more often."

"Mind giving it to me?"

"Sure thing." He recited the number, and I jotted it down.

I rose from my seat, thrusting out my hand. "You have been exceptionally helpful, Mr. Henry. We're doing every-thing we can to find Jacob. We've got a lot of people on his disappearance, so don't be surprised if other law enforce-ment officers drop by to ask you more questions."

"Glad to help out, ma'am. You have yourself a great day, okay?"

"You, too." Gathering up the photo albums, I headed out the door, got into the Corvette, and dumped the albums on the other seat. Backing the car out of the driveway, I checked my mirrors, narrowing my eyes at the silver SUV that slowed as it drove by Peter Henry's home.

I kept my speed to the limit and pretended I didn't notice the vehicle tailing me. Changing my plans of hitting a hotel right away, I led the vehicle on a merry chase, stopping at every red light, stopping at the yellows despite annoying drivers behind me, and keeping to below the speed limit.

When they grew tired of tailing me and pulled up along-side my Corvette at a red light, I leaned out the open window and blew a kiss to the two uniformed officers within. "Have yourselves a good day, officers! Keep up the good work."

They stared at me, and I waggled my fingers and blew them another kiss before the light turned green and I eased the sports car through the intersection.

Daniels never said I couldn't taunt anyone while giving them the slip. Not that I'd ever admit it to his face, but he was right about the paint job. Yellow really did make the car go faster, and I enjoyed testing its acceleration the instant I could no longer see the cops in my mirrors.

Chapter Fifteen

PLAYING IT SAFE, I drove over two hours to Albany before I found a hotel and got a room. With a Corvette to worry about, I ended up spending more than I liked for a hotel room, although it had perks, including a jacuzzi.

I would enjoy handing over the receipts for my expenses. If I couldn't douse Daniels in gasoline and light him on fire, I'd make him explain the charges to the accountants who would be out for his blood when it was time to balance the books. He hadn't listed spending restrictions as a part of my rule breaking, and I had a signed sheet of paper stating I was to break most of the FBI's rules at their expense.

Between driving the car and a license to make my own rules, I was enjoying myself for the first time since leaving Baltimore.

It took two trips to ferry my things into my new room, and I didn't bother to unpack before grabbing the albums. I lounged on the big bed, lying on my stomach so I could flip through the photo albums in search of answers. Having access to Peter's wife would have simplified the process, but true to Peter's word, names, dates, and locations were written on the back of each picture in clear, neat hand-writing.

The album told a sad story from the first page. No one smiled, not the two boys in the pictures, who flanked their fathers on opposite ends of the family. The wives stood side by side in the images, and neither looked too happy to be together.

The images had been taking in September, shortly after the Twin Towers of New York fell. Shadows of grief dark-ened the eyes of both men.

"Right after their mother's death," I murmured, grabbing my notepad and jotting down a note.

My phone rang, and I grabbed it out of my pocket, checking the screen. After confirming it was Daniels, I answered, "Hello?"

"Good morning, sunshine!"

"Daniels, what do you want?"

"What sort of trouble are you causing me?"

"Me?"

"Some cops ran the plates of the Corvette."

"I figured. They followed me around earlier. I blew them some kisses and told them to have a nice day."

"You flirted with the cops?"

"Sure. I didn't break a single traffic law, which they were clearly waiting for. If they hadn't been so painfully obvious about tailing me, maybe I would have given them a reason to pull me over."

"You are enjoying yourself a little too much, Agent Johnson."

"Why are you bothering me?"

"I have some information for you."

"I have a pen and a notepad ready."

"Your crazy conspiracy theory regarding money flow was correct. Henry has access to the accounts for monies owed for contract work for the project."

"Which means what?"

"He knows how much is being spent, what it is being spent on, and who is being hired for the work." Daniels sighed. "In short, you have connected the two cases. That means I should be pulling you off this case, Johnson."

"I really will quit if you pull me when I've just gotten started," I warned.

"It's not safe for anyone to be going solo. No one. No agents will be going without a partner on this case."

"So pull a partner out of your ass. If he—or she—can catch me, I'll tolerate them taking up room in my Corvette. If they play by my rules. Which are currently modified to my liking. I want to keep this car."

"I've created a monster, haven't I? You promised you wouldn't become a criminal. Remember? You promised."

"I did no such thing. I never once said those words. I stared at you. That is not making a promise."

"Now you're just being difficult."

"I'm not letting you wuss out on our wager, Mr. Daniels."

"Delayed for a different case—a safer case."

"Hold on, let me refer to my magic ball." I paused. "No. The magic ball says no."

"Your file mentioned something about you having a tendency to become difficult at times. Is this what your file meant?"

"Consider yourself fortunate, Mr. Daniels. Do you know how I normally deal with people I don't like?"

"Enlighten me."

"I don't say a word and I stare. I stare until they get really uncomfortable. Then I keep staring. I will watch my back. I will activate the emergency beacon on my phone if it proves necessary. But I am not giving up without a fight, sir."

"You found a lead, didn't you."

"I'm looking through legally gained but illegally handled evidence," I replied.

"Humor me."

"The Henrys are a family of four. Three brothers and one sister."

"We're aware of this information."

"Their mother was killed when the Twin Towers were destroyed, sir."

There was a long moment of silence on the line. "You're not joking, are you?"

"No, sir. I am looking at a photograph taken shortly afterwards. This is the last time Peter Henry took his family to meet with his brother's. The reason for it, however, intrigues me."

"Go on."

"Peter didn't like the type of people who were keeping his brother company. Called them 'his kind of people.' Apparently, these individuals favor black SUVs."

"Black SUVs?"

I patted the album, shifting on the bed so I could cradle the phone between my ear and shoulder. "Apparently, this photo album has pictures of them. Peter's wife enjoys photography, and apparently she takes pictures of everything. I have two full albums to sort through, and somewhere in here are images of Henry's sort of people."

"You took these albums into your possession?"

"I did, sir. The Henry brothers all seemed concerned. The real deal when it comes to family treating family right. It may not be relevant, but I was informed Amelia was somehow responsible for their mother's death. The woman wouldn't talk about it, and I kept it to Jacob, but you might want to find out exactly what they meant by that. It could be a motive."

"How did you stumble on this information?"

"I asked a naked man the right questions."

"I'm sorry, but you *what*?"

"Winston Henry answered his door in the nude, sir. He didn't feel it necessary to put on his clothes. It's his house. If he wants to walk around naked, who am I to judge? Nice fellow, seemed genuinely concerned for Jacob's well-being. That said, I noticed a patch of drywall that had been filled in with plaster near his landline. Line could have been tapped."

"Good eye. Notice anything like that at the other properties?"

"No. I did ask Winston if he spoke to Jacob often enough for the boy to recognize his voice. Winston seems to have developed a close relationship with the boy—close enough if he called and asked him to come out of the house, I'd bet my badge he would."

"Why did you ask that?"

"I was theorizing again, but it was one of the better ideas I had, and it fit. A group as professional as the one behind the Greenwich case could easily pull the trick off. If the line has been tapped, they could have easily recorded Winston's voice and made a clipping to lure Jacob out. If they made arrangements during a call, mimicking Winston's voice—or using Winston—then I could see it working. A burner phone and a recording is all it would take. Of course, this is just a theory, but I think it's worth pursuing. I asked because I trust my gut instinct, and that patch in the wall caught my attention."

"I really should pull you from this case. You're a potential target."

"We could write bait on my forehead. See who comes out to take a bite."

"No. I'm trying to prevent you from being assassinated, not encouraging this group to take you out once and for all."

"That would be a sad end to my career."

"So is quitting when you get pulled off a case that could cost you your life."

"We could argue over this all day, or you could find me a new partner and add them to the team that is supposed to be trying to hunt me down *without* you telling them where I'm at. If you don't want me without a partner, then you better find a partner who can keep up with me."

"There isn't exactly a wide selection of CARD qualified agents available to take up the mantle of your partner."

"So give me someone who isn't in CARD for this job. It's not like they need CARD training. They just need to be a special agent with experience."

"I'm going to make a note in your file that you are obnoxious and easy to dislike, Agent Johnson."

"It wasn't already there? How disappointing."

"It does mention you are exceptionally difficult to find suitable partners for."

"I don't appreciate when my back isn't watched. It tends to get me shot."

"So your file says."

"So find someone who understands the concept of watching their partner's back. If they're competent and let me do my job, I won't have a problem with them."

Daniels sighed. "I find that difficult to believe."

"I'm going to look through this album, get some sleep, and start fresh in the morning. No telling anyone my location, and no telling them what I'm driving. If they want to find out, they need to get the information themselves. Understood, Mr. Daniels?"

"You're going to sit tight in a secure location until tomorrow morning?"

"As secure as reasonably possible," I confirmed.

"Okay. We'll do it your way. But the instant this turns dangerous, call for backup. It'll give my agents a chance to find you, I suppose. And give me a few hours to find a partner you might be able to work with. We'll renegotiate for the Corvette. There's too much at stake now."

"How about you give me the Corvette for connecting the cases?"

"Don't push your luck." Daniels hung up on me. I snorted, tossed the phone aside, and returned to the tedious task of checking through hundreds of photographs for clues.

PAGE BY PAGE, I flipped through the photo albums, checking each and every image as well as the descriptions Peter's wife had left. I was halfway through the second book when I spotted the first SUV.

There were three of them parked on the street opposite the Henry home. Each vehicle had contained two men, and Peter's wife had gotten face shots of them all. I didn't recognize any of them, but I pulled out my phone and took photos of the photos, sending them to Daniels.

My phone rang after I sent the fourth image. I didn't

recognize the number. Narrowing my eyes, I ignored the call.

Moments later, a text from Daniels ordered me to pick up the phone. When it rang, I answered, "Hello?"

"Miss Johnson," Andrew said, his voice carefully neutral.

I contemplated someone's murder, and I wasn't sure who I wanted to kill more: my purported team mate or Daniels. "What?"

"Would you please reconsider?"

"Reconsider what?"

"Quitting."

Reconsidering my reconsideration of quitting sounded like a better and better by the moment. "Not interested in doing any reconsiderations of anything at this point in time."

"We could really use you."

I counted the seconds, wondering if they would try to use the live line to trace my position. "Look, I'm pretty busy right now. You know, doing the updating the resume thing. I'm sure I can get a job doing secretarial work for some nice corporation. They pay better."

I hung up, and when my phone rang again, I ignored it. Within five minutes, I expected Daniels to call or bother me. I filled the time by sending him more texts of the images from the photo album.

It was on the last couple of pages I saw a face that chilled my blood and had me dialing Daniels's number.

"Your team just called me saying they made an attempt to get you back—"

"I'm looking at a picture of one of the men who kidnapped me and Annabelle."

"Which one?"

"The one I took down to get out of the cabin. Called himself Phil."

"You're positive it's him?"

"I'm positive."

"You're off the case."

"Daniels!"

"It's in the list of rules you're not allowed to break. You're off the case."

"I want on the case."

"Not an option."

"Why not?"

"Because you'll be a prime target?"

I smacked my open hand against the photo album. "And would you have gotten this information without me on the case?"

"Probably not," the man admitted.

"So you're pulling the person who is actually making progress on the case. That's so smart."

"You can't help anyone if you're dead."

"I'm not going to sit around and let them kill a kid."

"We have no proof the group is the one behind his disappearance. We have circumstantial evidence they may be involved with the Henry family. If Henry is their informant, why would they kidnap his son?"

"Winston said his brother sounded more annoyed than concerned," I offered. "When he called asking if Jacob was with him."

Daniels sighed. "There is zero chance of me permitting you to remain on this case without a partner."

"Find me a partner who can track me down, and I'll let them warm the passenger side of the Corvette. But you know what happened the last time I backed down? A kid died. Not this time, Daniels. Not this time. Don't kick me off this case."

"You'll go rogue if I pull you off, won't you?"

"Can't say I have a whole lot to lose at this point."

"I can make a list for you. Let's start with your very successful career with the FBI."

"I'm not walking away from this case."

"Then accept the partner I assign you without wasting time playing hide and go seek."

I stiffened, my brows furrowing. "Wasting time playing hide and go seek."

"Of all the things I expected you to say, that was not it. What are you thinking?"

"Something Winston told me."

"Elaborate."

"In the file, it mentioned they were staying in Johnstown because they wanted to enroll him in the school system there."

"Correct."

"Then why would Winston Henry be so worked up about Jacob wanting to go to school but being unable to?" I asked. "Winston said the last time he spoke to Jacob was two weeks ago."

"Two weeks ago, Jacob would have already been enrolled —would have been enrolled for a while, probably," Daniels replied.

"Did anyone check if he was actually enrolled in the school system in Johnstown?"

"On it. What are you going to do?"

"I need sleep. After that, I want to look into who Jacob might have gone to play a game of hide and seek with in Johnstown."

"The CARD team is still in Johnstown, you know."

"They don't need to know we're sharing space. Really. They don't. If they really wanted my help, they wouldn't have benched me."

Daniels sighed. "I'll find you a partner and have them meet up with you tomorrow. Your team could use a fifth member anyway."

"Sounds good. That means when I quit or request a transfer elsewhere, they'll have their precious fourth member. I'm going to bed." I disconnected the call, plugged the phone into its charger, and stacked the photo albums on the nightstand.

If Daniels thought I was going to sit around and waste time, he was about to learn a bitter lesson. It was true enough I intended to stay at the hotel room for a little while.

I really did need sleep, a good dinner, and time to make a plan. Tomorrow, I'd be pounding asphalt to cover as much ground as possible, and I had every intention of putting my youthful appearance to good use.

If Jacob had run away to have a chance to be with other kids, it was entirely possible there was a very elaborate game of hide and seek going on. I didn't know if the group who had kidnapped Annabelle Greenwich would also be hunting for Jacob Henry. If they were, I'd be willfully jumping out of the pan and into the fire.

Some risks were worth taking.

Chapter Sixteen

A LOT of FBI special agents I knew had rituals. I liked to think I was immune to superstition, but in reality, I was as guilty of rituals as other agents.

In my two months with CARD, I had developed the habit of eating nothing but pizza when we were working a case. As a result, my diet consisted of nothing but pizza—pepperoni pizza light on the cheese and heavy on the meat, the way Jake liked it.

Between my night swims at the pool and foraging for cold pizza I didn't even like, I was going to be nothing but skin, bone, and a little bit of muscle holding everything together. When I had been involved with kickboxing, I had eaten a lot more. I had also eaten a variety of things thanks to Jake's ravenous appetite.

The man knew how to pack food away, and he didn't like when I picked at mine.

I had tried to avoid thinking of my ex-partner. When I slipped, I was left with nothing but regrets gnawing away at me.

Instead of acting like the adult I was supposed to be, I ate his favorite pizza and pretended I wasn't an emotional mess. I didn't do a good job of pretending everything was okay when it wasn't, but I would've made Jake proud at the damage I did to my dinner.

Once upon a time, my comfort food of choice had been Ma's mashed potatoes and chicken gravy. I had never managed to duplicate how she made it; I was too busy trying to be a good FBI agent to become a good cook. I managed, but that was about the extent of my cooking talents.

So instead of trying to stay healthy, I ate pizza, and something about it kept me hanging on when I wanted nothing more than to let go.

Before I had joined CARD, my choice of poison had been maxing out as many toppings as possible on my pizzas. The changes to my eating habits should have tipped someone off I was primed to blow.

Jake would've known with a single look.

I should have recognized my slow and steady dive into the deep end long before I had gotten to the point of quitting. Except for my meeting with Daniels, I hadn't had anything other than pepperoni pizza for two months.

I ate my way into a food coma, treating the pepperoni pizza like it was a lifeline, and didn't wake up until my phone rang the next morning. Fumbling for the device, I recognized Daniels's number. I considered it a miracle I didn't hang up on him while attempting to answer.

"Bwuh?" I asked in my effort to remember the English language.

"You haven't flown the coop on me yet?"

I tried to ask what time it was, but it came out as an incoherent mumble.

Apparently, Daniels spoke pre-coffee agentese. "It's six in the morning."

Willing my brain to take control of my mouth, I managed to croak, "I will douse you in gasoline and light you on fire."

"So cruel, especially when I have good news for you. I have found you a partner. I was up until two in the morning searching the FBI to find someone who might be suitable. Aren't I amazing? I'm amazing. I performed a miracle just for you."

I stretched, groaning as my back popped and creaked. It tasted like something had died and rotted in my mouth, and I shuddered. "Okay. I'm getting up and heading towards Johnstown. Don't talk to me until I've had coffee. Actually, just stop talking to me. If this partner wants to warm the passenger seat of my Corvette, they'll just have to hunt me down in Johnstown."

"You could be nice to me and pick up your partner from Albany's airport. It would only delay you by two hours."

"I need coffee, and I need to work. Fly my partner to Pittsburgh and make him or her drive to Johnstown."

If Daniels knew how badly I needed to be in the field doing something useful, he wouldn't have even considered routing me in the wrong direction. He didn't deserve the brunt of my agitation.

None of what had happened was his fault.

"Him."

I sighed. "Why can't I ever have a woman for a partner?"

"Your file indicates you do not play well with other women in the field." Daniels chuckled. "This was underlined and highlighted. In fact, a note in your file went on to say that you had zero tolerance for FBI agents who spend more time on their makeup than they do cleaning their guns. This was also highlighted and underlined."

It *was* something I'd say, which made me worry about what was in the file given to New York's headquarters. "For some reason, I really have my doubts anything like that was written in my file."

"This report about you being pistol whipped by your—"

"Has everyone heard about that?" I yowled.

Damn Jake, haunting me in CARD while he was probably doing the job of his dreams in HRT. The work suited him far better than CARD suited me, and I hoped his fortunes were far better than mine.

"It does appear I'm looking in the right file, then."

"I need coffee before I can deal with this. Please."

"Have breakfast, too."

"Okay, Ma."

"Something other than cold pizza."

Had the comment been a shot in the dark? It didn't matter; Daniels had managed to wake me all the way up with his well-aimed jab. "Why would I have cold pizza for breakfast?"

"We were trying to figure out what your favorite food was so when you're back in New York we can have your celebratory 'I quit but got talked into staying' party. We do it for all new agents here. When you return, you have an appointment with a nutritionist, who will try to impress upon you the importance of a healthy, balanced diet involving something other than pizza. Our investigation has determined pepperoni, but we're following some leads that might give us something more interesting to work with."

"I hate you." I hung up, screamed my frustration, and got ready to drive to Johnstown.

IN MY EFFORT TO act like a functional human being, I hit a fast food joint and indulged in a breakfast sandwich.

Apparently, a stomach accustomed to pepperoni pizza really didn't like sausage, egg, and cheese. By the time I made it to Johnstown, I regretted every bite and considered finding a hotel so I could be sick in relative comfort.

A distance that should have taken me six hours to drive took eight, and I swore off food altogether, determined to survive on a diet consisting solely of coffee.

Coffee would never betray me.

A little after two in the afternoon, I eased my Corvette through the winding streets of Johnstown, wondering why Daniels had called the place small. Any city with three colleges and two high schools didn't count as small, not in my book. Small was the town where I'd grown up in Georgia. It boasted a gas station and a church. It didn't even count as a one-horse town; the only horse had died of old age the year before we moved to Vermont.

According to my phone, Johnstown had three elementary schools, and one was within a five minute drive of the Henry household. I used the car's sound system to call Daniels.

"Oh, it's Agent Johnson. You're still talking to me? I feel so loved. So, so loved."

I breathed. I breathed until Daniels probably thought I was a psychotic serial killer out for his blood. If Daniels wanted to play, I'd play. "You don't need me to love you, sir.

You're too in love with yourself for me to have any hope of holding your attention."

"That's a good one. I'm going to write that one down and tell my wife. Wait, I better not. She'll use it on me. I assume you're calling me for a reason?"

Given different circumstances, I'd probably like Daniels and his twisted sense of humor. "You said you'd tell me if Jacob was enrolled in the elementary school system here."

"Did I say elementary?"

"No, I did."

"How did you guess he was in elementary school?"

Was Daniels testing my basic knowledge? I frowned but decided it'd waste too much time to call him out on his stupid question. "Ten year olds are traditionally entering the fifth grade, sir."

"I knew there was a reason we hired you."

"Is he enrolled in school, sir?"

"No, he is not."

The running away theory was gaining a lot of steam. I tightened my hold on the steering wheel so I wouldn't punch the defenseless Corvette. "Has CARD investigated the local schools?"

"Only enough to confirm he wasn't enrolled."

"Thanks."

Daniels sighed. "You're not going to wait for your partner before sticking your nose in places it doesn't belong, are you?"

"This is why they pay you the big bucks, sir." Pulling over, I let my hair down, opened the top of the Corvette, and picked up the makeup kit I had grabbed at a Walmart on the way, using the mirror to apply the makeup in a style favored by teens. Fortunately for me, the style page I had found on the internet included step by step instructions on how to avoid looking like a clown. "Anything interesting for me before I start poking my nose in places it doesn't belong?"

"How about an itinerary of your activities so your partner can locate you without me having to remotely activate your beacon?"

"I'm going to take a look at the local elementary, middle, and high schools. I'm going to try something."

"Define something, please."

I stroked on my lipstick, puckered my lips, and blew a kiss at the rearview mirror. "Don't feel like it."

"You're worse than a rebellious teenager."

"How would you know anything about rebellious teenagers?"

"I have two. One is eighteen, the other is fifteen."

Daniels had two kids that old? He hadn't looked nearly old enough for him to have any kids at all. "Did you have them while you were in middle school, sir?"

"My oldest is twenty-one, and since meeting you, I have earnestly prayed she decides against using you as a role model for her life."

Ouch. I understood I was an emotional mess crammed between a rock and a hard place, but did Daniels have to be so blunt about it? "How old *are* you, sir?"

"Isn't it rude to ask a gentleman his age?"

"What gentleman? I'm twenty-nine. I prefer satin over lace, and my bra size is—"

"Forty-three. I'm forty-three, and I don't need to know your measurements, Agent Johnson."

I smirked. "Good to know I'm not the only member of the club."

"What club?"

"The 'Get Carded Until I Die' club."

"I'm a founding member."

"Good to know. Now, if you're satisfied I'm not doing anything dangerous, can I please get back to it?"

"You're just going to scope out the local schools?"

"Might talk to a few kids, but that's about it. Unless kids are now dangerous criminals?"

"Last time I checked, petty crimes only."

"When does school start here?"

"Already started."

"Really?"

"Really."

"Great. I'm going to go talk to some kids, then."

"Let me know how that works out for you. CARD already tried approaching some. The children weren't impressed with them."

"Sir, those three are about as approachable as dynamite— dynamite that has been lit on fire and has a short fuse."

"You think you can do better?" Daniels challenged.

"Sir, if I'm not pulled over at least ten times before I'm done, I'll be shocked. I'm driving a bright yellow Corvette, and I look like I escaped from the local high school. I'll leave you to do the math, since it'll probably take you a while to figure it out." Hanging up, I shook my head and finished applying my makeup.

To finish the humiliating act of making myself look as young as possible, I tied my hair back in twin ponytails, draping them over my shoulders. I was ready to take on one of the most dangerous and bewildering elements of American society: its youth.

I STOPPED at the elementary school nearest the Henry house as school was letting out. I parked the Corvette, drawing the attention of every teacher and student in sight. When I stepped out of the vehicle wearing heeled boots, shorts, and a halter top that probably broke every single rule in the dress code, people gawked.

As a precaution, I had left everything in my trunk when I left Albany, and behaving like a reckless teen, I didn't close the convertible top.

It was far too nice of a day. It also made me look like a badass. If I had been at a high school, I would've taken a little more care, but until I lured someone to me long enough to ask a few questions, I'd risk the FBI's car.

I made it three whole steps before the first curious kid came running over to stare at the Corvette. She didn't say a word, her eyes wide open.

Cute kids like her, wearing ponytails a match for mine, always served to remind me why I had worked so hard to join CARD.

I slipped my hands in my jacket pockets, grinning at her. "Like it?"

"So cool," the girl blurted.

Retreating back to the car, I unlocked it and opened the door. To keep the teachers from panicking and assuming I was a kidnapper, I leaned against the vehicle, keeping my posture relaxed. "I know, right?"

"Can I look?"

"Just don't touch any buttons."

The Corvette wasn't going anywhere without the keys, which were safely in my pocket. With a brilliant smile, the girl skipped to the car, standing on her toes to get a better look inside. "So cool."

"Hey, can you point me in the direction of principal's office?"

"I can show you!"

"Sweet. I'm Kitty," I said, waiting until the girl was clear of the Corvette before reaching inside, putting the keys in the ignition long enough to close the roof, and lock the car.

Since I had gotten a kid to talk with me, I could afford to lower my badass levels to protect the FBI's property—my property, if I had my way.

"I'm Elizabeth. Did you get into trouble?"

"Not today," I quipped, winking at her.

"Did you leave school early?"

I faked a long and heavy sigh, hoping the sound would help convince the girl I hated what I was about to say. "I'm homeschooled."

Elizabeth frowned, although it looked more like a pout to me. "That's sad."

"I know, right? Dad's always an ass about it. Is it too much to ask to go to a regular school for once in my life?"

Cursing lost me points with the teachers hovering nearby, and I was aware of their glares. Elizabeth, however, thought it was the funniest thing anyone had ever said, dissolving in a giggle fit so strong she doubled over.

"You're not supposed to say that," she chided me in a whisper.

"Well, shit."

Elizabeth's next giggle fit didn't ease until we were at the doors leading inside. "The principal's office is over there, Kitty!"

"Nice. Thanks."

Grabbing hold of my jacket sleeve, Elizabeth gave a tug. "You don't like being homeschooled?"

I wrinkled my nose. "No way."

"Oh. Is it bad?"

Shrugging, I positioned my body so I was pointed in the direction of the principal's office while able to talk to Elizabeth. More teachers had gathered, and they were watching me like a hawk.

"You bet. I better get this over with," I muttered, forcing another sigh.

"Melly doesn't like it either."

"Melly?"

"She's my friend. She lives down the street." Elizabeth pointed to a line of single-family homes across from the school. "The other kids call her Skunky, but I don't like it."

It never failed to amaze me how cruel children could be to each other. "No shit. Skunky? That's just rude."

"I know! She doesn't like it. She's all by herself during the day, so I try to go over and play."

"That's pretty nice of you, Elizabeth. I better get this over with. Thanks for showing me where to go."

"Anytime. Bye-bye!" With the energy only a child could possess, Elizabeth tore off in the direction of one of the busses near the end of the line. The first were already starting to file off the school grounds.

I chuckled and strode towards the glass-fronted office. The teachers glared at me. When I reached them, I smiled, flashed my badge, and said, "FBI. I need to ask you some questions."

"We already spoke to people from the FBI," a woman replied, her body tensing.

I offered my badge for her to inspect. "We're attempting a different approach to resolve the disappearance of Jacob Henry. Your cooperation would be appreciated."

I liked the way the woman looked over my badge and identification, comparing the picture to my face before nodding and replying, "I'm the principal, Faith Partridge. Of course I'll cooperate. Can never be too careful these days."

"Definitely. Sorry for disturbing you, but I had some questions about the kids who attend here."

"Please, come into my office. Can I interest you in a cup of coffee?"

"Please."

Faith lifted her hand and held up two fingers to the short, stocky woman seated behind the desk in the reception area of the office. She scrambled to obey while the principal led me through a maze of offices. "As I told the other FBI agents, we don't know a lot about Jacob Henry. He's not a student here."

"While I'd love any information on Jacob you have, I'm actually here about the students attending your school."

The principal's office was smaller than my cramped space at the FBI with barely enough room for two chairs in front of her cluttered desk. Gesturing for me to sit, she squeezed around her desk and sank into her chair, which squeaked. "Why?"

"We have reason to believe Jacob may have been involved with some of the local children. I'd like to find out who and ask them some questions. It might give us the break we need."

Faith stared at me for a long moment before smiling. "That's one of the most intelligent things I've heard anyone say to me since this started."

"Is there a large homeschooling community in the area?"

Shaking her head, the principal drew a deep breath and sighed. "While I don't have numbers for the whole area, of course, it's a pretty low percentage of the population. Most of the homeschooled children come from affluent parents. Johnstown isn't exactly a hotbed of the rich and famous. We have a few, of course, but most kids here attend one of the public or private schools."

"Is there any overlap between the kids in your school system and the homeschooled kids?"

"Organized sports and summer camps. They're open for homeschooled children since Johnstown doesn't have a large enough population for two leagues."

"Is there any way to get a list of the kids attending these sports and camps?"

"Yes." Faith reached for a filing cabinet, but instead of pulling out a list, she handed me a sheet of contact numbers. "These are the organizers. I have copies, so please keep that one."

I picked up the sheet and folded it up, slipping it into the inside pocket of my jacket. A knock at the door announced the arrival of coffee. I accepted the mug with a grateful smile and waited for the woman to leave. "Elizabeth mentioned a girl named Melly? Do you know of her?"

"Melly? Ah, Melanie Shepherd. Yes, we know Melanie. We've had... some problems with her."

"What sort of problems?"

"Last year, she would show up at school and try to get into classes during the day. It hasn't happened yet this year, but we expect it to start soon. It happens sometimes. Some homeschoolers enjoy how they're educated."

"Some don't."

"Correct. Some don't. Melanie is one of them."

I jotted down Melanie's full name. "Do you have a contact number for Melanie's parents?"

"I do." This time, Faith reached for a Rolodex and halted on a card before reading off a phone number, which I wrote down. "Not sure if you'll get anything out of them, though. They don't like brushing elbows with people like us."

"Affluent?"

"Yes. They believe only in homeschooling or private education. As Mrs. Shepherd doesn't work, she handles Melanie's homeschooling. There are quite a few private schools in the area, but the Shepherd family won't consider public or religious-affiliated education for their daughter."

"Any idea why?"

"I don't know, but they opted against the local Catholic or Christian schools."

I nodded, made a note, and moved onto something potentially more relevant to Jacob's situation. "What sorts of sports are going on this time of year?"

"Swimming, field hockey, lacrosse, football, soccer, and volleyball. We don't have track and field until middle school. Winter sports start up in November."

"Any overlap between the fall sports and summer camps?"

"Complete crossover," the principal admitted. "Can't tell you much more than that; all I do is clear the use of our facilities over the summer, and honestly, someone else in the office usually handles that. I just sign off on the final forms."

I drank my coffee, looking at my notepad without really seeing anything I had written. "What's the most popular sport here?"

"Football for the boys, and field hockey for the girls. Soccer is pretty popular with both the boys and the girls. They had a co-ed camp this year, actually."

It wasn't a big first step, but it would help. I jotted down the names of the sports and the gender brackets. "How do the kids usually spend their time during the summer and after school?"

Faith leaned back in her chair, sighed, and held her coffee mug with both hands. "While I'd like to say I know everything about the kids we teach, I don't. Some join sports teams and go to summer camp. Some stay home and play on their computers or phones. Some play around the neighborhoods, but that's decreased a lot since there are so many over-protective parents in the area. Some head to the playgrounds, but a lot less than ten years ago."

It matched what I expected, although I was still disappointed in the lack of an area where local kids gathered. When I had grown up, the mall had been the popular hangout. "No popular hangouts, then?"

It was worth a shot even if it didn't amount to anything.

"Actually, there's Haynes Street; there's a bridge with art beneath it. It's the overpass for Route 56 in Kernville, which isn't too far from here. Pretty heavily trafficked, so it makes a good place for kids to gather without parents panicking over it. It's one of the first places the police look when a kid goes missing."

CARD had probably looked into it with the local police department, but I jotted it down as a note. "Anywhere else?"

"Conemaugh Gap; it's a gorge along Route 56. It's one of the local forbidden fruits. It's pretty dangerous, though."

"How far away is it?"

"It cuts right through town."

"How much territory are we talking about here? Is it just a small section?"

"The whole river goes through it, and there are steep

sections all around here. Outside of town is pretty heavily forested."

I made a note to ask Daniels if SAR had been called in to check the gorge. "That's really helpful. Thanks. I appreciate your assistance."

"Anything I can do to help, ma'am." Faith rose and held out her hand. "Can I ask you one question?"

I drained my coffee, set the mug down, and rose, shaking with her. "Of course."

"How on Earth did you manage to pull off looking like a middle school or high school student?"

Laughing, I reached up and twirled one of my ponytails. "A little makeup and the right clothes go a long way."

"Unbelievable. I really wish you the best with your investigation, ma'am."

"No, thank you," I replied, and I meant it. "You have one hell of a hard and important job yourself."

Faith's radiant smile warmed me. Grabbing a card from her desk, she offered it to me. "If there's anything at all I can do to help, give me a call."

Chapter Seventeen

SOMEONE WAS WATCHING me when I left the school and headed to the Corvette. I slid inside, locking the door before starting the engine. I pulled the list of names out of my coat and looked it over. It was organized by camp and sport, and I circled the organizers for the sports the principal had mentioned.

A tap at the window drew my attention, and I glanced out of the corner of my eye to see a cop holding his badge to the glass. I marked a tally on the notepad, lowered the window, and showed him my badge and FBI identification card without a word.

He blinked at the badge and card, blinked at me, and didn't say anything for a long moment.

Taking pity on him, I asked, "One of the teachers called?"

"I guess you aren't a high school student who took a very expensive car out on a joyride, are you?"

I laughed. "Afraid not. Do me a favor?"

"What do you need?"

"Don't tell your buddies I'm undercover, please. I want to see how many times I can get pulled over today." I paused, grinned, and continued, "Okay, I just don't want my cover blown."

"You got it. What story do you want me to use?"

"Homeschooled, got the car with my license."

"You got it. Good luck."

"You, too." I waited for the cop to step away from the car before rolling up my window, backing out of my spot, and hitting the road. My first stop would be the Route 56 over-pass to check out Haynes Street. If I busted there, I would start giving the organizers a call and see what I could find.

Within a minute of leaving the school, I picked up a tail. Drumming my nails on the steering wheel, I studied the sporty silver two-door matching me turn for turn. Like my Corvette, its windows were tinted too much for me to make out the driver.

Instead of heading to Haynes Street, I got onto Route 56, merging into the light traffic. I kept an eye to my right to get a feel for the landscape. The gorge cutting through John-stown sloped to the river, and as I cut north of town, it opened to enough forest to make any SAR efforts a challenge.

The silver car followed me, keeping one or two cars behind me in an effort to be discreet.

There were three ways I could handle the car tailing me. I could lead the driver on a merry chase, or I could attempt to lose them in a busy area. Either way, I'd lose time. The third option, parking in a place with a lot of people, would be the safest option until I could figure out who was following me and why.

A scenic overlook caught my attention. The parking lot

was packed, leaving only a few free spots. I pulled in, squeezed my car between a truck and an SUV, and killed the engine. Hopping out, I joined the crowd peering over the protective railing, which kept people from falling into the gorge.

I stood on my toes and leaned forward, shuddering at how deep the damned thing was. I stood on the precipice of one of my worst nightmares. The fall would smash my body to a pulpy mess before I hit the ground and bounced into the river far, far below.

Choices, choices: face the stalker driver in the sporty silver car or risk falling to my death.

Why couldn't I have picked a safe, sane job? Next time I had a psychiatric evaluation, I was going to inform the doctor I was off my rocker for even considering a career in the FBI.

Then again, the doctor would likely argue the fact I recognized I was insane for being a willing participant in a high-stress job was a strong indication I was a fully func-tional, mentally sound adult. Thanks to my height—or lack thereof—I was able to rest my elbows on the middle rail with my chin on the top rail, staring out over the forest.

My heart tried to pound its way out of my chest, and I shook from the stress of trying to stay in place without revealing my fear of falling. I fisted my hands and clenched my teeth.

The only thing that could make my situation any worse was if a slug made an appearance. With my luck, the gorge and its forest were filled with the disgusting, slimy creatures hellbent on sending me to an early grave.

Shuddering, I forced my attention to the case. Would a child run to such a place? While it classified as one of my worst nightmares, the spot had potential. It was, in theory, walking distance from Johnstown. If he had hiked to the gorge and its forest, I imagined he was hungry, tired, and discovering civilization was far more comfortable than the woods this time of year, especially after dark.

The trees were pretty enough I had no problems wasting a few extra minutes staring at them.

My phone rang, and I dug it out of my pocket with shaking hands to look at the display. Daniels again.

It took two tries for me to swipe my thumb over the screen. "Hello?"

My voice trembled, and I hoped Daniels wouldn't notice.

"Did you loan the Corvette to someone?" Daniels sounded pissed.

The question startled me enough I blinked, looked over my shoulder, and stared at the yellow vehicle parked nice and snug between two far larger vehicles. "Why would I loan my Corvette to someone?"

"Are you seriously telling me you let someone steal the Corvette?"

Confused, I held the phone so I could check the display to confirm I was connected to Daniels's phone. I was. Returning the phone to my ear, I replied, "I don't think so. Why?"

"Where are you? Someone who doesn't match your description was seen driving it. It was just called in."

I choked back a strained, hysterical laugh and cleared my throat. "Hold on. Can I call you back in a minute? Let me check on the car."

"One minute," Daniels snarled before hanging up.

I headed to the Corvette, sat on the hood, leaned back, and took a selfie of myself on the car. Sliding off, I headed back to the rail, hesitating at having to come so close to death again, and sent Daniels the image before calling him back.

"Did you get the picture?"

"Sec." A moment later, I heard him snort. "What the hell are you wearing?"

"I thought it was sexy in the slutty high school teen sort of way." I pouted.

"What did you do to your hair? Is that a wig?"

"Extensions. I had my hair done before I left New York. I didn't want to make it easy on your team, Daniels. Why wouldn't I would pull out all the stops to get to keep my Corvette? So, who thought I had stolen my car? Is it the driver of the silver two-door that tailed me out of Johnstown?"

"Ah, you noticed him."

"Does my file have anything about heights in it?"

"Highlighted and underlined notation you shouldn't be sent on ledges or agent-eating staircases."

"Whoever wrote the notes in my file was an asshole. This gorge is pretty deep. I came here because there are a lot of people looking around, and I didn't know who was following me. I was trying to play it safe, just like you wanted. Can I return to my car and get out of here, then? I don't like this spot. I don't like it at all. I don't want to be here."

"Take a few deep breaths, Agent Johnson. You can step away—carefully—from wherever you're standing. You have nothing to worry about. The driver of the silver car is your new partner."

While the railing offered a small sense of security, I felt a lot better backing away a few steps in the direction of the

Corvette. "He sucks at tailing."

"Why don't you give him a chance to say hello?"

"He's on the line, isn't he?"

"Maybe."

"You're an asshole, Mr. Daniels." I sighed, turned, and came nose to nose with a very tall someone wearing dark shades, a clean-cut suit, and a smirk I knew all too well. Like me, Jake held a phone to his ear.

"No fucking way." I lost the ability to form a coherent sentence, trying to figure out how—and why—Jake was standing in front of me. My brain refused to accept what my eyes were telling me.

Lifting his hand, Jake pushed his sunglass up to reveal his dark brown eyes. He straightened, looking me over from head to toe. "Well, well, well. Isn't this interesting?"

Jake's voice echoed in my ear, and despite the evidence of his voice coming out of the device and his mouth, I shook my head in denial.

"Interesting is one way to put it," Daniels replied. "I'll let you two get reacquainted. Leave your car, Agent Thomas. I'll have someone come pick it up."

"Yes, sir," Jake replied. Hanging up his phone, he slid it in his pocket. Daniels likewise disconnected the call, but I stood frozen in place, still holding my phone to my ear.

"It is customary to put the phone away after you're finished using it." Jake took the device out of my hand, looking me over again. "Where the hell do you hide things when wearing that little? Do you even have pockets?"

I somehow managed to force my mouth into motion, although I failed to master the art of speech. Snorting, Jake tugged open my jacket, discovered the interior pocket, and slid the phone into it. "I see you found a place to hide your gun."

"What? How? Why?" I blurted, pointing at him.

"Why don't we talk somewhere a little more private?"

When I didn't move, Jake grabbed my elbow and dragged me to the Corvette, stealing the keys out of my pocket so he could unlock the car and shove me into the passenger seat. Years of habit made me buckle my seatbelt despite the fact I was having trouble stringing two thoughts together.

"Jake?"

"It seems you remember my name. Amazing."

I opened my mouth, snapped it closed, and did a good impression of one of his huffs.

Shoving the seat back as far as it would go, Jake settled behind the wheel. How the little sports car fit such a big man, I had no idea, but he seemed comfortable enough in the Corvette. While he started the engine, he left the vehicle in park. "At one in the morning, right when I got home after a long shift, I get a call from my boss. He tells me I'm being transferred to a case, drops your name, and says that a car was going to pick me up in ten minutes."

While I was still stunned Jake had been called in, I fell back on my old habit of staring.

His familiar annoyed huff coaxed a smile out of me.

"At that point, I had no idea what was going on, so I grabbed my emergency bag and a suit from the closet. Sure enough, a car shows up ten minutes later. I'm told there's a flight waiting for me at a private airstrip and I'm expected in New York. That wasn't at all comforting, since I knew it had *something* to do with you, but no one was telling me what. A helicopter dropped me off on the roof of your building, where I'm met by three cranky upper management."

He paused, glaring at me. "Will you quit smiling? This is not funny."

Lifting my arm, I stared at my skin, picked a fleshy spot, and pinched myself as hard as I could. It hurt like hell, and my nails made a pair of crescent-shaped indentations.

"What are you doing?"

Pain indicated I hadn't fallen to my death, although I wasn't quite willing to eliminate it as a possibility. I hadn't even held the tiniest bit of hope Jake would show up.

Our days as partners were supposed to be over.

"Karma?"

I pinched myself again. "I'm testing a theory."

"What are you talking about?"

"If I fell in the ravine and died, would I still feel pain? I'm pretty sure the only way you'd show up here right now would be over my dead body."

Jake had worked hard to get into HRT—as hard as I had worked to get into CARD.

He kept his narrow-eyed stare focused on me. "Maybe that's what I thought I was dealing with. Did that thought occur to you?"

It hadn't. I frowned. "That doesn't change anything. You're not supposed to be here."

"Why the hell not?"

"You're in HRT. You worked hard to get into HRT."

"You worked hard to get into CARD. From my understanding, you quit. You. Quit. Not only did you quit, you did so during an assignment." Jake sucked in a breath through clenched teeth. "Do you care to explain yourself?"

I swallowed, clasped my hands on my lap, and stared at my white knuckles. "I snapped."

"So it seems." Jake put the car in reverse, pulled out of the spot, and got onto the road heading back towards John-stown. "We're booked in a hotel in Pittsburgh. We are going there to have a very long talk."

"What about the case?" I whispered.

"We're going to Pittsburgh, where we're going to have a long talk. We'll evaluate the situation then."

I shut my mouth. There were a thousand things I could have said, but I lacked the courage to utter a single word.

I WAS SHAKING by the time we reached Pittsburgh, and Jake knew it. When he thought I wasn't watching him, he stared at me under the guise of checking his side mirrors.

The hotel was on the outskirts of the city, surrounded on three sides by forest. It was the type of place that put me on edge; would-be shooters had plenty of places to hide. While I understood the chances of someone tailing us, getting ahead of us to get into position, and taking the shot was slim, tension cramped my muscles.

Jake found a spot near one of the hotel's doors, got out, and circled the vehicle to check the trunk, leaving me alone. It took me a lot longer than I liked to force myself into motion, unbuckle my seatbelt, and slide out of the Corvette.

"Need these albums?"

I nodded and joined him at the back of the car. He already had both of my bags in his possession, leaving me to grab my briefcase and the photo albums. Once he locked the Corvette, he headed for the doors, shuffling his hold on things to swipe a key card to gain access to the building.

Our room was on the second floor, and Jake opted for the stairs instead of waiting for the elevator. Two months hadn't been long enough to erase my memories of his habits, and his impatience warned me he wasn't in the mood for any bullshit from me.

If I was reading his mood right, he was beyond huffing angry, speeding right by it to a whole new level of rage, the kind I had only witnessed from him when I had done something particularly stupid, including getting unnecessarily shot. I carried scars on my leg from early in our partnership, when I hadn't quite accepted Jake really did have my back. If I had trusted him a little bit more, I wouldn't have gotten caught in the crossfire. I'd been so busy trying to watch my own back I had missed something right in front of me.

Without Jake, the bullet likely would have lodged in my skull instead.

When the dust had settled, he'd been too angry to huff, opting for silence while his body quivered from tension.

Jake opened the room to our room and growled, "Wait."

I stared at the carpet while he did a sweep of the room. When he grunted his satisfaction, I stepped inside, eased my way past him, and set my briefcase and albums on the desk, rolling the computer chair out of the way. The room had two double beds, and Jake's bag was sitting on the one closer to the window. As always, the curtains were closed to prevent anyone from getting a look at us.

Jake secured the door and dropped my bags on the empty bag. "Haven't you figured out I'm not going to bite your head off?"

"You're pissed," I pointed out.

"Damn straight I'm pissed. Still not going to bite your head off. I will, however, refuse to listen to your input for what we order in tonight."

My stomach still wasn't entirely happy with me for my

adventurous choice of breakfast sandwich. "Good luck with that."

"Explain."

"I engaged in a very bad relationship with an egg and sausage sandwich this morning."

Jake snorted. "You've been throwing your guts up all day, haven't you?"

"Not all day, just until noon."

"Eat anything else?"

"Coffee."

"Coffee isn't food, Karma. You've lost weight."

I hadn't exactly had a lot of extra weight on me to begin with, and cold pizza couldn't keep up with my tendency to count my distance doggy paddling in miles rather than laps. "You're looking good. Nice suit."

"Maybe you haven't been kickboxing, but you've been doing something with those legs of yours."

"Would you believe I still can't do anything other than a very bad doggy paddle?"

"Without hesitation."

"Three miles."

"Pardon?"

"My longest lap."

"You doggy paddled for three miles." At the incredulity in his tone, I shrugged and remained silent. "Who was spotting you?"

"No one."

"You swam by yourself."

"Even went into the deep end and everything."

Jake sighed. "I can't tell if you're stupid, brave, stupidly brave, or completely out of your right mind."

"Well, I probably wouldn't pass a psych eval right now," I admitted ruefully.

"I already had that impression. Daniels briefed me on the situation, but I'd rather hear it straight from the horse's mouth."

I eased my way out of my jacket and tossed it on the back of the computer chair before wiggling out of my holster. "Two months of anchoring. First case we did together, I didn't push a point hard enough. It got the girl killed."

"Daniels briefed me about that case, and the rest of the work you've been doing with the team. You did your job. It's not your fault they didn't do theirs."

"If I had—"

"Karma."

I sighed. "Well, it's true."

"You knew going in you'd win some and you'd lose some. You knew CARD wasn't going to be easy."

Grunting, I dropped onto the chair, grabbed the photo album with the SUVs, and flipped through it without really seeing any of the pictures. "Anchor is a nice word for secretary. I did an entire case from the gym swimming pool several weeks ago. I didn't even deploy. I had my phone on the ledge, on speaker, while I fucking doggy paddled a mile listening to them chatter. Then I kept on doggy paddling. Three miles later, I figured out I was looking at the rest of my life in the FBI. A doggy paddling secretary. I've spent too much time guzzling crap coffee taking up some poor cop's desk, pretending moving papers and filling out forms actually made a difference."

"Daniels mentioned something about at least one deployment when you managed to stay in New York without anyone noticing you hadn't actually left with the rest of the team."

"They noticed when they went looking for the printouts of some forms, and a cop at the local station handed them the faxes, a week and a half after they had deployed."

"Ouch." Jake sat on the foot of my bed, and I felt him staring at me. "If they were trying to force you to quit, that's a good way to go about it."

"What has Daniels told you about the case?"

"Not much. He seemed more concerned about how you're, and I quote, 'a stick of dynamite with a short fuse that's been lit on fire.' You're more of a risk to yourself than others, according to him. That's something, right?"

I located the page with Phil's photograph and set the opened photo album on his lap before retreating to the safety of the computer chair. "Look familiar?"

"A little younger, but yeah. I know who he is. He's one of the assholes who kidnapped you."

"Jacob Henry's aunt took those photos."

"Jacob Henry's the boy we're looking for?"

I nodded.

When I didn't elaborate, Jake flipped to the first page of the album and started browsing through the pictures, halting when he came to the first image containing a black SUV. "They like black SUVs, don't they?"

"Seems like it."

"Daniels told me you quit kickboxing."

"Yeah. I figured I'd find a studio after moving to New York, but it didn't work out."

"You didn't want to draw attention to yourself, did you?"

"Pretty much."

"I heard the story about the contacts."

Grimacing at the reminder of how I had quit, I shrugged and stared at my hands so I wouldn't have to look at him.

"You earned yourself a reputation, you know. Again."

I spun in the chair to face him and forced myself to look him in the eye. "Do I want to know?"

Jake was the perfect image of neutrality. "Patron Saint of Patience. You have a lot of curious co-workers on your floor. When word spread I had been your partner on violent crime cases, they came to visit me while I was snooping around in your office."

"Find anything interesting?"

"Beyond the hundred or so receipts for pepperoni pizza?"

Had I really ordered that many pizzas? Probably. I had spent most of my time at the office, returning home to shower, change my clothes, and sleep. "What does everyone have against pepperoni pizza?"

Jake sighed, crossed his arms over his chest, and shook his head. "Nothing, except I know you like every topping you can possibly get on your pizza, including anchovies. You also like your pizza fresh, because you have a belief no human being should eat linoleum, which is what pizza becomes if sits for more than thirty minutes without being consumed."

"So maybe I went a little overboard with the pizza thing."

"Maybe?"

"Fine, definitely."

"That's a good start. Anything else bothering you?"

"When Daniels said he was going to find me a partner, I never thought for an instant you'd show up." Saying the words was a lot easier than I expected, and once they were out, it felt like a weight had lifted from my chest and shoulders.

"I'm always up for a challenge."

"That *is* why you applied for HRT when I applied for CARD."

"We all make mistakes."

While I couldn't deny applying for CARD had led to the worst two months of my life, it didn't stop his words from cutting deep. It took every bit of my will to keep my expression neutral when all I wanted to do was crawl under the bed, curl up in a fetal position, and cry.

Jake sighed. "There you go, assuming the worst as usual. My mistake was applying for HRT instead of CARD. With my background and experience, I would have made the cut. With our track record, there was a damned good chance they would have assigned us to the same team."

I stared at him, my mouth dropping open while I tried to comprehend what he was talking about—and why. "What?"

"When Daniels called me in, he gave me a choice: I could work the case as an extension of HRT, serving as a protective detail for you while you tried to get yourself killed being stubborn, or I could join CARD."

So many emotions boiled under my skin I couldn't figure out which end was up. "They offered you a spot in CARD?"

"Something like that."

"Are you joining CARD?" My voice rose an octave, and Jake arched a brow at me.

"No, I'm not joining CARD."

Disappointment surged through me, smothering the rest of my emotions until I felt cold, empty, and devoid of life. "Oh."

Jake was right to avoid giving up his position with HRT. He had worked too hard for it. So had I, but unlike Jake, I had drawn the short straw. I didn't even know if things would get better or worse after the Jacobs case was wrapped up.

I couldn't afford to think about it.

"I'm not joining CARD because I've already signed all the transfer forms, got a new identification card, and even an access pass for the building. Hard to join something twice. Though, I suppose if it makes you happy, I could join a second time. I'm sure Daniels would humor me. I can't imagine why, but he actually likes you."

Chapter Eighteen

IT TOOK me almost two hours to process everything Jake had told me, and he spent the time calling the organizers of the kids' sports programs while I gaped at him from the computer chair.

It wasn't one of my better moments.

When he finished the final call, I was still trying to figure out which question to ask first. He stared at me, grinned, and hopped to his feet to lean over me. "Your jaw has to be aching, since you've been trying to catch flies the entire time I've been on the phone."

I snapped my teeth together.

"Are you really that surprised I showed up?"

I liked yes or no questions. I could nod, which I did over and over until Jake set his hand on top of my head to stop me.

"I should be offended by that, you know."

Jake had a good hold on me, which preventing me from

canting my head to the side. "You'd be stunned if I showed up for HRT."

"I'm more stunned you actually tried to quit. Ask Daniels."

I reached for my phone, deciding dealing with Daniels was a better option than trying to make sense of my emotions. After dialing his number, I held my phone to my ear.

"Is there a problem?"

"I need to verify some facts, sir." Calling Daniels to regain some of my standing with Jake wasn't entirely underhanded. Jake had challenged me to do it.

I was just doing what I was told—and testing to find out just how angry Jake was with me.

"Okay, go for it."

"Jake claims he was stunned I quit."

There was a long moment of silence on the other end of the line, which was followed by a snorted laugh. "He froze up like a statue, turned almost as pale as you, and stared so long I waved my hand in front of his face to see if anyone was home. That was when he started bellowing."

"Bellowing?" I blurted.

If Jake was bellowing, he was beyond angry enough to start pistol whipping me. I worried, shifting my weight in the chair, wondering how I'd be able to patch things up enough with the man to get through the case.

Stealing the phone from my hand, Jake held it to his ear and said, "There is no need to tell her about that, sir."

The theft of my phone distracted me from my thoughts and worries, as did the fact Jake was pushing down on the top of my head to keep me seated. "Hey! I was using that."

Jake arched a brow at me. "Now I'm using it."

"I can't ask Daniels questions if you have my phone."

"Quiet, woman. I'm trying to listen to our boss."

I crossed my arms over my chest and glared up at him. "You're being an asshole, Jake Thomas."

"You earned it. I thought I was being nice. I gave you the chance to verify the fact I was, indeed, stunned by your decision." Pausing, he listened to something on the phone. "He hung up on me." Jake handed my phone back to me. "Nice phone. Much better than that old piece of shit you had. I could actually hear things without static. Anyway, Daniels said we should resolve our differences like the adults we are and stop bothering him. He'll update us tomorrow morning unless there's a break in the case. He's busy coordinating between CARD and other divisions."

Reality reasserted itself. Breathing helped, steadying my nerves and allowing me to turn my attention back to work. "We're wasting time."

Jake's mouth twitched. Breathing only helped if I remembered to do it. When Jake's twitching resulted in a smile, I relaxed. "What's so funny?"

"You. Look, CARD's on the move, and there isn't a whole lot we can do tonight unless you have specific places you want to look. We may as well get an early start tomorrow and a good night's sleep. Breathe. And for the love of God, please put some clothes on."

I stared down at my shirt and realized my skimpy top had slipped, revealing a little more cleavage than I had intended to show. Adjusting the material only shifted which sections of skin showed. "I have clothes on."

"You wore more when you were kickboxing, and that's saying a lot. Are you supposed to be undercover as a prostitute? If so, I have cash in my wallet and handcuffs in my pocket. I've never hired a prostitute before."

I smacked his hand away from my head. "I am not a prostitute. I'd be wearing leather or something if I were posing as a prostitute."

"If you're not an underaged prostitute, what *are* you?"

"High school student?"

Jake took his time looking me over head to toe. "Please put some real clothes on," he asked, his voice strained.

"I don't see what your problem is. I'm covered, even when I bend over. I know because I checked."

Jake coughed. "I didn't need to know that."

"What? It's important to know the limitations of my clothing when working. If I can't move well, I can't watch my back. Don't tell me you don't check your clothes when you're getting ready to work. I know you do. I've seen you stretching like a giant cat."

Pinching the bridge of his nose, Jake sighed. "You're killing me here, Karma."

I furrowed my brows and double-checked my gun was on the desk still in its holster. "No, if I were killing you, you'd be bleeding out on the floor."

"Karma."

"What?"

Sometimes, I just had to push Jake's buttons as hard as he pushed mine, and the fact my legs and exposed stomach bothered him so much made it so easy.

He sighed again. "Never mind."

"Are you sick? You keep sighing."

"You're doing this on purpose, aren't you?" Turning away from me, Jake ran his hands through his hair before taking his jacket off and tossing it on his bed.

"I was wondering when you'd relax enough to get out of your jacket."

"I'm going to end up with gray hairs because of you."

"Jake, relax. You've seen me naked before." Granted, the first and only time he had seen me completely naked, a perp we had been hunting had come calling in my hotel room while I had been in the shower, resulting in a very tense few minutes and an awkward arrest.

When Jake had burst into the room after hearing the gunfire, I had been straddling the perp's back, my weapon held to the back of the man's head, still dripping wet from my interrupted shower, in the process of reciting my would-be killer's rights.

I had been covered in blood, too, a result of defending myself. Watching my own back had saved my life; if I hadn't carried my gun into the bathroom with me, I wouldn't have lived to tell the tale.

Jake had insisted on sharing a room after that.

"You're practically naked now." Jake pointed at my chest. "Your bra is showing. Since we're discussing your lack of attire, are you wearing pink panties? Is that thing made of strings? I don't think Daniels meant for you to violate basic decency laws."

I stared down at my cleavage and realized in my effort to adjust my top, I had made things worse. How had my under-wear crept up over the top of my shorts? "He never said I couldn't."

"He didn't say you could, either."

"Unless he said I couldn't, I can."

Jake knocked his knuckles on the top of my head before crossing the room to his briefcase, which he opened, digging through it until he produced two sheets of folded paper.

"Fortunately for me, I have a copy of the waiver here. Let's see what we're allowed to do."

"He really gave you a waiver?"

"He said something about not pissing off the rogue agent. He then went on to say if I were under different restrictions, I couldn't keep you out of trouble. Now, be quiet, woman. I'm trying to find the clause here that says you can't dress indecently." Jake scanned the pages. "No unnecessary killing has made the top of the list. Daniels is a wise man. No exposing government secrets. No betraying any law enforcement or government employees."

"I wouldn't even with a waiver," I grumbled.

"There's a note that any lethal force rules may be violated in life-or-death situations."

"Is it highlighted and underlined?"

"No."

"It probably should be. That seems important."

"No grand theft auto? Ah, specific to the Corvette. Wait, why is it specific to the Corvette?"

"Flight risk?" I suggested.

"I can't say I'd blame you if you ran off with the Corvette."

"Is the same clause on your list?"

"Our waivers are identical."

I propped my feet up on the edge of my bed. "I haven't heard a single thing about indecent exposure yet."

"It's gotta be here in somewhere," Jake muttered.

"I don't see what the big deal is."

"Maybe I don't want people looking at your legs and getting any ideas," he snapped.

I reached down, grabbed hold of my ankle, and lifted my leg to get a better look at my calf. "So many hours practicing my doggy paddle really did some nice things for my legs, didn't it?"

Jake glanced away from the sheet of paper in his hand, and his gaze locked on my leg. "I can count your ribs."

"You're not looking at my ribs," I pointed out.

Jake cleared his throat and turned his attention back to the papers in his hand. A hint of red spread across his cheeks. "I could count them if I wanted."

Relieved Jake didn't seem angry with me anymore, I relaxed and lowered my leg to the bed, reclining in the chair and making myself comfortable. "All the rules involve things like stealing money from people, damaging property, and anything that makes the FBI liable outside of normal operating procedures. I read them several times. I can expose myself as much as I want."

"That's really not fair."

"I could even prostitute if I wanted. That waiver is my free ticket to a very successful illegal career. I could make a fortune on the side before Daniels remembers he needs to cancel the waiver."

"I have cash in my wallet and my handcuffs in my back pocket. Nothing in this waiver says I can't put you in protective custody." Jake wrinkled his nose, flipping to the second sheet. "He really didn't include anything about prostitution or indecent exposure?"

"I tricked that elementary school principal. And cops. I have the rebellious high school girl act down to an art."

"Is there a reason you decided to dress as an underaged prostitute?"

"Hey, it got Elizabeth to talk to me."

"Elizabeth?"

"Kid from the elementary school. Tomorrow, I want to

have a talk with a girl named Melly; I got the contact information from the principal. I'm hoping there's a home-schooling network in this town."

"Pursuing the runaway angle?"

"In part. If he has been picked up by Henry's SUV-driving associates, I want to establish the timeline. If he hasn't, I want to find him first."

"You're worried he hasn't been grabbed yet."

"That's right." I sighed. "I feel like I should be out looking for him. Now."

"You need a real meal, good sleep, and time to relax. Unwind. You're tense." Jake tossed the papers onto his bed. "You look like hell, and not even all that makeup is able to hide it. You could have called, Karma. You know my number."

"What would calling have done? What would whining have accomplished?"

"You wouldn't have had to shoulder all that on your own."

Calling Jake had crossed my mind when I had lowered my guard, forgot myself, and thought about the man, which had been every time I had ordered a damned pepperoni pizza.

I was truly pathetic.

"Come on, Karma. Talk to me."

"I'm supposed to be able to handle anything."

He huffed. "Haven't you figured this shit out yet?"

I glowered at him. "What the fuck is that supposed to mean?"

Without any effort on his part, Jake picked up my feet and shoved them off the bed before standing over me, his hands clutching the armrests of my chair. He leaned over until he looked me directly in the eyes, so close I could count his eyelashes.

Damnit, the man's lashes were about as pretty as his eyes.

For a long time, I stared at him and he stared back, and I forgot I was supposed to breathe.

Jake sighed again. "It means you call me. For anything. If it's four in the fucking morning and you need someone to talk to, you fucking call me. You pick up that fancy phone of yours, you dial my number, and you call me. If I don't pick up, you leave me a message, and I will call you the instant I get the message. Text me to call you, too. Have I made myself clear?"

Spluttering, I tried to lean back, but Jake held my chair in place. "Don't you think that's a little ridiculous?"

"Not particularly."

"But why?"

"We're partners, that's why."

"Hard to be partners when you're in a different state in a completely different division of the FBI," I reminded him.

"And I'm saying that's bullshit. You should have called me. Here, there, wherever, you're still my partner. You watch my back, I watch yours."

"Bullshit. You didn't call me, either."

"You never retrieved your phone from evidence and no one—you, in case it wasn't clear—thought, 'Hey, maybe I should give Jake a call and give him my new number.' *You moved to New York.* You didn't even give your *parents* your number. I've talked to them more than you have!"

I stiffened as the realization he was right sank in. Calling my parents had been something I'd done from unlisted numbers, and once I knew I was destined for a dead-end career serving as an anchor for a team that didn't want me, I had stopped calling.

Shame was easier to carry when as few people as possible knew about it. At first, I had kept my number private because I had been busy. Then I had kept it private because I didn't want anyone to know my dream job was slowly killing me.

For better or worse, the FBI didn't just hand out numbers to people unless there was a legitimate reason. "Shit."

"I think you have something to say to me."

Damn the man for being right. I slumped in the chair, closed my eyes, and mumbled, "I'm sorry."

"That's a start."

Jake was worse than a dog with a bone, chewing, chewing, chewing until he reached the marrow and ate up every last scrap. While I had mastered the art of the silent stare, he wouldn't back down when he knew without doubt he was right. Sometimes he had the grace to say his piece and allow me to stew on it until I came to the conclusion he had been right all along.

The rest of the time, he kept on chewing until I acknowledged the truth of his words.

"You're a son of a bitch, you know that?" I couldn't open my eyes. If I did, the misery I'd been carrying around would bubble out. My unhappiness would probably manifest as tears.

When I cracked and cried, it was ugly, ugly, ugly. My face would splotch, I'd inevitably throw up, and the unavoidable headache would flatten me for hours.

No one needed to see that.

"All right. All right. I'm a son of a bitch." Jake pressed his thumb to my cheek and wiped, and to my horror, I realized my face was wet. "They really did a number on you, didn't they?"

I breathed until the trembling stopped and my eyes didn't burn quite so much. Admitting the truth Daniels had so directly told me hurt. "I did it to me."

"There you go accepting all the blame again. You really need to stop doing that."

"It's true. I could have done a lot more. I didn't have to accept being a stupid sunken anchor. I should have requested a transfer to a different division." I rubbed the back of my hand against my face, relieved there didn't seem to be any more tears leaking out.

Jake snorted and gave one of my ponytails a tug. "I really didn't recognize you dressed like this."

"That was the idea," I mumbled, grateful for the change of subject and too embarrassed to do anything other than go with his flow to safer waters.

"You probably would make a fortune as a prostitute. If you're looking for a side job, I *do* have cash in my wallet."

The safer waters were a lie, a very tempting lie. Jake had seen me naked, but it was a two-way street, and I had seen him, too. There was a very good looking man lurking under his crisp white shirt and dress slacks. I worked very hard to never, ever think about Jake like that.

That road led to very dangerous places, places I should never explore with a partner. "You couldn't afford me." Somehow, I managed to sound confident when I wanted to run away and hide. With luck, my tears would have made a mess of my makeup, which in turn would cover the blush undoubtedly turning my cheeks red.

When I did blush, there was zero chance of hiding it with my skin as pale as it was.

"You might be surprised how much I'd be willing to pay," Jake whispered in my ear. "Try me."

"F-fraternization," I stammered.

"Waiver."

"Fraternization!" I repeated, my voice rising an octave.

"I read the waiver at least three times. You can't kill people without just cause, you can't commit any major felonies—prostitution is not a major felony—and you can't compromise the government or any of its employees. Fraternization is an internal rule within the FBI. We could fraternize all night long, and we have a wonderful, wonderful piece of paper saying it's a-okay. And anyway, the FBI has surprisingly lax rules when it comes to fraternization. There are plenty of married couples within the Bureau." Jake made a pleased sound. "I'm liking that waiver more and more."

"*Jake!*"

"What? Karma, have you ever looked in the mirror? Ever? Even once? Jesus, woman."

"What is that supposed to mean?" I was proud of myself; I didn't shriek.

"It means you're a damned beautiful woman, that's what."

There were moments in my life when I felt like I had slammed into a wall, coming to a full halt as reality hit me like a speeding truck. Receiving confirmation of my acceptance into CARD had been one of those moments.

I spluttered, but my tongue twisted, and I couldn't force out a word. The burn of my blush intensified. Finally, I gasped, "Jake!"

"What?"

"Shameless. You're shameless."

"You haven't started screaming or trying to kill me yet. That's promising. As an added bonus, you're not crying anymore, either." Jake pulled on my ponytail a little harder, then I felt his hands working at the hairband. After a few muttered curses, he freed my hair before working on the second ponytail. "How long have you been a redhead?"

"Since I went to New York. I used to wear contacts, too."

"To turn your eyes brown. I heard one of those assholes on your team took a potshot at you over it. He managed to piss off everyone in hearing distance, too, and then once word spread, the rest of the office was in a bit of a snit over it. Honestly, I'm a little tired of hearing about how you pulled out your contacts, stared at him with the fires of hell burning in your pretty amber eyes, and quit."

I cracked open an eye. Jake's attention was focused on my hair, which he was playing with. He had a lock wrapped around one of his fingers, rubbing the strands together.

Like all office gossip, someone had blown the entire thing out of proportion. "A bit of a snit?"

"They were pissed. Lots of folks there seem to like you despite the fact you haven't talked to hardly anyone. You do your job, you don't complain about *anything*, and you don't make things difficult for anyone who doesn't deserve it. Thus, you're the Patron Saint of Patience." Jake huffed. "You should have kicked their pathetic asses. They weren't watching your back, and you know it."

"I know."

"You'll just have to deal with me watching your back. If you don't get your act straightened out, I'm going to pistol whip your ass so hard you won't be able to sit for a week. I'll keep doing it until you set that so-called team of ours straight. I'm not going to do it for you, but I'll be right there with you the entire time. Got it?"

I swallowed, knowing he was right. Some things I needed

to do for myself. Respect had to be earned, but if my hard work hadn't been enough, it never would be. Jake was right about too many things. I should have stood up for myself, refusing to accept being made the weak link, nothing more than a paper-shuffling anchor. "Got it."

"Good." Jake untangled his hand from my hair. "You need a nice hot meal and a soak. I may have picked this hotel because it has rooms with jacuzzis. After everything you've been dealing with lately, I thought you could use a little bit of luxury."

If Jake was trying to make me cry, he was doing a good job of it. I gulped down a few breaths and blinked until my eyes didn't sting quite so much. "You're being too nice to me."

"That's a pretty lame thing to complain about."

"Well, you are!"

"I'm going to give you a choice, Karma Johnson. You can go take a nice hot soak and let me order you something good to eat. Then you'll put some clothes on. Real clothes, not those slutty scraps of fabric imitating clothes. You can do so without complaint."

"Or what?" I demanded, rising to his challenge despite the fact a soak in a jacuzzi sounded pretty good.

"I wasn't really planning on giving you a choice," he admitted cheerfully.

I scowled. "And how exactly were you going to accomplish that?"

"Handcuffs?"

"Why are you asking me? That's not supposed to be a question. Why did you phrase that as a question?"

"It's a very hopeful question? I'm pretty sure you would try your very best to kill me if I tried to handcuff you without your consent. I know exactly how dangerous you are."

Jake was doing a pretty good job of confusing me. "What the hell are you talking about?"

"The subtle approach doesn't seem to be working." Jake matched my scowl with one of his own. "You're really going to make me say this, aren't you? You're going to make me say it, and I'll be giving you a reason to try to pistol whip or kill me."

"Murdering my partner is listed on the waiver as something I'm not allowed to do."

Jake leaned forward, his cheek brushing against mine as he whispered in my ear, "Fine. Since you're either being deliberately dense to drive me insane or you're even more clueless than I thought, let me spell this out for you. Put on some real clothes, or I'm going to handcuff you and have my way with you. That outfit is killing me in all the right ways. I want you so much it hurts. Is that clear enough for you?"

"Oh." I'd heard every sexual joke about handcuffs in the book, and as a general rule, they annoyed me. In reality, handcuffs weren't comfortable to wear. They were designed to be unpleasant. Something about the thought of Jake handling the handcuffs, however, had the blush on my cheeks spreading down my neck.

I took a moment to consider my situation very carefully.

Thanks to the waiver, fraternization was legal for us. Jake in a suit killed *me* in all the right ways when I was woman enough to admit the truth.

When had been the last time I had wanted to sleep with someone? It had been too long. Had I still been in college? Probably. It certainly hadn't been during my days in the FBI. I'd been used as bait one too many times, and my partner back then hadn't been fast enough to save me—and hadn't cared.

Jake was one of the few men I didn't flinch around; he made me feel safe.

To make matters worse, Jake had definitely been the last man who had seen me naked. Then, I had been covered in blood and handcuffing a criminal who had tried to kill me.

Had Jake always been attracted to me? Had I never noticed? I frowned.

Despite his proclamation, I still felt safe. With Jake, no meant no.

He wouldn't touch me unless I wanted him to.

Most men would have been impatient, but Jake simply kept leaning over me, his breath warming my throat while he waited. How often did a good man who was ready and willing to wait come around?

Not often. I'd seen enough violent crimes, enough rapes, and enough murders to understand just how volatile people could get. I'd been on the receiving end, too, emerging with scars I hid from the world.

While I had joked about taking the sexy high school approach on the phone with Daniels, I hadn't considered Jake would actually find me that attractive in it. He was right; I *was* dense.

"I think that was pretty clear," I admitted, realizing I had left him standing there for at least a couple of minutes.

Some things couldn't be rushed *too* much.

"Are you going to go change your clothes?"

All field agents injured or traumatized in the line of duty saw a psychologist, and mine had wanted me to expand my boundaries, especially with men. Jake met every last one of his suggested criteria for overcoming my emotional traumas.

He worked within law enforcement, he had a sterling record, and had the build of someone who could easily overpower me.

If I could handle any form of intimacy with Jake, the wounded part of me I hid from everyone, even him, would heal. If I found the courage to test the waters, I could find out just how close of a partner he could be.

I understood the risks I ran by even considering having sex with him; there were reasons for fraternization rules, and no one wanted to watch a partnership melt down because of sex. Would we work well together when morning came? I thought so.

If Jake had been driven by sex, he would have made a move long before we had gone our separate ways. The thought of making love with him intensified my blush. Once upon a time, before I had joined the FBI, I had enjoyed sex, and his close proximity reminded me of that fact.

If I wanted him, he was mine to take. My breath caught in my throat.

Jake waited.

I angled my head so I could whisper in his ear, "What are you going to do if I don't, Thomas? Arrest me?"

There were advantages to being short and flexible. I slid my way off the chair. The instant I hit the floor, I rolled through Jake's legs and jumped onto my bed, turned to face him, and blew him a raspberry. "Catch me if you can, Officer."

Jake's brows rose, and he reached into his back pocket to pull out his handcuffs. "You have the right to remain silent— if you can."

Chapter Nineteen

I WAS GOING to have to review the FBI's rules on fraternization very, very carefully.

"Marry me." I rubbed my wrists to restore circulation after spending a rather long time wearing my own hand-cuffs. While Jake had his own, he had stolen mine during my efforts to evade him. If anyone had told me running around a hotel room to avoid being handcuffed could be so much fun, I never would have believed them.

Jake had narrowed my world to the thrill of the chase. When he had finally caught me, he left no room for anything other than passion stronger than anything I'd ever experi-enced. My psychologist had been right; finding the *right* man would make all the difference in the world for me.

I hadn't laughed so hard in a long time, and I sure as hell couldn't remember when I had felt so damned relaxed.

I glanced at my handcuffs, which Jake had set on the dresser within easy reach. Did Jake even believe in marriage?

I hadn't asked—hadn't considered the possibility of wanting to spend my life with anyone.

If I married Jake while the waiver was valid, what would it mean for our careers? How could I have been partners with him for so long without realizing he had every last quality I wanted in a man?

Damn, I really *was* dense.

Jake smirked at me and said, "Okay."

"Wait, what?" I froze, then realized what should have been a very, very private thought had popped out of my mouth.

"Yes, I accept your proposal of marriage." Jake whistled a merry tune and headed into the bathroom. "You need to soak or you're going to be sore tomorrow. I'll call for room service. I should have called for dinner first."

"It's okay." My stomach betrayed me by gurgling its demands for food. Jake leaned out of the bathroom and glared at me. "What? Is it possible to get room service this late?"

"It better be, or we're going to have to get dressed and find something open. Get your pretty ass into the jacuzzi and soak. We have an early day tomorrow."

I flopped my way off the bed onto the floor, landing on my stomach with a grunt. Drumming my fingers on the carpet, I considered whether or not I had enough energy to get up and walk. Crawling could work.

I could doggy paddle for three fucking miles, but Jake had managed to tire out every last muscle in my body. "I'm done. I can't move. You win."

From my prone position between the beds, I got a good look at Jake's legs. Mine were definitely better, but he had been working out during his time in HRT, and I appreciated a man with muscular legs.

He leaned over so he could stare at me. "I didn't hurt you, did I?"

"In all the right ways," I reported. "Satisfied? Now could you please help me up?"

Laughing, he crossed the room, bent over, and worked his arm beneath me, lifting me up by my waist and tucking me to his side. His laughter died away. "You don't even weigh a hundred pounds."

I squeaked and grabbed hold of his arm so he wouldn't drop me. "How the hell did you do that!"

"I might spend some time at the gym to keep in shape. Unlike you, I also eat a suitable diet."

"Apparently."

"Are you all right?"

"You probably don't want to marry me," I confessed, maintaining my death hold on his arm. I wasn't *that* far from the ground, but the carpet didn't look very welcoming, and I had already landed on it once. "We both know I'm married to work."

I was ready to file for a divorce from it, too, although Jake's reappearance in my life and career gave me some hope I'd be able to salvage the mess I had made.

Jake chuckled. "Oddly enough, so am I. It's perfect. We can be married to our work while married to each other. Anyway, it's too late. I already accepted your proposal."

Maybe I hadn't been the only one to snap since I had joined CARD. "You're insane, aren't you?"

Jake set me on my feet long enough to get his arms under my back and knees. He picked me up again and unceremoniously dumped me in the jacuzzi. "My first act as an engaged man is to do my sacred duty of hunting food for my woman while she enjoys the nice hot bath I prepared."

I spluttered, wiping water and soap suds off my face. "I didn't mean to say it out loud, damn it!"

"I am not above taking advantage of your moment of weakness, especially when it works so well in my favor." Jake strutted out of the bathroom, and a moment later, I heard him speaking to someone on the phone. When he returned, he was wearing his dark gray bathrobe and had his phone in his hand. "I'm afraid you're stuck with me now. Don't worry, it'll be business as usual with the addition of certain amusements when we're forced to share a hotel room, a practice I already told Daniels was non-negotiable. That said, I'll buy you a ring. You can use it to drive our co-workers insane as they try to discover the identity of the man lucky enough to win you."

Sometimes, ignoring Jake's insanity worked best. "You told Daniels about the shower incident, didn't you?"

"It's in both of our files, remember? However, I may have drawn his attention to that case. He was both horrified and impressed, then he started looking rather worried."

"That was a close call, one I never want to repeat." I paddled my hands on the surface of the water, relaxing under the influence of the rumbling jets. Most of Jake's attention was focused on his phone. "What are you doing?"

"Looking up the logistics of acquiring a marriage license so I can marry you. I thought that was obvious."

I frowned. "You jumped from buying a ring I could use to torment our co-workers to marriage really fast."

"I'm not taking any chances. A beautiful, smart woman asked me to marry her. Yes, you're the beautiful smart woman. Just go with the flow. Everything will work out."

"Jake!"

Jake kept his attention focused on his phone, grinning as though he had won the lottery. "If we head out of here by six-thirty in the morning, we can get to a courthouse in Ohio by eight. Ohio doesn't have a waiting period for the license to become valid. No blood tests, either. That'll put us back in Johnstown no later than eleven—maybe even earlier, if I can find a place right by the state line. You can conduct some of the initial interviews by phone, right?"

"I could," I confessed, narrowing my eyes as I considered Jake. "I can't tell which one of us is crazier; you for saying yes or me for even thinking about going along with this stupid idea."

"Crazy together is better than crazy alone. We both know how damned well we work together. You already know what sort of man I am, and I already know what sort of woman you are. It's perfect and you know it."

Before joining CARD, I had been different—a lot different. I had thought things through, taking my time before acting. Jake represented everything I needed in my life—that I needed in CARD and hadn't found. I had worked hard to maintain an appearance of stability, something I needed and my partner had provided.

The man had a point; we worked well together on and off shift. Marriage hadn't been something I'd considered. Men had wanted one thing from me: sex. After learning that lesson, I had abandoned dating and marriage as viable options.

Some men were a lot more aggressive about getting sex than others. Jake had spent four long years putting up with my shit without acting like he wanted anything other than a partner he could trust.

I wasn't doing a very good job of talking myself out of marrying Jake.

When Ma and Pops found out, they were going to skin me alive and drape me from their porch railing. My parents were the type who took marriage seriously; if my guess was right, they were waiting for the day I bothered to date anyone or take an interest in having a husband. If Ma had her way, she'd plan a nightmare of a wedding for her enjoyment. Pops would go along with it, because he enjoyed the idea of marrying me off almost as much as Ma did.

I snapped my fingers. "There's a flaw with your plan. You still need someone to handle the actual marriage part of things."

"Already have a plan for that. I'll waylay a judge. I'm not above waylaying a judge at the courthouse. I'll make sure we arrive a few minutes early, abuse the privileges of my badge, and con one into handling the legalities." Jake glanced up from his phone and smiled at me. "You're not getting away from me that easily."

"You know, a normal woman would be running for the hills screaming in terror right now," I pointed out.

"Why the fuck would I want a normal woman?"

"That's a very difficult point to argue," I conceded. "Fine. Answer me this, at least. Why?"

"A woman like you comes around once in a man's lifetime, and we're a lot of things, but we're not stupid."

I lifted my brows, braced my elbow on the edge of the jacuzzi, and propped my chin in the palm of my hand. "Oh?"

"See? This is exactly why you should marry me. You call me out on my bullshit. For that alone, you should take a detour to a courthouse in the morning with me and make me the happiest man alive. Take responsibility for your actions, Karma Clarice Johnson."

I faked a heavy sigh. "I suppose, if I must."

"I'm afraid you must. I'm holding you responsible, after all."

"Worst marriage proposal ever," I muttered.

"Yeah, it was pretty awful, Karma, but I'll forgive you this once. I'm generous like that. I'm sure you'll make it up to me somehow."

"You're such an asshole, Jake."

"I'm pretty sure that's what you like about me. Who else is going to put up with your shit?"

The man had a point.

"Well, when you put it that way..."

TWENTY BEFORE EIGHT in the morning, Jake parked the Corvette at a small courthouse near the Ohio and Pennsylvania border. I yawned, reaching for my coffee only to discover my cup was empty. "Well, shit."

"Can you last thirty minutes?"

"Do you value your life?"

Jake laughed, grabbed his coffee, and handed it to me. "Maybe if you hadn't eaten like a starved beast this morning, you wouldn't still be half asleep. Drink mine so you don't hurt someone, yourself included."

"It's your fault. You exploited my weakness for waffles."

"Did you really have to steal mine, though? You're not feeling sick, are you? I was going to order bacon and eggs but then remembered your unfortunate incident with the breakfast sandwich."

"It isn't even eight in the morning, and I'm sitting in a Corvette with my FBI partner waiting for a courthouse to open so we can, apparently, get married. I'm pretty sure that waived your rights to your waffles. I'm fine."

Unlike yesterday, the introduction to foods other than pepperoni pizza wasn't haunting me yet. Dinner hadn't settled well, but I had managed to keep my chicken where it belonged.

Jake reached over and gave one of my ponytails a tug. "We're buying you new clothes on the way to Johnstown."

I batted his hand away. "Shut up, Jake. I'm dressed like this for a reason."

"I don't have to like it. At least you're wearing more than you were yesterday. Couldn't you wear a knee-length skirt or something?"

"What sort of rebellious high school student wears a knee-length skirt?"

Sighing, Jake shook his head. "You make a good point."

"Why are we doing this again?"

"I'd go with the madly in love with each other angle, but you'd probably laugh at me."

"Probably?"

"Definitely. You'd definitely laugh at me. We'll just say I'm madly in love with you. You took pity on me and agreed to marry me so you wouldn't have to watch a man cry."

I checked the clock, unbuckled my seatbelt, and got out of the car, taking Jake's coffee with me. Bending over, I narrowed my eyes and glared at him. Like yesterday, he was wearing a suit, and I liked the way the dark blue looked on him. "It's your fault I kept eating pepperoni pizza."

I shut the door and headed for the courthouse, which was connected to the local police station. A cop was standing on duty near the building, and his eyes narrowed in suspicion as I headed his way.

I'd add the tally to my notepad later. Before he could say a word, I whipped out my badge and FBI identification card. "FBI. Any chance you can get us in early?"

"Us?" The cop looked over my badge and card before handing them back to me.

I pointed in the direction of the Corvette, glancing over my shoulder to see Jake walking towards me, his hands in his pockets. "He's my partner."

The cop chuckled and unlocked the door, waving us inside. "Sure, I can let you in. No problem."

I smiled. "Thanks."

"Who handles civil applications?" Jake asked.

"What sort?"

"Marriages, divorces, and so on."

The cop pointed to the reception area. "That way, sir. The lady behind the counter over there can help you."

"Thanks." Jake planted his hand between my shoulders and pushed me in the direction of the counter. "You can't run away now, not after telling me you ate pepperoni pizza for two months straight because you missed me."

"You're never going to let this go, are you?"

"Not a chance in hell. Just hurry up and marry me so we can get back to work."

THE INSTANT the clerk realized she was issuing a marriage license to two FBI agents, she called over the judge. By the time we were finished with the basic paperwork, we had an audience of curious civil servants. The judge, chuckling between advising us of the legalities of what we were doing, married us on the spot.

I had lost my mind somewhere but decided it would take too much work to go find it, especially when Jake seemed to be enjoying himself so much.

My partner grinned and laughed his way through the entire process. Within twenty minutes we were finished, escaping the courthouse and the amused men and women who wished us well and good luck.

I was going to need all the luck I could get.

"Did we really just do that?" I demanded on the way to the Corvette.

"We sure did, Mrs. Thomas."

"I filled out the name change form, didn't I?"

"You did. It was the bright yellow one. Weren't you paying attention to what you were signing?"

"I haven't had enough coffee yet," I confessed.

"You've had three and a half coffees so far today. How many do you need to function, woman?"

"I'd normally be on my second pot by now. I think. Maybe third. We done here?"

"One stop left," Jake said, unlocking the Corvette and sliding behind the wheel. "For the record, those shorts are killing me, Karma."

"I guess it's a good thing you're going to be watching my back, then. If the stop involves a clothing store, you won't live to regret it."

"Your waiver clearly states you are not allowed to kill me."

"Jake."

"Jewelry store. We need rings."

"Rings?"

"You know, wedding rings? They're typically metal, worn around the left ring finger, and are used to indicate the wearer is unavailable for romantic pursuits."

"You were serious about the rings? Jake, if we both show up in New York wearing rings, they won't need to investigate anything."

"I'll keep mine in my wallet in the meantime."

"Why do I have to be the one to wear the ring? Why can't you?"

"I'm not nearly as gorgeous as you are. You have a reputation of being very secretive about your personal life, thus it's plausible you were seeing someone. It's no secret I don't date, and there are a lot of people who can verify I haven't been seeing anyone. Therefore, you should be the one to openly wear the ring."

I tried to make sense of Jake's logic and decided it wasn't worth arguing about. "Do the rings come with coffee?"

"I suppose the rings could come with coffee if necessary."

"I need coffee, Jake. I need coffee now. I have a lot of phone calls to make, and I can't handle them without coffee."

Laughing, Jake backed the Corvette out of the spot and went on a hunt for a coffee shop. Five minutes later, I had coffee, and once the first few sips were in me, I got on the phone and gave Daniels a call using the Corvette's sound system.

"Good morning," Daniels answered. "What do you need?"

"You promised us an update. Anything new on the wire?"

"The rest of your team is headed to New York to question Henry's relatives."

"They're slow."

"Too slow."

The anger in Daniels's tone warned me of trouble. I

didn't know my supervisor's boss that well, but I'd been in the FBI long enough to know he was about to start issuing orders I wouldn't like.

"You're considering taking the team off the case," I guessed.

"The team is about ten minutes from being dissolved. This is unacceptable." Daniels inhaled, was quiet for a long moment, and exhaled long and slow. "You and Agent Thomas will remain a permanent pairing. I'm in the process of looking for a CARD team able to take you both."

If the CARD team was dissolved and reassigned, we'd be off the Henry case, which didn't settle well with me. "I have some leads I want to follow."

"I haven't nullified your waiver yet. Until I have a new CARD team to take over, your team is still on the case. Once the new team takes over, I'm going to have to call you both back in."

"How long do we have, sir?"

"You have twelve hours. Make the best of them." Daniels hung up.

Once we were kicked off the case, we'd be cut out completely; while the possibility existed we'd learn the outcome of the case, neither one of us would be permitted to help find Jacob or interact with the replacement team.

If we were lucky, Daniels would assign us to the team taking over the case, but I doubted it.

"I'm going to go out on a limb here and say something happened," I announced, staring at my phone, wondering what I was missing.

"Sounds like a solid assumption to me. What isn't he telling us? More importantly, why isn't he telling us?"

"Hell if I know. Time to put this Corvette to the test." I

reached under my seat and searched around for the magnetic light stashed there. When I found it, I lowered my window and plunked it on the roof before plugging it into the cigarette lighter. "Do you remember how to drive, Jake, or do I have to show you how it's done?"

Chapter Twenty

I TOOK care of notifying the local police we were on the move, giving them a description of the Corvette and our planned route while Jake handled the driving. We got lucky with traffic, and despite the fact we hit Pittsburgh at rush hour, the car's sirens and magnetic light cleared us a path. I was starting to believe yellow paint really did make the car go faster, because we made far better time than I could have hoped for.

An hour and a half after leaving the courthouse, we reached Johnstown. I killed the light and hid it under the seat. "Our first stop is Haney Street; it's beneath the Route 56 overpass. The principal said it was a popular spot with the kids."

"Okay. What do you want me to do?"

"Guard my car and watch my back. You're dressed too pretty for this. Pretend you're my dad or something. You're smart. You'll figure something out."

"You are such a bitch sometimes."

"Why are you stating the obvious?"

"It amuses me." Jake made his way into town and exited the highway, driving to the parking lot near Haynes Street. "Got your gun?"

"Gun, badge, handcuffs, phone, wallet," I replied, patting myself down to confirm I had everything. Most of my things were in my coat pocket since there weren't many places in my shorts to stash things.

I wasn't ready to stoop to using my cleavage for storage quite yet.

"If you need help, scream."

"If you hear gunfire, assume I'm screaming in my head and forgot to vocalize."

"That's not comforting."

"Don't go scaring people off. If anyone asks if you're Kitty's dad, the answer is yes. Tell them I'm researching an art project or something."

"Kitty?" Jake made a show of shuddering, earning a punch to the arm. "Heaven help me. I have a daughter named Kitty? Do I look old enough to have a daughter named Kitty? I don't want to name my daughter Kitty."

While I hadn't asked him if he wanted kids, Jake loved them almost as much as I did; it was part of what helped me accept him as my partner. "Man up, Jake. Don't start whining on me now. Kitty is the name I gave one of the elementary school kids. Why would a girl like me hang out with a guy like you unless you're my father? At least you look like you should own a Corvette."

"Okay, fine. I have a daughter named Kitty. Fill me in so we're on the same page."

"I told Elizabeth, one of the elementary schoolers, that I was home schooled; something about my father giving me the Corvette. I probably stole it out of the garage, but you have me on your insurance, of course. You're smart enough to know I'd steal it anyway. Saves a lot of hassle if I'm legally permitted to drive it."

"You're a terrible daughter. I must lose a lot of sleep over you."

"You'll live. Just play along."

"Roger. Call me if you need me for anything. I'll be watching up here, probably cursing you for making me stop here for whatever reason you contrived." Jake got out, leaned against the Corvette, and glared at me, his arms crossed over his chest.

I nodded, got out of the car, and headed beneath the Route 56 overpass, marveling at how Johnstown had turned what was typically considered an eyesore into a work of art. Green lawns and flower beds contrasted with the mix of statues and artistic graffiti decorating the pillars of the bridge.

It had been far too long since I had gotten anywhere near something I'd classify as a crime scene. Very few people were out, although I noticed a few adults with younger children likely in elementary school. As I wanted, I drew attention, and I strolled around the green space, noting the older homes and more industrial buildings nearby. The pillars and the underlying structure of the bridge would offer me the most opportunity for clues if there had been any sort of violent crime in the area; with so much time having gone by since Jacob's disappearance, it'd be difficult to find useful evidence unless I got lucky and stumbled on something Jacob had left behind.

Pulling out my phone, I took pictures of everything,

hoping to get a chance to blow the images up and have a closer look at them later.

I explored beneath the bridge, aware of people watching me as I examined everything, making certain to keep as bored an expression as possible. Within five minutes, a middle-aged woman with blonde hair starting to go silver at the roots approached me.

"Aren't you supposed to be in school?" she demanded, putting her hands on her hips.

"This is for school," I complained, stuffing my hands in my jacket pockets and making sure I kept my coat closed so my gun wouldn't show. "Art."

"Then where is the rest of your class?"

The best part of acting like a rebellious high school student was not having to hide my annoyance when people bothered me. I lifted a brow, met the woman's glare, and snorted my disgust at the entire situation. "It's a class of one. I'm home schooled, lady. Don't like it? Complain to my old man." I took my hand out of my pocket and pointed in the general direction of the Corvette. "He's by the yellow car if you want to take it up with him. I'd like to get this over with sometime today, if you don't mind."

I couldn't tell if I had offended her, shocked her, or both, but she backed off and headed in the direction I had pointed. Biting my lip so I wouldn't smile, I resumed my examination of all the pillars and sculptures, making a point of taking a picture of everything.

Halfway through, I spotted something odd about one of the pillars, which was partially masked by the boughs of a pine planted nearby. I stepped closer, pretending to look at the abstract pattern painted on the bridge support. Bullets made a distinctive mark when they struck concrete, and the damage was recent enough the powder from the impact hadn't washed away. The design of the art did a good job hiding the marks, and it wasn't until I got close I realized one of the bullets was still lodged in its hole. I crouched and examined the entry points, which were around three feet from the ground.

The paint, which was a mix of browns, reds, and yellows, had masked the presence of blood spatter. I snapped photographs while the sinking feeling of dread cramped my stomach. I scooted closer to the pine, searching for the second bullet.

The base of the pillar, which was concrete leading up to the grass of the yard, was clean—too clean, likely to remove the blood. Someone had scattered some dirt from around the pine in an effort to hide that the section no longer matched the rest of the concrete beneath the bridge.

I found the second bullet half buried in dirt near the pine, and from the looks of it, it had been caught up in the effort to hide the clean spots of concrete. I took a photograph of it, rose to my feet, and backed away a few steps so I could take another picture of the pillar, the hole, and the bullet in the same frame.

Then I called Daniels, clutching my phone so my hand wouldn't shake.

"What do you have for me?"

"Two fresh bullet holes and blood spatter, one round still in the pillar, a second on the ground nearby. Looks like someone cleaned the concrete near the pillar and used nearby dirt to hide their activities. Location is the Haynes Street pillar park, which is beneath the Route 56 overpass. I can't tell you the age, but there is still concrete powder around the holes."

"Have you touched anything?"

"Of course I haven't touched anything, I'm not geared for a crime scene investigation. I don't even have gloves. I have taken pictures, and that's it." I focused on my breathing. "Bullet holes are about three feet from the ground. Looks like 9mm rounds."

"Quantity of blood?"

"If the attempted cleanup is any indication, substantial. Give me a sec." I got closer to the concrete, narrowing my eyes as I worked to distinguish blood from paint. "There's spatter on the art here. I'm going to guess the vic was close to the pillar when shot."

"Fatal amount?"

"I don't know, sir. Forensics might be able to figure it out. Without knowing the vic's age and body size, I can't really answer your question. Have there been any reports of anyone else missing in the area?"

Daniels was silent for a long time, and I chewed on my lip.

Waiting was always, always the hardest part, even though I knew the possibility of someone else going missing in the same town in such a short period of time was low at best.

"Not that I know of," he finally replied.

"Fuck," I hissed through clenched teeth.

"Any idea how long ago?"

"When was the last time it rained here?"

I heard the distinct sound of typing on the other end of the line. "The day before Jacob's disappearance."

"I really doubt it has rained since these bullet holes were made. The bullet on the ground looks like it was caught up in the sweeping, and the coverage is thin enough any decent rainfall probably would have washed it away."

"Have you completed your walkthrough of the area?"

"No, sir. Not yet. I called you right after I found the holes and photographed the scene."

"Keep me in the loop. Call me when you're ready for me to bring in the local police." Daniels hung up.

I sat back on my heels and stared at the holes. Nothing added up. If the men behind the Greenwich case had kidnapped Jacob Henry, why hadn't there been a ransom request? The evidence of Henry's connection to Annabelle's father was a strong indication Henry knew—or had—something the perps wanted. But, if that was the case, why was there blood spatter in a place elementary school kids hung out?

Who had been shot? Why?

I didn't want to believe the victim had been Jacob Henry, but I had a hard time denying the circumstantial evidence piling up. The holes were about the right height for chest or head shots against a ten year old boy. On an adult, the holes would be closer to an abdomen hit, which didn't bode well for the victim, either.

I checked the holes one more time to examine the angle of entry, hoping the shot had been taken from higher ground to eliminate the possibility of the victim being a child.

My hopes were short lived, and with a heavy sigh, I stood, stepped away from the pillar, and resumed my walk around the park, making sure I took time to examine the rest of the art as thoroughly as I had the pillar with its two bullet holes and bloodstains.

I found several blood spatters leading to a nearby street, where the trail went cold. Dialing Daniels's number, I stared at the park, wondering where I'd begin unraveling the mess.

"Find anything else?"

"Blood spatters leading to a nearby street. Looks like they carried the body to here and left. No rubber marks, and I can't see anything else of use. Send in the cops. Maybe they'll notice something I missed."

"On it. Take pictures of your shoes and footprints and send them to me so they can be accounted for. If you think you've gotten any evidence on your shoes, bag them and leave them for forensics."

I considered where I had walked, but doubted they'd find anything of use on my shoes; others had already disturbed the park, too. "Roger. I doubt there's anything on my shoes of use. Lots of people come here, so the site has been disturbed already. Do you want us to start doing the ground work?"

"I'm going to toss this to a violent crimes task force and the local police. I'll advise you on how to proceed."

"Roger." I hung up, stuffed my phone in my pocket, and trudged my way back to Jake and the Corvette, cursing every step of the way.

I STOMPED the dirt off my shoes when I reached the Corvette, aware of Jake glaring at me from his post leaning against the car.

"You sent that nag up here on purpose, didn't you?"

"Can it, Jake. I found two bullet holes, blood spatter, and a trail to a road on the other side of the bridge."

Jake made a sound suspiciously similar to a growl. "Fuck."

"Daniels is kicking it to folks on the violent crimes task force and the local police. He said he'll advise us how to proceed." Closing my eyes, I sighed, shook my head to clear it, and thought through our options. "This is not how things are supposed to go."

"Get in the car," Jake ordered, circling to the driver's side.

I cracked open my eyes, yanked open the passenger side door, and slid inside. "I took a lot of pictures. Bullet holes were approximately three feet from the ground, fairly level entry points from what I could tell. Found one bullet lodged in the hole, and the other was in the stirred up dirt. Happened since the last rain, and someone had taken the time to clean up the blood."

"What sort of idiot cleans up the blood on the ground but leaves the bullets behind?"

"I haven't gotten that far yet," I confessed. "I was stuck on trying to figure out how they did such a good job of cleaning blood off the concrete without anyone noticing. Or, you know, calling in the sounds of gunfire. There are houses around here."

"Probably happened at night when no one was around, then. There are a lot of older cars around here, so maybe people assumed it was an engine backfiring?" Grunting, Jake started the car and pulled out of the parking lot. "Where to next?"

"Should I assume the vic was Jacob Henry, or hope it was someone else and the kid still might be around somewhere? That's the question. If I assume the vic is Jacob, we're stuck playing the waiting game. I don't think Daniels intends to let either one of us get involved with a potential murder investigation."

"At least not this specific investigation. It'll get kicked to those in charge of the Greenwich case, probably. Sorry, Karma."

"Probably," I agreed.

"What I want to know is why the CARD team didn't find that. What the fuck are they doing? Didn't they ask any questions at all? Didn't they check anything out at all? Fuck. Anyone from the violent crimes division would've found those bullet holes. They're supposed to be better than this. It wasn't hard for you to find where the local kids hang out, was it? Why didn't the *cops* scope the place out?" Merging onto the highway, Jake flexed his hands against the wheel. I kept quiet, staring out the window.

"Those are some questions I want to ask Daniels. You have any ideas?"

"While the cops check out the crime scene, we should check out potential dump sites. Let's hold off on talking to Daniels until we've done our search." Jake hesitated. "I'm surprised he hasn't pulled us off the case yet. Your find changes everything."

"Give me a few," I requested.

As always, Jake nodded and settled in to wait for me.

I needed five or ten minutes to think, focus, and make a plan. In our years together, we had set up a rhythm. While I thought about the situation, Jake handled the groundwork. If Jake didn't have anything to do, he quietly waited for me to get my shit together.

That period of time I needed to sit back and reflect was both a weakness and a strength. His patience was part of why I liked working with Jake. He didn't question the time I took to think things over before dedicating to a plan. I liked reviewing the facts for a few minutes first.

It was part of how I'd gotten a reputation for being calm and collected. It wasn't because I was actually calm or collected, but rather because I needed the time to think, and

I did my best thinking when I took a step back, calmed myself, and stayed quiet.

Once it became a habit, it stayed a habit. Jake could handle the initial few minutes, getting us headed in the right direction.

Jake cleared his throat.

"What?"

"It's not much, but I want to check out that scenic over-look I tailed you to. I was a bit distracted when I picked you up yesterday. Think someone could toss a body over without anyone noticing it for a while?"

I grimaced at the reminder of the gorge. "Easily. Lots of trees and rocks down there. It's at the top of my list of potential dump sites in the area."

"Let's start there. If we don't find anything, we'll regroup and decide what to do next. That should give you a chance to think about other potential sites."

I really hoped we wouldn't find anything; since joining CARD, our failures had far outnumbered our successes.

Jake reached over and gave my knee a pat. "We win some, we lose some, Karma. If we lose this one, we'll do better on the next one, okay? Don't write the kid off yet. Stranger things have happened."

"Like what?" I demanded.

"I'm particularly fond of this one: an FBI agent freshly trained for child rescue gets kidnapped with an infant in a freak coincidence. Not only does she survive to talk about it, she rescues the baby. Both agent and infant emerge from the incident relatively unscathed. Stranger things have happened, and until we find a body, I'm not going to give up. I didn't give up on you even though everyone else had. I don't give a shit about the team's performance until this point. You and me. Here and now. That's how we used to operate, and that's how we'll operate now. If we lose, what do we do?"

"We win next time," I dutifully replied.

"Damn fucking straight, Mrs. Thomas. We win next time. Now, let's get to the overlook and do our jobs."

"But, Jake—"

"No buts."

"But I'm—"

"Didn't I just say no buts?"

"Goddamnit, Jake, you know I'm afraid of heights!"

"Oh for… how bad can it be?"

Chapter Twenty-One

"HOW BAD CAN IT BE?" I mocked, hands on my hips, ten feet above Jake, who was lying on his back. Without my partner's help, I doubted I'd ever make it to the bottom of the gorge, but it beat falling into a mud bath likely infested with woman-eating slugs.

The Conemaugh Gap was truly one of my worst nightmares. Why hadn't I said no? Why had I let him coax me over a mile from the scenic overlook to take some death trap of a goat path leading down the slope?

Why had the trail ended in a nightmare of jagged, broken stones designed to send us falling to our deaths?

The gorge had already claimed Jake, and I was stuck between a rock and a hard place.

Crying was starting to sound better and better.

"I'm not dead, Karma. Actually, it was a pretty soft landing. You can just jump down if you don't mind getting a little dirty. Nice, soft mud. Come on, it's fun. I'll even catch you."

"I hate you," I snapped at him. "I hate you, I hate you, I hate you. I hate you."

"Come on, darling. Don't be like that on our honeymoon."

"Don't you even darling me, Jake Thomas. And don't you honeymoon me, either. You just want to cash out my life insurance policy, don't you? That must be it. You lured me down here to kill me. It's how killers operate. They lure their victims to a secondary location. You picked this as the dumping site for my body, didn't you?"

"You're kidding, right? I lost my footing and landed in the mud. It's not the end of the world."

Tears burned in my eyes, and I stared up and up and up at the slope I had somehow managed to crawl down without dying. How had I come that far? There was no way I was getting back up without divine intervention. "You're going to leave me here to die, aren't you?"

Jake grabbed a handful of mud and threw it at me. It hit the rocks at my feet. "Laying it on a bit thick, aren't you?"

"You've lured me to my death."

"Now you're just overreacting."

"So what? You lied to me, Jake. You said everything would be just fine. You fell. Everything's not just fine."

"I'm fine, Karma. Do I look dead to you?"

"You're lying on your back in the mud!" I shrieked.

"I'm moving. I just threw mud at you. I can throw more at you. Damn, woman. You're making a mountain out of an ant hill." Jake lurched upright, and the mud sucked at him and his clothes. He shook his arms and hands, sending mud and water spraying everywhere. "I'm no longer lying in the mud. Are you satisfied?"

"No."

"Why not?"

"I can't get down." More accurately, I refused to budge from the safety of the solid rock. Determined to stay safely in place, I clung to one of the boulders, which was probably the only thing keeping me from falling the rest of the way into the gorge.

"Jesus Christ, Karma. It's ten feet. You have one big rock to slide your way to before you can walk the rest of the way down." Jake approached, sighed, and lifted his arms. "Come on, then. I'll lower you down."

"No way. I'll fall."

"Just because I tripped and ended up in the mud doesn't mean you're going to fall. If you fall, you'll land on me. I'll protect you, okay?"

I shook my head. When I refused to budge, Jake sighed again and climbed up the rocks to join me. "All right, all right. Look, I'm right here. Only a little way left to go."

"No."

Jake huffed, grabbed me by the waist, and pulled me away from the rocks. Struggling didn't get me far. The man had muscles like steel. Tossing me over his shoulder, Jake took two steps and jumped.

Mud splashed up, and he went down to his knees without dropping me. I clutched at his back, shaking as I stared at the mud, struggling to believe Jake had jumped so far while carrying me. "Holy shit."

Laughing, Jake slid me down his chest until my feet ended up in the mud. My boots would never be the same, but I didn't like them much anyway.

Only an idiot wore heeled boots while descending into a gorge.

"Breathe."

I obeyed, closing my eyes until my heart rate slowed.

"Better?"

Instead of speaking, I nodded.

"Good. We've got work to do. The river's right over there, which worries me. A body could easily end up in there if tossed from the top." Jake wrapped his arm around my shoulder and guided me to the drier ground fringing the shore. "Mind holding my stuff? I don't want to get mud all over it."

I frisked Jake, ridding his pockets of anything that could be damaged by water and mud. His wallet was ruined, and I liberated his damp cash before sliding it into his jacket pocket. His cell had survived unscathed, although there was an odd red icon blinking in the corner. "Hey, is your phone supposed to be doing this?"

"What?" Jake wiped his hands on the front of his jacket to dry them before grabbing the device. "Fuck!" He unlocked his phone, browsed through his contacts, and made a phone call. "Jake Thomas reporting in," he said when the call connected. "Uh, sorry. I fell."

"Into a gorge," I snapped.

"Not helping," he told me.

"It was *your* bright idea to go into a gorge, asshole."

"No, sir. Everything is fine."

Jake grimaced, and judging from his expression, someone was scolding him. After a few minutes, he sighed and slid the phone into his jacket pocket.

"You deserved it for trying to kill us," I informed him.

"It was not that bad!"

"It was. You fell."

"You didn't fall, so everything is fine."

"No, everything is *not* fine. You fell."

"All right, all right. I'm sorry. I'll be more careful, okay?

I'll even find a better spot to climb back up once we've checked everything out here." Jake checked his wallet and arched a brow. "You really took all my cash."

"A fine for making me go down that... that death trap."

"If you pick up that side career as a prostitute, I need cash to pay you." With wide eyes, he stared at me, and I could tell by the twitching of his mouth he was trying not to grin.

"I'm considering it bribe money to keep me from killing you for that comment."

"It's those shorts. I'm sorry. It's those damned shorts."

Shaking my head, I reminded myself my waiver didn't allow me to kill my partner. "Let's get this over with. Also, don't you even *think* about pushing me in the mud. You're already taking a dip in the river because there is no way you're getting mud in my Corvette."

Jake laughed and hurried to catch up, his shoes squishing every step of the way. "Understood. I'll scout from here to the river. You sweep to the cliff."

"You're taking the easier side," I observed, glaring at him. "I'm in heels."

"Last time I saw you near a river, I really thought you were going to drown before I got to you. No thanks. I never want to experience that again."

"This is my hell, just so you know."

"No, Karma. Your hell includes slugs. Let's just get this over with, okay? Yell at me later."

"Trust me, I will."

IN THEORY, we could have called for people to help comb the gorge beneath the scenic overlook for a dumped body. It would have cost time, but it would have saved me trudging through the muddy forest in heeled boots.

After more than two hours, I was seriously contemplating sitting in the mud until my body ached less. I was ready to ditch my boots and deal with walking barefoot in the woods.

"For somewhere that hasn't seen rain in a few days, this is seriously wet," I complained, watching the ground for any sign of disturbance. "If the cops decide to check this out, they're going to see our tracks and think a pair of lunatics came down here."

"Or they'll believe the FBI decided to check the gorge as part of the investigation, which is a very logical assumption." Jake trudged over to join me and bumped me with his elbow. "You have mud on your nose."

"Eyes on the ground, Agent Thomas. I don't want to be here after dark."

"It won't take us longer than a couple more hours to scope out the rest of the place. Plenty of time."

"We're on a twelve-hour time limit. We don't have a couple of hours. March."

"That's more like the Karma I know and love."

"What, ready to kick your ass or wanting to do my job?"

"Both."

"You are such an asshole. I've had it." I stopped, bent over, and went to work peeling out of my boots. "These fucking things are driving me fucking insane."

Jake whistled. "Nice."

"March, asshole!"

"Yes, ma'am."

When he didn't move, instead watching me fight with my shoes, I snarled a curse, yanked the first boot off, and flung it at him. My aim was good, but he stepped out of the way before it could hit him. The second boot fell short.

"Am I supposed to be impressed?"

I sighed, retrieved my boots, and tucked them under an arm, returning to my search. By the time we were finished, we'd both have to take a dip in the river so we wouldn't track mud into the Corvette. Then again, giving the car back to Daniels covered in mud might be suitable revenge for pulling us off the case.

I forced myself to focus on inspecting the forest, brush, and rocky bottom of the gorge for any sign of a body. The vegetation was thick with a canopy overhead; I had to check my feet and the trees above for evidence of a falling body, which slowed my progress.

Instead of watching where I was walking, I scanned the ground in an arc, paused to look up, and took several more steps forward. The method worked right up until I tripped and fell into a thorn bush.

I wasn't the first to fall prey to the thorns, but unlike the bush's other victim, I was alive to tell the tale. Corpses weren't new in my line of work, but as a general rule, I had warning before I saw them.

Then again, I normally didn't end up sprawled over a corpse. My first coherent thought identified the size of the body—what was left of it—as far too large to be a child's. My relief was short lived, however. The realization I was lying across someone's rotting remains slammed into me right along with the smell of decay. My shriek was cut off by my gag reflex. Lurching back, I ended up flat in the mud, a shudder running through me.

I choked and pressed the back of my hand to my mouth

to keep from throwing up. I panted until the nausea abated enough for me to speak.

"Jake." In my effort to keep from retching, I wasn't able to speak his name very loud, but my call summoned my partner.

"What is it? Something wrong?"

If I closed my eyes, I'd probably faint. That had been a hard-learned lesson. I was covered in something far, far worse than mud, and it was taking every bit of my self-control to stop myself from sprinting for the river and jumping in, washing away any evidence I might have accidentally picked up. "There's a body, and I found it with my face."

Jake stared at me, blinked, and searched the ground nearby, his gaze fixing on the bush I had fallen into. Stepping forward, he leaned in the direction of the vegetation and winced.

Coming to me, he took hold of my elbow and dragged me to the river. My entire chest and stomach were wet, as were my chin and cheek. Jake helped me out of my coat, peeled me out of my shoulder holster, and checked my pockets before pointing at the water. "It's shallow enough there even for you from the looks of it. Don't drown."

All thoughts of evidence fled my mind, and I was never so happy to enter a body of water in my life. Shuddering from more than the cold and wet, I went to work scrubbing my hands clean before dunking my face in the water and scouring my cheeks, chin, and mouth as though my life depended on it.

Thanks to my lessons, I could hold my breath underwater a long time, and I didn't emerge until Jake grabbed me by one of my ponytails and pulled me up. "I said *don't* drown."

"I got corpse on my face," I whispered.

"I know." Jake pointed at his cheek. "You missed a spot."

Shuddering, I submerged my head and rubbed until I was convinced I had taken off several layers of skin. Jake once again pulled my head up. "You got it. Neck next," he advised. "If you lie on your back, you can probably scrub it all off and let the current help without trying to drown yourself."

If it meant I could get everything off, I'd do anything, even lie in the water and let it slough all the skin from my body. "I don't think he was in one piece, Jake."

Jake crouched beside me, resting his wrists on his legs. "I saw."

"I fell on him."

"I know. Get the rest off you. I'll call this in."

I jerked my head in a nod. "I fell on a corpse, Jake."

Sighing, Jake pointed at a spot on his throat. "You have… a chunk sticking to you there."

The thought of having something more than blood or some other bodily fluid on me had me scrambling deeper into the river, my hands clawing at my neck to make sure I took off several layers of skin along with whatever was contaminating them. "Gross, gross, gross. Oh God, gross."

"Yeah. I'd be doing the same thing if I were you." Jake pulled out his phone, dialed a number, and said, "Daniels, we found a body. I'm guessing male, cause of death uncertain. He's… been mauled. Karma found him by falling on him." There was a long pause. "No, sir. I meant it literally. She fell on him. Face first. We're in the gorge below the scenic overlook I met her at yesterday. I thought I'd check the bottom to see if there was a body."

I checked over my arms, legs, and stomach, and when satisfied I was as clean as a river could make me, I stood and lifted my sopping shirt. There were dark splotches all over it. I ripped it off and flung it at the shore. My bra, fortunately, had survived unscathed.

"And she just took off her shirt. I believe it had... evidence on it. Our waivers will cover us for destruction of potential evidence, right? She got bits of our vic on her face. I'm sorry, I panicked and took her to the river. I accept responsibility."

"Just shut up, Jake," I pleaded.

"Hold on, sir. Let me make sure Karma gets out of the river without drowning herself."

I flipped him my middle finger and got out of the water. I recognized the cold clammy feeling as shock or hypothermia setting in, and I bent over and put my head between my legs, forcing myself to take long, deep breaths. "I'll be fine. Just give me a bottle of gin, enough rubbing alcohol to decontaminate myself, and a few minutes."

"He wants me to describe the body and take pictures," Jake replied. "Let's not ruin the rest of the evidence."

Once I got my heart rate down to a tolerable level, I waved him off. "Go."

Jake nodded and headed back to the body. Following after him, I freed my hair from its ponytails so it could dry. The last thing I wanted to do was go anywhere near the body until I had better control of my nerves and stomach.

With a body found, I could divert my attention to searching for more evidence and figuring out how the victim had fallen into the gorge without tearing through the canopy, which I had been checking for. Had the man rolled off the side and into the bush?

Determined to make myself useful while Jake dealt with the initial examination of the corpse, I headed for the rocky incline making up the gorge's side. The height of the jagged stone hill—more of a wall or a cliff than a slope—explained the tattered state of the corpse.

It was a long, long way to fall.

When I tripped again, I caught myself in time to land on my back instead of my chest. I clenched my teeth, choking back my scream of disgust and frustration. I blamed my lack of shoes for my clumsiness, growled curses under my breath, and got to my feet. Clenching my hands into fists, I turned and stared down at the ground to see what I had fallen over.

My mouth dropped open.

Could someone really have bad enough luck to land on *two* bodies?

Closing my eyes, I pinched the bridge of my nose, inhaled through my mouth, and held my breath until my lungs burned. I exhaled long and slow. The second body had to be a lie, a conjuration of my overactive imagination or a symptom of shock. I could buy into such a theory with little effort.

When I opened my eyes, there wouldn't be a second body. A log was more probable—a log I had, in my twisted, shocked psyche, transformed into a corpse.

I peeked through my lashes, determined to prove my theory right.

The man was wearing dark, baggy clothing similar to the formless outfits my kidnappers in Baltimore had worn. Unlike the first victim I had found, he was intact—at least, I thought he was until I got a good look at his throat.

Someone, or something, had ripped it out.

With far more calm than I felt, I marched towards Jake. The third time was always the charm. I noticed the body half obscured by a rotten log and managed to step over the extended arm rather than tripping on it. When I reached my partner, I inhaled, remembered to keep my eyes open so I wouldn't faint, and announced, "I fell on another corpse."

"And Karma found another body."

"Two," I corrected. "I didn't fall on the third one. Barely."

"Okay. Apparently, we have a few bodies down here, sir."

"I'm going to go drown myself in the river now."

Jake dropped his hand on top of my head. "You don't have anything on you that I can see."

"I'm not buying what you're selling. My back is covered in the rotting remains of a dead white male dressed in dark, baggy clothing remarkably similar to the attire worn by the men in Baltimore. Something tore his throat out."

"It seems the second corpse is dressed in the same fashion. Please dispatch a paramedic with the investigators, sir." Jake hung up, put his phone in his pocket, and released my head to grab hold of my arm. "Come on. I'll make sure there's nothing on your back, okay?"

When I tripped over the fourth body obscured by the underbrush, Jake caught me before I could fall. He tossed me over his shoulder and carried me the rest of the way to the river's shore.

Chapter Twenty-Two

THE INSTANT JAKE slipped and took his attention off me, I waded deeper into the river and submerged to my chin. Two months of spending so many hours in the pool after work made the water far more comforting than the illusion of safety the shore offered.

Until the area was swept and all of the corpses were found, I had zero intention of leaving the water.

Jake discovered I had left his side and spat a curse. "Karma?"

"The water is warmer here than in Colorado." While it was the truth, the water was still cold, and I was going to give myself hypothermia at the rate I was going.

Hypothermia was still a better option than coming into contact with another corpse. I ran my fingers through my hair, spreading the strands to make sure the water could clean them.

"What are you doing? Get out of there."

"Miso something or other."

"Pardon?"

"Misogi. That's it. Misogi. It's a Japanese purification ritual. Ask Pops. He'll tell you all about it. He thought if he told me a bunch of things about Japan I might consider taking up his branch of martial arts. I think it's supposed to involve a waterfall."

"Okay." Jake pulled out his phone, tapped the screen a couple of times, and held it to his ear. "Good afternoon, Mr. Johnson. It's Jake. Could you please tell me what Misogi is by any chance?"

I scowled, lowered myself until my mouth was submerged, and blew bubbles in the river water. I lifted my head enough to say, "You're an asshole. Have I told you that today? Asshole. Complete and total cheating asshole. I wasn't suggesting you actually call Pops."

Jake dismissed me with a wave of his hand, although he kept an eye on me, probably to make sure I didn't drown. "I see. Let me run a scenario by you, if you have a minute?"

"Don't you dare."

Judging from the fact Jake directed his middle finger in my direction, he wasn't going to listen to my threat. "Let's assume you were involved in a situation where you found a body and you tripped over it, resulting in close contact with the corpse. Would you use this Misogi to purify yourself?"

"You are such an asshole, Jake Thomas."

In the distance, I heard sirens approaching. Jake glanced in the direction of the scenic overlook before returning to his watch-Karma vigil. "I see. Bleach has rather toxic consequences on the human body, sir. I'll keep that in mind. Thanks for the info."

"Such an asshole," I muttered.

"I'd like that. Let me call you back with details. Thanks again." Jake hung up and pocketed his phone. "You realize your father heard you calling me an asshole, right?"

"Well, shit."

"Just get out of the water, Karma. You're going to catch your death in there."

"I'm not clean enough."

"The paramedics will take care of everything. We can sterilize you from head to toe if you want, I promise."

"I don't want to go to another hospital."

"I'll be with you the entire time. I won't let them unnecessarily take you to the hospital."

"Fine." I didn't move, but I did turn my attention to the scenic overlook. "There are people staring at us."

"They're probably staring at you, Karma. You're in the river, and you don't have a shirt on."

"I'm wearing a bra."

"That's a lot of perfect porcelain skin to admire."

Scowling, I got up and marched to shore. Before I could reach for my jacket, Jake shrugged out of his and held it out for me. "I promise it's not contaminated."

"Fine." I slipped my arms into the sleeves and let him wrap it around me.

"What have we learned from this experience?"

"The water here is warmer than in Colorado, but it's still fucking cold," I replied through chattering teeth.

"And there's the first signs of hypothermia. Surprise, surprise."

"I might be in shock," I offered.

Jake sighed. "I guessed as much. That may have influenced my decision to request a paramedic."

After so many years with the FBI, I should have been used to seeing corpses, although I had never fallen face first into one before. "I'm never going to live this down."

Jake snorted. "When I saw him, I was a split second from throwing up. You have balls of steel. You *touched* him. You don't have to live anything down. I promise you at least one of the investigators is going to end up puking his guts out. No one is going to remember you destroyed evidence when the other investigators puke and ruin everything. Anyway, Daniels said he'd cover us. You have nothing to worry about —or be ashamed about, either."

While I didn't believe him, I nodded. "There's a problem."

"What?"

"How are we getting out of this gorge? I'm done. There is no fucking way I'm climbing anything. It's not happening. I'm *done*, Jake."

"Right." For once, he didn't argue with me, for which I was grateful. If he had, I would have gone from unnaturally calm—probably thanks to shock—to hysterical.

I handled hysterics about as well as I did crying. If I broke, things would get ugly. I did know one thing for certain.

For better or worse, I would never forget the day I married Jake Thomas.

JAKE'S PREDICTION PROVED CORRECT; at least three men ended up polluting the river with their vomit when they saw the bodies for the first time. I was pretty sure one didn't make it to the river before losing his lunch. We were so deep in the gorge it was difficult to get people down, resulting in rescue and investigation personnel hiking almost a mile to reach us.

The paramedics brought blankets, a dry change of clothes, and a first-aid kit. The sweats were far too big for me, but they beat my soaked clothing. Jake had tried to convince me to change under the cover of the bushes, but until we found all the bodies, I wasn't leaving the shore. Instead, I changed under Jake's jacket. I was tightening the draw string on the sweats when my phone rang.

Jake retrieved it from my coat and offered it to me.

"Hello?" I answered without looking at the screen to see who was calling.

"This you, darlin'?" Winston Henry asked.

"Sure is. What can I do for you?"

"Jacob's at my place, he wandered in five minutes ago."

My entire world froze as I comprehended what I heard. "Really?"

"Really. He's… he's covered in blood, ma'am, but he don't seem hurt any."

"Hold on a sec." I turned to Jake. "Phone. Phone! Stay on the line, sir," I ordered to Winston.

"Yes, ma'am."

Jake handed his to me, and I dialed Daniels's number.

"What ar—"

"Jacob Henry is at Winston Henry's house. Just showed up five minutes ago."

"Jesus Christ." Daniels hung up on me.

Offering Jake's phone back to him, I turned my full attention back to Winston Henry. "Winston, I want you to get him warm and wrapped in a blanket. Make sure he stays warm, okay? Do not let *anyone* in your house unless they identify themselves as law enforcement. When they show you their badge, demand to see their full identification."

"He seems right scared, ma'am."

"Warm him, get him bundled up, keep talking to him. Don't take him anywhere. Try to talk about something—anything—other than what happened to him. There will be people coming over to help, okay?"

"I trust you."

"On my way," I promised, already moving to grab my holster, which I slid into. I double-checked my gun.

"That a gun, ma'am?"

"FBI," I gently reminded him. "If you own a gun, sir, make sure you have it put away. Don't want any misunderstandings, okay?"

"Ma'am," he replied, and judging from his tone, I thought he was consenting to my demand. "Anything else I should do?"

"Take care of Jacob." Hanging up, I turned to Jake and said, "Call Daniels back and tell him to make sure there's either a woman or the gentlest male agent possible. Do *not* send the current CARD team. Henry's probably armed and is freaking out. Jacob showed up covered in blood. We're going."

"Roger." Jake went to work while I finished gathering the rest of my things and checking my pockets.

The paramedics stared at me as though I had grown a second head.

"What's the fastest way out of this death trap?" I demanded.

As one, they pointed behind them.

One of the police investigators, a man almost as large as

Jake, stepped to me, his hands on his hips as he glared down at me. "Where do you think you're going?"

"To do my job," I snarled back, showing him my badge. "My one and only priority is to that little boy, Officer. I'll be back to answer your questions after I've dealt with him." Pulling out my notepad, I ripped out a sheet, jotted down my contact information, and gave it to him.

"Shouldn't you be going to the hospital?"

I couldn't help it. I laughed in his face. "I'm needed in New York. Jake, move it!"

"Moving, moving," my partner called back, coming to my side, my boots in hand.

"Leave those damned things. Let's go."

"If you follow the river, the gorge slope becomes easier to climb about a mile from here. There are cruisers up top. Someone can drive you to your car," one of the paramedics said.

I took off at a jog, my attention so focused on getting back on the road and headed to New York I didn't even notice the pain of running barefoot over stones or care I had to climb more damned rocks in order to reach the road.

All that mattered was getting to Jacob.

I WAS GOING to return the Corvette to Daniels covered in filth with damaged leather, but I was beyond caring. When Jake tried to get behind the wheel, I snarled a wordless threat at him, stole the keys, and took the driver's seat. I put the portable light on his seat and called in our route to the police so they would be aware I was going to break just about every traffic law in the book.

The instant Jake had the magnetic light in place and flashing, I turned on the siren, tore out of the parking lot for the scenic overlook, and sped north and east.

"Please don't crash," my partner begged.

"I didn't criticize your driving when you blitzed here. Don't criticize mine."

"I didn't fall on a corpse."

"Do yourself a favor and shut up, Jake."

"Right."

I understood his concern, but I had no time to think about anything other than getting to Winston Henry's house in one piece. Advanced driving skills were a part of FBI training, and thanks to training for CARD, I was fresh on the maneuvers required to navigate roads at high speeds.

The Corvette handled a hell of a lot better than the cruisers we practiced on. By the time we arrived in Winston's neighborhood, his street was blocked by a lot of parked cars and an ambulance. I slammed the brakes at the end of the line, killed the engine, and left Jake to deal with the car. I flashed my badge and slowed my pace long enough to get a nod from a nearby officer before heading to the house at a run. I had my hand lifted up to knock on the door when someone opened it.

The female officer looked me up and down. Before she could say a word, I had my badge out. "FBI. CARD," I announced.

Relief smoothed her tense expression. "Kitchen's that way. The boy's giving us problems."

"Problems?"

"He's terrified of us, and his uncle can't get him to cooperate."

"Are the officers armed?"

"Of course."

"Trauma," I explained, double checked my weapon was concealed, and marched to the kitchen. Four cops, three of whom were women, were near the door while Jacob Henry hid near the refrigerator, clinging to his uncle.

I displayed my badge to the cops. "I'm from CARD. Everybody out." No one argued with me, although Winston tensed. "Not you, Winston."

"Thanks for comin', ma'am."

"My name's Karma," I said, stowing my badge and approaching as close as the table. Once there, I sank to the floor, making sure I was lower than Jacob's height. Height was important for kids. While I wasn't much taller than the boy, I wanted him looking down at me rather than up.

Sometimes, little things like that made all the difference.

"Thanks for calling. Why don't you introduce me to your nephew?"

"Jacob, this nice lady has been lookin' for ya. She's Karma," Winston said, shifting to the side to give me a better look at the boy.

I could see where Winston had tried to help Jacob get cleaned up, particularly his face, but he was still splattered with old, dried blood and a lot of mud. I clenched my teeth at my oversight; I should have told Winston to avoid cleaning away any potential evidence. Jacob's clothes were so dirty and torn I couldn't tell what he was wearing beneath the layer of filth covering him.

At first glance, the mud was the same color as the muck found in the Conemaugh Gap. I heard footsteps behind me and glanced over my shoulder in time to see Jake in the kitchen doorway. I held my hand up to halt him, and he stayed put.

Jacob stared at me with wide hazel eyes, but I wasn't sure he really saw me.

"Hi, Jacob," I said, careful to keep my voice calm and soothing. "How are you?"

"You're dirty," the boy whispered.

I glanced down at the sweats, which were far too large for me. Running a mile through swampy forest had done a number on them. My feet were caked in mud a match for the gunk covering Jacob. "I sure am. Looks like we're both in need of a shower." I pointed with my thumb at Jake. "He was rolling in the mud earlier, too. That's Jake. If you ask him, he'll show you his back."

"I'm a Jake, too," Jacob whispered, his attention turning to my partner.

Jake took that as his cue to step into the kitchen until I felt his legs press against my back. "It's a good name, kid, although I can't say my parents were nice enough to give me as cool of a first name as yours. You got Jacob. Nice. Don't tell anyone, but I'm a James."

Biting my lip so I wouldn't snicker at my partner's dislike for his real name, I watched Jacob watch Jake.

During our time together dealing with violent crimes, we had dealt with numerous situations involving kids. Sometimes, kids preferred me, finding my small size and gender comforting. Other times, Jake was preferred, as his build gave the illusion of security.

I couldn't read Jacob. When he wasn't gawking up at Jake, he was staring at me. I smiled for the boy, giving my leg a pat. "It looks like you've had a pretty rotten day, Jacob. Want to talk about it?"

Jacob glanced up at his uncle, which I took as a promising sign. Winston was the known authority figure, and the boy respected that—and was aware enough of his surroundings to comprehend familial structure.

"Go on," Winston said, giving the boy a pat on the shoulder. "She's one of the good guys."

I always took the patient approach with kids. It worked well with the fosters; giving a child the chance to decide for themselves always helped in the long run for me. By giving them a chance to handle things on their terms, I found it easier to develop a sense of trust with them rather than trying to force them to bend to my will.

With a little luck, Jacob would warm up to me or Jake before the adrenaline rush ended. Once it did, I'd be useless until I got some rest and a solid meal. Until Jacob was in medical hands and under guard, I couldn't afford to break down.

Jacob didn't leave me waiting long, and once he decided to move, the little boy was fast. Some kids took the slow and careful approach. Others hit like a truck. The force of his impact with my chest and stomach knocked me against Jake's legs, and my partner steadied me with a hand to my shoulders while I made sense of the tangle of arms and legs on my lap.

I kept still and let Jacob sort himself out until he hid his face against my stomach. Once he settled, I rubbed his back. Instead of talking, he cried, and I didn't say a word. I kept rubbing his back until the flood of tears ended, and when it did, Jacob slipped into an exhausted slumber. I checked his pulse, breathing a sigh of relief at the strong, steady beat.

"I'm going to take him to the ambulance, Mr. Henry," I whispered.

Jacob's uncle nodded. Once I had a good hold on the boy,

Jake helped me to my feet. Understanding I had no intention of releasing the child until he was in the hands of the paramedics, Jake tailed me, hovering in case I needed help.

Winston followed us, wringing his hands together and shifting his weight from side to side in his nervous anxiety.

"Everything's going to be just fine," I assured the man, stepping to the back of the ambulance. The waiting pair of paramedics gingerly took Jacob out of my arms. "Go with him to the hospital. Until his parents arrive, you're the closest kin."

"Don't got me his insurance," Winston mumbled.

Considering the way the man stared at his feet, I had the feeling Winston didn't have insurance himself. "You let his parents worry about that." I took a deliberate step back from the ambulance to indicate I trusted the paramedics to do their jobs.

That first step was always the hardest. Maybe I wasn't the most feminine of women, but whenever I saw a suffering kid, every instinct demanded I latch on and guard them to my dying breath.

The paramedics would handle the rest of the work. Maybe I hadn't found him, but my work was done, and the relief was so intense I wanted to burst into tears.

At my encouraging gesture, Winston climbed into the back of the ambulance, as did a police officer and an FBI agent. Confident the pair could handle guarding Jacob as well as the evidence collection, I watched the vehicle pull away and navigate the maze of cruisers and other vehicles on the street, after which the shaking started in earnest.

I focused on slowing my breaths, but it didn't help at all. I flexed my hands, aware one of the worst headaches in my life was about to slam me right between the eyes. Digging out my phone, I thumbed through my contacts and called Daniels.

"What's the situation?" he demanded.

"Jacob's on route to the hospital with his uncle. You'll want to send his parents there. Do you want me to handle the questioning?"

"Your voice is shaking, Agent Johnson."

"I ran a mile and averaged one twenty-five getting here, sir. You were right. Yellow really *does* make the car go faster." My stomach churned, and I swallowed until the nausea faded enough I could speak without throwing up. "Where do you want us?"

"The hospital for a thorough examination. No excuses, Agent Johnson. Hand Agent Thomas your phone." I sighed but obeyed, listening to my partner talk to our boss. Within two minutes, he hung up.

"Time to go to your favorite place in the world," Jake said, patting his hand against the middle of my back. "Just be glad he's letting me drive you to the ER in the Corvette. He could have insisted on an ambulance."

I surrendered with a sigh. If I didn't cooperate, Jake would toss me over his shoulder or find some other way to physically restrain me until I did exactly what he wanted. Like it or not, I'd be going to the hospital. Fighting it would only make the consequences of my adrenaline rush worse. "Let's get this over with."

"It's a miracle."

"Fuck you," I hissed.

"Later."

"You are such an asshole, Jake Thomas."

"You'll like it, I promise."

I stormed off in the direction of the Corvette, cursing my partner every step of the way.

Chapter Twenty-Three

SINCE MY SWEATS had come into contact with Jacob's clothing, they were confiscated as potential evidence. The Corvette would likely be treated as evidence, too, since Jake had come in contact with me at the gorge, and we had both been in close proximity to the mauled corpses. At the rate I was going through clothing, I would be forced to buy an entire new wardrobe or run the risk of indecent exposure charges.

Daniels's first act upon confirmation we had arrived at the hospital was to nullify our waivers. Jake snorted at the development, huffed a couple of times, and finally smirked when no one else was in the hospital room with us.

At least I wasn't the only one going through an examination—or the indignation of losing clothes. Jake's suit had been confiscated, too.

"I am so glad we decided to take an early morning drive this morning. Learn from this, Karma. When an opportunity presents itself, take it." Jake stretched his legs out on the hospital bed. I had opted for sitting in the chair beside him, flat-out refusing to lie down on another hospital bed despite the nurse's protests.

My partner had cooperated, probably to set a good example for me.

My understanding of my limitations kept me seated upright, alert enough despite my sleepiness and pounding adrenaline-withdrawal headache. If I stretched out, even for a moment, I wouldn't want to get up again. The last thing I wanted to do was provide the hospital with any ammunition to keep me an instant longer than necessary.

"You don't look happy, Karma. You should be happy."

The quiet wouldn't last; someone would eventually remember we were here, and the real grilling would begin. I'd be reamed for jumping in a river and washing away potential evidence. Daniels covering for us wouldn't prevent it; it'd only spare us from either losing our jobs or some other official reprimand. I'd use my waiver to protect myself, although I should have had the presence of mind to remember my job.

Washing away evidence was a big no-no, and I deserved someone screaming down my neck over it. I had so many problems I wasn't sure which one I wanted to address first.

I'd start with the one I would never forget. "I fell on a corpse, Jake."

"I know."

"And then I washed away the evidence."

"I know."

"The evidence, Jake. And I forgot to tell Winston not to wipe anything from Jacob. I lost us more evidence."

"I know."

"If Daniels doesn't kill me, Malone will," I whimpered.

"Daniels already said it wouldn't be a problem, Karma. If you think you have it bad, one of the cops threw up on the corpse. Poor guy isn't going to live that down for years. If Malone values his life, he will keep his mouth shut. If he's wise, he'll smile, nod, and let Daniels handle everything." Jake huffed. Twice.

"Have you even met Malone?"

"No. Don't want to, either."

"I still lost evidence."

"Karma, you fell onto a corpse face first. Considering I saw a cop puke on a corpse and witnessed four other men contaminate the river with their vomit, I think you were justified in your reaction. Fine, you lost some evidence. Frankly, that corpse had been there for at least two days, had been sitting in the bushes, and had probably been chewed on by animals. The chances of obtaining good evidence from the decomposition material transferred from him to you is pretty slim. I don't envy the team put in charge of examining that crime scene."

The man had a point.

We fell into silence, and while we waited, I checked my email on my phone, scanning through the messages, grimacing at the ones from my CARD team. While Andrew hadn't tried speaking to me again, everyone had emailed me several times.

I forced myself to read their emails. Between the three of them, they had tried every angle, ranging from guilt trips to blatant begging. The guilting worked, but not for the reason they likely wanted.

If I had acted sooner, if I had done things differently, I might have made a difference in all the cases we had lost. If I had been bolder, stronger, and better at my job, things would have been different.

Then again, Jake wouldn't have been called in, either, and I didn't know what I thought about that possibility. No one else understood me like Jake did.

"Agent Johnson?" a man asked from the doorway of the room.

I lifted my hand, staring at my screen as I tried to decide if I wanted to reply to any of the emails.

"I think he wants you to look at him instead of your phone," Jake said.

"I am in my unhappy place, Jake. Let me stay in my unhappy place for a few more moments."

"You have it backwards again. You're supposed to be in your happy place. People customarily retreat to a happy place in situations like this."

I sighed, diverting my attention to the low-battery icon. "I need to hunt down a charger before the damned thing runs out of battery anyway. Daniels said I couldn't let the phone run out of battery, Jake. I don't even know where its charger is anymore."

I hated whining, but I couldn't make myself stop.

Jake reached over and dug his knuckles into the top of my head. "It'll be okay. I'm sure we can find a charger somewhere."

The man in the doorway cleared his throat. "Agent Johnson?"

Since I lacked pockets to stash my phone, I tossed it onto the bed beside Jake. "Yes?"

I'd get around to looking up eventually. Something about being stuck in a hospital while waiting for the ax to fall and chop off my head brought the worst out in me. I heard a sigh of frustration.

"Please forgive her. She fell on a corpse today and performed a very close examination of the remains."

Jake really was an asshole.

"I… see."

"It was only a couple of days old."

I chewed on my lower lip so I wouldn't giggle. Maybe Jake was an asshole, but he was a funny asshole. Whoever was at the door was either someone Jake knew and thought could handle the disgusting mental image, or it was someone he knew, abhorred, and hoped to give nightmares.

Jake usually gave his victims a chance to introduce themselves before revealing just how much of an asshole he could be.

My partner knew me too well. Maybe my coping mechanism of indulging in morbid humor wasn't politically correct, but it beat crying. Time and distance gave me the chance to twist the horrific into something a little easier to swallow.

I made a show of taking deep breaths, although I used the exercise to stop myself from laughing. Lifting my chin, I stared in the direction of the door.

The suit didn't surprise me, but the man's close resemblance to Jake did. I blinked, turned my head to stare at my partner, blinked again, and returned to inspecting the intruder from head to toe.

If it weren't for the fact I knew Jake so well, I might have mistaken them for twins. I talked more about my family than Jake did, although I knew his parents were still alive somewhere.

The man's age puzzled me; his features, skin tone, and

lack of wrinkles spoke of youth, placing him firmly in his early thirties at most, but there was something about his dark eyes that made him feel so much older to me.

"Jake, he stole your face," I observed.

"He's a face-thieving bastard like that."

My suspicions were immediately stirred by Jake's answer, and I narrowed the playing field to an older brother or his father.

"Now who has it backwards?" the man demanded, confirming my suspicions. If the man wasn't Jake's father, I'd be shocked.

Jake had been right about one thing: when an opportunity presented itself, taking advantage of it was wise. "Ah, yes. You and your daddy issues. Should I leave you two alone for a few minutes so you can hug and kiss while maintaining your illusion of masculinity?"

The twin huffs of annoyance broke me, and laughter bubbled out of my throat, spilled from my mouth, and refused to be contained. Doubling over, I waved my hands in front of my face in a futile effort to take back control of my nerves.

"You may as well come in and sit. We might be a while waiting for her to regain her composure. Close the door behind you. Should I be worried they sent you?"

"Nothing to worry about, kiddo. I drew the short straw because they assumed I could cut through your bullshit. I told them they were setting the bar for their expectations far too high, but they seemed confident in my abilities to get answers out of you."

"Kiddo?" I choked out.

"I would like to establish we had a waiver, so the fact we

may have washed away evidence can't be held against us," Jake announced.

"I know."

"There's two of you, Jake." My attempts to swallow my laughter resulted in snorted giggles. "S-sweet, sweet baby Jesus, there's two of you."

Jake's father frowned. "Should I be concerned?"

Jake reached over and knocked his knuckles against the top of my head. "No, she'll be fine. We're down to the laugh or cry stage. Give her ten minutes. She'll be able to answer your questions like an adult once she's worked it out of her system."

"Very well. So, are we going to play games or can we get straight to business?"

"Karma, do you want to toy with him or make this quick and painless?"

I took a deep breath, fought my giggles, and exhaled when my lungs burned. "Why are you asking me that? You're the instigator, not me. I only instigate when people imply I'm a suspect."

"Good to know," Jake's father said.

"So, who are you?"

"Sebastian Thomas, Agent Johnson."

"A pleasure to meet you, Mr. Thomas."

"Same."

If Jake's father wasn't going to be forthcoming with information, I was prepared to ask questions of my own. "So, who are you, and why are you asking us questions?"

"You already know who I am."

"I know your name, but that doesn't tell me who you are. It doesn't tell me whether or not you actually have the authority to ask me questions." I smiled my sweetest smile.

After four years of Jake, I figured I'd handle my partner's father the same way. Either I'd infuriate the man into giving me a straight answer or frustrate him into leaving.

I had no problem with either result.

"I see you play by the book, Agent Johnson."

"It has its benefits."

"Unless she's—"

"I won't hesitate long before punching you in the kidney, Jake. Milliseconds if that."

My partner shut his mouth with a clack of teeth.

"I'm the Deputy Chief of Staff in charge of CARD." Sebastian Thomas dug into his pocket, pulled out his badge and identification, and offered them to me.

Taking them, I looked over his details, narrowing my eyes at his age. "This says you're sixty-two."

"I aged well, like a fine wine."

"Did they dunk you in formaldehyde and let you preserve for a few years when you were in your thirties?"

"Something like that. Did you come out here after elementary school closed for the day? Perhaps I should call the school and inform them you're guilty of truancy."

I handed Jake's father his identification and badge. "Are you the reason I almost had a heart attack when I saw Agent Thomas behind me yesterday?"

"I may have signed the final approval for Agent Thomas's transfer into CARD. Considering the circumstances, it seemed like a good usage of available personnel."

Jake sighed and rubbed his forehead. "I should have known."

"We notice when certain partnerships bear excellent results. Considering the abysmal performance of a certain CARD team, I may have delivered a file to someone's office in New York—in person." While Sebastian Thomas was smiling, there was nothing friendly about his expression.

"I changed my mind, Jake. Your father is terrifying. When he smiles, I feel like he's a great white shark and dinner is about to be served. Unfortunately, I'm the dinner."

"Yeah. You figured that out quick."

"Gut instinct. Didn't even have to think about it for long this time. What floor are we on again?"

"Fourth."

"That's too high to jump, isn't it?"

"Would you even get within two feet of the window in the first place?"

"That shouldn't be relevant to this discussion."

Jake laughed and shook his head. "You're something else."

"If you two are finished, could we begin?"

"Of course, sir," I replied, glancing out of the corner of my eye at the empty bed. If I indulged in the temptation to lie down, I'd probably be out like a light within ten seconds of my head hitting the pillow. Would a loss of consciousness get me out of another questioning session? If the father was anything like the son, it wouldn't work.

If the father was anything like the son, I was about to step into the darkest depths of hell.

AFTER THE THIRD hour of being questioned, I lost track of time. There were a few minutes of respite when Jake's father ordered someone in the hall to hunt down a pair of chargers for our phones. In addition to the cables, two bags with clothing were brought in.

One day I would have to find out who was in charge of

providing clothing to female agents and educate them about the impractical nature of skirts. The fact Jake was forced into another suit almost made it worth while. Almost.

Over and over, I repeated the same answers to the same questions. I'd probably end up mumbling the answers in my sleep. I couldn't even force myself to complain.

Sebastian Thomas was doing his job.

The devil was in the details, and he grilled his son with the same intensity I suffered through, which made it tolerable. If Jake wasn't going to whine about it, neither was I.

Mercy came sometime after I began punctuating every other word with a yawn. I was aware of Jake and his father staring at me.

"What?" I asked through a yawn.

"I think we're done here. Gather your things, and don't forget your phones," Jake's father ordered, heading to the door. He leaned against the doorframe, watched us both, and waited.

"Jake, we shouldn't let him take us to a secondary location. That's his plan," I whispered.

Bursting into laughter, Jake shook his head, grabbed his jacket, and shrugged into it. "He's many things, but my father isn't a serial killer, Karma. You're safe. Look, I survived my entire childhood with him—somehow. You'll be fine."

A phone rang, and I was so tired I checked mine before I realized it was coming from the doorway. Jake's father answered, stepped out into the hallway, and turned his back to us.

"Not buying what you're selling. Let's go. Out the window. Quick."

"Fourth floor," he reminded me.

"Stop using your shitty logic on me, Jake Thomas."

"You are so tired."

"If he asks me one more question..."

Jake's father stuck his head into the room. "Tacos okay with you two?"

Before I could launch myself across the room and show Jake's father I still knew a lot of kickboxing moves despite being rusty, Jake placed his hand on top of my head. "Tacos are fine. Anything but pepperoni pizza."

Snorting a laugh, Sebastian Thomas shook his head and disappeared into the hallway.

"He'd kick your ass, Karma. Once he was done kicking your ass, you'd still end up having tacos for dinner, because the man simply doesn't understand the meaning of the word no." Jake leaned over and whispered in my ear, "Whatever you do, don't mention anything about this morning."

I flushed. If I had my way, the only people who knew about this morning would be me, Jake, and everyone at the courthouse in Ohio. Playing along, I placed my hands on my hips. "So you're saying he's the one who taught you to be such an asshole?"

"Yes, I guess I am."

"Why did he ask us about tacos, anyway?"

"Because we need to eat dinner?"

"Wait, what?"

"Just nod, smile, and accept you're about to have dinner with my father, Karma. At least he probably had one of his minions deal with our discharge papers so we wouldn't have to. There's that, right? Tacos instead of discharge papers. Look at the bright side."

The first signs of panic manifested as dryness in my throat and a trembling feeling that inched its way down my spine to my toes. I hissed at him, "What about Ohio, Jake? What about Ohio?"

His breath tickled my ear. "Best moment of my life happened in Ohio. Don't you go maligning Ohio on me. Crying won't save either one of us, Karma, so you may as well accept your fate. Remember: you are a dignified and professional FBI agent. You'll be fine."

Jake's father cleared his throat from the hallway. "Are you two coming?"

"Yes, sir," Jake replied, placing his hands on my shoulders and propelling me out of the room.

Chapter Twenty-Four

JAKE'S FATHER snatched the keys to the Corvette out of my hand. For a long moment, I stared at my keys, the fact they were no longer in my possession filtering in through the exhausted haze clouding my thoughts.

Handing over the Corvette's keys had been part of my original plan, but having the choice taken away from me snapped my fraying patience. I slipped my feet out of my heels, hopped to the asphalt, and spun. Smashing my foot into Sebastian Thomas's hand, I sent my keys arcing into the air to land somewhere in the parking lot twenty or thirty feet away. Metal clattered, and I hopped out of range, my breaths coming fast and hard as I shifted my weight side to side.

Jake's father stared at his hand, blinking at the absence of my keys.

"I'll just go hunt those down," Jake muttered, shaking his head. Far too fast for my liking, Jake disarmed me and got out of my kicking range. "There. While the parking lot of a hospital is the ideal place to critically injure someone without killing them, it's still a crime. Unfortunately, he's your boss's boss's boss's boss, which means he's your boss."

"He took my keys."

"I know."

"My keys, Jake."

"I know."

I stalked Jake as he crossed the parking lot to hunt for my keys. After ten minutes, he found them beneath a van. He handed them to me. "Here."

"I'm too tired to drive," I admitted.

"Trust me, we all know it. That's why he took the keys. I'm not driving, either."

Following after Jake, I fumbled with the ring attaching the car keys to my house keys. The metal resisted my attempts, and I clacked my teeth together from frustration. Jake's father's gaze followed my every movement.

I finally gave up and held my keys out to Jake. "Fix it."

Sighing, he separated the Corvette keys before giving the rest back to me. "What have we learned here?"

Jake's father frowned. "We're really going to do this?"

"I value my life. Do you?"

"All right. Next time, don't touch the woman's car keys."

"That's part of it. Ask Karma for her keys next time. She's actually a reasonable woman who does recognize when she's too tired to drive." Jake handed over the Corvette's keys. "Someone is going to need to give the whole thing a cleaning."

"I'll take care of it. Now that you have managed to delay us, can we go before your mother gets upset we're late?"

Jake froze. "Wait. You said tacos. You did not say tacos with Mom."

"Did I forget to mention that?"

"Dad, Mom's in Washington."

"I would hope so; that's where I left her yesterday."

"Dad."

"What?"

"We're in New York."

"I'm aware."

Jake groaned. "You're dragging us to Washington?"

"You said it yourself, son. I'm your boss's boss's boss's boss, which means I'm your boss. Get in the car, you little shit."

I looked Jake over. "Little?"

"Damnit," Jake grumbled, walking to the pale SUV his father directed us to.

"Take the front seat, Agent Johnson."

Some arguments weren't worth having, so I climbed in and buckled up. "Yes, sir."

"I will be back in five minutes. Don't touch anything." Jake's father glared at us before heading back to the hospital doors to talk with someone wearing an FBI jacket.

Jake reached between the seats and tapped my shoulder. "I will make this up to you."

"I'm not talking to you right now," I informed him. "Think he'll fire me before he has me arrested for assault?"

"I thought you weren't talking to me."

"I'm evaluating the pros and cons of making a run for it."

"Don't bother, Karma. He'd just have fun chasing you down and forcing you back into the car. Trust me, I know. Dad's not the type to file assault charges, anyway, not when he provoked a tired, cranky woman. He knows he fucked up. He might not apologize for it, but he won't try to steal your keys again."

I groaned and slumped in the seat. "I should have just crawled on the bed and passed out. They would have kept me for observation. What was I thinking?"

"You weren't."

TWO HOURS after leaving the hospital, we arrived in Albany, where we caught the last flight to BWI. We were ten minutes late, but 'mechanical problems' delayed takeoff long enough for us to blitz through security and board.

When they took my gun, I began plotting how to get away with murder. Jake wisely said nothing.

Security let him keep his.

To add insult to injury, I ended up crammed between Jake and his father, a move they must have somehow planned to prevent me from trying to escape their unwanted company. Neither man spoke, probably aware I wanted to kill them both and hadn't yet decided which one was going to die first.

When we touched down and made our way to the terminal, my weapon wasn't returned to me. I halted, clasped my hands behind my back, and waited.

Jake noticed I had stopped first, turning to face me, his expression puzzled. "Karma?"

It took all my will to keep my voice pleasant when I replied, "Did they change the pickup location for law enforcement's checked firearms?"

Jake closed his eyes and adopted my habit of controlled breathing. "If you're not going to tell her, I will."

Jake's father shrugged. "Your firearm has been confiscated until you pass your psychiatric evaluation."

My last straw crumbled away to dust. The rage over

having been singled out faded to a cold, bone-deep numbness. It could be days, weeks, or months until the government got around to scheduling me in for an evaluation,
especially since it was a decision made by my direct
supervisor.

Ian Malone would probably enjoy making me rot, especially when he found out his team was to be dismantled due
to poor performance.

I should have had a little confidence in my job's security
because the FBI had gone through the effort to transfer Jake
from HRT to CARD, but I knew better. It'd be easy for them
to transfer him back.

Anyone who ate nothing but pepperoni pizza for two
months and could doggy paddle for three consecutive miles
needed an evaluation and therapy. I recognized the wisdom
of the decision.

A little courtesy, however, would have been appreciated.
That my partner knew I was losing my gun before I did
stung.

Arguing, however, was pointless.

"Understood, sir."

Without my firearm, there would be no field work for
me. An indeterminate amount of time with a desk job
loomed in front of me, and once an agent's weapon was
confiscated, getting it back would take a lot of time and
effort. I would have to qualify again, a process I had breezed
through several times.

When Jake's father led the way, I followed, not paying
much attention to where I was going. Having flown in and
out of BWI countless times, I knew the way out of the
airport better than I did my own apartment in New York.

Outside the terminal, a cold wind blew. A car was waiting

for us, and Jake's father took the front seat. I slid into the back and stared out the window, ignoring the murmur of conversation between the driver and the Thomas family.

If I handed in my badge and emailed my resignation, I could at least end my career in the FBI on a high note. With a notice of evaluation in, the resignation process was easy; I had no loose ends to close. Without a firearm, I was not a field agent, which meant I didn't have to go through as lengthy of a procedure to legally resign or quit.

Leaving for good was a single email away, and it'd be for the better. I hadn't made any real contributions to Jacob Henry's recovery, but I had done some good. I had found a break in the case dealing with Annabelle's kidnapping.

It wasn't much, but it would have to be enough. Everyone had limits, and I had found mine. In the morning, I'd finish what I had started in New York.

What was the point in wasting resources on an evaluation I'd likely fail? I had been a fool to hold hope for the future. As always, hindsight was perfect, and I had paved a yellow-bricked road to my career's grave.

I MAINTAINED appearances by working through my emails, answering each and every message on my phone despite knowing my effort would mean nothing in the morning. Manipulating Jake into believing I was disappointed but would bounce back was simple enough; I gave him my best silent stare whenever he tried to talk to me, gestured with my phone to indicate I was busy, and went back to work.

Jake's father lived on an estate forty minutes away from the airport, and when we arrived, I met Jake's mother, a woman almost as tall as her son. She had a bright smile, a faint silvering to her hair, and equally contributed to Jake's curse of eternal youth.

Holding out her hand, she said, "I've heard a lot about you, Karma. It's nice to meet you."

After pocketing my phone, I shook with her. "The pleasure's mine, ma'am."

"Pauline. You have got to be tired. Dinner's almost done, and there's a guest room ready when you want to get some sleep."

While I wanted to just give up on the day and go to sleep, I knew better. Someone who had her head on straight would eat. "Thanks. It's been a long day."

"So I've heard. The investigative business isn't easy, is it? You're CARD, right?"

I nodded. It was true enough. Until tomorrow, I belonged to CARD.

"So, you little shit. What is this I've been hearing about a gorge?" Jake's father demanded, turning on his son with a scowl.

Jake flinched. "It's no big deal."

Turning to me, Jake's father asked, "Agent Johnson?"

"Ten feet, landed in a mud puddle," I reported, careful to keep my tone neutral. "As he said, no big deal."

"Sebastian, you leave that boy alone. He's had a long day. Come to the kitchen."

The kitchen was larger than my apartment in New York and included a dining room table capable of seating twelve. I was relieved when Jake sat at the island close to the counters and stove. I picked the stool on the end so I would have space, pulled my phone out of my pocket, and went back to work answering emails.

"You're just like Jake, grabbing every last second you can to deal with paperwork." Pauline sighed. "Do you ever take time off?"

"I've worked in the field for less than a week in the past two months. That probably counts as a vacation," I replied without looking up from the screen. Two full days counted as less than a week.

Without clearance to work in the field, my anchor had disconnected from the ship and was on a one way trip to the bottom of the ocean.

"You were already pulled from field work?" Jake's father asked.

I glanced up from the screen, arched a brow, and replied, "Why are you asking me? You have access to my file, sir."

Jake groaned and slumped over the counter, covering his head with his arms. "It's too late to fight."

"Your file states you were active duty since your transfer into CARD."

"Did my file neglect to mention I have been serving as anchor, sir?"

"As a matter of fact, yes. Jake? Were you aware of this?"

When I said nothing, Jake sighed and replied, "She was notified of her assignment after the Greenwich case broke."

"How many days of field time have you had since you transferred into CARD, Agent Johnson?"

I turned my attention back to my phone, selected an email from Daniels updating me on the Henry case, and replied, "Two. Today and yesterday."

"And what, exactly, were you doing during your team's deployments?"

"I'm willing to bet there's no CARD team within the FBI with such neat records or prompt filing of paperwork." In the grand scheme of things, it wasn't an accomplishment I was proud of. "I'm also willing to bet it's the worst-rated team in the FBI."

"That I was aware of."

There wasn't any point in hiding my intentions, not with the issue already brought up for discussion. "Then you can probably guess why I will be handing in my resignation and badge in the morning."

Silence answered me, and while I wanted to believe it was because everyone was stunned by my proclamation, I couldn't help but believe I had been railroaded into it.

I WENT through the motions of eating dinner, quietly went to the guest bedroom, and ended up staring at nothing until five in the morning. My body craved sleep, but I couldn't stop tossing and turning long enough to find relief from my own thoughts.

The memories from dinner stabbed through me. Jake's father claimed he understood. Jake said nothing at all, and his mother had offered a small, sad smile that told me far more than words.

Shit happened.

Giving up on sleep, I got up, made myself presentable, and emailed in my resignation, heading to the kitchen to leave my badge for someone to find.

Jake's mother was at the island reading a book.

"If there's one thing I've learned over the years, it's that my husband loathes having the wool pulled over his eyes," Pauline said without looking up from what she was reading. "Your intent to resign took him by surprise, and he does not like being surprised. It's good for him. It reminds him the people he manages are individuals, and that behind success and failure are circumstances he can't see."

I set my badge and phone on the island. "I'm finished with being walked on. There are a lot of eager agents waiting in line for a spot in CARD."

"That may be so, but are they good enough to replace you?"

"I guess they'll find out, won't they?"

"You look like you're ready to hit the road. Where are you going?"

"The airport. It's time I took a vacation, anyway. A change of scenery sounds like a good idea right now."

Pauline reached for a bowl in the center of the island and pulled out a set of keys, which she tossed to me. "Take my car and park it at the airport, dear. I'll have Sebastian drop me off on the way to Washington in a few hours to pick it up. Park it anywhere you want; it has a tracker in it, so I'll be able to find it. It's the Jag. You go take some time and clear your head. That's the spare set of keys, so just give them back when you're done traveling."

I stared at the keys in my hand, baffled by her offer to take her car. "Why?"

"Are you kidding? If you think airport parking fees are horrific, you should see the cab fare to get to the airport from here. It's brutal." Pauline chuckled and returned to her book. "I'm all about letting my husband and son learn life's hard lessons through experience, dear. After you went to bed, we had a little talk. Sebastian confessed he had approved the evaluation request based on certain recommendations, but he lacked the backbone to confiscate your weapon directly. It seems a woman who is capable of kicking hard enough to knock keys out of his hand intimidates him."

"I see. What I don't understand is why they were discussing this with you."

Pauline smiled. "I'm in the FBI, too. Technically, I'm Sebastian's boss, although he gets a little twitchy whenever I get uppity and remind him of that fact. I'm in upper management of Human Resources. You have yourself a nice vacation, dear. The alarm's off, so you can just trot yourself out the front door. I already moved the Jag out of the garage, so you can leave without waking anyone up."

"Thanks, I think." I frowned at the keys, stared at Jake's mother for a long moment, and shrugged. I had a feeling I was missing something, but I had no idea what.

"I knew you were a smart one. Have a safe drive."

I left without looking back.

Chapter Twenty-Five

WHEN I ARRIVED AT BWI, I was disgusted by how far away I had to park from the international departure terminal. I had no idea where I was going, but I was determined to leave everything behind for at least a week.

In a week, I'd be better equipped to evaluate what I wanted to do with the rest of my life. Staying would kill me one way or another. I'd already lost all control of my temper.

Kicking a supervisor had started the death throes of my career. Kicking Jake's father had crystalized something in me, although I couldn't quite figure out *what*. Until I did, my best move was to get as much space and distance as possible so I could think.

I had gone from calm, cool, and calculating to volatile in two months, cracking open wider and wider each day until my caged rage spilled out. The instant I had started pursuing a career in CARD, I had known it wouldn't be easy. I had known working in the violent crimes division would leave as many emotional scars as physical ones.

The confiscation of my weapon bothered me. However, the fact no one trusted me to turn in my gun was the blow that broke me.

No one trusted me, not even Jake. If he couldn't trust me, no one could.

I wasn't like Jake, who acted on some gut instinct I lacked. I had to stop and think. I crept forward and made up for my weaknesses with caution—or I was supposed to, at least. Once I committed, there was no room for hesitation or doubt. The five or ten extra minutes I took to plan had saved my life many times.

I should have taken a hell of a lot more than five or ten minutes to think about marrying the bastard. I filed the mistake as one I'd never repeat for the rest of my life. Until I figured out what I'd do about it, I'd pretend it had never happened.

All I had to show for it was a new last name and some signatures on a piece of paper.

For the first time since I had turned twenty-three, I lacked the protection of my badge, the right to carry a firearm, and the comfort of having the ability to protect myself. When I took a shower alone, I wouldn't have a gun nearby.

I certainly didn't have a partner to watch my back, not anymore.

I would be like most other women in the world, and I would do the best I could with what I had. It wasn't much of a start, but it was a first step.

The departure terminal was quiet, and I headed for the ticketing counter. Somewhere in the world was a place for me, just for a week or two, somewhere I could escape, regroup, and have the time to really think.

The woman behind the counter looked up as I approached and offered a smile. "How can I help you, miss?"

I pulled out my New York driver's license along with my passport since my government identification card was no longer valid. "I'm looking to go somewhere exotic and warm. Any suggestions with a flight that leaves soon?"

The woman accepted my identification, looked them over, and went to work on her computer. "There's a flight to Morocco that leaves in an hour and a half. You should have time to get through security. You will have to change airports in London to make your connecting flight, however."

"Book it, please," I said.

Morocco sounded as good as any other place in the world. My global geography wasn't a strong point, but it was either in Africa or the Middle East. I had never been farther beyond America's borders than Canada.

"Coach?"

"First class if available, please."

The woman tapped a few keys. "Yes, I can book you in first class."

"Cost isn't an issue." I handed over my credit card. If what I had heard of international flight was true, I'd be in the air for at least ten hours. She charged my credit card, handed me my booking pass, and gave me directions to the security gate.

I headed for security, looking over my receipt. Two thousand dollars to reach freedom was both a huge and a small price to pay. I'd probably regret the decision later, but I'd just add it to the mountain of regrets and bad decisions I had piled up in the past two months.

What was one more? I hadn't touched the profit I had made from selling my home in Baltimore, and my lackluster diet of pepperoni pizza hadn't done a whole lot of damage to my bank account. Sitting around doing paperwork for the men living my dream had paid well enough, if I cared about the money.

If money had been my main concern, I probably would have been happy with my job. I would have been content with doing *my* job, not caring the failures of the others on my team had caused so much harm.

I probably would have been a lot better off if I hadn't cared so much.

If it meant I could think of something to do with myself or find a little peace, I wouldn't miss the cash. I navigated through security in a numb, tired daze. I had a bad moment when I forgot my federal identification card was tucked in my passport, but it got me past the TSA guards without any problems.

I'd take scissors to it when I found a pair. I should've left the damned thing along with my badge.

Stopping in one of the after-security shops resulted in a carry on filled with the basics. Once I reached Morocco, I'd dress like the locals and disappear somewhere calm and quiet. Maybe I'd find a garden and waste away the days, allowing myself to think of nothing.

Maybe I'd find a beach and dip my toes in the ocean. Maybe I'd swallow my fear and be brave enough to wade in for the first time in my life. A world of possibilities stretched out in front of me.

All I had to do was get through the flight.

I marched back to the store and bought a handful of books. If I broke down into hysterical giggling, at least I could blame the book. If I got lucky, I'd have a talkative seat mate, preferably one who had zero interest in what I did for a living. Maybe I'd find one who liked talking about television.

I couldn't even remember the last time I had watched a show. Hearing someone ramble about a plot or favorite character would fill the hours. When I reached the correct gate, they announced the boarding for my flight, and I discovered the first perk of flying first class. I was belted in with a book in my hand and my bag stuffed under the seat before general boarding began, sparing me from the frustration of dodging people.

When my seat mate sat down, I glanced up from the novel I wasn't reading. I swallowed my resigned sigh at the sight of his black suit, white shirt, and black tie. Old habits died hard, and I had him identified as a middle-aged white male, probable businessman, before I remembered I wasn't supposed to be profiling anyone anymore.

I survived the flight without having to say more than a handful of words to anyone. Sleep claimed me most of the time, and when I woke, the sun over the clouds seemed a little brighter, the sky a little bluer, and blankets of white hid the world from me.

For the first time in my life, I was grateful I couldn't see the ground or feel it beneath my feet.

The change of airport in London went a lot smoother than I had hoped, and I was relieved when the final stretch of my journey to Morocco came to an end.

When I thought of Africa, I expected heat, but the bright colors of the buildings and the architecture of a vibrant past caught me by surprise. My worries about clothing eased at the staggering variety of people. It wouldn't be hard to find a balance between modest and comfortable.

Despite being weary from the long flight, I exchanged the cash I had on me and went on a hunt for clothes.

The cash's origin opened the wounds I had tried to leave behind. At least I rid myself of the bills I had swiped from Jake's wallet after he fell in the mud.

Damn the man, anyway. Why hadn't *he* trusted me? I could understand his father, but why hadn't Jake even tried?

I had been a stupid fool to trust him with everything.

Melancholy tightened my throat, and armed with local currency, I searched for something to distract me from the reasons I had run away. Africa was supposed to be my escape, not a prison full of reminders.

I scoured Marrakesh for peace, but all I had to show for my efforts was a pair of slippers, clothes favored by the locals, and a heavy heart.

SLEEP HELPED, but I woke up aware I was alone in bed.

I missed Jake's warmth. I missed the scent of the coffee he made, and how he always managed to have a fresh pot ready right when I needed it.

Even coffee made me think of him. Determined to forget everything about him, I drank tea instead.

It reminded me of minty grass.

The hotel I found catered to tourists, and I had taken a cheap, cramped room with a view of the neighboring building. After checking out, I let my feet carry me where they would.

In the maze of merchants eager to haggle, I found a bead vendor. While the bright blue of turquoise caught my attention, the chocolate-colored spheres a match for the brown of

Jake's eyes enthralled me. In broken English, the merchant hawked his wares, ranging from the beads to the string and metal threads needed to bind them together.

I stared at my wrist. I hadn't replaced my watch, something I had been meaning to do but hadn't gotten around to. I bought a handful of the spheres, arguing with the man until he sold them to me for half the amount he had pitched me. Instead of running away, I was clinging to Jake's memory again, and disgusted with myself, I stuffed my purchase in my small bag.

How was I supposed to find peace if I insisted on thinking of Jake and purchasing frivolous things destined to remind me of him every time I looked at them? Cursing myself, cursing him, and cursing the circumstances leading to my flight to Africa, I abandoned Marrakesh.

I couldn't bring myself to even try to make a bracelet.

In Casablanca, I found crowded beaches and blue seas. I took off my slippers and waded in to my knees. The billowing material covering my legs swirled in the water, and the waves tugging at me encouraged me to venture in deeper.

While I'd find peace of a different sort there, that wasn't what I was looking for.

I stayed long enough in the port city to book a flight away from Africa. The choices were few and far between, leaving me the option of returning to London or venturing to Moscow.

I chose Russia, and three hours later, I was in the air.

When I thought of Russia, I thought of snow. Instead, I got the brisk chill of autumn, and it reminded me of Baltimore on the brink of winter. My frustrations grew, and instead of leaving the airport like a wise woman, I searched through the departing flights for something—anything—that resonated.

London seemed like the type of city I would want to visit with someone, so I discarded it as an option. All it'd do was make me feel even lonelier.

Why was even running away so damned hard? I picked the next flight out headed to mainland Europe.

Flying wasn't working, so I'd drive. Maybe by the time I finished roaming around Europe, I'd have so many stamps in my passport they'd have to staple in new pages. It gave me something to look forward to. How far could fifty thousand take me?

I laughed so I wouldn't cry. I couldn't even vacation right.

From Moscow, I flew into Germany, staying the night in Berlin before renting a car. Determined to walk away from the trip with something positive, I selected the best Mercedes they'd give me.

If I was going to put hundreds of miles behind me, I'd do so in comfort and luxury.

On the Autobahn, I found freedom but little else. In the stretches without speed limits, I pushed the Mercedes and enjoyed the purring roar of its engine. My life narrowed to nothing more than the moment, the skill needed to keep from crashing the vehicle, and the adrenaline rush from zipping over a hundred miles per hour on empty roads in the dead of night. Each time I passed through a city or stopped to sleep, I filled up on gas.

Two or so weeks later, I returned to Berlin without having left Germany, the backseat of the Mercedes littered with Christmas ornaments and other pointless knick-knacks. I had no idea why I had purchased them or what I was supposed to do with them, so I boxed them up and shipped them to my parents.

Maybe they'd enjoy them. They loved Christmas. They loved everything about the holidays. The last thing I wanted to do was crawl back in defeat with nothing of substance to show for having finally managed to join CARD.

Instead of the peace I needed, my guilt over everything I had done grew until it smothered me. I checked into a hotel connected to the airport and barely made it to my room before the tears I had refused to shed caught up with me.

It took three days before I managed to crawl out of the depths of my misery and force myself to put one foot in front of the other.

Tired of Germany, tired of traveling, and tired of everything, I booked a flight for London. While waiting for my flight, I acquired a cell phone and a data plan. According to the device, I had left the United States almost three weeks ago.

Flitting from city to city aimlessly had done nothing more than damage my bank account. Sighing, I checked my personal email, staring numbly at the hundreds of unread messages waiting for me, each one a reminder of the life I had left behind.

Maybe I'd find something in London. If I didn't, I'd bow my head and return to the United States. Where, I didn't know—not New York, not Vermont, and definitely not Baltimore.

I had to find a new place to call home.

THE FIRST THING I noticed about London was the fact people spoke English. In Morocco and Germany, I had been surrounded by the babble of language unfamiliar and alien. Many people spoke some English, but few spoke it well, and I hadn't minded the solitude. It hadn't helped me, but it hadn't hurt me, either.

I followed the signs to get out of the terminal but didn't make it far before someone caught hold of my elbow.

"Excuse me, miss. Are you Karma Johnson?"

I didn't know the man in his early thirties, but I recognized his FBI badge all too well.

"Well, shit." I sighed, shifted my bag on my shoulder, and shrugged. There was no point in hiding the truth. "Yes, I'm Karma Johnson. What do you want?"

"Please come with me."

If he were following protocol, he would have introduced himself. I shook my head. "Name and identification first."

The man chuckled, pulled his identification card out of his pocket, and offered it to me. I dug my passport out, found my card, which I really should have taken scissors to, and compared them. If it was a fake, it was a good one. I handed them back. "Thank you, Agent Miller."

"Can't be too careful these days."

I shrugged and followed him through the terminal. An unmarked car was waiting near the curb, and Miller held open the back door for me. I slid inside, shoving my bag between my feet, regretting having chosen London as my destination.

Why couldn't the FBI just leave me alone? I had resigned and left my badge and phone. Did they want their damned identification card back? If so, I'd happily give it to them before walking away.

Three weeks should have done something to ease my bitterness, but I circled like a vulture over a rotten corpse. When I thought of the FBI, without fail, I thought of Jake. When I thought of Jake, I couldn't think about anything other than the fact he couldn't trust me enough to ask me to relinquish my gun and agree to evaluation.

"Comfortable, Agent Johnson?"

"I'm no longer in the FBI," I replied, proud of how calm my voice sounded. "Miss Johnson or Karma, if you must."

Maybe I had found something in Germany after all: my voice, the one I had built my reputation on. Calm, cool, and collected.

I didn't even have to focus on my breathing.

"A resignation made under duress can be challenged or postponed during an investigation of circumstances," Agent Miller countered.

I glanced in the direction of the driver, another younger man who was dressed in the same style of suit. "Are you saying my resignation has been challenged, sir?"

The numbness settled into my bones again, and I shivered. To hide the shaking of my hands, I pulled out my phone and scrolled though my unread messages without seeing any of them.

"Both challenged and postponed, Agent Johnson."

"Am I under arrest?"

Without a waiver, failure to present myself for duty could land me in a set of handcuffs. I kept on scrolling without truly seeing the screen.

"I was hoping to take a more civil approach with this situation, Agent Johnson. Your cooperation would be appreciated."

I read between the lines. As long as I behaved, Agent

Miller and his partner wouldn't arrest me. That was something at least. Not much, but something. "Understood, sir."

"We're expected at the embassy. It's about an hour drive from here if traffic cooperates. If you need anything, let us know."

Flicking my finger up and down the screen of my phone, I stared at the scrolling messages in silence.

Chapter Twenty-Six

WHEN THE FBI agents riding in the front of the car didn't break the silence, I forced my eyes to focus on my emails. I couldn't quite bring myself to read any of them, but I sorted them by sender and started counting. I turned off the ability to preview the opening lines of the messages so I wouldn't have to cope with what they said.

My parents had sent me fifty-three messages, and the subjects warned me of hell to pay the instant I set foot on American soil. Most of them boiled down to threats of death when they got their hands on me. I was grateful I had turned message previewing off.

It was bad enough knowing how angry they were with me.

There were a handful of messages from girls involved with the Baltimore kickboxing circuit, which I ignored. A few had tried to keep in touch with me, and I had given half-hearted replies, just enough to keep them contacting me, though not enough to entice me into finding a New York circuit.

Two hundred and three messages were from FBI employees, and most of the subjects indicated a desire to know my whereabouts.

Three hundred and sixteen messages were spam, which I systematically deleted.

One message was from Jake, and he had sent it over two weeks ago. It had a blank subject heading, which hurt almost as much as his lack of trust. What was the point of emailing me at all if he couldn't be bothered to put in enough effort to add a subject?

A little over an hour after leaving the airport, we arrived at the US embassy. Windows offset in a checkered pattern gave the building an odd sense of rigidity while having an industrial air.

The giant sculpture of a bald eagle far overhead seemed ready to fly off the embassy roof.

Pulling through the gates, the car parked in front of the building, and while I stared in resignation at the embassy's doors, Agent Miller got out and opened my door.

"This way, Agent Johnson," he ordered. "Dillan will join us after he parks the car."

I slid out, grabbed my bag, and followed after him.

"Do you have any weapons or anything else to declare?"

I stared at him. Despite having spent three weeks traveling, all I had to show for the journey was a bag of beads, some string, and metal wire, which I informed him of.

Everything else had ended up in the box with the Christmas ornaments, not that I had a whole lot to show for my trip.

"Is that it?" Agent Miller frowned. "You were in Europe for three weeks."

I shrugged. "I shipped some things to my parents."

"What sort of things?"

If my selection of things to buy wasn't a solid indication I had no business in the FBI, I had no idea if they'd ever figure it out. "Mostly Christmas ornaments."

"Interesting."

That was one way to put it. When I made no effort to elaborate, Agent Miller led me into the embassy. The inside was the stark elegance I expected from a United States federal building, both intimidating and comforting in its familiarity. An armed guard checked through my bag, and when he discovered nothing more than a few changes of clothes, slippers, some odds and ends, and the beads, string, and wire, he stared at me as though he couldn't believe what he was seeing.

Then he offered a smile and went back to his work. It was hard enough to keep from frowning. If anyone wanted more from me, they were going to be disappointed.

Too many people were smiling, and the last thing I wanted to do was pretend I was happy.

Agent Miller led me to a conference room on one of the upper floors, and when he gestured for me to sit, I sank down onto one of the chairs, dropping my bag to the floor. "Coffee, Agent Johnson?"

I shook my head. Coffee had been one of many things I hadn't bothered with after landing in Africa, although it had been readily available. I had gone beyond not bothering with it. I cringed at the thought of drinking it.

Jake had ruined coffee for me. I declined the water, soda,

and a long list of other drinks the man kept insisting on offering.

Agent Miller made himself scarce, leaving me alone in the wood-paneled room. When he returned, he had a stack of empty glasses and a pitcher of water in hand. His partner was with him, as was a young woman wearing a blazer and knee-length skirt. She carried a briefcase with her, which she set on the table.

"Agent Johnson, I'm Dr. Mellisa Sampson." The woman pulled out a seat across from me and sat down. "I can take this from here, gentlemen."

With bright blond hair and blue eyes and a slim but curved figure accented by her blazer jacket and skirt, Dr. Sampson could have easily made the front cover of a fashion magazine. She regarded me with a calculating stare, silent until both men had excused themselves.

"Do you know why I'm here?"

I set my elbows on the table, clasped my hands together, and rested my chin on them. "I'm no longer in the business of guessing motives, profiling people, and trying to deduce next moves, Dr. Sampson."

"That is up for negotiation, Agent Johnson. I've been assigned as your psychologist. I'm also a psychiatrist, so I've been put in charge of your evaluation. There are specific rules in place dealing with agents who have been coerced into handing in their resignations. This is one of those cases." Opening the briefcase, she pulled out a thick file and set it on the polished wood. "This is a part of your file."

The stack was over two inches thick, and I pitied anyone assigned to the task of searching through it. Unable to guess what the woman wanted, I shrugged. With the exception of forgetting to turn in my FBI identification card, I had followed protocol. I had emailed a formal resignation in addition to notifying management directly of my intent to resign. "I wasn't coerced to resign, Dr. Sampson."

"Management and Human Resources disagree. I have all day, Agent Johnson. Where would you like to begin?"

I kept staring at her, and to her credit, Dr. Sampson didn't seem to care. "With all due respect, Dr. Sampson, can we skip directly to the part where you ask me if I feel I should pass my psychiatric evaluation so I can say no? Your time is valuable, and I would rather not waste it on something unnecessary. I wasn't coerced. It was established I was prepared to quit prior to my official resignation."

"We can start with discussing your psychiatric evaluation if you'd like, Agent Johnson. Please elaborate on why you feel you would fail." Dr. Sampson clasped her hands on the table in front of her, her body leaning towards me to give the illusion she was interested in what I had to say, and waited.

"I thought taking an unexpected flight to Africa before going to Russia and then spending several weeks driving in circles in Germany was sufficient evidence I am not of a sound mind, Dr. Sampson. If you consider the circumstances leading up to the first time I quit and up to when I handed in my badge and filed my resignation, I think you'll find all the evidence you need to support a failure of a psychiatric evaluation."

"Agent Johnson, you have not taken a substantial vacation since you joined the FBI when you turned twenty-three. In fact, the only time you took more than two consecutive days off work was when you or your partner were recovering from injuries sustained during the line of duty."

There was no point in denying the truth, so I nodded.

"It comes as absolutely no surprise to me you would have adverse reactions to being, essentially, forced into a support role when you have dedicated your entire career to field work. Frankly, no one in their sound mind expects an agent to remain stable under such conditions for an extended period of time, especially without an established timeline for a return to duty. It's a little like working with police dogs, Agent Johnson. When you give a good police dog an excellent trainer and challenging work, you will not find a better partner. Transfer that same dog into a quiet home expecting him to become a couch potato, and you are asking for trouble and a fortune in destroyed property."

I understood the analogy well enough; some breeds of dogs simply needed work, and the ones favored by the police and military tended to be happiest when given a job to do. "I follow."

"Why would anyone expect anything different from a highly successful FBI agent? We have programs to transition retiring agents for a reason, Agent Johnson. When an agent has an expectation for meaningful work and is relegated to a supporting role, there will be problems." Dr. Sampson pulled out several sheets of paper from my file and set them in front of her. "Mr. Daniels's decision to set you loose with a rather unique set of conditions was a rather unusual approach to dealing with the problem. While I'm not sure I approve of the specifics of his method, the method itself is sound."

I frowned. "In short, give the highly trained dog a job to do and watch the problem sort itself out?"

"Essentially. Unfortunately, I think Mr. Daniels underestimated the severity of your situation. Rebellion and insubordination are common symptoms of psychological strain, especially of the sort you have undergone. Of course, no one expected some of the circumstances following him cutting you loose."

"The Henry case and the Greenwich case," I muttered, shaking my head.

"In part. In short, Agent Johnson, you were expected to be volatile, unpredictable, and potentially dangerous, which was the reasoning behind bringing a stabilizing factor into the situation." Dr. Sampson coughed, and the corners of her mouth twitched up in a smile. "Of course, no one predicted you and your partner would visit a courthouse in Ohio and take advantage of the state's laxer laws regarding marriage. Would you prefer if I called you Agent Thomas?"

I stiffened in my seat and felt the blood drain from my face.

"The FBI has, in recent years, adopted some rather casual rules regarding fraternization, in part due to the higher success rate of couples within certain divisions. Unsurprisingly, with the way CARD currently operates, it is one of those divisions. Motivation matters, and married couples tend to have even more drive to resolve cases. Of course, it is something carefully monitored and handled on a case-by-case basis. Considering your exemplary success rate with your partner and your long-term experience working together, I hold the opinion this benefits the FBI in more ways than one."

In the end, I couldn't escape Jake no matter what I did. "With all due respect, Dr. Sampson, I think I need a stiff drink before I can handle this conversation."

"Water?" the woman offered.

"Is it spiked with vodka?"

"I'm afraid not. Would you prefer me to refer to you as Johnson or Thomas?"

"Dr. Sampson, Agent Thomas did not trust me enough to ask me to hand over my firearm and agree to an evaluation. What do you think?"

"If you had been given the opportunity to do so, what would you have done?"

"I would have handed over my firearm and agreed to an evaluation, Dr. Sampson."

"Oh really?" The scorn in the woman's voice dug at the wounds that had been festering in my chest ever since I had fled the United States.

All my anger and bitterness welled up and poured out of me. I was on my feet before I realized I had moved. "Never once—not *once* in my career—have I willfully or intentionally ever put my partner or any other member of law enforcement at risk. Even when my partner was responsible for me being shot, even when my partner's neglect put everyone else on the team in unnecessary danger, I have *never* even *considered* taking action against them. Never. Why the fuck would I start now?"

Something in me snapped under the strain, and it wasn't until Dr. Sampson sucked in a breath through clenched teeth that I realized I had slammed my fist into the table.

My finger definitely wasn't supposed to bend at that angle, and surging waves of pain radiated from my wrist. "Well, shit."

ACCORDING TO THE X-RAY, I had severely broken two bones in my hand and wrist. To add to my misery, I also had hair-line fractures in two others. Dr. Sampson accompanied me through almost the entire process, leaving only when the surgeon was busy piecing me back together.

Thanks to a hefty dose of painkillers and anesthetic, I lost a significant number of hours, so when I was finally coherent enough to comprehend what was going on around me, Dr. Sampson had changed into casual clothes.

"Nice jeans, doc," I slurred.

"Thanks. How're you feeling?"

"I broke my hand," I reported. "I think it hurts. Yeah, I'm pretty sure it hurts."

"I see."

I glared at the splint immobilizing my hand and wrist. The painkillers did a good job of numbing me to a tolerable dull, persistent throb. "I thought people got casts when they broke stuff. I got short changed. Where's my cast? Did they lose it somewhere? They must have. Damn them, losing my cast."

"They gave you a splint instead of a cast, Agent Johnson."

"I'm so disappointed right now, Dr. Sampson."

"I'm sure you are." Taking the chair beside the bed, the woman set her briefcase on her lap and started flipping through pages.

While I didn't mind the silence, I'd lost count of the number of times Dr. Sampson stopped what she was doing, looked at me, sighed, and shook her head. I had no idea how much time passed, but when the woman finally decided to start talking, my head felt a lot clearer.

Unfortunately, my hand and wrist were starting to feel a hell of a lot worse. I found it an unsatisfactory exchange.

"You know, most people would have screamed or cried. You? You uttered a single vehement curse and took out your phone with your left hand. What did you do then?"

"Asked you who I should call to wrap it?" I blinked at the woman. "Isn't that what normal people do when they hurt themselves? They call someone for help?"

"There should be limits on how calm and collected you can be in a situation, Agent Johnson. You broke your hand in multiple places."

"If I had been calm and collected, I wouldn't have broken my hand hitting the table," I countered.

"I'm satisfied you are of sound enough mind to return to duty when your hand has finished healing. However, that's only after a one to two week vacation, Agent Johnson. A proper vacation, rather than indulging an overactive flight instinct. Upon your return, I will do another evaluation. Even when I deliberately provoked you, you displayed a remarkable amount of restraint. Of course, I would have preferred if you hadn't used enough force to do lasting damage to yourself, but I neglected to consider your background in martial arts. For that, I am sorry."

"With all due respect, Dr. Sampson, that's a pretty fucked up way to do a psychiatric evaluation. I also never said I conceded to my resignation being challenged or postponed."

"Are you sure you want to discuss the issue of your resignation while you are under the influence of morphine?"

"I'm in tolerable possession of my faculties, enough for this conversation at least."

"I am of the opinion you were coerced and manipulated into filing a resignation. At least one member of your former CARD team was involved in the final decision to confiscate your firearm. This has factored into my professional opinion regarding your resignation, Agent Johnson. As a result, I will be confirming the postponement of your resignation until you are capable of returning to full active duty. At that point, there will be a formal interview to discuss the situation. In the meantime, I will be monitoring you during the progression of your recovery. Should you qualify with your left hand, I am willing to sign the approval to have your weapon reinstated and you assigned to light, low-risk duty."

I frowned. "Do I have the option to reject this proposal?"

"I'm afraid not, Agent Johnson. You're far too valuable to the FBI to waste like this. We pay attention to agents with a high success rate, especially when dealing with violent, organized crimes. Your partner is already on route from the United States, and upon his arrival, we will have a session to discuss the situation further."

Jake was coming to London? "Oh, hell no. No, no, no. No. Absolutely not. Toss the rat bastard off the plane and make him swim back to the United States. *No.*"

Dr. Sampson laughed. "I'm afraid I'm going to have to disregard your request, Agent Johnson. This is a perfect opportunity to resolve this situation. I take a great deal of pride in my work. In many ways, we're very similar, you and I. We both thrive when we are allowed to take pride in what we do. Neither one of us has a high tolerance for situations where we can't be actively working on something that is meaningful. You found your limit, but once you stop thinking about today, tomorrow, and next week, I think you'll figure out you'll never forgive yourself if you quit now. At the risk of sounding unprofessional, get your head out of your ass and stop wallowing long enough to logically evaluate your situation."

Something about the doctor cursing made me giggle, and

once I started giggling, I couldn't stop. When Dr. Sampson sighed, my giggles grew into tear-inducing laughter. Sometime after the hiccups started, the woman threw her hands in the air and left the room.

I blamed the morphine.

Chapter Twenty-Seven

TEN HOURS after arriving at the hospital, I was discharged. I had a long list of restrictions which boiled down to avoiding the use of my right hand, no driving, and taking my medication as prescribed.

Dr. Sampson refused to budge, ignoring me whenever I mentioned I really didn't want to see my so-called partner. Through clever tactics involving silent stares and disgusted expressions, she had talked me down from never again to maybe in a couple of years.

"You are a hard negotiator," I complained. The morphine the doctor had given me before my discharge wasn't helping me deal with Dr. Sampson at all.

"Maybe if the matter were open to negotiation, I would negotiate with you, Agent Johnson. But, since I've already worked you down to a couple of years, why don't we narrow the time frame to ten minutes?"

I glanced out the window of the car, which was speeding along at a decent clip into the British countryside. "It would be fatal if I jumped out and made a run for it, wouldn't it? Also, why have we left London? I think the embassy is back that way somewhere. Can we go back to the embassy? I liked the embassy. It's a very nice embassy."

"A pleasant, quiet location will help facilitate your healing."

"You're luring me to a secondary location to murder me and ditch my body, aren't you?" I sighed.

In the front seat, Agent Miller snorted. "Are you always so colorful, Agent Johnson?"

"Her file is definitely colorful," Dr. Sampson muttered. "Your previous supervisor seemed to enjoy highlighting and underlining key points. Considering the number of notes praising Agent Thomas for his ability to work with you, I'm truly astonished management approved placing you two into separate divisions. You truly have high standards, and finding a partner who matches well with you isn't easy. It's admirable, really. I think your supervisor used a color coding system, too. I haven't quite cracked the meanings behind the different colors yet, though."

"Let's not talk about the highlighting and the underlining," I pleaded.

"I will agree not to mention anything highlighted or underlined should you agree to my terms. Ten minutes, Agent Johnson."

"That's confidential information, you know."

"As your psychologist *and* psychiatrist, I have the privilege and right to inform relevant parties of certain elements of your file. It is currently in your better interest to reveal these notations."

With my right arm trapped in a sling to keep me from

using my hand, I couldn't even cross my arms over my chest like I wanted. "That's harsh, Dr. Sampson."

"Have you considered therapy for your fear of heights?"

"Low blow, doctor. Low blow," I mumbled.

"You're afraid of heights, Agent Johnson?" Miller twisted around in his seat to stare at me. "You don't strike me as the type to be afraid of anything."

Dr. Sampson grinned. "The human psyche is an amazing thing. There are at least twenty pages of incidents involving heights in her file."

"They did *not* include those in my file. You're bullshitting me. You have got to be bullshitting me."

"Your supervisor has a reputation for filing unnecessary but interesting paperwork."

I groaned and leaned against the door. "Torture is against the law, Dr. Sampson."

Clearing her throat, Dr. Sampson lifted a page out of her briefcase. "Of all the cases I have handled, yours is probably the funniest one. This part of your file is highlighted, circled, and underlined. At the top of the page, someone has made several notations. Remember, they might need to act on this information to safeguard you until your return to the United States. As an employee of the United States government, your safety and well-being trump any patient confidentiality rules in place. You will cooperate and peacefully meet with your partner—your husband, if you need a reminder—or I'll tell the lovely agents in the front what this says."

"Stop reminding me that he is my husband," I hissed through clenched teeth.

All the reminders of Jake's betrayal did was make me want to cry.

"I can't tell if I envy or pity the man," Miller said in a false whisper.

"Now, now," Dr. Sampson chided. "The choice is yours. If you accept my generous offer, I won't have to divulge the information in this file, instead transferring the protection of your person to your partner and spouse."

"You're manipulating me."

"That's a part of my job description."

"Do you have to look like you're having fun while doing it?"

"Slugs," Dr. Sampson declared, depositing the page in her briefcase before closing the lid. "Agent Johnson has a disabling phobia of slugs."

"You're a horrible person, Dr. Sampson," Miller said, shaking his head.

"It's not like I run into a lot of slugs." I was really proud of myself for keeping my voice so calm. "Fine. I'm afraid of slugs and heights. So what?"

Dr. Sampson sighed. "You may as well give up. I already told you this wasn't up for negotiation. Things aren't nearly as bad as you think they are. Stop worrying."

THE HOTEL HAD ONCE BEEN a castle, and I stared at the massive stone structure, my mouth gaping open. "Why is the hotel a castle? Why are we at a castle?"

"I'm just following orders," Dr. Sampson replied. "We're here because you will be staying here for the next week with your partner."

"This might be the best international case I have ever been assigned to," Miller announced. "Thank you for disappearing in Germany for two weeks, Agent Johnson. Because of you, we get to stay in a castle."

"You're so very welcome, Agent Miller."

Dillan sighed. "Don't mind my partner. Can I call you Karma?"

"Sure, but only if you tell me if Dillan is your first or last name."

"Last." The agent laughed. "Call me William or Will; your choice."

Dr. Sampson cleared her throat. "Perhaps, instead of sitting in the car, we could get out and go inside. I'm afraid you'll have to accept temporary imprisonment here, as I'll be taking the car back to London this evening."

Unable to think of a single way to delay the inevitable, I unbuckled my seatbelt with my left hand and fumbled with the door. I got it open, slid out of the vehicle, and discovered one of the side effects of the painkillers.

My legs wobbled. The world circled around me, a lot like it did when I got too much water in my ears and stood up too fast. I was so focused on trying to keep from ending up on the cobbles in a trembling heap I was only partially aware of the slap of shoes on stone.

I didn't need to see Jake to recognize his big hands when he grasped my shoulders and held me upright.

Damn the man for coming and saving me from eating dirty rocks lined up in nice, neat little rows in front of a castle. Everything would have been easier if he let me fall; I could have hit the ground like an idiot, and he could have laid into me for being stupid. Running away to Africa, then going to Russia and failing to leave the airport before fleeing to Germany counted as stupid, foolish, and idiotic.

Why did Jake always show up when I was in the process of making a fool of myself?

It was almost enough to make me cry.

I had known I would be forced to face him, but I had thought I'd have at least a little more time. My first instinct was to retreat to the car, but the illogical part of me that hadn't been drugged into a stupor along with my common sense had different ideas and full control over my mouth. "I broke my hand."

Why couldn't I say something normal? An 'I'm sorry' would have been a good start. An accusatory 'why didn't you have my back?' would have been better. A tirade, one so intense I flayed every bit of skin from his body with the power of my voice alone, would have been best.

Instead, I hiccuped, and I recognized the opening volley of either throwing up or bursting into tears. I wasn't sure which.

The sound Jake made was a mix of a huff and a sigh. "Where have you been? I've been worried sick." He paused. When I didn't say anything or move, he gave my shoulders a squeeze. "Karma?"

"Hello, Agent Thomas. I'm Dr. Sampson. I'm afraid she's rather heavily medicated at the moment."

"You didn't tell me she was hurt." Jake's tone dipped in pitch, and when he huffed, it was so soft I barely heard him.

The anger I expected from him was showing, but it was directed at the wrong person. I tried to reach for him, and it took me longer than I liked to realize my right arm was still bound in a sling.

I forced myself to look up enough to focus on his chest. Why was he wearing a suit? It was a long flight from the United States. Had he changed?

The shirt looked really, really white and pleasant against the rich blue of his jacket. I lifted my left hand enough I could grab him so he wouldn't focus his fury on the doctor, when I was the one who deserved to get yelled at. I ended up with a handful of silk, and I tugged at it to get his attention.

Jake wrapped his arm around me and pulled me so close my nose pressed to his shirt, which smelled faintly of his spiced cologne. "Karma?"

"I broke my hand."

"What happened?"

"My fault," Dr. Sampson declared, and a whimper escaped my throat before I realized I was making the sound.

"No. I'm the one you're supposed to be mad at. She didn't do it. Just doing stupid job. Her job is stupid. Stupid job."

"Just what sort of drugs do they have you on?" Jake pushed me away and held me at arm's length, leaning down until his nose touched mine.

Damn, the man did have pretty eyes. I blinked, aware I was supposed to be answering a question of some sort. I was also supposed to be mad at him, but the reason for my anger had vanished along with my common sense.

Dr. Sampson replied, "Morphine. They gave her an injection right before they released her. We picked up the prescriptions on our way here. Why don't we get her inside?"

Jake slipped his arms under my knees and back and lifted me up.

"No." My whined protest fell on deaf ears. While my head wanted me to break free so I could walk on my own, my body rather liked not having to do any work. "Not fair."

"This again? Karma, you can barely stand. Haven't you broken enough things?"

"Don't use your shitty logic on me, Jake Thomas."

"What happened?"

"I was under orders to test her volatility towards others and deliberately provoked her. She hit the table with her fist, broke two bones rather badly, and fractured two others. The surgeon managed to repair the damage without any hardware, but we'll have to see how well she heals over the next few days."

"That sounds pretty volatile," Jake replied, and the subtle change in his voice betrayed his worry.

I remembered why I was angry at Jake. He didn't trust me. No one trusted me.

Another hiccup slipped out.

"Agent Miller, Agent Dillan, if you would please excuse us for a few minutes?" Dr. Sampson gestured towards the hotel, and both men walked away. "Get in the car. It's probably better if you let her sit instead of carrying her."

"I'm perfectly comfortable," Jake replied.

"Let me spell this out for you: sit her in the car nice and easy before you make her throw up from jostling her." Dr. Sampson held open the back door. "It'll be more comfortable for all of us, and I'd rather no one overheard confidential information."

Jake huffed but obeyed, and once I was seated upright on the backseat, my vertigo eased to a gentle sway. There was no escaping, however, as Dr. Sampson slid into the car beside me, trapping me in the middle.

"I'd like to say something." I leveled my best glare at the woman, but I only made her smile.

"By all means, Agent Johnson. We're listening."

I opened my mouth, and the words spilled out of me. "He's not supposed to be nice to me. It's too hard to be mad at him when he's being nice. That's not fair. How can I have my fit of righteous wrath if he's being nice? It's like kicking a puppy, and I can't kick a puppy."

Dr. Sampson sighed. "Morphine can cause excitatory responses in some patients, and Agent Johnson happens to be one of them. These periods seem to be coupled with moments of calm clarity and normalized behavior."

"Karma, I'm over six feet tall. I'm about as far from a puppy as a person can get. I can handle anything you throw at me."

"It's your stupid pretty eyes, just like a puppy's," I informed him. "All big and brown. Chocolatey brown. Shut up. Puppies are stupid. Why can't I kick puppies? I'm mad at you. Stupid."

Dr. Sampson cleared her throat. "Admittedly, I'm a little concerned about the degradation of her vocabulary and difficulty maintaining coherent thought."

"You should have seen her on Demerol. We had to handcuff her so she wouldn't be a threat to herself and others. Unfortunately, the handcuffs did nothing to stop her mouth. She was very vocal. Let's just say they changed her to a different medication." Jake chuckled, shifting beside me. When he reached over and rested the back of his hand against my forehead, I frowned at him. "I thought so. You're running a fever."

"Likely a combination of injury and stress. As long as it remains low-grade, it shouldn't be a concern. Now, can we get to business?"

"Of course."

"Jake's an asshole, Dr. Sampson."

"Let's try to keep the discussion civil, Agent Johnson."

Jake chuckled. "I'm pretty sure she's just telling you the truth, ma'am. If it makes her happy, let her. I'd be more worried if she wasn't calling me an asshole. It's her favorite."

"Very well. Let's begin with the issue of her firearm confiscation."

I slumped in the seat and wished I could disappear. "Well, shit."

"I was a stupid asshole, under stress, and didn't think through the consequences of my stupidity. I should have refused to cooperate. Better yet, I should have told her the instant I found out, recommended she just hand over her firearm and cooperate, and taken a few minutes to figure out what was going on and why. I fucked up."

"Agent Johnson seems to have substantial trust issues when it comes to her partners, and it seems this incident has triggered old trauma." Dr. Sampson patted her briefcase. "Almost all FBI agents have faced trauma of some form or another, of course. Unfortunately, this could have long-term consequences."

Jake tensed beside me. "This conversation will remain confidential?"

"This conversation is confidential, there are no recording devices being used, nor am I taking any notes. Anything said in this vehicle remains between us."

Sighing, Jake shifted on the seat so he could better face us, although it was a tight fit with his long legs.

"You're a giant with puppy eyes. Should cut you off at the shins so you fit in tight spaces better," I complained, moving my feet out of the way.

"I can't say she's wrong, Agent Thomas."

"Until Karma joined the FBI, she was your average pretty young woman. Someone once told me she dated, could probably talk anyone she wanted into having sex with her, the pretty thing she is, and what have you."

"Who the fuck told you that?" I demanded, narrowing my eyes so I could glare at Jake. "I did not."

"Father of the Shrimp," he replied.

"Pops told you *what*?" My voice rose an octave. "And why were you talking about my sex life with Pops?"

"Karma, I wanted to know what had happened with your previous partners. Of course I talked with your parents when I found out where they lived. I visited them several times within the first few months of our partnership. How can I watch my partner's back if I don't know about her?"

"You sneaky rat bastard. You seduced Pops with your puppy eyes, didn't you?"

"I actually told him I was your new partner and needed to know your circumstances so I could best watch over you in the field. Your parents were very cooperative."

"Tricky bastard."

"She stopped dating anyone after her second or third month in the field. Around the same time, she developed a rather cold and withdrawn reputation. She handled people she didn't like by simply refusing to talk to them unless absolutely necessary." Jake sighed and shook his head. "It's tough being a woman in the field to begin with, and when your partner doesn't give a shit what happens to you as long as he looks good, bad things happen. She took the brunt of it. After she was shot four times over six months, her psychologist ordered her partner to be transferred."

I echoed Jake's sigh. "He liked using me as bait, and he didn't pay attention or watch my back. Fine. I have trust issues."

My first partner hadn't just used me as bait for gunfire, either.

"I've seen your file, Agent Johnson. I understand."

If anyone else had tried to tell me they understood, I wouldn't have believed them for an instant. However, I suspected Dr. Sampson understood a lot more about my circumstances than I ever wanted to admit to anyone. Maybe she hadn't walked in my specific shoes, but her job was to make sure I could wear them and survive the experience intact.

I wondered if I'd remember that little gem of insight when the morphine wore off.

"Her next six or so partners just didn't understand what it meant to watch someone's six. Karma did. She was so busy trying to watch theirs and her own at the same time that she was shot several times. I was number eight's replacement. The first picture I ever saw of Karma was showed to me by her parents. She was unconscious in a pool of her own blood, and her so-called partner was responsible. Went rogue. The first time I met her, she informed me I was a stepping stone so she could make her way into CARD. She warned me our partnership was temporary, and she had no appreciation for those who couldn't do their jobs."

"That doesn't sound like a promising start to a partnership."

"I found it a very promising start, actually. She made her expectations clear. Once she relaxed a little, she gave me an opportunity to present my own concerns and expectations. It wasn't until she tried to get herself killed during a bad case that she finally figured out I was actually watching her back. As I said before, I fucked up. I know exactly what sort of woman she is, and I knew full well there was no justification for confiscating her weapon."

"So why did you participate?"

"Ma'am, she fell face first onto a corpse. She fell on a second corpse shortly after. Just prior, she had climbed down into a bloody gorge trying to discover the truth of a little boy's disappearance, convinced she'd be finding his body. By the end of the day, I'm pretty sure we were both primed to blow. I fucked up."

"Taking my keys out of my hand without asking was a shit move," I muttered.

"Next time, let the fucker have the keys without kicking him."

"Maybe the fucker shouldn't have fucking stole my fucking keys, then I wouldn't have had to fucking kick him."

"Mom asked me to tell you she's very sorry, and she has properly disciplined Dad for his actions."

"And what about you?" I demanded.

"We're going to be here a while, aren't we?" Dr. Sampson pinched the bridge of her nose. "Perhaps holding this discussion in the car was not as wise as I thought."

"Honestly, all I want to know is where you were for the past three weeks, Karma. Mom said you were getting fresh air for a *week*. You didn't contact anyone. You vanished without a trace, and no one would tell me anything, not until some asshole showed up at my door, forced me into a suit, and dragged me to his car by my ear, took me to the airport, and shoved me in the security line so I could fly to London."

"Some asshole?"

"Dad."

"Oh, that asshole."

"Yeah, that asshole."

"I'm not sorry." I really wanted to cross my arms over my chest, but the sling hampered me. How could I express my annoyance properly while my arm was trapped in a sling?

"I know. I was wrong, and I'm sorry. You deserved better."

"You didn't trust me."

"Just because I'm a stupid idiot doesn't mean I didn't trust you, Karma. If anything, I didn't trust my father. He's an even bigger idiot than I am, and he simply isn't ready to handle the immense amount of stubborn pride packed into that little body of yours. I was fucked no matter how I looked at the situation."

Letting go of an unwanted grudge was easy.

Jake had nothing to prove, and I should have remembered that from the beginning. "Morocco sucked, but I went to Casablanca and waded all the way to my knees in the ocean. I didn't even leave the airport when I got to Russia, and I spent two weeks driving in circles on the Autobahn in a Mercedes-Benz I should have just bought outright. I probably would have saved money. Then I got to London, and the FBI picked me up and told me my resignation was postponed because someone's an asshole."

"That asshole would be my mother."

Bursting into tears, I wailed, "I married my way into a family of assholes!"

Chapter Twenty-Eight

NOT EVEN THE morphine spared me from a skull-splitting headache. Sobbing must have contributed to the painkillers wearing off; my hand throbbed along with my head. I choked back the worst of my tears, my entire body shaking from the effort.

"Now would probably be a good time to take her to your room, get her medicines into her, and give her a chance to rest. You are checked in, right?"

"Yes, I'm checked in, though I haven't been to my room yet."

"Give me your key. I'll walk with you and get the door open and bring her bag."

The thought of anyone seeing me made me shake my head, which only added to my headache and growing nausea.

Jake took a tissue and wiped my face. "Karma, everything'll be fine, okay? You can hide in our room until you feel better."

While I protested, Jake ignored me, slid out of the car, and waited for me to join him. The man somehow managed to lure me out of the vehicle, but the instant I tried to stand, everything spun around me.

I lost a lot of time somewhere, because when I could finally crack open my dry, gritty eyes, I was cocooned in a warm blanket. The soft material had me wiggling my toes. Moving woke the pain in my hand, which hurt enough to warn me the painkillers had worn off.

"Hey. You actually awake this time?"

It took me a moment to realize I wasn't alone in bed. Jake wrapped his arm around me and tucked me close to him.

A yawn slipped out, and I mumbled, "No."

"Breakfast comes with coffee and painkillers, but you have to get up to have any of it."

"It's breakfast time?"

"It's a little after seven. You slept right through dinner and the night. Dr. Sampson said to let you sleep for as long as you needed. Something about stress fatigue. She then told me I should do the same for the same reasons. That woman's pushy."

"You're an asshole, Jake."

"There's the Karma I know and love. How are you feeling?"

"I haven't had coffee in three weeks."

For such a large man, Jake moved fast, and he was out of bed on route to the room's coffee maker before I had a chance to do more than blink.

"This kingdom is hell. Apparently, they don't believe in coffee. I had to specifically request a coffee maker. The only other way to get coffee? Room service. They would have brought it in a tea pot. In teacups. Gold-rimmed teacups." Jake sighed. "We're stuck with the gold-rimmed teacups. At least they believe in cream and sugar here."

It wasn't until Jake turned to face me, the coffee brewing, that I realized he wasn't wearing anything.

While I thought he looked great when he wore a suit, damn the man looked even better when there was nothing between me and a good look at his skin. There were a lot of different types of men in the world, and Jake was definitely my type. While he was tall and had muscle, he balanced masculine bulk with a leaner build. When he wanted to show off muscle, he could—and did.

I had some very pleasant memories of just how he could put his strength to good use. The emotions I expected, the anger, sting of betrayal, and all the negativity I had carried around with me in Africa, Russia, and Germany should have still been lurking beneath my skin poised to rear their ugly heads, but they came a distant second to my awareness of his beautiful body.

I wanted to do a lot more than run my hands all over him, which added to my confusing tangle of emotions. Men had made it clear what they wanted me for, and Jake being so relaxed frustrated me.

It wasn't supposed to be the other way around, and I had no idea how to bring out the playful and energetic man I wanted in bed with me.

Careful to avoid using my right arm, I lurched upright so I could figure out how to lure him away from the coffee maker. While I had no memory of changing, I was wearing a nightgown, the kind I hadn't worn since I was little a girl.

It had frills. Pink frills. "Why are there pink frills?"

"I was going to ask you that. It was in your bag."

Finding adult clothing in my size was often a challenge, especially after having lost so much weight. I glowered at the gown, taking a few minutes to consider the most satisfying ways to rid the Earth of it. "I would rather be naked, too."

"You need to stop losing your clothes."

"But maybe I like losing my clothes."

"That has to be the painkillers talking."

"You lost your clothes. Are you saying I can't lose mine? Look at you, all naked over there." I lifted my right arm and stared at the splint. "The painkillers aren't working anymore."

"Is there something you're trying to tell me, Karma?"

My face flushed right along with the rest of me.

Jake stalked towards me, leaning down until we were eye to eye. "Well?"

Why did the man have such pretty eyes? It had been the first thing I had noticed about him when we had met. He always managed to make me hyper aware of him and his eyes, and I had had to work hard to ignore those feelings.

"We're going to have to work on this," he murmured. "If you want something from me, all you have to do is ask."

If my face got any hotter, I'd combust. "Oh." I stared at the splint trapping my arm and sighed my disappointment. It was in the way, and until it was gone, there'd be no repeating what I had enjoyed so much.

Jake stared at me for a long moment. At first his expression was one of complete confusion, then he followed my gaze to my arm. Concern replaced confusion, and when the comprehension hit him, he laughed. "You're surprisingly shy. If *that's* what you want, don't you worry. I think we can come up with something."

We did.

"DO YOU HAVE A LIGHTER?" I eyed the pink frilly nightgown, which had somehow ended up discarded on the other end of the room. Despite being located within a castle, the room was mostly taken up by the large bed, the dresser currently serving as a place to make coffee, and the tiniest bathroom I had ever seen in a hotel. It was still a bit of a mystery how they fit the sink, toilet, and tub in such tight confines.

Despite the room's small size, it still managed to ooze opulence. The dichotomy amused and puzzled me. How could something so tiny still seem so elegant?

"No. Why?"

"I want to light that thing on fire in the bathtub."

"The painkillers have kicked in, haven't they?"

"Probably." I had a vague memory of Jake plying me with coffee and pills after he had finished having his way with me. If anything, he had been even more determined and enthusiastic than in Pennsylvania.

Men, especially Jake, confused me. Then again, I'd heard a lot of people discuss make-up sex as though it were a sacred thing.

It wouldn't take much to convince me they were right.

"If I order something, do you think you can keep it down?"

"I haven't thrown up my coffee," I reminded him. "These cups suck. I have to keep refilling my coffee every other minute. What is the deal with that? What happened to mugs? I need a mug, Jake."

"I think they intend for you to sip the coffee and enjoy it."

"I think they're crazy."

"So, we're good?"

I turned my attention away from my nightgown nemesis to stare at my partner. "We're good. Just don't do it again. If you even think about it, I will unload my weapon, clear the chamber, and proceed to pistol whip you into unconsciousness before turning it in."

"Preferable to having a hole drilled into my big toe so you can remove my internal organs through it, I suppose."

"Damn straight, Mr. Thomas. Don't you forget it." Holding out my coffee cup with my left hand, I waved it at him until he sighed and refilled it. "We're good?"

"We're good. If you ever scare me like that again, I will handcuff you to me so you can't leave my sight."

"That's a lame threat, Jake. The only eventful part of that trip was the Autobahn, and only because I rented a really nice Mercedes and it liked the roads. Actually, the entire trip has sucked. I hated it."

"If I hadn't been such a fucking idiot, you wouldn't have had to go anywhere at all. I'm sorry."

"I'm nauseous enough without you apologizing over and over and adding to it."

"Point taken. How's your hand?"

"Throbbing." I took a sip of my coffee. "Think we can get away with escaping this castle? I need clothes. Maybe a new watch. I've been wearing this same shit for days."

"I'll ask Dr. Sampson. I got a rental so I could get here, but I wasn't anticipating you having two FBI agents following you around. What's the deal with them?"

"Don't ask me. They just picked me up at the airport and implied they would arrest me if I didn't cooperate. After that,

I was sent to the embassy, and they've been around ever since. I didn't see them at the hospital, but they were there when I left. Miller slipped and said it had something to do with me disappearing in Germany." I shrugged. "They're overly determined to nullify my resignation."

"Can't say I blame them, woman. You're a good agent, and good agents don't just fall out of the sky."

"I've been a pretty terrible agent lately," I mumbled before draining my cup of coffee. "These cups are torture devices."

Jake reclaimed the cup and filled it. "I'm going to have to find you a proper mug before you start drinking straight from the pot."

"Might be an idea. What am I going to wear? I refuse to wear that pink frilly thing ever again. It would make me really happy if I could burn it, Jake."

"There has to be a fireplace in this castle *somewhere*."

"We could go explore the castle."

"Not naked we aren't."

"Put that suit back on. I like it."

"Considering it's the only thing I have to wear, I don't really have much of a choice. That asshole didn't think things through. Do you have any idea how hard it is to find clothes that fit me?" Jake grumbled and grabbed the travel bag I had purchased at the airport and set it on the bed. "Someone got you dress slacks and a blouse at least, but they're wrinkled."

"Do I look like I care about wrinkles?"

Jake frowned and pulled out a black box. "Is this makeup?"

"Looks like it."

"I'm concerned, Karma."

"I didn't buy it."

Jake sighed his relief and tossed it in the garbage can beside the dresser. "Someone took a lot of liberties with your bag, then."

After rooting around, he held up the bag of beads, string, and metal wire. "What's this?"

"I got them in Morocco. It was during a moment of weakness."

"Weakness?" Jake open the bag and scrutinized the chocolate and gold colored beads. "This is one of those female things I won't understand, isn't it?"

"I thought I'd make a bracelet with them."

"Do you even know how to make a bracelet?"

"Not a clue in hell. As I said, it was during a moment of weakness."

"I'm not sure I understand why you keep referring to these beads as a moment of weakness."

Scowling, I turned my head so I wouldn't have to look at him. "They match your eyes."

Jake laughed and set the beads on the bed. "That is the most feminine thing I have ever seen you willingly do."

"Just give me some clothes, Jake."

Dressing with one functional hand was a challenge. Jake sat on the bed, watched, and fought to keep from laughing at my struggles, but I won the war without having to ask for his help. When I finished, he smiled at me, reached over, and gave my blouse a tug to straighten it. "Not bad. You even got the buttons right."

"When you're good, you're good."

"I have been told we will be staying here a week. If you don't feel up for it, I can go do the shopping. No one deserves the nightmare that is finding clothing in my size."

"I broke my hand, Jake. I'm not an invalid."

"Karma, you may as well accept it. Until you're back over a hundred pounds, I'm going to treat you like you're made of glass. If you had been in shape, you never would have broken your hand hitting a table." Jake huffed and ran his hands through his hair. "Fine, but I'm clearing it with Dr. Sampson first—and whoever the hell your surgeon is."

Pulling out his phone, he browsed through his contacts before connecting the call. "Dr. Sampson? Jake Thomas. Can I take Karma out shopping? We both need clothes and some odds and ends."

While he talked to the woman, I got up and hunted down my Moroccan slippers. They didn't match my outfit, but I didn't care. They were comfortable.

I regretted I only had one pair.

"I'd prefer if we could go on our own." Wrinkling his nose, Jake adjusted his hold on the phone and made a strangling motion with his other hand. "Is there a reason we need an armed guard?" After several long moments, he laughed. "Karma, she wants to know if you're taking me to a secondary location."

"I thought we were going to a clothing store."

"That's what I thought, too."

"Just tell her no. Too much work."

"Dr. Sampson, she says it is too much work. No, we are not going to go on an impromptu honeymoon. We are going to have lunch, see if we can find reasonable clothing in our sizes, and probably have dinner. No, I don't know where we'll be going. We haven't gotten that far in planning anything."

"London is supposed to have good shopping, Jake."

"London is over an hour from here."

"I'm not driving, so I'm fine with that."

"Apparently, Karma wants to shop in London." He listened for a few more minutes, tapping his foot. "Yes, we have thoroughly resolved our differences, Dr. Sampson."

Several seconds later, he made a choking noise. "That's none of your business!"

"She's asking if we kissed and made up, isn't she?"

Jake sighed and nodded.

"Just tell her repeatedly, Jake."

He stared at me and sighed again. "Repeatedly. Are you satisfied?"

Smirking, I blew him a kiss. Loud enough I was certain the woman on the phone could hear me, I said, "Why yes, I am. Thanks for asking."

"Goodbye, Dr. Sampson. I am going to take my satisfied partner to London now." Jake hung up. "That was awkward."

I frowned. "I thought men enjoyed having the praises of their prowess proclaimed."

Someone knocked at the door, and with my coffee in hand, I went to answer it before remembering I had only one functional hand. Sipping my coffee, I manipulated the knob with the thumb and palm of my injured hand and somehow managed to open the door with minimal pain.

Even under normal circumstances, I would have been alarmed by the presence of my mother at my door. When she came calling, it was for a reason. I stared up into her narrowed eyes, aware of her darkened cheeks. Anger always made her blush, and on a black woman as dark as my mother, it turned her skin coal black.

I forgot how to swallow, and my coffee burned my mouth. When the pain registered despite the little pills Jake had given me, I did the absolute worst thing possible.

I spit coffee in Ma's face.

I went cold with horror as the liquid dripped down her cheeks to the stone floor.

Far too calm for my comfort, Ma reached into her pocket, pulled out a tissue, and wiped her face. "Karma Clarice Johnson, what *exactly* do you think you're doing?"

Where Ma went, Pops wasn't far behind. Instead of crossing his arms over his chest when angry, Pops put his hands in his pockets, straightened his back, and stared down his long nose at me. Like Ma, his skin darkened with emotion, though he never managed to get quite as black as Ma.

I backpedalled into the room and bumped into Jake, who took possession of my coffee before I could drop it on the floor.

My mouth moved, but I couldn't say a word. There was nowhere to retreat to; with Jake behind me, I couldn't even reach the bed. With Ma and Pops looming in the doorway, I couldn't get past them without one of them catching me first.

"Help," I begged in a desperate whisper.

"There's two of them, and I don't have a gun anymore, remember? What am I supposed to do?" he whispered back.

"Think of something!"

Ma cleared her throat. "Karma."

I whimpered. "Yes, Ma?"

"I asked you a question."

"S-shopping. In London. I-I n-need new clothes. In London."

Jake nudged me to the side so he could step around me, thrusting his hand out. "Mrs. Johnson, it's a pleasure to see you again. Please forgive Karma. She just had some painkillers."

Ma wound up and slapped Jake across the face so hard his head snapped to the side. "And just what do *you* think you're doing with my daughter, James Thomas?"

I covered my face with my hands and wished I could disappear.

Chapter Twenty-Nine

IT WAS SURPRISINGLY spacious beneath the bed. Whoever was in charge of cleaning the room had done a stellar job. Despite my close examination of the stone floor, I couldn't locate even a single dust bunny to be friends with me.

The only things missing from my safe haven were a nice warm blanket and coffee. If I wanted to risk discovery, I could pull the blanket off the bed and drag it into my lair. A lair was so much better with a blanket.

I curled up beneath the head of the bed, closed my eyes, and pretended I couldn't hear Ma murdering my partner. Maybe Jake was already dead; he hadn't said a word despite the fact my ma had slapped the sin right out of him. If she had balled her hand into a fist, she would've cleaned his clock and floored him.

Maybe Pops knew enough martial arts to kick my ass, but all Ma needed was her slap to defend herself—or murder my partner.

I'd miss Jake.

My guilt for sacrificing him to my ma would last a long time. If she took her time killing him, maybe she'd forget I existed. Ma liked things nice and neat, so she'd definitely dispose of his body first. Once she finished with Jake, she'd come after me.

I had some time. It'd take her at least a few hours to find a good place to hide Jake's body.

Pops cleared his throat several times. I could imagine him with his hands in his pockets, his expression neutral, waiting patiently for his turn. Ma always went first. If they were playing Rocks-Paper-Scissors, Ma would be the scissors to Pops's paper, and Pops was as smart as he was wise.

Pops would let Ma finish with my partner before taking care of the leftovers. For the first time, I realized my pops was like a vulture. He was circling, just waiting for the predator to finish with her share before coming in to devour the scraps.

The room would make an interesting crime scene. They'd find all sorts of evidence of what Jake and I had been up to, assuming it wasn't obliterated by Ma and Pops.

Pops cleared his throat again.

"Can't you see I'm busy here?" Ma didn't shriek. No, Ma's voice pitched low and growly, warning anyone stupid enough to get in the way of her target.

I wanted to help Jake, but Ma would skin me, too, then she'd have two bodies to hide.

"We've got company, darling dear," Pops said, his voice calm and dangerously polite. "They've been waiting right patient, too. Rude to leave them waiting at the door, don't you reckon?"

I'd been little when we'd moved from Georgia to

Vermont, but sometimes Pops slipped. When Pops slipped, it meant bad news for someone—Jake.

"Oh dear. How rude of me. I'm so sorry. Blessed be, come on in. Please forgive our rudeness," my ma chirped in her most pleasant sing-song voice. She liked to call it her Sunday Best.

I thought of it as the Wrath of God.

It suited; the only thing capable of saving my partner was divine intervention.

"Nothing to forgive, Mrs. Johnson. Please don't mind us. We can wait our turn. I'm finding this very educational," Pauline Thomas replied, and like Ma and Pops, her voice was calm.

"Mr. Johnson. Mrs. Johnson," Jake's father greeted.

At least I wouldn't have to explain Jake's death to his parents. Would they help hide his body? If they did, I doubted anyone would find Jake for a long, long time.

"If you don't mind the interruption, is your daughter around? I was hoping for a chance to speak with her," Pauline said.

There was a long moment of silence.

"That blasted girl, too clever for her own good. I see. She sacrificed her partner so she could escape," my ma muttered. "Well, she didn't go out the window, not at this height. Sweet baby Jesus, that's what I get for not paying enough attention. Darling, which way did she go?"

Maybe Ma was the scissors to Pops's paper in most matters, but when it came to stupid questions, Pops was the rock to her scissors. "Why are you asking me? You said you would handle everything."

Ma sighed. "She must have sneaked on out while we were

having a talk with the boy here. Damn that girl, doing exactly what she wants. Where did we go wrong? She was such a darling little thing when she was just born, so sweet and never fussing unless there was something truly the matter."

"Are we talking about the same woman here?" my partner asked.

Why did he sound so amused? Didn't he know he was about to die?

"Now you look here, Jake Thomas! Don't you go maligning my little girl like that," Ma snapped.

"She could be halfway across the country by now if we let her give us the slip." Pops sighed. "I keep warning you to stop underestimating that child, but no. You keep insisting she's the perfect little angel until she goes and does something stupid. She had you fooled the instant you saw her."

"She wouldn't go far, would she?" Jake's mother demanded.

"Oh, goodness me. No, no. I reckon she's gone and found herself a place to hole up. She likes up a tree the best," Ma reported, and like Pops, her Georgia roots showed through. "Terrified of heights, that one, but sure enough, she'll go right on up like a scared house cat when we're fixing to give her a scolding. Without fail, one of us has to go on up after her to get her to come down. She never learns, her. At least she stopped crawling her way into holes, not after that one time we had to take her in for rabies shots because she crawled her way into a vixen's den. That's when we decided it was high time to move to Vermont."

I really wanted some coffee. Maybe I could choke on it and put myself out of my misery. Once she started, Ma wouldn't stop until she was happy, and by the time she was finished, Jake's parents would know every last one of my childhood shames.

When Ma got a hold of me, she'd torture me before forcing me to dig my own grave. Then she'd bury me in it and give me a nice funeral.

Ma had always promised she'd give me a nice funeral when I got myself killed doing stupid, dangerous things. Invoking her wrath counted.

"I have the feeling your daughter still managed to find trouble despite your efforts," Jake's father said, his tone wry.

Ma used her best long-suffering sigh, the one that tended to make everyone in a twenty-foot radius stop in their tracks. "Oh, the stories I could tell you, Mr. Thomas. But first, there's the matter of this boy here."

"Indeed. Don't let us interrupt you. Best finish with him before we hunt down the girl."

"Dad," Jake protested.

"I have one word for you, James: Ohio."

"I'm a dead man, aren't I?"

"You have no idea."

I COULD STAY CURLED up under the bed forever. Stone shouldn't have been so comfortable. The cold floor worked well with the tiny painkiller pills Jake had given me, keeping me pleasantly numb.

My hand didn't throb, which worked for me. I lost track of time listening to Ma grill Jake while Jake's parents offered their insights. Like me, Jake had gotten himself into a lot of trouble as a child, and Jake's father seemed to enjoy telling my ma about it.

"Shouldn't we be looking for Karma?" Jake pleaded. I'd lost count of the number of times my partner had sought a way out of my ma's interrogation and flaying. "The painkillers have to be kicking in by now. It can't be safe for her to be alone."

"Don't you even think about taking that tone with me, James Thomas," Ma warned. "She's probably up a tree waiting for someone to rescue her."

"With a broken hand."

"Details," Ma replied, her huff so similar to Jake's I had to swallow a giggle before it slipped out.

"I think we should discuss how your daughter broke her hand. James, what did you do to that girl?" Jake's mother demanded.

"It wasn't me!"

"Really. With how angry that girl is at you, you think I'm going to believe that?"

"The doctor did it."

There was a long silence before Jake's mother spluttered, "The… what?"

Jake sighed. "I tried to tell you."

"Explain," Pauline ordered.

"There's this thing called patient confidentiality, Mom. Here, I have Dr. Sampson's number. She can explain how she broke Karma's hand. If you close the door, I'll put it on speaker. You can talk to her directly."

My partner was such a smart man, sacrificing my psychiatrist to our parents. I nursed a little hope he might survive.

"Do it," Pauline ordered.

Several moments later, I heard the ringing of a phone. "Dr. Sampson speaking."

"It's Jake again. Sorry to bother you, but there are a few people who want to ask you about Karma's hand."

"A few people?" the woman asked.

"Her parents and my parents."

"I see."

"This is Sebastian Thomas, Deputy Chief of Staff of CARD. Agent Thomas tells me you're responsible for Agent Johnson's broken hand?"

"Yes, sir."

"Yes?"

"Yes, sir. I'm responsible."

Dr. Sampson was a smart woman. I wondered if she'd survive the combined forces of Jake's family and mine. It'd be a shame if she didn't. When she wasn't breathing down my neck, I liked her.

"Explain."

"Mrs. Thomas ordered me to do the provocation evaluation."

"Pauline," Jake's father rumbled. "Would you care to explain?"

"Don't you take that tone of voice with me, Sebastian Thomas. Have you forgotten I'm your boss?"

After clearing her throat, Dr. Sampson said, "Agent Johnson passed her initial psychiatric evaluation. Unfortunately, I misjudged how sensitive she would be to my choice of words and she took her justified agitation out on the table. She hit the edge with a substantial amount of force. I was very impressed with how calmly she handled the resulting situation. I'm surprised Agent Johnson hasn't informed you of this herself. She's a very forthcoming woman when she's asked questions."

"Agent Johnson has probably climbed a tree somewhere,"

Jake reported, and I recognized the glee in his voice. "Is there rabies in Britain?"

"Excuse me?"

"Rabies. It's—"

"I know what rabies is, Agent Thomas. Why are you asking me if there's rabies here?"

My partner coughed. "Just wondering."

"Are you trying to tell me you've lost track of your partner?"

"She's a very smart woman. Had I known she was planning to sacrifice me to her parents, I would have run, too."

"James," my partner's mother warned.

"Mom always tells me to tell the truth, but when I do, I get in trouble. Could you explain this phenomenon to me, Dr. Sampson?"

"Since I have you on the phone, Mrs. Thomas, I have already notified Agent Johnson I would sign the authorization forms for her firearm to be returned conditional to her qualifying with her left hand. Would you like me to make the arrangements?"

"Please do," Jake's mother replied. "Thank you. I'll take care of the situation here."

"Agent Thomas, I recommend you postpone your trip to London until tomorrow. She is scheduled for a new x-ray in the late afternoon at the hospital. Agent Miller has the details for you."

"I have no problem with making two trips. It's still early enough in the day. But, seriously… is there rabies here?"

"No, Agent Thomas. Rabies is not a problem here. I am, however, concerned about why you are asking me this question."

"Long story."

SHORTLY AFTER DR. SAMPSON hung up, there was a brief but
fierce argument between my parents and Jake's, which ended
when they left the room.

The bed creaked as someone's weight hit the mattress. A
moment later, an upside-down Jake appeared. He grinned at
me. "You have the strangest parents."

"You're still alive?"

Snorting a laugh, he rolled off the bed and flopped onto
his stomach. "I won't lie. I had some doubts for a few
minutes there. How the hell did you squeeze under there
anyway?"

"Very carefully."

"Come on out. I texted Agent Miller that I knew exactly
where you were and asked him to cover for us while we
escape. All we have to do is make it to my rental without
getting spotted, and we'll be free and clear. We'll get a hotel
room in London for the night. Sound good?"

I nodded, uncurled, and wiggled my way out from under
the bed. Once my head and shoulders were clear of the
frame, Jake helped pull me out the rest of the way. Smiling,
he kissed my forehead. "You're sneaky, you're clever, and I
think I just fell in love with you all over again."

"Why?"

"You let me watch your back. You also used me as a living
shield in a life-threatening situation. I'm so proud of you."

"I think you're the one who needs a psychiatric
evaluation."

Laughing, Jake herded me to the door, slowing long
enough to grab my bag of medications, stuffing them in my
purse before handing it to me. "We'll leave our bags here and

get stuff for the night in London. When Mom railroads the hotel management into giving her a key to our room, they'll think we're still around here somewhere. That should keep them off our trail for a few minutes."

"You're adding fuel to the flames," I accused. "On purpose."

"Damn straight. Fuck, your ma hits like a truck. Does she work out? I might have to get my jaw realigned. You can make it up to me by running away to London with me."

"Yoga, actually. Please don't charge her with assault."

Jake snorted. "I'd never. She was just trying to protect you, I think. Either way, I worry my parents told yours I married you in Ohio. They're going to find out eventually. I honestly didn't believe my mom and dad would stay in the dark for long. After the marriage certificate was filed through the courthouse and into the legal system, my marriage status in my file would've been updated, and while they might not check your file frequently, I'm sure they check mine."

Sucking in a breath, I stared at my partner. The blood drained out of my head and pooled in my feet. "Fuck. Oh, fuck. Fuck, fuck, fuck, fuck. Fuck shit. We're dead, Jake. We're dead. We're so dead. We're going to be crucified."

"Why?"

I whimpered, peeking out the door to check the hallway for any sign of our parents. When I didn't see anyone, I gestured for Jake to follow me. "I ruined Ma's dream of me having a big wedding, Jake, and you helped me do it. When she finds out, we're dead."

WITH AGENT MILLER'S HELP, we left the castle and reached the SUV Jake had rented without our parents noticing us. Jake drove nice and slow to prevent drawing attention to us until we reached the road leading to London.

"They're going to kill us when they figure this out," I informed him, torn between laughter and tears. "We're going to have the lamest obituaries. The headlines will be worse than when I was kidnapped with Annabelle. I can see it now: Couple elopes, killed by parents. A lesson for the modern generation."

"I'm pretty sure Mom knew you were still in the room somewhere."

"Why?"

"You're joking, right? As if I was going to let you out of my sight after you walked out and took that trip overseas. Mom's not stupid. Maybe Dad is, but Mom? No. Mom saw I was still in the room while your ma was dressing me down and decided to enjoy the entertainment. Now, Mom has her blind spots, but she's of the opinion there is no way I would stick around if you weren't nearby. That said, she won't anticipate me leaving the castle right out from under her nose. Dad would expect it, but since he probably thinks you're up a tree somewhere, he's not going to say anything. Once they put their heads together, they'll figure it out."

"We're so dead."

"Hey, Dr. Sampson told me she *recommended* we postpone until tomorrow. She didn't forbid it. My parents didn't forbid it, either. Neither did your security detail. We'll be fine. They'll only kill us a little."

"Explain how they can only kill us a little."

"Very carefully, Karma. Very carefully."

"If we call Dr. Sampson and beg, do you think she'd

smuggle us back to the United States? Maybe she could set us up with a change of identity. We could become hermits somewhere."

"I don't mind having a big wedding if it comes with a stay of execution."

"That might help with my parents," I conceded.

"You don't mind?"

"You're kidding, right? I hate dating. Where else am I going to find a man who'll marry me without dating me first?"

"So cold, Karma."

"You like it."

Jake laughed. "Heaven help me, I do. I still remember the first time you set eyes on me and treated me like you do slugs. I couldn't tell if you were terrified of me or wanted to riddle me with bullets."

"I don't like how people think I'm going to shoot them all the time. Why, Jake? I don't understand. I'd never do that. I'd never kill someone without just cause."

"Oh, Karma."

"Explain it to me, Jake. I don't understand."

"When you stop and take a long look at someone, you're thinking. Behind those bright eyes of yours is someone who is thinking, who is watching every move, and analyzing to predict what will happen next. Most people just react. I do it, Mom does it, you don't. No, you take those few extra seconds to stop and think, and that makes you beautifully dangerous."

"Dangerous," I echoed.

"Wise men fear a strong, smart woman. I'm wise *and* smart, so instead of fearing you, I fell in love with you."

Chapter Thirty

JAKE CONFUSED ME, and I spent the entire drive to London trying to make sense of my tangled emotions.

I came to one conclusion: I was a defective human.

The emotion I felt for my parents counted as love—at least, I thought it did. They had dedicated a great deal of their lives shaping mine, and I appreciated it. If they were to disappear, I would miss them. I had a healthy dose of respect for them, though part of that was born of the fear they'd kick my ass if I strayed off the straight and narrow path they wanted for me.

I'd already done a lot of straying by choosing to become an FBI agent, although they had accepted my choice readily enough. I was doing something good with my life, and while they didn't approve of it, I liked to think I made them proud.

I had friends, but I hadn't thought too much about how much I loved them. Was there some invisible measuring stick used to gauge the emotion? When did respect, appreciation, and a general enjoyment of someone's company morph into love?

The night in Pennsylvania and the morning in Ohio had changed things. Until that night, Jake had never called me anything other than my name or partner. I hadn't realized he had crossed the threshold into friend territory. His lack of overtures, romantic or otherwise, kept me from realizing he was far more to me than just another co-worker.

Did I love the man, or was I just grateful to have a partner who was able, willing, and ready to put up with my shit? I enjoyed his company. Despite my doubts, I knew I could trust him to watch my back. When I needed him, the man had an uncanny ability to show up at just the right moment, wanted or not.

We were entering the outskirts of London when I tired of thinking and decided to take the direct approach. "You confuse the fucking hell out of me, Jake."

"Do I get a context, or will I have to start making guesses?"

"I don't understand how it is even remotely possible for you to decide you fell in love with me after speaking to me for five minutes."

"All right. Deep conversation that could possibly result in my body being tossed in the Thames it is."

"I thought we already discussed that, Jake."

"But I like when you narrow your eyes at me. You're so pretty when you're cranky with me."

"You're a masochist, aren't you?"

"Only for you."

"See, there you go confusing me again."

"This explains why you don't appreciate dating. You don't

get the point, do you? Jesus, am I ever glad I decided to just watch and wait for my chance to make you mine."

"Sex."

"Pardon?"

"That's what every man I've ever dated has wanted from me: sex."

I wasn't quite ready to tell him how much more I enjoyed sex with him than the other men I'd been with.

Jake sighed. "You're a gorgeous woman, Karma. You always have been. You're the kind of woman that makes a man stop and stare because he just can't believe you're real. Of course men want to have sex with you."

"You, too?" I winced at the hint of disgust in my tone.

It wasn't Jake's fault.

"Babe, I wanted every bit of you since I met you. Give me a break here. Those brains partnered with that body? You were my dream come true from the start. Of course I wanted to have sex with you."

"I had no idea."

Sighing again, Jake shook his head. "Of course you didn't. I didn't want to scare you off. I wanted to know why you seemed so damned skittish, which was why I had a talk with your parents. I'm being completely honest with you when I say I wanted to beat the shit out of whoever made you flinch away from people so damned much. I had been warned you had problems settling with a partner, but no one would give me any more details than you had been shot."

Being shot hadn't helped matters, but it wasn't the main reason I had feared a new partner. Acting as bait to lure out predators had been one of the worst decisions I had ever made. I had gone in knowing the risks, I had accepted them, and as a result, I had emerged relatively unscathed, but the experience had solidified my opinion I wanted nothing to do with men or sex.

Then Jake had come along and changed everything. How had he gotten under my skin? It was like I had a button and he knew exactly where it was and took a gleeful delight in pressing it. Once he pressed it, I was helpless. I didn't even want to resist him.

Was it because he had waited?

I guessed his patience was part of it. Four years of him watching my back gave me something I didn't share with many others. He gave me a sense of security. I could sleep with only one eye cracked open instead of both. I could take a shower in peace, knowing he was on guard. When he was in a hotel room with me, I had a few minutes to relax, safe in my knowledge he was there watching over me.

If I had been partnered with anyone else, the thought of my gun being confiscated would have driven me straight into a panic attack, and the realization startled me.

It was easier to think about my disastrous sex life than cope with the thought of losing my gun.

"I wasn't a huge fan of sex even before I joined the FBI," I admitted.

"There's nothing wrong with that you know."

I shrugged. "That's not what other men have told me."

"Their loss. If they didn't put in the work making sure you were the happiest woman alive, they didn't deserve you in the first place. I've been waiting for my chance with you for four years. There was no way I was going to risk blowing it by being an inconsiderate bastard."

"Am I supposed to feel guilty for making you wait so long?"

I did, at least a little.

"No."

"Why not?"

"You told me what you wanted to do with the rest of your life. You told me your dreams, and you told me exactly what you were risking by partnering with me. I respected that—I still do. That's why I transferred into CARD to come after you. You're my partner. I wasn't about to let some rat bastard ruin what you worked so hard for. When we go home, I'll do everything I fucking can to make sure you get your dream job without someone trying to destroy it for you. If I have to steal Dad's gun and pistol whip him until he makes it happen, I will."

My sense of guilt strengthened. "Isn't it supposed to be a two-way street? What have I done for you? What do you want me to do?"

"The only thing I want from you is for you to keep being you, Karma. You don't have to do anything. Keep on calling me an asshole when I annoy you. Keep watching my back, because there's no one else I'd rather have doing the job. If you said you never wanted to have sex with me ever again, fine. I won't go anywhere. I'll cry myself to sleep each and every night, but I want *you*, not your body. Okay, who am I kidding? I'm lying. I desperately want to keep having sex, but I want it because it's with *you*. Great. Look what you've done to me. You've turned me into a sappy idiot. Good job, Karma."

I couldn't help but laugh. "Sorry."

"I can think of ways you can make it up to me."

"I'm sure you can," I muttered, flipping my middle finger at him. I would have flipped him off twice if the splint hadn't stopped me.

"I'm looking forward to discussing this later."

IT TOOK Jake almost forty minutes to find somewhere to park. After consulting with his phone, we discovered he had parked several miles away from where he wanted to be. For some reason, I thought walking was a good idea.

I blamed the medication for my stupidity.

While I had done a lot of wandering when I had fled the United States, two weeks of driving around Germany and neglecting my health had damaged me far more than I thought possible. It took less than a half mile for me to feel the burn of unused muscles.

When I started wheezing, Jake paled. "Karma?"

How could I have gone from being able to run several miles to asthmatic in a matter of three weeks? "I think I need to stop for a minute."

The words came out a lot easier than I thought they would. Jake took hold of my left arm in his hand, his grip so tight I worried he'd leave a bruise. Closing my eyes, I concentrated on my breathing until I was able to fill my lungs despite the tension in my chest and throat.

"How long has that been going on?"

"Hasn't. Never."

"I'll call Dr. Sampson."

I cracked open an eye in time to watch Jake pull out his phone. Any other time, I would have argued with him.

"Dr. Sampson, It's Jake. I took Karma to London. We were walking to the shops, and she started wheezing." The worry in his voice upset me, and I shifted my weight from foot to foot. With his death grip on my left arm, I wasn't going anywhere, and I wasn't quite brave enough to use my right.

Even with the painkillers, my hand still throbbed.

"Karma, she wants to know if you're feeling light-headed or dizzy."

I shook my head. "Just felt like I couldn't get a good lungful of air. That's it. I'm already feeling better. Stopping helped."

Jake relayed my words, and as he listened, his hold on me eased. "Not Demerol. She turns into a frenzied serial killer with a foul mouth. We were able to contain her the first and last time she was on it. We had to handcuff her. My desk was never quite the same afterwards. Don't know of any other problem medications."

"I still think you made that up," I muttered.

"Okay, Dr. Sampson. Text me the number and the other details." Jake hung up and sighed. "She's going to talk to your surgeon and have a new painkiller prescribed. She's going to try to get you straight morphine, apparently, since it only makes you talk a lot and become deathly calm in random intervals. Until then, we wait for this stuff to wear off, and I'm to keep an eye on you. If you start wheezing a lot, I'm to call an ambulance."

"Joy."

"Are you going to let me carry you?"

"Fuck no. Just walk slow and let me take breaks, I guess. Medication's fault?"

"Medication's fault."

"So it has nothing to do with my pepperoni pizza diet and the fact I ate like shit while globe trotting?"

"I'm going to say no, but only because I have every intention of supervising what you eat until you are back to a hundred and ten where you belong—or a little heavier."

Some things weren't worth arguing over. "Okay."

"You tell me at the first sign you have any trouble breathing. Understood?"

"I got it, Jake. I like breathing as much as the next person. Remember, can't swim worth a shit? I've almost drowned how many times?"

"You're the only person I know who can't swim worth a shit that counts her doggy paddling laps in miles. And don't remind me of your attempts to drown. We're near a river. And the ocean. We're on an island. Fuck."

"We could just go shopping. And no, I'm not going to let you carry me. Non-negotiable. And no more hospitals. I'm done with hospitals."

"Then you better not wheeze again, because if you do, we're going. I will handcuff you and toss your skinny ass over my shoulder if I must."

"You have no idea how badly I want to pistol whip you in the ass right now, Jake."

"I'm a little disappointed neither one of us is armed."

"You are such an asshole."

JAKE TOOK me to a pub and fed me until I couldn't tolerate even the thought of another bite. Somehow, I managed to keep all my food down. When he was convinced I wasn't going to starve to death, Jake took me to King's Road.

In the first boutique, I discovered Jake's dark and dirty secret: he liked his clothes expensive. In a way, I was relieved he had chosen a store for himself first. It gave me a chance to come to terms with him spending more on a single suit than I did on the rental car in Germany for my entire two-week drive on the Autobahn.

He bought three suits, two of which needed to be tailored to fit him. The third, by some miracle, fit without requiring a single adjustment. While they were ringing up his order, which had more zeros than I could readily accept, Jake got on the phone to find us a hotel.

The shop delivered, and by the time we checked in, his new suit would be waiting for him.

"I can't believe you spent that much on suits," I muttered.

"Wait until you see how much I intend to spend on your clothes."

"Wait, what?"

Jake smiled, linked his arm with mine, and pulled me out of the shop. "My mother calls it a severe birth defect. Dad thinks it's funny."

"They think *what* is funny?"

"My enjoyment of helping women shop for clothes. The prettier the woman, the better it is. While Mom's a pretty lady, she doesn't hold a candle to you, and I've been waiting for this moment for years."

"Wait, *what*?"

"Don't argue, Karma. Just let me buy you clothes and think about all the damage you're doing to my wallet. View it as my punishment for my bad behavior."

"How is it punishment if you like it?"

I HAD no idea what I was going to do with so much clothing; some things fit me, and some would fit me when I regained weight. Some had been purchased because Jake started gaping and lost the ability to speak, and I figured the outfits would come in useful sometime in the future.

Jake insisted on going into a jewelry store on our way to our hotel. I would have been fine without adding the cost of rings to the substantial amount Jake had managed to spend in three hours, but he was a man on a mission, and he wasn't going to leave King's Road until I had rings on my finger.

"You're a fiend," I complained as he dragged me into an upscale boutique featuring more diamonds than I could readily accept.

Jewelry wasn't my thing. My ears were pierced, but I only put in earrings for formal events, and I avoided those whenever possible. I sometimes wore a pair of studs so the holes wouldn't close. One ring I had been willing to wear for him, but two was pushing it.

At least he'd be wearing one, too.

"You're just awed I'm manly enough to own up to actually enjoying this."

"I'm awed, all right."

Jake glared at me.

Inside the store, Jake went on a hunt for rings while I followed along, either shaking my head no, shrugging, or nodding when he pointed out rings he liked. A helpful representative measured our ring sizes, which helped us narrow the field to rings we could wear right away instead of needing them resized. His phone rang while we were making our first circuit of the store.

"Uh oh. Mom and Dad noticed," he announced before swiping his finger across the screen to answer. "Hi, Mom."

"Only an idiot would answer that call," I told him, heading across the store to escape having to listen to the inevitable argument. I flagged down the sales rep, and she smiled at me.

Two could play the shopping game, and within moments,

the nice lady had my credit card in hand, ready to do excessive damage to my limit.

If Jake was going to spend his time convincing his parents not to murder him for fleeing the castle, I'd just have to buy his wedding ring for him. I had noticed a set of bands I liked, a simple and elegant design with clean lines. My ring would be a little bit loose, but when I regained weight, I suspected it would fit. Unlike most wedding bands, which were a little too plain for my liking, both bands had tiny diamonds circling their centers.

They sparkled, and if I was going to wear a ring for the rest of my life, I wanted a bit of shine. "These," I whispered to the representative. "And an engagement ring that matches."

"I know just the ring in your size," she whispered back, pulling out the bands I had chosen before sliding her way along the counter.

The ring she selected startled me; instead of clear stones like the wedding bands, a yellow diamond was ringed by tiny brown stones matching Jake's eyes.

I was so, so weak when it came to that man's eyes.

"Yellow and brown diamonds. Bigger isn't better, and with hands as small as yours, one of those big rings will get in the way. Small stones, but they're unusual, right? With the way you're buying your rings, you come across as an unusual couple."

I somehow managed not to burst out laughing. Unusual was one way to put it. "I'm afraid to look at the price tag."

"Not nearly as bad as you'd think; hard sell, yellow and brown stones. They've been waiting a long time for the lady to do them justice."

"That was smooth."

"Want to try it on?"

I held out my left hand and wiggled my fingers, glancing at Jake, who was still on the phone, leaning against one of the counters. At the rate he was huffing, I expected him to explode at any second.

The sales representative slid the ring onto my finger. True to her claim, it was the same size as the wedding band, just a little bit loose without running the risk of falling off my finger.

I really was a sucker for the color of Jake's eyes.

"Put them on my card."

While the sales rep went to work finalizing my purchase, I stepped to Jake, listening to him huff and sigh.

"Mom," he complained.

I had to stand on my toes to reach his phone, which I stole out of his hand. He gaped at me, and I stepped away, putting the cell to my ear.

"Hi, Mrs. Thomas," I chirped. "Bye, Mrs. Thomas!" I hung up before his mother had a chance to say a word. Moving back into arm's reach of my partner, I slid his phone into his pocket. "When she calls you back, don't answer."

"And you accused me of adding fuel to the fire."

"I bought you a ring."

"Wait, what?"

The sales representative approached with a ring box and my credit card. While she held the box for me, I worked the lid off, grabbed his ring, and held it out to him. "Ring."

"You're so sneaky." Jake took the ring and worked it onto his finger. Taking the box, Jake pulled out my ring and slid it on my finger to join the engagement band. "There. Now everyone will know you're all mine."

I lifted my left hand so I could admire the rings. "Just remember, Jake. By making me buy these rings, you've accepted full responsibility for your actions. *You* get to deal with my mother."

Jake laughed, wrapped his arm around my shoulders, and pulled me out of the store. "A small price to pay."

"Explain to me again how this happened?"

"I dazzled you with my masculine charms, tricking you into proposing to me. You're mine now. Didn't I tell you when you first left to go to CARD? You'll always be my partner."

His declaration flustered me, but at the same time, it gave me a warm, fuzzy feeling. "I don't know how to respond to that, Jake."

"Just fall back on your usual. When in doubt, call me an asshole."

"I'm pretty sure I don't want to call you an asshole."

"You'll figure it out. Take your time and just enjoy the fact we're off duty and can fraternize all we want without getting in any trouble." Jake grinned at me, leaned down, and gave me a kiss.

I blamed my medication for how much I enjoyed it, standing on my toes to get closer to him. At first, I was puzzled when he pulled away, but then he wrapped his arms around me and held me close.

"People are staring at us," I whispered.

"Let them. I'm—" Jake stiffened, straightening as something caught his attention behind me. I spun around, my world narrowing to isolating the threat.

The black SUV captured my attention. Instead of hitting me in the back, the round caught me in the shoulder. Pain tore through me, and before I could do more than draw a breath, numbness spread, cold and relentless.

One, two, and three shots rang out, but it wasn't my body

that thumped to the ground. Jake's arm spasmed around me and fell away.

I sank to my knees, staring into a pair of cold eyes. Someone screamed, then their voice was lost to the silent dark.

Chapter Thirty-One

A SHARP SLAP to my face woke me, but it was the burning throb in my shoulder that jolted me to awareness. Cloth in my mouth choked off my scream and muffled the sound. Something was wrong with my nose, and I panicked at how difficult it was to breathe.

A second slap snapped my head around, and agony pulsed through me.

Somehow, I managed to blink open my eyes, but so many white bubbles danced and burst in my vision I was essentially blind.

"Don't kill the bitch yet," a man snarled. I didn't recognize his voice, and through the pain burning through my shoulder, I remembered.

Four shots had been fired, and only one had hit me. Four shots had been fired, and my body hadn't been the first to fall.

A deep chill enveloped me until all that remained was the memory of Jake's arm spasming around me. It had been the convulsive jerk of life leaving the body, something I had witnessed far too many times working in the FBI.

A small part of me wanted to deny it, to harbor a tiny flame of hope my partner still lived. The rest of me, too experienced and hardened by reality, knew better.

Jake was gone. One bullet was enough to kill someone; I'd taken a round in the shoulder, and I didn't need anyone telling me I'd die sooner or later. With medical attention, there was a decent chance I'd recover, but nothing more than a chance.

Life was a fragile thing, so easily broken.

Someone grabbed hold of my chin, forcing my head to turn. The movement triggered nauseating, pulsing pain in my shoulder. The spots in my vision faded enough for me to recognize the dark eyes of the man in the SUV, the one who had shot me and taken Jake's life.

Confident in his victory, he wore nothing to obscure his features. Pockmarked scars scattered over his face accompanied longer gouges marring him from ear to chin. White male, mid-thirties, with brown eyes several shades lighter than Jake's.

No matter how brutal the crime, I had worked hard to find justice for victims and their families. When I stared into my killer's eyes, one certainty rose above all others.

Jake was gone, and the man who had killed us both would die with me. Instead of a fire burning bright, my rage was a cold, numbing ice, bringing out the calculating logic I used to hunt murderers, criminals, and rapists.

The man before me was nothing but prey, and it was my turn to be the predator.

"Don't worry," my killer said. I should have been afraid of

the viciousness of his smile. "She'll be singing like a canary before I'm finished with her."

"Get the answers first. Then play with her however you want. Don't be long about it. We need to get out of here before we're tracked down."

"You worry too much. They're too busy dealing with the explosives, the dead agent, and the chaos we left behind to pick us out of the countless black SUVs in London. Even if they got pictures of our tags, they won't find us. Not with six other cars exactly like ours."

The chill in my bones intensified as my fury grew to new heights. He was happy he had killed Jake.

I would turn his joy to terror. I felt myself smile, and I bared my teeth. Before we had left Georgia, I had bitten Pops so hard I had drawn blood. I couldn't remember what he had done to drive me to it, but I had never forgotten the taste on my tongue.

That had been the day I had invaded a vixen's den to escape Ma's wrath, my face stinging from where she had slapped me. It hadn't been until she had struck me that I had let Pops go.

The vixen had bitten my shoulder in the same place I'd been shot, hard enough to draw blood. Tiny scars still marked where her fangs had sunk in. It had been a warning bite accompanied by her harrowing warning cry—a cry that still haunted my dreams sometimes.

"Just ask her the fucking questions before she bleeds out, and we went through all of this effort for nothing."

My killer's grip on my chin tightened. "Who tipped you off, bitch?"

"It'd help if you removed the gag first."

The fabric was yanked out of my mouth and left to

dangle around my neck. I licked my lips and tasted sweat and blood.

I remembered the taste of blood.

I hadn't remembered I liked its mix of sweet and metallic. The vixen's harrowing call echoed in my head.

"Who tipped you off, bitch?" my killer snapped, lifting his free hand to strike me. "How'd you and your fucking team know we were making the Baltimore hit?"

I should have cared more the man in front of me had been part of Annabelle's kidnapping. I opened my mouth, but instead of the words he wanted, the vixen's cry burst from my throat. The warning call was followed by short, chittering cries. I recognized them as the sounds the vixen had made the instant before she sank her teeth into my shoulder.

My gaze locked on the man's exposed throat.

He had taken Jake from me, and he would pay for his crimes with his blood.

MY FIRST MEMORIES had been of dreams. I couldn't pinpoint the moment my childhood obsession with foxes had begun, but I clearly remembered the day Ma had beaten it out of me.

Before Ma had knocked the sin out of me, I had dreamed, and in those dreams, I had hunted, and I had cried for a companion who never answered my calls.

It was that lonely scream that burst out of me, and I knew it would remain unanswered.

Jake was gone and could no longer hear me.

Human teeth couldn't do what I needed, and my rage

melded with my despair. I sank into my old dreams, the ones Ma had beaten out of me, and shifted from prey to predator.

My name was Karma, and for every bit of bad in the world, there was a balancing of good, for every wrong dealt, there was right to be found. I would even the scales, taking all of the good I had done and exchanging it for the justice I'd take with me to the grave.

First, I would deny what my killers wanted from me. Then I would sink into the dream of tearing their flesh with my fangs, their blood staining my fur. Unlike the red fox vixen I had met so long ago, who had warned me away with her barks, her chattering cries, and her scream, my fur would be black for the darkness I embraced while my paws and the end of my tail would be white as a reminder of everything I had lost.

In my dream, their bodies would lie with mine, their lives stripped away from them as surely as they had stripped away mine.

The blood on my tongue was hot and warm, but instead of the sweet taste I had enjoyed in my old dreams, it was bitter from my fury and regret.

Someone screamed. The pleasure of my teeth closing over delicate bones, crunching and tearing until the sounds died away to nothing, was matched in equal part by the aching hole burning through my chest.

I screamed a vixen's lonely cry, but Jake was gone and could no longer hear me.

Just as I had started to understand what Jake had been trying to show me, death had claimed him. A chasm the size of his life tore me in two.

When silence surrounded me and my prey cooled, I lost interest in them. I waited for the rest of my prey to come and find me. I had taken blood as payment, but it wasn't enough.

It would never be enough.

Every last one of them would fall to my fangs, and it still wouldn't be enough. Blood soaked my fur and weighed me down. I shook out my coat, prowling my prey's den, waiting for when the rest of their skulk would return seeking their own.

Once the rest of my prey fell, my dream would end.

With Jake gone, it already had.

MY PREY CAME in twos and threes, and I took them by surprise. The first always fell before he realized death had come for him. My fangs ripped through the black clothes obscuring their faces from me. With one bite, I eliminated the threat, and I turned my wrath on the others.

Gunfire should have frightened me, but the stench of their terror partnered with the acrid bite of gunpowder drove me into a frenzy. It didn't matter if they struck me.

I would not fall until they died.

I was aware of a distant pain in my shoulder and paw, but I ignored it, hunting, waiting, and hunting more only to have to wait again. When no more prey came, I ventured outside their den, their blood dripping from my coat.

Dark SUVs parked on the green lawn gave new life to my fury. Without living prey to tear apart, I directed my rage at the vehicles. Anything I could tear away and destroy, I shredded, broke, or dismantled. My claws gouged paint, and I tore at the metal beneath. I screamed, but I knew my cries would remain unanswered.

The nightmare began when the dream should have ended, when I should have slipped away into the eternal dark, but I remained.

When I scattered plastic, metal, and rubber over the lawn, when nothing remained for me to destroy, I staggered several steps, braced myself, and shook the dried and drying blood from my fur, sending it raining from my coat.

Night fell and the darkness stretched on, then the dawn rose, but the sun didn't bring an end to the nightmare. Whether I was a fox or a human, whether I lived or died, none of it mattered.

Jake was gone.

With my head hanging low and my tail dragging on the ground, I dragged myself step by step into the shadows of the forest to wait.

For what, I wasn't sure.

A STREAM MEANDERED through the forest. I slipped into the cold waters until nothing but my eyes and the tip of my nose remained above the surface. The chill soaked into my fur and washed away the blood. The current tugged at me, reminding me I lived.

I had ripped my prey to pieces, but instead of the calm quiet of death that should have been my reward, I rested in the water. It welcomed me in its embrace, held me down, and numbed me until the pain in my shoulder and paw grew distant.

In the distance, a wolf howled, and its cry was as lonely as mine.

Baring my teeth and pinning my ears back, I scorned the

presence of a wolf in my woods. What use was a wolf to a fox?

I wanted a human. I had been a human. I was a human.

I was a human who dreamed of foxes, one who had once hidden away with a vixen until I had been too old to fit in her den. I remembered. I hadn't invaded her den. She had welcomed me until the day she had driven me back to the humans who had beaten the dreams of being a fox out of me.

I remembered.

Ma hated the fox in me, the animal lurking beneath my frail human skin. When my cries were more fox than human, she beat the sin out of me. When I refused to speak in words instead of growls, Ma forced the human back into me.

I remembered Ma crying with each blow. The fear of Ma had remained, but I had forgotten why. I had forgotten I belonged in the forest instead of within the house. I remembered I had enjoyed lying in the water, paddling human hands when I should have had paws, watching the cycle of life go by around me, learning from the other wild things in the world.

I remembered why I couldn't swim. The water liked me too much. It welcomed me in its embrace and held me when no one else would. I was happiest where the water met the shore, because I was treasured by both. The earth, the mud, and the muck worked its way into my fur and clung to me while the water stroked me and offered what comfort it could.

The water soothed me, and the earth welcomed me home.

The distant wolf howled once more. Its melancholy lingered long after it fell silent, and I twisted an ear back in annoyance. I was a fox, and foxes did not mingle with wolves. Lesser foxes stole what the wolves left behind, but I was no lesser fox.

My teeth were meant for hunting, for fresh prey—not for scavenging. Wolves were competition, rival predators. A pack of wolves posed a danger to me. Without a skulk, I would turn from predator to prey.

I was not a lesser fox, and I did not leave my own kind, even the lesser ones, to face wolves unaware.

Where there was one, there were more, and my voice carried farther than a mere wolf's. Lifting my muzzle free of the water, I barked a warning.

Other foxes picked up my cry, and they scattered to the four winds. Pleased they had obeyed me, I lowered my head back into the water leaving my eyes and nose above the surface.

On the cool wind, I smelled the wolves draw near.

FIVE WOLVES SLINKED through the trees, and the smallest of the lot was the weakest link in the pack. My nose told me four of them were male and one was a female. The female was the largest, and she ruled over the pack with claw and tooth.

They had my trail, but the stream seemed to puzzle them.

The earth welcomed me, and because it did, it hid my fur from their watchful eyes. The water loved me; it washed away my scent so the hunting wolves wouldn't be able to find me with their noses.

If I were wise, I would use the earth and water's love for me to slip away, sliding through the shallows, leaving behind no evidence of my presence. Instead, I watched the wolves.

The female was brindled white and gold, and the male she nipped, shouldered, and showered with her affection was mottled brown, white, and red. The next male was solid red with a white ring around one eye and a single black paw. One wolf looked like I expected, gray with brown, although his fur was shedding, and the coat beneath was more black than gray with spots of red.

The smallest wolf was injured, and he limped with every step. When he whined, the female sidled up to him and groomed his fur, pausing every now and then to drape her larger head and neck over his. His fur was a rich chocolate brown, and his chest and underbelly were a vibrant tawny gold, as were his paws and the tip of his tail.

His coat was the finest of them, gleaming in the sunlight.

I was puzzled the wolves had brought a hurt wolf on their hunt. Did wolves not leave their sick, injured, or dying in their den, foraging for them until they healed? Did wolves not care for their own?

Foxes always cared for those within their skulk until they were ready to be driven away. I remembered that lesson well, and the scars marked my human shoulder, tiny pinpricks on my pale skin.

Such scars didn't show in my black coat tipped with white, nor would they again. What use did I have for a human body?

All that was left for me as a human was grief.

Because of me, Jake was dead. I had no reason to return to the world of humans, not when the earth and the water welcomed me. I remained still and watched the wolves. The injured one flopped on the ground and whined. The female stood over him, nudging him with her nose.

The other wolves sighed. It was the female's mottled

brown, white, and red male who approached the water to drink. I flattened my ears as he drew closer, tensed and poised to strike.

I was a fox, smaller than any wolf; the ones encroaching on my territory were far larger than they had any right to be, even the smallest of them. My size was always a disadvantage, but I would make up for it with savagery.

I would teach the wolves the error of their ways; the stream and its shores belonged to me.

The wolf sighed and dipped his muzzle to the water. I waited until he drank to strike, surging out of the water to latch my fangs around the fur of his throat.

His startled yip drew the attention of the rest of the wolves, and I chattered and clawed at him, pulling tufts of fur out, shaking my head in my effort to dig at his neck.

I hated wolves and their thick fur, so difficult for me to dig my fangs into. My aggression manifested as a chuffed, throaty huffing, not quite a growl but not as menacing as a wolf's snarl.

When the wolf lifted his head, I dangled from his throat.

The rest of the wolves stared at me, their tongues lolling in their amusement. I dropped, hackles raised and my fur standing on end. I barked to warn them away.

They kept staring at me. I braced my legs and shook the water and mud out of my coat, drenching the big male, who turned his ears back. When he didn't back away, I lunged and closed my fangs over the tip of his nose in rebuke.

The wolf yipped, shook his head, and threw me off. I landed in the stream with a splash, sinking straight to the bottom where it was deeper than I was tall. As a human, I understood how to make my body fight the water's love for me so I could breathe.

As a fox, the earth and water conspired against me, holding me down and smothering me with the weight of the entire world. The shallows were the cradle of life, but the depths were my death. I should have fought it, but I had no reasons left to fight.

Jake was gone, and it was my fault.

Fangs closed over the back of my neck, seized my scruff, and dragged me out of the water.

The wolves were laughing at me, and I thrashed in the big male's hold, screaming my outrage at their mockery and at being robbed of the peace of death.

Chapter Thirty-Two

NO MATTER HOW I THRASHED, screamed my fury, or struggled to bite him, the big male wolf didn't let me go. When I couldn't dredge up enough strength to even kick my paws, I hung limp, panting to catch my breath.

My nose was reporting a myriad of scents, but I had no idea what most of them meant. There were three smells I recognized: wolf, blood, and cinnamon.

The spice baffled me. Where was the cinnamon coming from? The blood I understood; I had tracked a lot of it from where I had hunted the humans and killed them as they had killed Jake. There was a fresher source, which likely came from the injured male.

The female wolf trotted to me, her ears pricked forward. She stared down the length of her nose at me. While I was too exhausted to struggle, I displayed my fangs.

She licked me. Offended by a wolf daring to lick me, I made an effort to break free, twisting my head to evade her.

Unperturbed, the female kept dragging her tongue over me, starting with my muzzle and working her way down my neck. When she reached my shoulder, the pain I had forgotten burst back to life. I yipped and tucked my tail, shuddering.

The female's ears turned back, and she made a noise in her throat. The male lowered me to the ground, but before I could get my paws under me, he stepped on my neck and pinned me. My paws twitched to the throbbing beat in my shoulder. The female continued dragging her tongue over my shoulder, separating my fur in her effort to examine me.

My whimpers drew the attention of the other wolves, who crowded the female to get a look at me. Even the injured male joined them, sniffing at me with his ears perked forward in interest.

They were probably deciding how best to divide me when they got hungry.

The brown and gold wolf licked my muzzle before turning to the female.

Wolves weren't supposed to wag their tails, but the small wolf's whipped back and forth so enthusiastically his entire body swayed. The female huffed, nipped the male's neck, and returned to dragging her tongue over my fur.

Had she been a fox, I would have found her attention comforting. Was she tasting me to decide if she was going to share me with the rest of her pack?

Not only did wolves annoy and frighten me, they confused me, too.

When she worked her way to my right forepaw, I yipped at the throb her licking woke, reminding me once again of my human body.

I didn't want to remember it or the reason I hurt.

The small wolf growled, and his ears turned back. The female sighed and shook her head. I had no idea how they communicated with each other, but the biggest male grabbed hold of my scruff in his teeth and lifted me up so he could follow after the female. The smallest wolf sidled up to me, bumping me with his nose and licking at my muzzle again.

I snapped my teeth at him.

He snapped back, voicing a short, deep growl.

I chittered threats at the wolf, and he snarled and warbled back at me. His ears alternated between perking forward and laying flat in annoyance. I lost track of time as I fought with the wolf, threatening to rip his muzzle off whenever he came close in his effort to lick me.

Why couldn't wolves keep their tongues to themselves?

Eventually, the small wolf's strength flagged, and he stumbled to a halt, his sides heaving as he fought to catch his breath. The other wolves stopped, watched, and waited. I sighed, and despite being carried, I was exhausted, too. My head nodded as I fought my need for sleep.

The female licked the small wolf's muzzle and rubbed her head against him until he forced his wobbly paws into motion.

The rest of the pack matched his wearied pace. The big male carrying me didn't even seem to notice my weight, no matter how many times I mustered enough energy to struggle in my attempt to free myself.

THE STENCH of blood and death filled my nose, and I recognized the early smell of rot hanging in the air. My fur stood on end, and I struggled in earnest, thrashing in my effort to free myself from the male's hold.

My instincts warned me of danger. The part of me that was human wouldn't stay sleeping if I got closer; that part understood the significance of the scents. I barked, and when my cries were ignored, I screamed. The wolves stared at me, and the small male's hackles rose, his tension stiffening his body.

I screamed again and didn't stop until the female shoved the entirety of my head in her mouth. Biting down hard enough for me to be aware of each and every one of her teeth, she didn't relent until I made a distressed, whimpering cry.

The small wolf echoed me with a whine of his own, which earned him a bite on the shoulder from the female. Yipping, he darted back, tucked his tail, and lowered his head.

The big wolf holding me released me, catching me by surprise. I hit the ground hard, the air whooshing out of my lungs. The pain in my shoulder and paw stabbed through me before lessening to a dull throb.

Tucking my tail and retreating seemed wise, so I did. I didn't make it far before the big male prowled forward, set his paw between my shoulders, and pressed down until I dropped to my belly. He stayed with me while the other wolves left.

The female had to drive the smallest one away with nips, growls, and several harder bites.

Once they had left, the male took over the female's job of grooming me, smoothing my fur with long strokes of his tongue. I flattened my ears, squirming in my effort to pull free.

I would have had more luck trying to move a mountain.

Sighing, I surrendered, laying my head on my paws, ignoring the pain from my right one. When I submitted to the indignity, the male wolf rubbed his nose along my neck.

Not only were wolves obnoxious, they had terrible breath.

The snap of a branch nearby had me lifting my head in alarm, barking a warning. The wolf growled, shifting until he stood over me. The pose was one I recognized; if anyone came too close to him—or to me—it would end in a fight.

The wolves had to be toying with me. I was nothing more than a small snack for one of them.

I had so much wolf slobber on me I would never get my fur clean, assuming they stopped licking me long enough for me to undo the damage done by their attentions. Another branch cracked in the woods.

I had lived far too long as a human not to recognize one, and I bared my fangs at the unwanted reminder. I had accepted my dream had morphed into a wolf-filled nightmare, but why did there have to be more humans?

Humans weren't food, and I was hungry. Hunger was a detail that shouldn't have existed in my nightmare.

Why couldn't I just finish dying? I had done everything I had needed to do. The evidence of my revenge clogged my nose and deadened me to the other scents in the forest.

The human was a female, a fact I determined more from vision than smell. She placed her hands on her hips and glared down at the wolf. "Don't you snarl at me."

I recognized her voice, and I canted my head to the side.

The wolf snarled at her.

"Don't you even start with me right now. I'm tired, I'm hungry, and I'm pretty sure I'm going to have to burn these clothes. Our puppy needs your help to change. Hand her over and go do your share of the work."

Sighing, the wolf straightened, backed up a pace, and grabbed me by the scruff of my neck. He lifted me off the ground and offered me to the human like I was a living toy for their amusement.

I displayed my teeth in warning. The woman crouched. With no sign of fear, she took hold of my muzzle so she could get a better look at my fangs. "They say seeing is believing, and I can easily see how these teeth could do a lot of damage."

Grabbing hold of my scruff, the woman took me from the wolf, one hand supporting my chest and belly while the other one kept a firm grip on my neck to keep me from mauling her.

Unlike the humans I had torn to shreds, the woman had no trouble holding me at bay. I chattered threats at her, but she ignored me. The big male sighed and took off at a lope.

"You're a serious pain in my ass, little lady. You better be grateful for this later. Why couldn't that pup of mine pick a sane one? Damn him. He just had to have the lunatic earth witch with multiple personality disorder."

Witch? I was a fox. I clawed at the woman in my effort to get her to release me, and she gave me a shake so strong it rattled my teeth together.

"Stop that. You've caused me enough trouble for one day. Couldn't you have left one alive for questioning? Was that too much to ask? Just one?"

I twisted enough in the woman's grip to regard her with an eye. The memory of who the female was lurked beneath the surface, but I recoiled from the knowledge.

If I remembered her, I would remember other things—the painful things foxes didn't care about. As long as I rejected everything about humanity, I wouldn't have to face why there was no answer to my calling screams.

Knowing there wouldn't be an answer—that it was all my fault he was gone—was already too much for me to handle.

"Come on, then. Maybe Mellisa can figure out what to do with you, because I'm fresh out of ideas. I should just dump you onto the pup's lap and make him deal with you."

I had no idea what the woman was talking about, which worried another whimper out of me.

"Oh, stop that. Haven't you figured out we're not going to hurt you?" The woman sighed. "I should be thanking you for snapping in a remote location. It makes cleaning up and hiding the evidence so much easier without curious Normals around."

One of us was crazy, and I wasn't convinced it was me.

MY GRAVEYARD of destroyed SUVs had a visiting group of humans, and I chattered my agitation at the pervasive stench of death in the air. The hum of conversation halted when the woman carrying me stepped out of the forest.

I counted eight humans, and they stopped sifting through the debris littering the lawn to gawk at me.

"Mellisa? Can I borrow your eyes, please?"

"Why can't you ask if I would take a look or something nicer? Whenever you say that, I think you're going to put my eyes in a jar of formaldehyde when you're done using them." A woman shook her head, and I recognized her.

I shied away from the memories that gave her relevance to me, and I flattened my ears.

The one named Pauline sighed. "What do you think?"

"I bet she sinks like a stone if you put her in water."

Pauline laughed. "Been doing that since the day that pup of mine met her. What else can you tell me?"

"She isn't a Fenerec. What she is, though, I have no idea. Her aura's clean, so whatever she is, she's doing it on her own—no sign of having stolen someone's abilities. There's a lot of fluctuation in her aura, and if my guess is right, she's suppressing."

"She bit Sebastian's nose."

"He probably deserved it. Come on. You can't just tell me something like that without elaborating."

"She was pretending to be an alligator, and he went for a drink of water a little too close. Didn't see her. When she couldn't get a hold on his throat, she latched onto his nose."

"How do you miss a huge fox hiding in the water?"

"Blended right in. She was fully submerged except for her nose, I think. I didn't actually see her until she was already on Sebastian and trying to drive him away from her territory."

"What type of earth witch likes water?"

"You'll have to ask my pup that."

"Out of the question. He's down and out for the count. Your mate's standing guard."

"How is he?"

"Tired, but he'll be fine."

Pauline sighed, and I suspected the sweetness in her scent was relief. "What's the plan?"

"We're going to tow the SUVs, pick up the evidence we can, torch the place, and sterilize it. Not much else we can do. It's a mess. From what we can tell, she ambushed them as they came in, probably in sets of two to four. It was pretty systematic. Went for the throat for the kills and did the rest of the damage after they were dead. Do you want my professional opinion?"

"Yes."

"She's the type to roll with the punches, as long as the punches are aimed at her. Those bodies told me one story: she wanted to watch the world burn, and I have no doubts she didn't care if they killed her. The instant she stops suppressing, it's going to get ugly. I'd rather not have to put her down. Take her to your pup. Maybe we'll get lucky and everything will work itself out. Once I figure out what she is, I can probably do something for her, but for now? It's your job to keep her from losing her shit and going on another rampage. Good luck. I have a feeling you're going to need it."

WHEN PAULINE CARRIED me to a pale SUV parked clear of the wreckage, a man's voice announced, "According to this, foxes live in family groups called skulks. I'm a little jealous, babe."

"Sebastian, what are you doing?"

"What does it look like? I'm educating myself about foxes. I don't think she's a red fox nor any of its color mutations. She's too muscular and broad in the chest. The closest I've found is a blue-coated Siberian arctic, but they're a lot smaller. Actually, I wouldn't want to meet the males of her species in a dark alley. Male foxes are a lot larger than the females, and she's already about the size of a coyote. The males are probably closer in size to wolves."

"Find anything out about her behavior?"

"That screaming she was doing was probably a call for her mate or skulk. Beyond that? The chittering was equivalent to our snarling or growling. It seems she was trying to warn us off and was willing to fight. The bark's a warning call."

"Mellisa said to keep her with our pup and hope for the best."

"She's given up already?"

"I think she just wants to start lighting things on fire so we can get out of here."

"Can't say I blame her. Hand the vixen over, then."

I should have taken advantage of the transfer to make a run for it, but I was too tired. Whenever I breathed, a pleasant, soothing scent filled my nose and relaxed me. The smell was of a male partnered with cinnamon and some other warm spice.

"Don't put her with him yet. Watch her. She's fixating on his scent."

Sebastian laughed, holding me close to his chest. I snuffled, pressing my nose to the man's clothing. His wasn't the male scent I liked, and I twisted my ears back. "I'm willing to bet my badge this is her first shift. At least she's not trying to kill me any more."

Humans confused me, but there was something familiar about both of them, and familiarity birthed a sense of safety and security. Humans were a better option than overgrown wolves. It was easier to submit and wait to see what would come.

As long as they didn't hurt me, I wouldn't hurt them. Until I rested and could hunt on my own, I would take advantage of their watchful eyes.

I was a fox, and foxes were opportunists. That much I remembered.

Satisfied with my plan, I closed my eyes and focused on the scent I liked and found comforting without knowing why.

Chapter Thirty-Three

I DREAMED JAKE LIVED, and he held me close and chased my nightmares away.

I wanted nothing more than my dream to be the truth, but I remembered. I knew better. Death was long in coming for me, but Jake was already gone.

All it took was a single bullet to kill someone, and I remembered the four cracks of gunfire and the sound of his body hitting the ground. No matter how many times I analyzed the situation, nothing changed. My body had shielded him enough the bullets would have struck his upper chest or head, decreasing his chance of survival. His arm had spasmed convulsively before he fell.

The first round had hit me. The rest hadn't.

The shooting taking place in such a public venue would have raised his chances a little. There had been witnesses. I remembered their screams.

How long did it take for an ambulance to reach someone in London?

If I could return to the water so it could numb me, things wouldn't be so bad. If I never woke up to a world without Jake in it, I wouldn't really be happy, but it was better than the alternative. His loss was my fault. They had wanted me.

Jake had been in their way.

The pain started as a deep throb in my right—my human —shoulder, and I counted the beats of my heart to delay waking up. I missed the comfort of having fur and the barrier it provided against the world.

If Ma found out I was dreaming about foxes again, she'd finish what the round to the shoulder had started.

"Go back to sleep." Jake's voice was whisper soft, a little hoarse, and had a rumble to it I didn't often hear.

I sighed. I must have died after all. Death wasn't supposed to be painful; I never thought those who theorized the afterlife was merely a continuation of life had it right. How long would it take for me to realize I no longer had a body?

I should have been at least a little embarrassed over how happy it made me to know we had found each other after death. Had I somehow not used up all my good karma getting my revenge on those who had killed us?

Then again, I had probably bled out before having a chance to get my revenge, which was a rather disappointing conclusion to my life, and I told Jake so.

Jake spluttered, then he laughed, and once he was done with his chortling, he held me closer and nuzzled my neck. "While I was shot, Karma, I'm not dead, and neither are you."

Denial made sense in the afterlife. We didn't want to be dead, so it was logical to deny the truth. "You were shot three times. Of course you're dead."

"Four, actually. The one round went right through you

and hit me, too. Haven't you figured out you can't get rid of me that easily?"

"I can tell. You found me in the afterlife," I informed him, rather pleased the myth about finding loved ones after death was the truth.

Jake laughed, and his breath both warmed and tickled my throat. "I'm going to have to have a talk with the doctor about your painkillers."

"Painkillers? There are painkillers in the afterlife?"

"No, painkillers are for living people only. You have a hole in your shoulder. If you take a look, you'll see you have a sling keeping you from moving your arm. Look on the bright side; we're sharing a bed, and it isn't in a hospital. You don't even have an IV. Granted, that's only because they stopped putting it back in after you ripped it out five times."

"You're taking the denial of our deaths thing too far," I complained, contemplating cracking open an eye to verify my surroundings. Little facts were filtering in through my head, and the throbbing in my shoulder rose to the top of the list. The steady rhythm of Jake's breath on my throat came a close second.

Birds were singing somewhere nearby.

Jake trailed kisses up my neck to my cheek. "You're ridiculous. You're alive, and so am I."

"But you were shot three times. I was shielding you. They could have only shot you in the chest, neck, or head. All potentially fatal. Three rounds? Very probably lethal."

"Four, Karma. One graze from the round that went through your shoulder and three through the shoulder, though one got a little too close to my chest for comfort. I'm sore, but I'm a lot better off than you are."

"You're telling me what I want to hear. That's more proof we're actually dead."

"You could just open your eyes and stop arguing with me," Jake suggested, pulling away from me. A moment later, I felt him poke my cheek. "You're being ridiculous."

"You found me in the afterlife to torment me, didn't you?"

"Yes, that is exactly what happened. I hunted you down in the afterlife to torture you for the rest of eternity."

"You're an asshole, Jake."

"Is there a reason you're refusing to open your eyes?"

I sighed. "I'm dead. I don't need to open my eyes."

"Says the woman who just sighed at me. How can you sigh without a body? Dead people can't sigh. They can't talk, either. Obviously, you're still alive."

My head was starting to hurt almost as much as my shoulder. "You're giving me a headache."

"Dead people don't get headaches, either. You're just going to have to accept you're still alive."

If I was alive, then I had to be dreaming, and I didn't want to wake up to the disappointment of reality. "So I'm dreaming then?"

"You're really being stubborn about this. Just open your eyes, woman."

"But you'll be gone."

Jake laughed and kissed my forehead. "I'll go get the doctor. Maybe he can talk some sense into you while he gives you some more painkillers."

The fear he'd disappear and never return choked off my breath. I reached for him, and the pain in my shoulder crested, the throb exploding into stabbing agony. A strangled cry escaped my throat.

Weight settled on my chest, and hands cupped my face.

"Stay still," Jake ordered. "Damnit, I wasn't going to go far, just to the door."

I shuddered and went limp, whimpering at the pulsing throb ripping through me. Tears burned my eyes, hot on my cold cheeks. "Don't leave."

"I'm right here. I'm not going anywhere, I promise. Lie still and breathe."

Breathing helped, but it also hurt. "This is proof you're dead and this is a dream. You're fine and I'm not. You were shot, too," I whispered.

Jake pressed his forehead to mine, and I cracked open an eye to peek through my lashes. A dim light illuminated the room enough for me to make out his features, although my vision blurred.

"You don't remember?"

"Remember? Remember what?" When he didn't disappear, I blinked, and he pulled away enough I could see his smile.

"Looks like you're not dead or dreaming. See? Still here." Jake rolled off me, propping himself up on an elbow. With his other hand, he gave his shoulder a pat, drawing my attention to his bare chest, which had a square bandage taped over his shoulder. A long, healing scab cut over his ribs and along his side.

Two scabbed over, circular wounds flanked the white patch.

I stared. His injuries had had a lot of time to heal.

"Here." Jake took my left hand in his and gently lifted my arm, pressing my palm to his chest. His warmth seeped into me, and I slid my fingers to the nearest scab. Jake's breath hissed through his teeth, and I jerked my hand away.

I'd been shot enough times to recognize Jake had been a

long time in healing. Turning cold from dismay, I gaped at him. "How long have I been out?"

Had I been in a coma? A thousand questions tumbled through my head until my fears and worries drowned them out and left me shivering.

Jake stretched out beside me and rested his head beside mine, nestling his chin against my shoulder. "It's all right. You're fine. We were attacked four days ago."

There was no way his injuries had happened four days ago. Careful to avoid moving my right arm, I pointed at his shoulder. "That's been healing for weeks, not days. Don't lie to me, Jake."

I couldn't force myself to voice my fears.

"It's only been four days, Karma. I swear it. You really don't remember anything?"

I remembered the pain and awareness of death coming for me before I had dreamed of life as a fox in search of vengeance. The dream had likely been hallucinations induced by blood loss, and once I'd been found, whatever painkillers they had me on likely accounted for the rest. "Nothing coherent," I admitted.

Jake sighed. "All right. Are you going to let me go to the door? You might be the toughest woman I know, but you can't hide the fact you're in pain, not from me. Anyone else would probably be screaming or crying right now. I want the doc to make sure you didn't hurt yourself."

With Jake nestled between my right shoulder and throat, I couldn't see over him, and I wasn't brave enough to lift my head to see how far away the door was. The giddiness of relief washed over me, and I swallowed a giggle.

If I let a single one out, I'd succumb to them, and I had no doubt laughing would hurt. Deep breaths hurt, too, but it beat turning into a giggling or crying mess.

Until my shoulder healed, which would take weeks at the very least, I'd be reliant on too many people, which would be embarrassing enough. If anyone found out about my afterlife conversation with Jake, I'd never live it down.

"Hey, Jake?"

"What?"

"Don't you dare tell anyone I thought we were dead."

Laughing, Jake lurched upright, leaned over to kiss my forehead, and rolled out of bed. He winced as he stood. A large bandage was taped to his back. When he rolled his shoulders, his joints cracked.

"Please?" I begged.

Jake stretched his arms over his head, and I admired the flex of his muscles. Once he finished raising both arms over his head and working out the kinks, he turned to me and pouted.

His expression coupled with his lack of clothes was so absurd a giggle slipped out of me. I choked back the second one, resulting in a snort. Instead of answering me, his pout shifted to a smirk. Scowling, I lifted my left hand and flipped him my middle finger.

"All right, all right. I won't tell anyone you were convinced we were having a conversation while dead, but you're going to owe me."

The man was going to drive me insane at the rate he was going. "I can't tell if I love you or love hating you," I confessed.

Jake's smile was radiant. "I love you, too."

Pivoting on a heel, he headed to the door while whistling a merry tune.

"It's just the drugs talking, you know," I called after him.

"Sure it is." He paused long enough to blow me a kiss before unlatching the door and sticking his head out into hallway. It didn't take him long before he made his way back to the bed, slid under the covers beside me, and snuggled close.

"You really went to the door naked, didn't you?"

"Got a problem with it?"

I thought about it. Did I have a problem with him prancing around naked?

I didn't have to think long on it.

"I'm the only one allowed to see you naked."

"Will doesn't care, Karma."

"No, but I do," I hissed at him.

"You're jealous, aren't you?"

"So what?"

Jake laughed.

I HAD no idea what was in the needle the doctor jabbed me with, but it didn't take long to numb me to everything and leave me in a half-awake daze. With my awareness flitting in and out, it was difficult to make myself care, even when the doctor stole Jake away, leaving me with promises of his return.

That's when my parents visited, and I was grateful for the painkillers. My parents weren't criers, but they sobbed at my bedside. The numbness kept me cocooned in a protective layer, cradling me from reality.

My nose was playing tricks on me; relief shouldn't have

had a scent, but it hung so heavy in the air it made it hard for me to breathe.

Maybe I was drugged, but I knew better than to say a word. If Ma found out I was dreaming about foxes again, she'd beat them out of me. I opted for the safest course possible: silence.

Tears were far better than rage.

The doctor returned without Jake, spending far too long discussing the miracle of my ongoing survival with my parents. While I was of the opinion the gray-haired man talked far too much, I waited it out. It was difficult to make sense of the conversation, but I came away with a few important facts.

First, I'd make a full recovery. I had no idea how; when bullets tore through the shoulder, they destroyed a lot of things. Real shoulders weren't like the ones on television; I wouldn't hop back to my feet at the end of the episode as though nothing had happened. In a few weeks—more likely a few months—the injury would heal, but it would leave behind scars and bones that would never heal quite right. Those scars would impair my movement in some fashion or another. If I got lucky, I would escape with minimal nerve damage.

In a few years, I'd find out how impaired my movement would be. Physical therapy would help, but I'd always carry reminders.

Second, I wouldn't be going anywhere soon, but the doctor somehow managed to talk my ma and pops into returning to the United States. I regretted not comprehending most of the conversation; I was able to focus my attention on exactly one thing at a time, and analyzing the reality of my injury and the doctor fibbing about a full recovery had consumed the little coherency I had.

Finally, once the doctor managed to drive my parents out of the room, he removed the splint from my wrist, winking at me as though letting me in on some joke. He set it on the nightstand beside the bed, which also held a tray littered with pill bottles, syringes, and clean bandages.

"You lied to them," I accused in a slur.

"The only lie I told was the period of time it will take for a complete recovery."

I was so focused on how I couldn't possibly recover completely, I had missed the part about how long it would take. "Huh?"

"Under normal circumstances, the injury you sustained would take half a year to a year for a full recovery with a substantial chance for impairment. However, thanks to your rather unique circumstances, I expect the entire process will take no longer than two months."

"That's impossible," I informed him.

"Under normal circumstances, it is. Frankly, under normal circumstances, I'd probably still be in the operating room searching for the missing pieces of your shoulder and trying to piece the fragments back together. For the moment, it's probably easier if you don't think about it. Enjoy the fact you're healing well, take your medication exactly as prescribed, and be grateful. I have instructions on your general care for the next week. My primary focus is on your weight. Until your nutrition problems are resolved, I can't begin a physical therapy regime for you."

I frowned. "How long?"

"For what?"

"Until physical therapy."

"Two to three weeks—maybe sooner, depending on circumstances."

"That's impossible."

Most doctors I knew would have been offended by my disbelieving tone. Mine smirked instead of getting angry. "I wouldn't hold on too tightly to your perceptions of what is and isn't possible, Mrs. Thomas. It'll make things easier for you down the road."

"What do you mean by that?"

"You'll see. For now, you should rest. As soon as your husband's parents are convinced he's on the mend, I'll send him back to you so you both can get something to eat and some sleep. Tomorrow, I'll be taking you to the local hospital for a new set of tests to confirm how well you're healing, and I'll reevaluate things from there."

The doctor was halfway to the door before I realized I didn't know his name. "Who are you, anyway?"

"I'm Dr. Sampson, ma'am."

"No, you're not. Dr. Sampson is a woman."

He laughed. "That Dr. Sampson is my daughter. If you think that's bad, wait until you meet my wife. *That* Dr. Sampson will be your physical therapist. Trust me on this, you will want to speed your recovery along as quickly as possible. She'll make your life hell if you give her half a chance."

I had a very, very bad feeling, but before I could say a word, the doctor swept out of my room and closed the door behind him.

Chapter Thirty-Four

DR. SAMPSON, Mrs. Dr. Sampson, and Mr. Dr. Sampson joined forces, and whenever I was coherent enough to realize all three of them were in the room with me, I snarled curses at them.

I thought they were having way too much fun confusing me. One of them I could handle. It was when there were two or more of them I had problems. When two or more of them came, they stole Jake away from me.

At first, they kept me so drugged I struggled to focus enough to be upset he was gone. When I complained, Jake smiled, kissed my forehead, and assured me he would return. Then the devil doctors drove him out of our room.

Only the knowledge they were helping my shoulder heal kept me cooperating.

I had no idea how much time had gone by, but the fact all three of them had come warned me of trouble.

"What?" I asked, tensing warily as they regarded me.

"We're going to give you a choice," Mr. Dr. Sampson announced.

Choices were bad. The last time they had given me a choice, it had resulted in pain, pain, and more pain—and a trip to the hospital for tests. I grimaced. "What choice, sir?"

"You can go to the hospital with us for tests without a fight, cursing, or trying to crawl under the bed to get away from us."

I waited for the second choice. It didn't take me long to realize there wasn't a second choice.

Even I could learn a new trick, and resisting would only result in pain and going to the hospital anyway. "Yes, sir."

All three of them stared at me.

"You're going to cooperate?" the youngest Dr. Sampson asked.

"Yes, Dr. Sampson."

"We're not going to have to drug you this time?" Mr. Dr. Sampson didn't sound like he trusted me one bit, not that I blamed him.

I was a terrible patient, especially when they sent Jake away. The fear he'd disappear had faded, but it didn't take long for the first trembling signs of anxiety to set in. Why couldn't they just let Jake stay in the room?

Better yet, why couldn't he go to the hospital with me?

I sighed. "You won't," I promised.

For once, I'd like to have some idea what was going on— and walk in and out of the place under my own steam. At least they were taking me to a smaller hospital for testing, which limited the number of people who witnessed my embarrassment.

Mrs. Dr. Sampson narrowed her eyes at me, placing her hands on her hips. "You're not going to try to climb out the window again, realize you're afraid of heights halfway out, and indulge in a fit of hysterics?"

Jake had *tried* to warn them what happened when I was given Demerol, but no one had listened to him. I had no recollection of the incident, but if the stories I kept hearing were to be believed, I had been a devil of destruction on a mission.

At least I wasn't responsible for the bill for the damages.

I lifted my chin. "That was *not* my fault."

Of the three Dr. Sampsons, my psychologist was my favorite, and she grinned at me. "It's true. We were warned. It's not her fault you didn't listen, Dad. When Agent Thomas warned you and backed out of the room when you disregarded his warning, you should have known."

"We can't keep giving her morphine. It's too much of an addiction risk," Mr. Dr. Sampson announced.

All three sighed.

"It's not my fault," I muttered.

Even the morphine derivatives turned me into a psychopath. Drugs that had worked before no longer helped without doing *something* to me. The nicest of them had induced hysterical giggles, which had disconcerted Jake so much he had begged the doctors to take me off it immediately.

Morphine did strange things to me, too, but I was a tolerable nuisance rather than a danger to myself and those around me.

"If you can successfully address us by name, you'll get to walk yourself to the car and in and out of the clinic today," Mr. Dr. Sampson declared.

"Mellisa, Arthur, Denise," I chirped, pointing at them in turn. "Psychologist and psychiatrist, orthopedic surgeon, and tort—ahem, physical therapist with a specialty in bone trauma recovery. All three of you are attached to London's United States embassy when abroad, and when in the United States, you service the Baltimore-Washington area."

Maybe they had kept me drugged, but when I was reasonably coherent, I paid attention to the chatter around me.

The doctors stared at me.

"What? You asked." I scowled. "You weren't expecting me to know, were you?"

Mellisa held her hands up in a gesture of surrender. "I warned you, Dad."

"So you did. Try not to embarrass yourself, Agent Thomas."

I caught myself looking for Jake before realizing the man had been talking to me. I doubted I'd ever get used to people calling me anything other than Agent Johnson, and I resented the reminder Jake wasn't with me. While I wanted to snarl a curse at the implication I couldn't handle walking, I breathed until I could force a smile.

Everyone had good reason to doubt me. If I managed to walk without tripping over my own feet, I'd be impressed.

I couldn't wait until they decided I was able to handle life without the medications clouding my head. "I think you're asking for a miracle, sir."

"Mellisa will help you get changed. Once you're ready, we'll head out. We'll try to make this as quick as possible, but we have a lot of tests to run."

I sighed. Some battles weren't worth fighting, and I recognized a lost cause when I saw one.

THE DRUGS HAD WORN off by the time we reached the small hospital in the British countryside. My shoulder ached, but it was a tolerable pain. My hand, which should have still hurt, didn't bother me unless I tried using it too much. When I did, the stiffness in my joints was the primary source of discomfort.

I had a feeling the only reason physical therapy on my hand hadn't already started was because of my shoulder. Even the act of wiggling my fingers made the gunshot wound throb.

For the first time I could remember since waking up in bed with Jake, the doctors didn't drug me, allowing the painkillers to work their way out of my system. The battery of tests did a good job of distracting me, although I couldn't stop checking over my shoulder. Without Jake around, my nervousness grew, and when the doctors took their eyes off me, I took advantage of the opportunity to get my back to the nearest wall, as far from the windows as I could.

They were so absorbed by my x-rays, the doctors didn't notice I had moved for at least ten minutes. When Mellisa looked up and noticed I was gone, she scanned the room and spotted me in the corner.

"What are you doing over there?"

I reminded myself I liked the woman. I reminded myself it wasn't her fault I hurt. Taking deep breaths to help calm the fluttering feelings in my chest and stomach, I matched her stare for stare.

Without Jake around to watch my back, tension cramped my muscles.

"I like it over here." I couldn't stop myself from glancing in the direction of the big window. A green lawn stretched to the edge of a forest, and the forest had too many places for people to hide.

Mellisa was a lot of things, but she wasn't stupid, and her gaze flicked to the window before returning to me. Her answering frown didn't last long, but she did get up and close the curtains. "You're going to have to deal with it eventually, Karma. Suppression is an excellent short-term coping tactic, but you have to face the underlying trauma eventually."

"I've been shot before," I reminded her.

"Yes, you've been shot before. Those injuries, however, were not nearly so severe or traumatic."

"I'm used to watching my own back," I muttered. "Fine. I didn't like the window. We *are* on the third floor."

"As long as you acknowledge the real reasons you do not like the window."

I clacked my teeth together. "Yes, Dr. Sampson. I'm uncomfortable with my back facing a window. Yes, I'm aware of the circumstances. Yes, someone tried to shoot me in the back, and I was only facing the shooter because Jake had noticed and reacted. Yes, I'm aware they shot him, too. I'm unarmed, and damn it, I miss my fucking gun." I huffed, wrinkled my nose, and poked at the sling keeping me from using my right arm.

"All things considered, you've been exceptionally patient." Mellisa smiled at me. "Why don't you come over here and have a look at these pictures? You can get a good look at your recovery. Unfortunately, the results are in, and my mother is going to have her way with you starting in about an hour."

With wide eyes, I rose and approached the table they

were using to examine images of my shoulder. Mellisa directed my attention to the x-rays.

One thing stood out: I couldn't spot a single broken bone.

"Whose x-rays are these?"

"Yours."

I shook my head. "No broken bones. That's impossible. Bullets through the shoulder break or shatter bones. I don't see any pins, rods, or anything else that should be there."

"I was unaware you have medical training, Agent Thomas," my orthopedic surgeon commented, his tone neutral.

I stared at him. "I don't. I've just seen x-rays of shoulders after a bullet has torn its way through. My instructors thought it wise for us to know what would happen if we got shot, sir. I thought it was pretty effective. Bullets to the shoulder usually impair mobility in the long-term unless it's a graze or misses bone."

In case there was any doubt, I pointed at my shoulder. "There's a lot of bone right there, sir. I don't need a medical degree to know that. There is no way those are my x-rays."

"They were broken," Dr. Sampson corrected, gesturing to one of the x-rays. "Look at this one, Agent Thomas. If you look here, here, and here, you can see where the damaged bones have fused."

Careful to avoid hurting my shoulder, I bent over the table to look at the image. At first, I couldn't see what he was trying to show me, but there were dark lines on the bones, which I assumed were the evidence of healed fractures. I tapped my finger against one of the marks. "Like there?"

"Yes, there. Now, look here." Dr. Sampson tapped on a different x-ray. I looked.

As far as I could tell there was nothing wrong with the bone. "I don't see anything?"

"That's today's x-ray. There's no longer any evidence you were shot. Your muscles, however, are the problem. Fatigue, malnutrition, and stress seem to be the primary factors in your delayed healing. While you've gained weight, it's time for you to begin exercising again to get back into decent physical condition."

I grimaced. "Physical therapy."

Mrs. Dr. Sampson sighed. "Initially, I wanted to use swimming, but your husband did not handle the suggestion well."

"I sink, ma'am."

"Yes, which makes swimming a very dangerous proposition. So, we're going to try something a little unconventional."

"Unconventional?"

When Mrs. Dr. Sampson smiled, apprehension shivered through me. "To begin, we're going to go to the firing range."

I straightened, staring at her with widening eyes. I couldn't remember the last time I had held a gun. Being armed when I had been shot wouldn't have changed anything, but I missed the security of having a firearm.

With a gun, I had the means to protect myself.

I snapped my head in Mellisa's direction, holding my breath in the fear I'd misheard my psychiatrist's mother.

"While they think I'm absolutely insane for authorizing it, I'm going to give you a chance to qualify with your left hand. They think I'm the one in need of a psychiatrist now, but I get how you FBI agents tick. They don't." Mellisa smiled. "If you qualify, you walk off the range with a permit to carry in Britain."

"She looks like she's about to cry," Mr. Dr. Sampson blurted. "She hasn't shed a single tear since I got my hands on her. Psychoanalyze that for me, Mellisa."

"She doesn't have a mental illness. I'm currently functioning as her psychologist, not her psychiatrist. There's nothing to psychoanalyze. Let me explain it in small words so you can understand it: little is as liberating for a victim as the ability to defend herself from becoming a victim again. You both have been pressing her buttons while she's been drugged trying to prove to me she is unstable. All you have to show for your efforts is an expanded vocabulary. Now, if you're quite finished doubting my abilities to do my job, would you please stop looking for bullshit reasons to delay the next phase of her recovery?"

I recognized a fight I did not want to be part of, and I backed away from the table. "It's not hard to press the buttons of someone under the influence of narcotics. Please don't give me any more narcotics."

All three doctors stared at me, but it was Mr. Dr. Sampson who replied, "You don't want painkillers?"

"It doesn't hurt that bad." It was the truth, too. "Don't tell my instructors I said this, but please, please, *please* let me play with some guns. Please. *Please.*"

"Look at her, Dad. How can you refuse such a face? If you refuse, I'm going to tell Agent Thomas you made his beloved woman cry after you stole her away from him."

In that moment, I realized the real threat was my psychologist, and not even her parents were brave enough to face off against her. I wisely kept my mouth shut, waiting for the final verdict.

"Don't make me regret this, Mellisa," Mr. Dr. Sampson warned.

Mrs. Dr. Sampson stared at me before turning her gaze to her daughter. "This is going to be interesting."

THE DOCTORS TOOK me to a firing range operated by the British military, and the supervising instructor handed me a Beretta M9 with a magazine loaded with live rounds. For the first time since I had woken up with Jake at my side, I was free from the sling immobilizing my arm. I went through the motions of stretching my shoulder, hissing at the stiffness and pain radiating from the joint. A bandage kept me from bleeding all over the place.

If I could shoot a gun, even for a few minutes, I didn't care if I set back my recovery.

A sheet of paper was about to become confetti, and I looked forward to every last second of it. I paid a minimal amount of attention to the instructor as I systematically dismantled the Beretta, checked it over, reassembled it, and loaded it. My right hand was so weak I doubted I'd be able to hold onto the gun no matter how hard I tried. With my mufflers in place, I stared at the supervisor and waited for his nod of approval to start firing.

When he gave his permission, I shifted the weapon to my left hand, took aim, and fired. I kept firing until I emptied the magazine. I dumped it, grabbed the spare from the sill, reloaded, and kept shooting. Five magazines later, I scowled at the empty sill.

Why couldn't standard magazines hold more than thirteen rounds? Sighing, I stooped, gathered the empty magazines, and went to work refilling them. When I finished, I lined them up on the sill, set my empty gun beside the magazines, and reached up to remove my mufflers.

My three doctors stared at me, their mouths hanging open. The supervisor pulled in the target, spreading it out over the sill.

The three holes outside the kill zones should have annoyed me far more than they did. I wanted to grab the sheet and hold it close.

"Agent Thomas, I was under the impression you're right handed."

I widened my eyes at the middle-aged man with bright blue eyes and sun-blond hair. "If I had been using my right hand, sir, I wouldn't have missed."

His gaze dropped to the sheet, focusing on the three stray rounds. "Ma'am, they're still within the silhouette."

"But they're not in the kill zones, sir."

"I don't suppose you'd consider defecting, would you?"

I blinked at him, but before I could come up with a reply, Mellisa clapped her hand over my mouth. "She politely declines."

"Pity. If this is her off hand, I would love to see what she can do with her main hand."

"Think you can handle a few rounds with your right?" my psychologist asked, lowering her hand from my mouth.

"Are we placing bets on how many shots I last before I drop the gun?" I replied, eyeing the Beretta warily. "I don't know if I'd be able to keep a grip on it after one. It's sore enough from stabilizing my left."

My left hand, shoulder, and arm ached from the effort of holding onto the Beretta after so long without practice.

"Let's not push our luck," Mr. Dr. Sampson spluttered. "Does she qualify, Lieutenant?

My supervisor, one Lieutenant Wilhelm, gaped at my orthopedic surgeon. "You're bloody fucking with me, aren't you? Damned yanks."

"Translation: don't ask stupid questions," I offered, stretching my hands in my effort to resist the urge to put my mufflers back on, hunt down another sheet of paper, and murder it as enthusiastically as I had the first. "Of *course* I qualified. What do I look like to you?"

"Someone who hasn't touched a gun in over a month," my psychologist replied.

In truth, since I had joined CARD, I had limited my range time to the mandated number of hours. Instead of telling them that, I shrugged. "I prefer a Glock. My Glock."

I wasn't above faking a sniffle while regarding the Beretta with disdain.

Lieutenant Wilhelm laughed. "Bloody hell, lady. You're something else."

Maybe I'd never have Jake's wide brown eyes capable of melting me from the inside out, but I did my best to imitate my partner's saddest stare, turning it onto the man overseeing my qualification. "Please, sir, can I have some more?"

"Oh, for fuck's sake. Just get it out of your system," my psychologist muttered, throwing her hands in the air. "Mom, Dad, we may as well go find coffee. She's going to be here for the rest of the afternoon." Narrowing her eyes at me, Mellisa put her hands on her hips. "And no, you may *not* defect. Lieutenant, please keep an eye on her. Someone erased the word moderation from her personal dictionary, and she has a great deal of pent up stress to work out."

Lieutenant Wilhelm waited unto the three doctors left the firing range before turning to me and asking, "Machine guns?"

"Machine guns," I agreed. Then I blinked. "Wait, machine guns?"

"We're all about the hospitality here, Agent Thomas. What kind of host would I be if I didn't show our guest our finest machine guns?"

"Of course. How silly of me. Please, Lieutenant. I would love to see your finest machine guns. How could I, in good conscience, refuse?"

Chapter Thirty-Five

HANDLING a machine gun was both heaven and hell, and I found savage joy in turning targets into confetti although handling the weapon hurt. After my stint with the machine gun, Lieutenant Wilhelm introduced me to a wide variety of weapons to test. I trembled from pain and fatigue, and I shook my head when he tried offering me a small handgun.

I wanted to take it and empty its magazine, but I had reached my limit. The fact the weapon was a Glock made refusing even more difficult.

"I'm done," I confessed, proud I didn't allow my voice to dip into a whine.

"Bloody hell, lady. I thought you were going to be done after the first stint with the machine gun. You're tough. Let me swap the paper and see what you can really do."

I scowled but nodded my agreement, taking the Glock from him and checking the weapon over. The model wasn't marked on the weapon anywhere, and while it had a serial number, it was different from any other Glock I had come across since joining the FBI. "What kind of Glock is this?"

It had unmarked settings on it, which stirred my suspicions.

"A special one. I think you'll like it." Once the paper was in place, Lieutenant Wilhelm took the gun from me, adjusted the settings, and handed it back. "Keep a firm grip on this weapon. It has an intense amount of recoil. I'd rather you didn't punch yourself in the face underestimating it. Small package, big punch."

I set the Glock down long enough to adjust my mufflers and stretch my throbbing body. I hurt, and I had no doubts the pain would be far, far worse later. Picking up the gun, I firmed my grip on it, took aim, and fired.

I dumped the entire magazine before I realized the weapon was fully automatic. Holding the trigger wasn't one of my finer moments, but the gun's recoil had taken me by surprise, and my instinct was to keep a death grip on the weapon so I wouldn't drop it or point it anywhere other than my target.

"Holy *fuck!*"

Lieutenant Wilhelm dissolved in a fit of helpless laughter. "Your face," he choked out.

Shock kept me staring at the target. When I recovered enough to blink, I stared at the little gun in my hand.

I wanted the weapon so much it hurt.

"Turn around for a moment, would you?" I begged.

The man snorted. "I know that look, Agent. You want that gun."

"You have *no* idea."

Laughing, he held his hand out for the weapon. "Sorry,

lady. I'm not authorized to give you any weapons. I'm just the qualifier. Actually, this isn't even one of our weapons. I just wish it were. It's a loaner, and I had permission to let you fire it."

"I'm so disappointed right now."

"How's the shoulder?"

"Don't ask."

"Hurts like a bitch, don't it?"

"Understatement of the year, sir."

"I'm sure those white coats will want to have a good look at you. Talk them into letting you pay us another visit. I'd appreciate another chance at talking you into defecting."

I laughed. "Some ally you are."

"If you ever change your mind..."

We had tried so many different weapons it took us almost an hour to check over the equipment and put it away. By the time we were finished, I was stifling yawn after yawn. To make matters worse, my stomach voiced complaints at my mistreatment of it.

The Glock was the only weapon that wasn't returned to the range's armory, and it took all my willpower to not stare at it in its holster, which Lieutenant Wilhelm draped over his shoulder.

"I should confiscate your weapon for poor transportation etiquette," I informed him.

He chuckled, shook his head, and guided me down a long hallway to a cafeteria.

My three doctors were seated at a table with Jake and his parents. I halted, blinked, and rubbed my eyes to confirm my head wasn't playing tricks on me.

Nothing changed.

"Huh. What are they doing here?"

"Who? Oh, the folks with the white coats?"

I pointed at Jake. "My partner." I turned my finger to his parents. "Parents of the partner."

"Ah, there's the owner of the Glock."

"What?" I shrieked, which captured everyone's attention. Instead of answering me, Lieutenant Wilhelm headed for the table, leaving me to stand around like an idiot or follow. "Well, shit."

I should have known; Glocks were the gun of choice for the FBI. Lieutenant Wilhelm offered the weapon and its holster to Pauline Thomas, who took it with a smile.

My mother-in-law owned the gun I wanted, and for a long moment, I contemplated how to get it out of her hands and into mine. Sighing my resignation, I strolled over.

Jake rose from his seat, his eyes narrowing as he inspected me from head to toe. "You're shaking."

While exhaustion played a big part in how much I trembled, so did the rush of handling more high-powered machinery in an afternoon than the FBI had let me operate in the entirety of my career. "Machine gun," I blurted. "*Rocket launcher.*"

Jake's eyes widened, and he jerked in Lieutenant Wilhelm's direction. "You let her use a rocket launcher?"

"A little one, and we fired it with blanks."

"Is there such a thing as a little rocket launcher?" Jake boomed.

"Jake." I grabbed his arm and tugged. "Jake, it was *beautiful.*"

"They said I could let her fire anything I thought she could handle," Lieutenant Wilhelm countered, pointing at the three doctors.

"I didn't think to ask if they had rocket launchers,"

Mellisa admitted. "I said no vehicles. Maybe I should have been more specific."

The psychologist didn't seem very concerned by her oversight.

"Did you enjoy yourself?" Pauline asked.

I sighed happily, closed my eyes, and savored the sore ache of muscles I had neglected for too long. I hurt, but I was free of the sling, I could use my right arm, and I could think without painkillers fogging my head.

"Karma?" Jake rested his hand on my left shoulder. "Are you okay?"

"What are you doing here, anyway?"

"You didn't come back to the hotel. I was worried."

"Machine gun," I told my partner. Did I really need to give more of an explanation?

"Why are you at a firing range?"

"You didn't ask that before you came here?" I peeked through my lashes and tilted my head to stare up at my partner. "Dr. Sampson required me to qualify with my left hand."

"Did you?"

I opened my eyes wide and stared at him. "You doubt me?"

"You're right handed."

I clacked my teeth. "I'm not speaking to you." I sat beside my psychologist and crossed my arms over my chest. The movement hurt, but my relief at having the freedom to do so outweighed the pain.

Jake followed me without letting me go. I wasn't about to admit it to anyone, but I enjoyed his touch.

"Do you think I'd let her handle a rocket launcher if she didn't qualify?" Lieutenant Wilhelm asked, his tone incredulous. "Of course she qualified. Her aim leaves a lot to be desired with the rocket launcher, though."

"You're supposed to aim them?" I blurted, staring at the man, widening my eyes to feign astonishment.

"If you defect, I promise you can fire the rocket launcher some more. Look on the bright side, you have a hell of a throw with your left hand, lady. You got some great distance with the grenades."

I couldn't help myself; I smiled. "Those were *so* satisfying."

"Grenades?" Jake boomed. "Are you *insane*?"

"You're not allowed to defect," Jake's mother informed me.

"Why do people keep telling me that?" I turned an accusatory glare at my three doctors. "You bring me to heaven and tell me I can't stay? That's mean."

"Grenades?" Jake's grip on my shoulder tightened.

"They're about this big," I said, using both hands to create the rough shape and size of a grenade. "When you pull the pin out and throw it, it explodes. The ones we were using made loud bangs and a bright flash."

"I know what a grenade is," Jake growled.

"Then why ask me?" I wrinkled my nose at him. To distract him, I showed him my right arm. "Look, Jake! No sling. I'm *free*."

"You're pale and shaking."

"It hurts like fucking *hell*, but I'm free, Jake. No more sling!" Euphoria at having a functional arm had me shifting my weight in my seat. "Jake, look. No sling."

"Jesus, what did you give her this time? So help me, if you gave her Demerol again..."

"For safety reasons, the painkillers were out of her system before we brought her onto the range. We confirmed residual quantities through blood testing before we left the hospital," Mr. Dr. Sampson reported. "I'm rather intrigued by her response to the lack of medication."

Mrs. Dr. Sampson grabbed my sling, which was lying on the table. "You should put the sling back—"

Ducking from beneath Jake's hand, I bolted out of my chair and headed for the door, determined to escape having to wear the confining sling ever again.

I MANAGED to evade Jake long enough to get outside before he caught up with me, tossed me over his shoulder, and carried me back to the cafeteria. I whimpered my protests between pants, ineffectively beating at his back.

"Put me down!"

"So you can run again? I don't think so." Jake secured his grip on me, one hand holding the back of my knees while the other gripped the back of my shirt. "What has gotten into you?"

I went limp over his shoulder. "I don't want to wear the sling."

"Your shoulder hurts like hell, doesn't it?"

"Don't you start with your damned logic, Jake. I've been wearing that thing for *weeks*."

"You've also spent most of those two weeks either unconscious, in a drugged stupor, or trying to kill everyone around you, thanks to them testing painkillers so you wouldn't become addicted to morphine. Strapping my wife to the bed so she doesn't commit homicide is not one of my favorite activities."

"If I don't remember it, it doesn't count."

Jake sighed, leaning his head against me. "What am I going to do with you?"

"Don't let them put me back in the sling. It's impossible to get off without help," I whispered.

"If the doctors say you wear the sling, you're wearing the sling, Karma."

"I refuse."

"You don't have a choice."

"That's unfair. It's my shoulder. I should be able to decide for myself if I wear the sling or not."

Jake carried me through the cafeteria, lowered me from his shoulder, and placed me on a chair, both of his big hands on my shoulders, pressing down hard.

It hurt like hell. Recognizing his tactic for what it was, I forced my sweetest smile despite the blood draining out of my face from the pain stabbing through my right shoulder.

Jake gave a little squeeze.

"You bastard," I hissed through clenched teeth, struggling to keep my smile fixed in place.

"Please forgive my partner," Jake said in his sweetest voice. "She seems to have an abundance of energy right now."

Clearing her throat, Jake's mother pulled her Glock out of its holster and systematically disassembled it, spreading the pieces across the table to examine each one in turn. I licked my lips and watched the woman's every move.

"Agent Thomas?"

I canted my head to listen to my psychologist. Jake replied, "Yes?"

"Just testing to see if she has come to terms with her marriage," Mellisa replied. "I'm a little concerned with her interest in Mrs. Thomas, however."

Jake leaned over, pressing his cheek to mine. "Until she has a weapon of her own, I'm pretty sure anyone carrying a firearm is going to be the subject of her interest. I may have had access to a gun for over a week—"

I sighed at the unfairness of it all, although I did understand.

"I haven't been carrying it, Karma. I specifically refused until you qualified and had your own firearm. What am I going to do with a gun in our room?"

"Shoot anyone who comes near me while I'm recovering."

"We have a security detail for that. We've had at least two armed shadows since the shooting."

I sighed again while Pauline reassembled the weapon before sliding a magazine into place. "It's so pretty."

Lieutenant Wilhelm cleared his throat. "Sorry to inter-rupt, but it does take a bit of time to fill out the paperwork. Dr. Sampson, if you'd please come with me?"

All three doctors rose to their feet and excused them-selves, leaving me with Jake and his parents. Pauline lifted the holster by its straps and swung the weapon back and forth.

I traced its gentle arc while Jake secured his hold on my shoulders. "I want it, Jake."

"I know you do. We'll get you your own soon," he soothed, letting go of my left shoulder to circle his arm over my chest. "Please don't do anything crazy, Karma. I don't want to get banned from flying back to the United States. I want to go home, and the sooner you're better—without sliding into a homicidal rage thanks to poorly chosen medications—the sooner we get to go home."

I straightened my back, pulling away from him enough I could stare into Jake's eyes. "When are we going home?"

"As soon as those three fiends clear you for air travel. You need to be able to last fifteen hours without—"

"Book us now," I demanded.

Jake gaped at me, blinking several times. "What?"

I flexed my hands, welcoming the pain in my shoulder. "I have some questions I want to ask once we're back in the United States," I ground out through clenched teeth.

Lowering the Glock to the table, Pauline released the weapon so she could prop her chin in her hand. She cleared her throat. "Have you forgotten I'm in upper management in the FBI, Karma?"

I narrowed my eyes at Jake's mother, wondering if I was prepared to cross a lot of lines. Did it matter if I was home or overseas?

The anger that sent me to the airport to buy a flight to Morocco revived. "I haven't forgotten."

"I can address any and all of your concerns."

"I would like to deal with my own problems without circumventing protocol and the chain of command." My first job would be to discover who had filed the complaint responsible for me having my firearm confiscated in the first place. Once I learned who and why, I'd figure out what I'd do about it.

I also had to think long and hard over the London shooting and sort out what were actual memories or hallucinations induced by blood loss. Without the drugs hampering my ability to think, I was puzzled no one had questioned me about what I knew of the shooting.

Then again, there were enough holes in my memories of the shooting and recovery it was entirely possible I had already been questioned without remembering a minute of it.

Jake chuckled and rested his chin on my shoulder. "You might buy your way into her good graces if you give her your gun, Mom. Otherwise, I'm not sure she'll bend in the slightest. When she gets like this, there's no point in fighting with her over it. She won't be happy until she has a chance to handle her problems on her own."

"Jake, why are you clinging to me?"

"I love my mother and do not want my beautiful wife killing her."

I frowned. "I thought we weren't supposed to discuss Ohio."

"A little too late for that. She found the marriage papers. She has absolutely no regard for personal property *or* my privacy, apparently."

"You brought them into my house, James Thomas. You only have yourself to blame. If you hadn't left your jacket on my floor, I wouldn't have found them." Jake's mother arched a brow.

"That was stupid, Jake."

"I know, but you'd run away from me. I was stressed and worried. Mom threatened to shoot me if I tried to leave the house. I didn't want to find out if she meant it."

Pauline snorted. "I did no such thing."

With a wicked grin, Jake's father clasped his hands in front of him on the table and leaned towards me. "She pistol whipped him when he tried to leave to find you. She's telling the truth. She didn't bother with the threats. She knocked him out cold and, to make sure he didn't cause her any more problems, she handcuffed him to the kitchen island. Then she told him he was banned from leaving the house to chase after you. He would have, too."

I gaped at Jake's mother. "You didn't!"

"She did," Jake grumbled, leaning his considerable weight on my back. I grunted and struggled to keep upright. "It was terrible. I was pistol whipped upside the head by my own mother. You should take pity on me."

"Why would I do that?" I sucked in a breath, my eyes widening. "Oh, God. Jake? Do my parents know?"

"I'm pretty sure they know."

"We're dead," I informed him.

"I'm pretty sure they intend to keep you alive. It's me I'm worried about. I've had to talk to them every day since they returned to the United States. I guess you don't remember trying to talk to them on the phone, do you?"

"I talked to them? What did I say?" I whispered.

"While I appreciate how much you adore me, Karma, did you really have to give them the details of our sex life?" Jake sighed. "I warned them not to put you on Demerol. I warned them what would happen. I *told* them you developed the most horrific language known on Earth. I told them you had no filters and had a tendency to become homicidal. If you aren't trying to kill someone, you're cursing them out and telling them exactly what you think. Did anyone listen to me? No. Your parents stopped asking to talk to you after that. I'm surprised they're still talking to me at all after learning *exactly* what we had been doing. Unfortunately, my parents were also in the room at the time, so even if they hadn't found the marriage certificate, you blew it."

I hung my head and groaned. "I've changed my mind. I'm going to find a place to hide and stay there until I die of old age."

"Everything will be okay," Jake promised.

I had my doubts, but I kept them to myself.

Chapter Thirty-Six

I REFUSED to wear the sling, and when Mr. Dr. Sampson threatened to jab me with a needle he pulled out of his coat and dose me with painkillers, it took Jake and his father working together to keep me from fleeing. Mrs. Dr. Sampson and Dr. Sampson watched in amusement.

"I'm rather awed, actually. You'd think we were trying to kill her," Mrs. Dr. Sampson observed. "Dear, stop tormenting the poor woman. I think it's obvious she's recovered sufficiently to decide if she wants painkillers. Prescribe pills and give them to her husband in case she needs them."

"Keep them away from me," I begged, grabbing Jake's shirt and twisting the material in my hands. "I try to kill people when they give me drugs. *Stop them.*"

"Could you please stop trying to make my wife kill people?" Jake demanded. "Leave her alone."

While I appreciated my partner snarling at the doctors in his effort to get them to leave, there was something disconcerting about the tension in his body and the way he was poised to act. I'd seen him in combat situations often enough to recognize the same alertness and readiness to take action.

For the first time since meeting him, I was relieved Jake wasn't armed.

"He might not be carrying right now, but my partner has a really mean right hook and watches my back," I stated, tightening my hold on Jake's clothes. "Please stop with the drugs. I don't want them. It doesn't hurt that much."

"All right, that's enough. She's made her opinion clear. Thank you for your help, doctors. I'll take it from here," Jake's mother announced, clapping her hands together. "If you could forward the documentation to the United States, I'll handle getting them home. I'll take care of the flight arrangements when we're ready to head back."

Mellisa chuckled. "I'll take care of it, Mrs. Thomas. Mom, Dad, let's go. I don't know about you two, but I *do* have other patients."

"You don't have to get mean about it, Mellisa," Mr. Dr. Sampson complained, capping the syringe.

"Why are you calling *me* mean? We're in the cafeteria of a British military installation. You're torturing an FBI agent because you can. At least I only torment people under orders. You're just getting in a last jab for the fun of it."

Jake, his mother, and his father groaned.

"You're encouraging her," I muttered.

"She's right, you know," my psychologist agreed with laughter in her voice. "Take care of yourself, Karma. I'll be checking in with you in a few weeks."

I sucked in a breath and brought my right hand to my chest. "Please, no."

Mellisa laughed, waved, and herded her parents to the door. The three doctors left, and I sighed my relief, leaning towards Jake and going limp against him. "Sweet baby Jesus, I never thought they'd stop."

Jake laughed. "I could really learn to like the Brits. They're trying so hard to be polite. Back home? Open betting."

"I'm pretty sure they were making bets; they're just more discreet about it. Up, up," Jake's mother ordered, clapping her hands together. "It's a bit of a drive back to the hotel."

Before I had a chance to get to my feet, Jake worked his hands beneath me and rose, picking me up. I gaped at him, clutching at his shirt so he wouldn't drop me. "Damnit, Jake!"

"But you're so pretty when you're angry."

"Just because you took advantage of your waivers to break the rules does not mean you get to openly fraternize at a government installation, James Thomas," his mother scolded. "Stop flirting and put her down."

Heaving a sigh, Jake set me on my feet. "We should elope, Karma. Run away while we can."

"We already tried that. You left the papers where your mother could find them," I reminded him, smoothing my clothes. Once I was presentable, I systematically stretched from head to toe. It wouldn't keep the stiffness at bay for long; I'd need to keep working to restore all I'd lost, but I didn't need a physical therapist to tell me the basics.

The stint at the firing range had done more than relieve stress. I resented how I tired so easily, I hated the weakness in my muscles, and I hated the knowledge I wasn't anywhere near my prime.

"Come along, kids. We'll have dinner at the hotel. Your forays to the hospital are enough to give your security detail nightmares. They're going to panic when they find out they have to protect you at the airport."

"What sort of doctors abandon their patient without checking to make sure she didn't ruin her shoulder firing a rocket launcher?" I demanded, stomping my foot. "And what sort of physical therapist doesn't even bother to give me a schedule or exercises?"

"Karma likes her physical therapy strict, routine, and under a defined schedule. She will also expect me to be at every session. If she has to suffer, so do I."

Pauline herded us towards the exit. "If you're quite done playing, let's go. We have things to do."

IT TOOK an hour to reach the castle. I would have preferred a chance to shower and change, but Jake's mother was on a mission. British hospitality only went so far, and I was well aware of the other diners in the hotel's elegant restaurant staring at me.

I didn't blame them. Gunpowder, oil from handling firearms, and sweat caked me in equal proportions. Black marks stained my hands, and I fled to the bathroom to scrub the worst of them away.

Pauline tailed me as though worried I'd climb out the window and make a run for it. If I could have fit, I might've tried.

"How is your shoulder feeling?"

I glanced at the window and sighed. My relationship with my mother-in-law hadn't started on the best foot, and my being responsible for her son's close brush with death didn't help matters any.

Dr. Sampson was right. I'd have to face everything eventually, including making sense of my fragmented memories.

"It hurts, but it's tolerable." Tolerable was a flexible word. I wasn't really lying; until I was at the point I was crying or screaming from the pain, I'd be able to cope.

"My son told me you don't remember much about what happened."

I shrugged and winced at the increased throbbing. I stared at my hands and scrubbed, hoping the sink wouldn't be too much of a mess when I was finished. The soap wasn't as good at cutting through the mess as I liked. "No one has questioned me yet?"

Laughing, Jake's mother grabbed a towel from the basket beside the sink and held it out to me. I took an extra minute and made one last ditch effort to get any remaining residue off in the hope the linen wouldn't end up ruined. "If you haven't been asleep, you've been either screaming profanities or attempting murder. Who knew you had such adverse and unique reactions to medications?"

"Jake knows. I definitely don't remember any of that."

"He knew about the Demerol, but not the others. He did try to warn them."

I was still amazed they had managed to get Jake to leave the room. My fragments of memory supported my belief my partner had resisted every attempt to evict him from our room. His absence had probably been necessary so the three doctors could experiment with my medications without him getting in the way.

I'd have to thank him for his efforts later.

"Is it true my parents have been talking to Jake?"

The woman's sigh worried me. "I'm sorry, Karma. I'm pretty sure after the call when you were on Demerol, they're just going through the motions to maintain appearances. You... were very vocal."

I took the towel, turned, and leaned against the sink, watching Pauline. The woman's expression was serious, and I really didn't like the hint of pity in her eyes. "Explain, please."

"Well, I learned you were *really* upset that your mother had slapped my son. I mean, I can't say I haven't taken my shots at the little shit. I did pistol whip him and handcuff him in my kitchen, after all. Now, granted, I was preventing him from committing a string of crimes certain to land him in a lot of trouble. He's usually good at curbing his reckless impulses, but not when it comes to you. He forgave me for restraining him after a couple of days. Anyway, you were very, very detailed about your relationship with him. While I'm quite proud of my child, there are some things a mother doesn't need to know—his skills in bed are near the top of the list. Then you explained, at length, how there was nothing wrong with him, and that he didn't need to have the sin beat out of him, too."

I felt the blood drain out of my face and work its way down to my feet, leaving me cold and shivering. "Oh, shit."

"You then explained, in detail, how you intended to deal with anyone who put their hands on your husband. It was very graphic, and that was about the time my son attempted to intervene. I did find it rather amusing you claimed it was your exclusive right to drill a hole in his toe and rip his intestines out through it. Do I even want to know? I was very impressed by how determined you were to start killing people. Sebastian had to help contain you. At that point, I decided it might be a good time to hang up the phone."

I tossed the towel in the bin with the rest of the dirtied linens. "I really don't remember any of that."

"The general consensus was that you likely wouldn't

remember. Your doctors gave a long explanation, but I ignored most of it. I couldn't spell half the words they were using, which made looking them up in the dictionary difficult."

"I can only imagine."

"I'd like you to answer one question for me, Karma. I'll leave you alone about the rest unless you want to talk about it."

There was only one good thing about the conversation; I could mark off a bathroom interrogation by my partner's mother from my bucket list. Bracing myself for the worst, I replied, "Ask away."

"What did you mean when you told your mother my son didn't need the sin beaten out of him?"

I had stepped into my personal hell, and I couldn't see a single way out of admitting the truth. While I could have refused to answer, I got the feeling Pauline wouldn't let it go until she found out what had happened when I had been a child.

In a way, the idea of telling someone lifted a weight off my shoulders. Telling her the truth wouldn't hurt me.

After all, they had only been dreams.

"I wasn't an easy child," I replied, shrugging. "Ma and Pops were determined to raise a little princess."

"That is never a reason to beat a child."

"I bit Pops hard enough to draw blood. I don't really remember it, but that was the same day I got bit by a fox and ended up needing rabies shots." I shrugged. "I deserved to have my hide tanned."

"Then why phrase it as having the sin beaten out of you?"

Tilting my head to the side, I tried to figure out what

Jake's mother was trying to hint at. "Because we lived in Georgia?"

She blinked. "Georgia?"

"Ma believes in wearing her Sunday best to church. How else would I phrase it?"

Some things Jake's mother didn't need to know, and the fact I had dreamed of becoming a fox was one of them. For all I knew, she might want to beat the sin out of me, too. But despite everything, I felt the need to defend my ma. "I wasn't an easy child to raise. Apparently, I was pretty obsessed with foxes, and I liked imitating the sounds they made. Not a good combination when Ma and Pops took us to church every service. There's nothing more to it than that."

DINNER WENT BY IN A BLUR. I ached, my shoulder hurt, but my worries over Jake's mother believing Ma and Pops no longer wanted anything to do with me consumed my thoughts. I ate enough to appease Jake and spent the rest of the meal moving my potatoes around my plate while pretending to pay attention to the conversation around me.

Near the end of the meal, while Jake and his parents were engaged in a debate over procedures for handling violent crimes, I excused myself and headed to the bathroom.

To my relief, Pauline didn't follow me. I dug my personal phone out of my pocket, still amazed it had survived through my stay in London. The only way I'd find out if Jake's mother was right about my parents was if I called.

It was a little like having a tooth pulled. The longer I waited, the harder it'd be when the time came to get it over with. I wanted to say it wasn't my fault, but while the medication had brought down my walls, I had spoken the truth.

I dialed home and connected the call before I fell prey to cowardice.

On the third ring, Ma answered, "Hello?"

"Hi, Ma."

"What do you want, Karma Clarice Thomas?"

I winced at the anger in my ma's voice, but the painful part was the removal of her last name from mine. Ma was the type who never let someone escape; she had once been eager to have a chance to four-name me.

"I just wanted to call and let you know I'll be coming back to the States in a few days."

"I see."

The static hum of a live line was the only indication she hadn't hung up on me. I swallowed, at a loss for what to say.

"Is there something you actually wanted?"

I wanted my ma back, but I didn't need to see the fire to smell the smoke. "That was all. Sorry to bother you."

She hung up.

I shouldn't have been surprised. Ma and Pops were proud. They fostered kids, and all I'd done was shatter the illusion of their perfect family. To make matters worse, I had done so in front of three members of the FBI.

If Social Services hadn't come knocking at their door for an interview, I'd be very surprised. Pauline had her dirty secrets, too, including pistol whipping her son to keep him out of trouble. Handcuffing him to the kitchen island put her on a whole different level. There was one key difference, and the more I thought about it, the deeper I sank into my misery.

Jake was a full-grown man who could defend himself and handle his mother however he saw fit.

I had been five.

Considering Jake's father was directly involved in CARD's general operations, I couldn't imagine the Thomas family letting go of what they'd learned about my childhood. Like me, protecting children was in their blood.

Lowering my phone from my ear, I stared at the device for a long moment, then took the ten minutes to cancel my phone's plan and deactivate the account. The frustrating conversation with a man with heavily accented English and limited vocabulary distracted me enough I avoided crying.

Just to make certain the number wouldn't come back to haunt me, I took out the SIM card, bent it in half, and tossed it in the trash. The phone joined it a few moments later. I washed my hands for the sake of appearances, forced a neutral expression, and returned to the table.

The Thomas family was still arguing about procedures, and I wasn't sure they had noticed my departure or return. I waited for a lull in the conversation before asking, "Want to go on a walk tonight, Jake?"

My partner stared at me before offering a small smile. "Sure."

"Armed and with your detail," Sebastian ordered.

Jake sighed. "Yes, sir. Do you want to go now? Might give us a chance to escape before they start asking for your opinion. Once they get started, they never quit."

Grateful for a chance to get some space and fresh air, I nodded. "If you'll excuse us?"

"Enjoy your walk, kids," Pauline said, waving her hand to dismiss us. "Take your phones with you. Karma?"

"Yes, ma'am?"

Pauline reached under the table, grabbed her oversized purse, pulled her holstered Glock out of it, and offered it to me. "I don't think I need to remind you it isn't a toy, right?"

Clearing his throat, Jake shook his head, likely in an attempt to warn his mother if she gave me her gun she'd never get it back.

Before the woman could change her mind, I reached over the table and secured a hold on the leather straps. "You don't, ma'am. I'll be careful with it."

After I walked off the worst of my misery, I'd take her gun back to the room, dismantle it, and lovingly clean every piece. With luck, Jake's mother would forget I had it. If I kept it out of sight, maybe she wouldn't remember.

Hip holsters were substantially more comfortable than the shoulder one I used when I needed to conceal a weapon.

Pauline meant for me to be obviously armed, and I appreciated the extra layer of protection. With a sigh, Sebastian unbuckled his holster and offered it to Jake. "Han shot first. If anyone comes calling, son, you be like Han."

"I'll be careful," my partner promised. After he buckled his father's holster in place, he linked his arm with mine, careful to stay to my left side. "We probably won't be too long."

"Take your time, kids. Check in every now and then," his mother ordered.

We escaped while we could.

Chapter Thirty-Seven

I WANTED TO RUN, and it took far too much willpower to walk at a sedate pace. Without the medication dragging me down, an abundance of restless energy worked its way through me.

When it wore off, I'd crash and burn hard, but I wanted to earn every bit of soreness in my muscles. The need to be doing something had me fidgeting despite my best efforts to remain calm.

Jake chuckled, freed his arm from mine, and drummed his fingers against the middle of my back. "You're a short fuse ready to blow right now, aren't you?"

"I don't want to push my luck." I'd already pushed it enough at the firing range, handling weaponry with enough recoil to stagger a horse. If I wasn't already bruised, I'd be black, blue, and green by morning, especially along my left shoulder, which had taken the most punishment.

"Did you really fire a rocket launcher?"

"I think it was made to disable or destroy tanks. It was like a grenade launcher, but so much better."

"He let you work with a grenade launcher, too, didn't he?"

"We could defect."

"We're not defecting, but I'm grateful you're considering me in your plans to commit treason."

With the disastrous phone call with my ma still fresh in my mind, I understood Jake was all I had left. "Of course I'd consider you in my plans to commit treason."

Jake worked his arm around me and tugged me to his side. Despite our difference in height, I fit with him, and while I lengthened my stride to match his, he shortened his to match mine. A year ago, if anyone had told me I would enjoy being so close to my partner, I would have laughed at them.

I should have felt awkward, but he had as much to do with my sense of security as the presence of his mother's gun against my hip.

"If it makes you feel better, I'll listen to your proposal for defecting."

"Jake, two words: rocket launcher."

"I bet Mom could hook us up with an instructor and a rocket launcher if we asked her really nicely."

I frowned. "Are you being serious?"

"I don't want to defect, Karma. We haven't been here long, and I'm already dying for a good steak. The Brits just don't get steak. Some of the food here is fantastic, but they commit crimes against steak. That's a deal breaker for me."

Laughing, I shook my head. "You've always enjoyed a good steak."

"That's right. I love a good steak, and I haven't had one

here yet. We can't defect. I'm sorry. Anyway, we have to go back to work."

The last thing I wanted to talk about was returning to work with the FBI. With my shoulder hurting as much as it did, I wouldn't be ready for field work anytime soon, which only added to my misgivings. I wasn't even certain I wanted to return to the FBI, in the field or otherwise.

"There's going to be an interview regarding my resignation at some point in the future, which is going to be coupled with another evaluation." Clacking my teeth from a mixture of disgust and frustration, I increased my pace, forcing Jake to lengthen his stride.

"I get to have an evaluation before I can return to active duty, too. Apparently getting shot four times put me on the fast track for one."

"Just don't let them take you to a secondary location. They might try to dissect you to figure out how you're still alive. Actually, I need to watch out for that, too. When they see my x-rays, I'll be on the short-list for a dissection."

"Something wrong with your x-rays?"

"No."

"Then I don't understand the problem."

"That *is* the problem, Jake. There's nothing wrong with my x-rays." I pointed at the bandage covering my right shoulder. "The bullet should have pulverized my shoulder. It should have left a fragmented mess of bone. I should have pins, rods, and screws or whatever it is they use to piece someone's shattered shoulder back together. The bullet went through me and my shoulder blade."

"And you don't," my partner stated, and I was aware he was agreeing with me rather than asking a question.

"Today's x-rays showed no evidence I'd been shot at all.

Nothing. There's not even a single one of those shadowy lines or blurry spots or anything. They showed me the x-ray. It's like I hadn't been shot, except I have this healing hole through me."

"Did your doctors seem worried?"

I frowned. "Well, no."

"So why are you worried? You're healing well. You qualified to carry a firearm again. My mother trusts you enough to give you her weapon so we could go on a walk without having them breathing down our necks. You're going to pass your evaluations just fine. What's the issue? Most people would be overjoyed they're healing so well."

"It's impossible. You've seen what happens to people when they're shot. I should still be in a cast, probably still in the hospital, looking forward to six months to a year to *possibly* recover enough to return to field duty. You, too. This is obvious evidence we're dead. Maybe I'm actually in a coma in a hospital somewhere."

Jake huffed. "You're being ridiculous again."

"You're the one being ridiculous."

"I am not."

"You're being ridiculous, Jake. This isn't possible."

"You're not dead, in a coma in the hospital, or hallucinating. What do I need to do to convince you? You're healing fast, that's all."

"I have a fully functional shoulder when I really shouldn't. You, too."

"Hey, leave my shoulder out of this. I'm quite happy with how mine has healed, thank you very much." Jake huffed again. "Don't put me in a coma or grave again, especially not having to deal with you on Demerol. I never wanted to kill someone as much as I did that stupid doctor.

Demerol, Karma. I dealt with you on Demerol. You owe me."

I narrowed my eyes. "You know I don't remember anything, Jake."

"I thought it was bad when you chewed on my desk and tried to kill everyone at the office. You were even worse." Coughing, Jake covered his mouth with his hand. He snorted. "Dad was shocked. It was one of the few times in my life I've ever seen my mother speechless."

"Was it my language or the violence this time?" I grumbled.

It was probably what they had learned about my childhood, but I wasn't ready to talk about that quite yet.

"You know I love you, Karma."

"I may have the romantic instincts of a rock, but even I recognize when something does not sound promising."

Jake laughed, faced me, and lifted me up by my waist, pulling me to him.

Squeaking from a mixture of shock and fear, I wrapped my arms around his neck and clamped my legs around his waist, clinging so he wouldn't drop me. "Don't do that. Put me down, Jake!"

"I was not expecting you to imitate a koala, but I like the results. Now I have you nice and close, right where I want you—and at eye level."

It was true, we were at eye level, and as always, his rich brown eyes derailed my train of thought. "Damn you and your pretty eyes, Jake."

"You could just shut up and kiss me," he countered.

I didn't have to think about it for very long. Kissing Jake was something I could get used to very quickly. I lowered my gaze to his mouth, which was curved in a smile. "I could."

"You should."

I made a show of thinking about it, shifting my gaze away from him and into the woods. Something in the trees caught my attention, and I stiffened, my hands flexing and grabbing hold of his shirt.

"What's wrong?"

"Just something in the woods," I replied, remaining tense and wary. "Do they have bears here?"

"I have no idea. They don't have rabies, though. Do you remember that?"

I scowled at the memory of my ma telling Jake and his parents about the vixen biting my shoulder, resulting in a move to Vermont and rabies shots. "Unfortunately."

Working his hands under the back of my shirt, he teased my skin, pressing his lips to my cheek. "You're worrying about the wrong animal. I heard you very clearly tell everyone I'm a beast in bed."

"We're not in bed, Jake," I reminded him.

"We could improvise."

I snorted. "I'm pretty sure there are people watching us."

"I'm strangely okay with them knowing without a doubt you belong to me."

"We have wedding rings for that."

Somehow, our rings had survived intact, although mine had required a thorough cleaning. I wasn't sure when they'd been returned, and I was genuinely surprised they hadn't been kept as evidence.

"Now you're just being mean."

Wherever the animal had gone, I couldn't spot it, but I kept searching the forest for a sign of it. "But Jake, there's an animal."

"A less secure man would probably be really offended right now."

"Why?"

"I have my hands up your shirt while trying my very hardest to get you to kiss me." Jake kissed his way along my jaw, and I tightened my hold on him, well aware he was trying to make me squirm. I was determined to resist him, at least long enough to see the local wildlife. "You're ignoring my kisses. That's not fair."

"But I want to see the animal," I complained. If he was going to tease me, I'd pay him back for it. "There is also no way I said you were a beast in bed."

"You really like what I do to you when you're handcuffed. That counts."

I did, and I probably should have been at least a little embarrassed by that fact. "I'm not sure what you're talking about, Jake."

"You just want me to remind you," he accused. "You want to use me, don't you?"

I did want him to remind me, and the truth of it made me happy. "Yes. Now, shh. You're going to scare off the animal."

"Aren't you supposed to be afraid of heights?"

"Are you going to drop me?"

"I'm not sure I could. You have a death grip on me."

The woods remained still and quiet, and I sighed my disappointment. "This is your fault, Jake. I wanted to see the animal."

"I would ask if you were under the influence of narcotics, but I know you're not, which is actually disturbing me. You don't like the woods. Slugs live in the woods. If you want to see animals so badly, I'll take you to the zoo. I have a better idea; I'll take us back to our room." He growled in my ear. "I'll show you how much of a beast I can be."

I bit my lip so I wouldn't grin—or worse, giggle. "Do you want something, Jake?"

"You, obviously. We're really going to have to work on this."

"But I'm right here," I replied, careful to keep my voice neutral.

"You sly vixen. You're toying with me, aren't you?"

I turned my attention away from the forest, gave him a quick kiss, and pulled away before he could react. "Yes."

"You win this round. I will behave until I have you back in our room. All bets are off then, though. My handcuffs are in there, and I think I need to put them to good use." Jake slid his hands out from beneath my shirt. "All right. Back on your feet, you."

If Jake thought I was going to jump down, he was crazier than I thought. "It's too high."

"I'd remind you it's only a foot or so you have to slide down, but there's no way you're going to jump, is there?"

"Not a chance. You picked me up, you put me down."

"All right, all right."

I took one last look at the woods using the extra foot of height. I tightened my hold on Jake's shirt, preparing for the moment he'd either lean forward or stoop so I could get my feet under me.

That was when the wolf stepped out of the trees. It bared its fangs, and its silence frightened me far more than its size.

"Jake."

"What?"

"I found the animal," I whispered, plucking at his shirt

while every one of my instincts screamed at me to run right up the nearest tree.

Trees were safe. Wolves couldn't climb trees. There were trees all around the path. All I needed was to make it the handful of steps off the trail to reach one.

Jake snorted. "It's a slug, isn't it?"

Fear had a way of making things seem far worse than they were, and the wolf was far too large and close for my comfort. I couldn't even tell what color its coat was; my attention was focused on its long fangs, which it showed off.

I'd dreamed of being a fox too many times. I knew what those teeth could do to me if it sank them in my thin skin. Without fur to protect me, I had no hope of facing off against a hunting wolf.

Angry wolves growled. Hungry, hunting wolves didn't make a sound. They stalked, they waited for the perfect moment, and then they ate their prey or goaded them into running. In my dreams, I escaped wolves by either diving into holes too small for them to follow or by bolting up a tree. My claws differentiated me from my lesser fox cousins; mine were hooked, and they let me climb high to safety.

Wolves couldn't climb trees, but I could.

Releasing my hold on Jake, I dropped. The instant my feet hit the trail, I headed for the nearest tree.

I heard Jake call my name, but I didn't slow. The bark scraped my hands and tore at my nails, but the pain was minor in comparison to the stabbing in my shoulder. Clawing my way upward, I didn't stop until there was nowhere left to go. With a whimper, I clung to the trunk, closed my eyes, and waited for the wolf to lose interest.

JAKE WAS SOMEWHERE FAR BELOW, and he was laughing at me. "How can someone so terrified of heights be so good at climbing trees?"

"The wolf's going to eat you," I hissed.

"No, she's not. Really, she's not going to eat me."

"How do you know it's a she? *It's a wolf, and it's hungry.*"

"What makes you think she's hungry?"

"Bared teeth, no snarling. Hunting wolves are quiet. They growl or snarl or snap their teeth when they're warning away other predators or driving wolves from their territory. If their pack is around, they'll do it when they're inciting their prey to run. It was obviously waiting for its pack so we couldn't escape. It didn't want us to run too early."

Jake snorted. "So you abandoned all sense and climbed a tree, leaving me to get eaten by a wolf."

"I'll miss you, Jake."

"You are such a bitch, Karma. First, you sacrifice me to your mother, now you're trying to sacrifice me to a wolf? Is that all I am to you? A living shield?"

If he wanted to play those cards, I had cards I could play, too. "When you're not serving as my living shield, you're a ridiculously handsome sex object—mine, in case you weren't certain. I need to get full value for my investment. It's not my fault you're too stupid to run from the wolf!"

"Wow, Karma. I'm not even sure what to say to that. On one hand, I'm never sure my pride will recover from such cruel objectification. On the other hand, I'm very, very interested in the benefits of being your ridiculously handsome sex object. Too bad I can't write 'Sex Slave' on my business cards. I'm strangely okay with being your sex slave. Will I be well rewarded for being very good or very bad?"

555555555555

"You will never know because you're about to get eaten by a wolf."

Jake laughed. "Before I'm terribly mauled, could you at least explain why you climbed up a tree?"

"Wolves can't climb trees," I hissed.

"Yet you, who is absolutely terrified of heights, climbed up that tree like you were born in one. I'm actually awed. I had no idea you were that agile."

"When I'm running away from a wolf determined to eat me, you better believe I'm agile."

"You're making assumptions. First, you're assuming the wolf is hungry. She's really not. She already had dinner. Second, she doesn't want to maul me. She adores me."

I could only think of one reason for Jake to be familiar enough with the wolf to know if she was hungry or not. "Sweet baby Jesus, Jake. Who have you been feeding to the wolf?"

"How the hell did you jump to that conclusion?"

"How else do you know if she's hungry unless you've been feeding her?"

"Shouldn't you be asking *what* I've been feeding her instead of *who*?"

"That's a confession. You've been waiting to take me to a secondary location so you could feed me to a wolf." I wiggled closer to the trunk, wincing when the branch I was straddling creaked. "Oh, sweet baby Jesus. My partner is going to feed me to a wolf. I hate wolves. I hate them. Their breath is disgusting, they can't keep their tongues to themselves, and they eat foxes."

"I'm not even sure where to begin. I'm not going to feed you to her or any wolf. I spent far too long hunting you down to feed you to a wolf."

"Wait, you lured me to a secondary location so *you* could eat me?" I wailed.

"I hunted you down so I could *marry* you, you idiot!"

"Who are you calling an idiot, idiot? You're the one who's still down there where the wolf can eat you."

"Son, would you please explain what is going on here?" Jake's father asked.

I groaned, bumping my forehead against the tree's rough bark. "Why? Why? Not only did he lure me to a secondary location, he brought in someone who could help him hide my body. I trusted you!"

"Damn it, Karma! I'm not going to feed you to a wolf. Why do you think a wolf is going to eat you?"

"Wolves are evil, that's why. If they don't kill you right away, they'll drag you off, lick you until they get bored, and *then* they'll eat you. That wolf is just waiting until she's bored. Once she is, she's going to eat you *and* your father. Why did you let him lure you to a secondary location, Mr. Thomas?"

"Good luck with her, son. You're going to need it. "

"Thanks, Dad." Jake sighed. "Would you care to explain this? Is there a reason you helped terrify my wife up a tree? She's absolutely hysterical, and I don't mean in the funny way."

Unable to stop it from emerging, I made a noise the blend of whimper and moan. "Just get away from the wolf before she eats you, Jake. I don't want you to get eaten by a wolf."

"Karma, she's not going to eat me."

"Not today at least," Jake's father added.

"I'm pretty sure you're not helping, Dad. You drove her up there. Figure out how the fuck we're getting her down."

"I'm assuming we'll climb up there, pistol whip her if she puts up a fight, and carry her down."

"Why does your solution to every problem have to include pistol whipping someone?"

I sighed. Had the wolf caught me before I had gotten up the tree? Blood loss was the only reasonable explanation I could think of for my situation.

"Says the little shit who got written up for pistol whipping his partner across her ass."

"Can we not do this right now?"

"It's not my fault your mother wanted to see what your cute little vixen would do. I really didn't think she'd actually climb a tree."

"Let me see if I understand this correctly: Mom, you wanted to see what my partner would do, so you gave her your fucking fully automatic handgun and sent her out into the woods, where you then deliberately tried to scare the life out of her? Dad, you encouraged her to do it, didn't you? Have you lost your mind?"

Jake's father snorted. "Try to be reasonable, son."

"You helped scare her up a fucking tree! I see no need to be reasonable."

"You're overreacting. The grounds are clear, and frankly, I'd *really* like to go on a hunt tonight. We're taking your woman with us, so get your scrawny ass up the tree and fetch her so we can go on a hunt."

There was a long moment of silence. Jake spluttered, "You want to *what?*"

"You heard me."

"No, I'm pretty sure I did not hear you correctly." Jake growled, and the sound was so wolf-like I shivered and clung tighter to the tree, every muscle in my body quivering from tension.

Why couldn't I climb any higher? I whimpered, cracked open an eye, and examined the narrow branch overhead, wondering if it would support my weight. A little higher would help me stay out of the wolf's clutches, as well as keep away from the two men insane enough to want to hunt with one.

"Family hunt. Now. Go fetch your woman. I'm hungry, and I'm tired of dainty British dinners. We're going hunting, and we're going hunting now."

Chapter Thirty-Eight

THE TREE CREAKED AND SWAYED. Reminding myself wolves couldn't climb trees wasn't enough to stop me from whimpering. My skin crawled as I imagined my final moments, which involved bouncing from branch to branch before smacking into the ground below.

"It's just me, Karma," Jake said, and his voice came from right below me. A moment later, he patted my leg. "It's safe to come down, I promise. I'll muzzle that damned wolf and lock her in a—"

"You will do no such thing, James Thomas," Jake's father barked.

"I'll muzzle you, too, asshole!"

"Don't you start with me, you little shit. You have to come down from there eventually."

"I'll lock you both in a cage, and if you're lucky, I might remember to feed you," my partner bellowed.

"I do not understand why you're being such a child about this."

"You scared my partner—my *wife*—up a tree. How can you not see the problem with this?"

I mourned for the calm quiet of my life. "I thought being disowned was bad, but I married into a family of lunatics." Sighing over my poor choices, I relaxed my hold on the tree, slumping in defeat. "I'm going to get eaten by a wolf. Of all the ways to die, it'll be in Britain, eaten by a wolf. I'm so sad, Jake."

"You're taking this a little too far," Jake complained. "Cut me some slack here. Look, I haven't been mauled or anything."

I risked stealing a glance at my partner. His head was beside my leg, and his face was wet. "Wolf slobber. On your face. She was tenderizing you for later consumption."

"Could you please explain why you're convinced you're about to get eaten?"

Sighing, I stared at Jake. "Wolves are predators. They eat anything they can catch. When they catch foxes, they eat them. What sort of animal eats a fox?"

"A hungry one," he replied.

"That's exactly my point. When that wolf gets hungry or bored, she'll eat us."

"This might be even funnier than watching her on Demerol," Jake's father called out.

"You're not helping, Dad."

"It's not my fault you picked a vixen. Not my fault at all. I was sensible and picked a good bitch. You? No. Despite all my best efforts, you're going to spend the rest of your life fetching your vixen out of trees."

"Did he just call your mother a bitch?" I blurted. Blinking, I thought over what Jake's father had said. "And why is he calling me a vixen? That's creepy, Jake. You should file a request for him to have a psychiatric evaluation."

"If you come down, I'll explain everything," Jake promised.

"No way in fucking hell. There's a wolf down there."

"I know."

"She'll eat me."

"She won't eat you."

I snapped my teeth together. "You're lying to me."

"I am not!"

"Prove it."

"If you won't come down, how am I supposed to prove it?"

Jake slid his hand up my leg and grabbed hold of his mother's holster.

I snarled at him, but it didn't stop him from taking the weapon. "You fucking bastard. Give that back!"

"If you want it back, come get it," Jake challenged, descending out of my reach.

A whimper escaped my throat, and I closed my eyes. Without Jake blocking my view of the ground, it was a long, long way down. "I'll die up here."

"If you make sure the chamber is empty and dump the magazine, you could pistol whip her with it," Jake's father suggested.

"I married into a family of assholes," I wailed.

"Wolves are assholes," Jake's father agreed. "But I don't really like the taste of fox, so you're safe, little vixen."

"Wait, what?"

"Dad," Jake protested, and his voice sounded weak.

"If you're not going to be a man and tell her, I will."

"What happened to easing her into this? Dad, this is *not* easing her into anything."

"Don't start with me, you little shit. Your mother didn't even snarl. All she did was show a little teeth. Give me a break; it's not my fault your vixen has an overactive flight instinct."

"Dad, wolves eat foxes in the wild. We're the ones being unreasonable here. Can you stop antagonizing her? Please?"

"Can we stop talking about this?" I shrieked. "Stop calling me a vixen."

"So come down here and correct me to my face," Jake's father shouted back. "Bring it, if you can. If you can't handle one little she-wolf, you're not woman enough for *my* pup."

"*Little?*" Fury burned at me, deep in my bones. I clacked my teeth, raging at the implication I wasn't a good enough partner for Jake. I screamed my anger and frustration, my world narrowing to my desire to claw the man's face off.

I had no recollection of climbing out of the tree, but my feet were on firm ground, and I launched myself at Jake's father, fingers curled into claws, ready to gouge his eyes out with my nails. Plowing into me from the side, Jake wrapped his arms around me, pinned my elbows to my sides, and picked me up.

"I'll kill him!" I screamed.

"If this is how she behaved when she was little, I think I understand better why Mrs. Johnson took the approach she did," Jake's father announced, his tone wry. "It seems foxes are just as territorial as wolves. I'm afraid you're stuck with her, son."

"Stuck?" Jake snarled, tightening his hold on me. Twisting around, I snapped my teeth at him in my effort to break free of his grip. Jake lowered his chin to protect his throat. "Karma, will you please stop? You can't kill Dad. Maybe he deserves it, but you can't kill him. Dad, stop making her want to kill you."

"It's like she has a little switch. If you flip it, she starts running on pure instinct. How do you turn her off?"

"How the hell would I know?" Jake bellowed.

A snuffling behind me had the hairs on the back of my neck rising, and I struggled in Jake's arms. He held me so tight I could barely breathe. I squeaked.

"Mom, don't you dare even think about pouncing me from behind." The snarls rumbling in Jake's chest made me tense, and I stilled in anticipation of having to react, flexing my hands. "Damn it, what is wrong with you two?"

"I got her out of the tree, didn't I?"

"Dad!"

"Well, I did."

"It's your fault she climbed up the tree in the first place."

"Actually, it's your mother's fault. I just came along to watch. Who am I to tell your mother she can't do something?"

"Karma's right. You *are* an asshole."

"Wait, what?" I demanded, my eyes widening. "What did you just say?"

"Dad's an asshole. I'm sorry, Karma."

"Not that." A tremor ran through me. "The wolf belongs to your mother?"

Jake sighed. "No, Karma. The wolf *is* my mother."

I HAD no memory of how I escaped Jake's hold on me, but there was blood on my hands and the taste of it was fresh in my mouth. My entire body throbbed, and my shoulder hurt the worst. The need to run surged through me, and I panted in my effort to catch my breath.

There was no way Jake's mother was a wolf. The impossibility of it partnered with my awareness I wasn't alone in the woods and drove me on. Wolves couldn't climb trees, but Jake could, and he had joined forces with *wolves*.

How could he dare side with *wolves*?

Once I made sure the wolves were gone, I was going to have a long talk with Jake about his choice of bad jokes. Then I'd bite him. Once I was done biting him, I had a lot of other ideas of what I'd do to him, and he'd probably enjoy them. I would.

My desire to drag him to bed confused me, filled me with lust and other conflicting emotions, and made me want to bite him even harder. The damned dreams were back again. That was the only explanation.

Whenever I dreamed of foxes, I wanted to bite. Ma had been right to beat the sin out of me. Biting led to nothing good.

I licked my lips, disconcerted the blood made me crave something more than running through the forest as a human. I wanted fur. I wanted to hunt. The dreams of hunting as a fox had infected me again, and the need to call for the skulk I didn't have itched in my throat.

Neither human nor fox could withstand a hunting wolf. I clacked my teeth, sucked in a deep breath, and ran through the trees. I searched the shadows for a place to hide. With distance, any tree would do, though one with a thick canopy to mask my presence would help.

A stream, deep enough to wash away my trail and scent, was ideal. Deep, but not too deep.

The water would welcome me and hide me, but it'd also drown me if I let it.

I smelled the water before I saw it, an undertone of the rich loam of the forest. I sniffed in my effort to pinpoint its direction, slowing my stride. I chittered my annoyance, taking another breath.

A twig snapped behind me, and I spun, but not in time to prevent Jake's father from plowing into me and slamming me to the ground. I shrieked and struggled beneath him, but he captured my wrists in one of his large hands, holding them over my head while using his legs to pin the rest of me down.

"Got you," he crowed.

Instead of words, chattering cries burst from my throat.

"Vicious little thing, aren't you? Quit struggling. It's pointless."

The man's laughter stoked my fury, and I fought to get a hold of him with my teeth.

"You're going to hurt yourself. I've been pinning that puppy of mine since he was old enough to put up a fight. Also, I bite back. Settle down. All struggling is going to do is tire you out, hurt your shoulder, and delay the inevitable. This is how this is going to work. Pauline's going to come say hello, and you're going to submit like a good little vixen. Once you learn she's not going to eat you, we'll figure out the rest. You may as well calm down and accept it."

I panted, showing him my teeth in a promise to bite him as hard as I could once I was able to reach him. Running seemed like my wisest option, but Jake's father had a grip of steel, and his knee jammed against my stomach hampered my ability to take deep breaths.

"You're going to bite the shit out of me if I loosen my

hold, aren't you? Pauline? Our son picked a crazy one. I'm pretty sure this is your fault."

I recognized the brindled white and gold wolf from my dream, and I tensed at her approach. When I had been a fox, protected by my thick winter coat, her size had frightened me. Trapped and unable to escape, cold terror swept through me and left me shaking.

Unable to run, my only option was to stay perfectly still, afraid to even breathe.

"Easy. She's not going to hurt you. Remember the whole 'too good of an FBI agent to lose' discussion we had? It goes against my interests to feed you to my wife—yes, my wife, who happens to be my mate, who also happens to be a beautiful wolf—this specific wolf, if you weren't certain."

I wasn't at all comforted by the man's words, not with a huge wolf breathing in my face, her sharp, massive teeth within snapping range. The brindled white and gold female had the foulest breath I'd ever encountered in any species, predator or prey.

Whimpering, I turned my head to avoid the smell.

That was when she struck. Pinpricks of teeth digging into my throat froze me in place, and I choked back a cry. With a single bite, the wolf—Jake's *mother*—would finish tearing a hole in my neck. I closed my eyes, shuddering at the relentless pressure of fangs pressing into my skin.

"Or we can skip straight to emotionally scarring our puppy's mate for life." Jake's father sighed. "May as well get it over with, I guess."

Rolling off me, Jake's father made room for the wolf, who pinned me down by flopping across my chest, all without releasing my throat. Jake's father kept my hands trapped in his.

Once she was satisfied I couldn't escape, the wolf tortured me with long, wet strokes of her tongue while Jake's father watched and laughed.

SOMETIME AFTER I was soaked to the skin in wolf slobber, I gave up hope of escaping.

That was when Jake's father released my hands. He turned his attention to my shoulders, which had stiffened from my hands being pinned over my head for so long. I whimpered as he dug his fingers into the stiff muscles so I could move my arms without screaming.

Jake's mother remained sprawled over me, her cold, wet nose pressed to my throat. The urge to run and scream fluttered through me, but I swallowed it back.

Laughing, Jake's father flicked a finger against the side of my neck. While he didn't hit me hard, a zap of electricity arced down my spine and curled my toes in my shoes. "If you run screaming from Jake when he comes calling as a wolf, you'll damage his fragile pride and ego."

I stared up at my partner's father in disbelief. "Are we talking the same Jake? Over six foot tall, all nice lean muscle? Does he have a fragile *anything*?"

I should have been more alarmed by the man's claim my partner was coming as a *wolf*. The pain in my shoulder was enough to convince me I was trapped in a horrible reality filled with people who became wolves. I should have been more skeptical. I should have questioned.

It was hard to question when I remembered why my ma had beaten the sin out of me. When I had been a child, I had run with foxes, I had dreamed of them, and I had dreamed of being one of them.

"I'm not sure I want to continue discussing my son's assets."

"Then don't you insult his ego and pride."

"I'm merely providing sufficient warning so you don't panic when you have to deal with two wolves instead of one."

I swallowed. "I won't scream."

"No, you'll just whimper, shake, and cringe, which is even worse than screaming."

I hiccuped. "I'm not a coward."

"No, you just recognize a bigger predator. Perfectly reasonable. Have you figured out we're not going to eat you, yet? If you promise you won't run, Pauline'll let you up and you can approach Jake on your own terms. No whimpering, no screaming, and please, no running. It's tiring chasing you down. You're quick."

Only an idiot agreed to sticking around to give more predators a chance to get closer. "Just make her stop licking me. I'll do anything. Just make the licking stop." My voice trembled, and another hiccup slipped out of me.

"All right. Let the poor girl up, Pauline. I think you've licked her into submission."

With a heavy sigh, the wolf got off me. I rolled and scrambled for safety, putting Jake's father between me and the oversized predator. "She was taste testing me for a future meal, wasn't she? Memorizing my taste to figure out how to best eat me."

"You realize I can become a wolf, too, right?"

"This is a nightmare. I'm really in a coma, aren't I? No, wait. I died, and this is my hell. My hell is marrying into a family of wolves. Wolves who like licking me." I drew in a deep breath and let it out in a sigh. "I knew it. Where did I go wrong in my life to deserve this?"

"This explains so much. Jake told me we should ease you into this. He said you wouldn't take it well. I had no idea, however, you would come up with such interesting ways to deny reality."

"Reality doesn't have people who can become wolves, Mr. Thomas." I pointed at my shoulder. "It is far more feasible for me to be a ghost in denial than it is for my partner's mother and father to become wolves."

"Your partner does, too." Jake's father pointed at nearby shadows. "Look at those sad eyes, Karma. How could you think those sad eyes belong in a nightmare? You're going to break my poor puppy's fragile heart."

The chocolate-colored wolf with gold chest and under-belly sat primly beside a tree, his gold-tipped tail thumping against the ground. Both of his gold-tipped ears were perked forward, and he watched me with big, brown eyes.

I was so, so weak against those eyes.

"That's cheating," I whispered.

"I *am* a wolf, Karma. I'll do anything to secure my victory."

What had *I* done to deserve my partner being able to transform into a wolf? Why couldn't I have dreamed of wolves instead of foxes?

Why did I want to be a wolf instead of a fox? Why couldn't I just be a fox?

If I were a real fox, I'd have already been eaten by the wolves. Instead, they were having fun torturing me. I sighed my surrender. "Well, if I'm going to get eaten by a wolf, at least Jake's pretty. That's something, right? If I'm going to get eaten by a wolf, at least he's a pretty one."

"I'm not sure whether I'm supposed to be offended or not."

"If I offend you, will you go away and never bother me again?"

"I'm afraid not. Not only are you wonderfully entertaining, but you're Mrs. James Thomas. That makes you family. Pack. Let me give you your first lesson about pack life: wolves don't abandon anyone in their pack, even stray vixens. So, you may as well get used to it. You're going to have a lot of wolf noses poking around in your business soon enough."

Chapter Thirty-Nine

IT TOOK me a long time to work up the courage to approach Jake, who remained seated with his ears pricked forward, his rich brown eyes watching my every move. Crawling at a snail's pace of an inch at a time, I kept one eye on him and the other on his mother, who watched me with the same interest.

I would never admit it aloud, but I was grateful Jake's father had decided to shut his mouth and keep it shut. What sort of idiot approached a wolf capable of eating them in a couple of bites?

When I got within arm's reach of Jake, I drew a deep breath, held it, and stretched my arm so I could press my finger to his nose. His eyes crossed as he tried to look at my finger.

I didn't lose my hand to his teeth. I froze, wondering what to do next. Would he bite me if I touched his ears? Did wolves even like being touched?

Jake shoved his head against my hand, leaning forward

until his breath warmed my throat. Losing my balance, I sat back hard, sucking in a breath. A moment later, he rubbed his entire head against my chest, shoulders, and neck, his long fur tickling my nose until I sneezed. I ended up with a mouthful of coarse fur.

He shoved me down with a paw and pinned me. For a long moment, he stared at me with his beautiful eyes, his ears pricked forward while he snuffled, a sound I recognized as him breathing in my scent.

At least he didn't lick me. I didn't have a chance to wiggle out from beneath him before he flopped over my chest, rested his muzzle against my shoulder, and sighed as though using me as a bed made him the happiest of wolves.

Damned wolves. Damned Jake. Damned Jake for being a wolf. How was it even possible? Men couldn't become wolves.

I really wanted to believe everything was a really bad dream, one filled with fox-eating wolves. In my psychosis, I had married one on a whim and liked him too much to kill. Then again, when I had married him, I hadn't known he was a *wolf*, one who was masquerading as a human.

Wait, was he a wolf pretending to be a human or a human pretending to be a wolf?

I should have tried to run away. Instead, I struggled to make sense of the wolf using me as a pillow while nuzzling my neck like an oversized dog who hadn't yet learned the concept of personal space.

If I thought of Jake as a very, very large and friendly dog, I could handle his sharp teeth being so close to my throat. It helped he seemed more interested in rubbing his muzzle against me.

While his fur wasn't soft, there was something pleasant

about its coarse texture, and I liked the cinnamon of his scent. As long as he didn't bite me, I didn't mind him keeping me warm, and I could live with his weight pinning me to the ground.

"You all right, Karma?" Jake's father crouched just beyond arm's reach. "Lesson two about us: never come between a mated pair. Lesson three: never threaten a mated pair's puppy."

"You're starting to freak me out, Mr. Thomas."

"I'm just starting?" The man's eyebrows rose towards his hairline. "And don't think about calling us werewolves. We're Fenerec."

"Fenerec," I echoed.

"Honestly, I have no idea what you are. I've never met a woman who could become a fox before."

I shook my head, cracked my jaw against Jake's, and yelped. "No. No, no, no."

"No?"

"No."

"No what?"

"No, don't involve me with your craziness. I just dream about foxes sometimes. It doesn't mean anything." A shiver ran through me. The dreams weren't real. They couldn't be real. "I'm—"

"Karma."

I shut my mouth with a clack of my teeth. I recognized the no-nonsense tone of voice warning me against arguing without listening first.

"Maybe Dr. Sampson thinks it's wisest to let sleeping beasts lie, but I know better. We're cut from the same cloth. I'm a predator. Pauline's a predator. Jake's a predator. You're a predator, too. Unlike us, you're a predator who has no idea what you are, and your instincts are running wild. You don't growl like a wolf when you're posturing or warning someone you're willing to fight. Your aggression warning is more of a chitter. Like us, you bark when you're warning others of danger, but unlike us, you scream when you're calling for your mate or skulk, the fox version of a pack. When you sense another predator, you head straight up a tree."

Jake huffed before nuzzling my neck. He shifted his weight on me and rested his paws on my shoulders. I shouldn't have found his presence or the feeling of being trapped beneath his warm body comforting, but I did.

With Jake sprawled on top of me, there wasn't any room for other wolves.

Maybe no one would get close to me. The thought appealed. If no one came near me, they couldn't hurt me, and I was tired of hurting.

I was just tired.

"Maybe we're wolves while you're a fox, but my puppy chose you, and that makes you one of us. You'll have to get used to it. We'll be sticking our noses in your business for a long time. Jake hates it, and I'm sure you will, too. Now, little vixen, I'm *really* hungry. I want to hunt. Jake could use a hunt, too. Why don't you show us that pretty fur coat of yours? Bring out that black and white fox writhing under your skin. Learn to hunt like a wolf."

I sucked in a breath, my eyes widening. The dreams weren't supposed to be real.

Ma had beaten them out of me.

Why would anyone want them to be a reality? Why would anyone want someone who once forgot what it meant to be human, living as a fox while trapped in a fragile, human body?

The years had dimmed most of the memories, and my fear had suppressed the rest, but I remembered enough. Ma and Pops had feared me, then, and had hated the demon they had brought into their lives. It had been Ma who had made me forget, and Pops who had found an outlet for the wildness in sports and fighting.

I wanted it, but I remembered, and because I did, I was afraid. Hiding my face in the thick fur of Jake's neck, I grabbed hold of him and refused to let go.

Jake's father sighed. "You can't hide forever, Karma."

When I didn't move, breathing in Jake's scent while his fur tickled my nose, Jake's father sighed again. "It's a start, I suppose. Guard your mate while we hunt, pup."

I didn't need to see my partner to know he rebuked his father with his glare. Instead of the anger I expected, Jake's father laughed. Then, in utter silence, he left us alone in the darkening woods.

THERE WERE two other wolves in the woods, but whenever I caught a glimpse of them moving through the trees or smelled them drawing close, I worried. Jake drove them away with warning growls and barks. His snarls and the snaps of his teeth should have worried me far more than they did.

Maybe wolves ate foxes, but I didn't feel threatened by Jake despite his unnatural size. His mother and father were far larger wolves, but Jake easily outweighed any natural dog I had ever seen.

Without so many predators breathing down my neck, I relaxed enough I could think. While I still didn't understand how it was possible, pieces of the puzzle fell together. In Colorado, the search and rescue dog hadn't been a dog at all.

He had been a man who could become a wolf, and he had followed me when I had fled with Annabelle. He had, except for his size, looked like a wolf. Jake's coloration was nothing like a natural wolf's.

What I didn't understand was how—or why—a Fenerec had been hunting me on the mountain in Colorado. Worry shivered through me.

If there had been Fenerec in Colorado, had they been in Pennsylvania, too? I didn't want to think of the bodies I had found, but the one had been torn to pieces, and I couldn't help but think something other than the fall into the gorge had killed him.

A wolf Jake's size could easily tear someone to pieces. I had dreamed of being a fox often enough to understand the relationship of predator, prey, and predator who was also prey. People didn't handle being a prey species well. Some became predators of their own kind, requiring organizations like the police force and FBI to restore order and protect others.

Some ran away.

I was a mix of both, hunting predators while running away from the predators too big for me to chew on alone. Hunting predators on my own had caused me problems enough in the FBI, problems resulting in me becoming prey. I would always carry the scars, even the invisible ones.

I wasn't quite sure how I had ended up with Jake curled around me, but he sighed and rested his muzzle on my side, staring up at me. As a wolf, the brown of his eyes was flecked with gold, and the bright bursts of color only made him prettier.

He made a warm and comfortable pillow. The tension I hadn't known was plaguing me eased out of my muscles. I wasn't supposed to feel safe near a wolf.

What other secrets was Jake hiding? I wasn't sure what to make of anything, of him, and of his father's belief I could, by my own choice, decide to become a fox like they became wolves. My dreams of living as a fox were supposed to be dreams, not reality.

If I accepted my dreams as the truth, I would have to accept everything that had happened after being shot in London. In my search for vengeance, I had hunted the humans who had hunted me, and I had tasted their blood, torn them apart, and left their bodies to rot.

If my dreams were truth, I had killed. I hadn't just killed, I had deliberately hunted those who had tried to take Jake away from me.

In that, at least, I wasn't any different from a wolf.

I FELL asleep in the forest to wake up in bed with Jake, who was stretched out beside me, his arm draped across my stomach while his breath tickled my ear. I grumbled a complaint at the sun in my eyes, rolled over, and came nose to nose with Jake's father.

I smacked the smirk off the man's face before realizing I had moved, baring my teeth.

Spluttering something incoherent, Jake tugged me closer to him. I didn't resist him, although the urge to bite had me clacking my teeth together.

"You deserved that," Jake's mother announced from the end of the bed. "Maybe if you slap him harder, Karma, he'll learn."

Some invitations I simply couldn't refuse, and it took three more swats before Jake's father retreated out of reach.

"What are you doing?" Jake grumbled, shifted beside me, and tightened his hold on me. "Go away."

Pauline sat on the edge of the bed, and I contemplated kicking to drive her away. Unfortunately, even if I stretched, I doubted I'd reach her.

The woman smiled, reached out, and gave Jake's leg a slap. "We need to get to the airport. Your father's been called back to the States, and we're going with him. It's time for you to get up and get dressed."

"I thought you were his boss," Jake complained, making no move to get out of bed. If anything, he held me tighter, making it clear he liked me exactly where he had me.

I didn't mind. The man radiated warmth, and I snuggled closer, moving enough to grab the blanket and pull it over my head.

"I am, and it's wonderful," Jake's mother replied.

"So why'd you call him back to the States?"

"The pack's whining."

Jake growled, his body going tense. "Let them whine over there."

Pauline chuckled. "We're going, so don't bother trying to fight it. Just admit you're worried they'll make moves on your mate."

"They'll try."

"Jake, you're an idiot," his father said, grabbing hold of our blanket and yanking it off us. "They're just eager to see you and make certain you're okay. They're also excited to meet your mate since you've been driving them away ever since the day you partnered with her. Now, get up. We're going home, and we're going home now."

Considering there wasn't a stitch of clothes between us, I thought my shriek was justified. Jake, however, had different thoughts on the matter, and he clapped his hand over my mouth to muffle me. "Fine, we're getting up, we're getting up."

"Good. There's coffee in the car, so get in gear."

Jake's parents left, and I snapped my teeth in my effort to free myself. Jake growled at me, soft and sensual, trapping me against him with his arm over my stomach and his hand covering my lips while he pressed his mouth to the side of my neck.

Maybe I was dense, but I didn't need a map to know exactly where we were headed, and I had no intention of resisting him—much.

The door of our room cracked open. "That's not getting ready to leave for the airport," Jake's father chided. "Move it, you two. We don't have all morning. Maybe if you hadn't tried to purchase half of London, thus giving us far too much luggage to pack, you'd have more time for recreation. We're leaving!"

Jake grabbed my pillow from under my head, sat up, and flung it at the door with a wordless snarl. It thumped against the wall and fell to the floor.

"You missed."

"I hate you, Dad," Jake growled.

"Hate me all you want, just get your scrawny ass out of bed before we miss our flight."

THE DRESS SLACKS, clean white blouse, and jacket warned me of trouble. Jake ended up in a suit, too, which didn't comfort me in the slightest.

After a fifteen hour flight, the last thing I wanted was to deal with anything official. If my other clothes hadn't been spirited away by Jake's parents, I would have changed.

"Get used to it," Jake advised me. I turned my nastiest silent glare on him. The second-to-last thing I wanted was to lower myself to accepting bullying from my unwanted in-laws—or have them pick my clothes for me.

As though sensing he was on thin ice, my partner lifted his hand in surrender. "I'm just saying they're obnoxious, stubborn, and too clever for their own good. I've been trying to thwart them since I was a kid. No success yet."

"They could have given us ten minutes," I complained, stomping around the room to do the last check. All things considered, I was a lot less sore than I had any right to be after the previous day. "Ten minutes."

"Do you really think ten minutes would be long enough?"

I glared at Jake, who leered at me before a sly smile curved his mouth. When I didn't reply, he laughed. I flipped him my middle finger and stalked my way out of the room to discover his mother waiting.

"He's right, you know. Ten minutes is not long enough."

Why had someone decided killing in-laws wasn't legal? I glared at her, too, and like her son, she laughed.

"You really need coffee. It's in the car. It might still be warm."

The car was an SUV, and Agent Miller leaned against the vehicle, waving at me as I approached. "Good morning. Looking forward to going home?"

"Coffee. I need coffee."

Agent Will Dillan poked his head out the driver's window. A moment later, he held out a Thermos. "An offering."

I grabbed it, opened the top, and breathed in deep.

"I hope you have three or four more of those," Jake teased, coming up behind me to massage my shoulders. "How're you feeling?"

"Like I haven't had coffee yet."

"If we take the middle seats, neither asshole can sit with us," Jake commented, opening the SUV's back door.

"Sold." I climbed in, set the Thermos between my feet long enough to buckle up, and began my long-neglected morning ritual of getting coffee into me as fast as I could without doing lasting damage to myself.

Why did people have to put too-hot coffee in the Thermos? What was the point of having coffee too scalding to drink? With the choice of no coffee or dealing with a burned mouth, I opted for the pain.

"I thought you two were supposed to protect me," I complained.

"Are you in trouble?" Agent Miller asked, sliding into the front passenger seat beside his partner.

"It's too early to go anywhere, especially an airport. I'm going to have to give you a failing grade."

He laughed hard enough I kneed the back of his seat. "I need my beauty sleep."

"You're plenty beautiful," my partner said, grinning at me.

"Not without enough sleep I'm not. I probably have raccoon eyes."

"Not once have I seen you with black rings around your eyes, which is a good thing, because you'd look like a domestic violence victim with your porcelain skin."

Jake either had a death wish or no fear, and I was sorely tempted to dump my coffee over his head. "You're being an asshole."

"Stop taunting your wife," Jake's father ordered, sliding by his son to get into the back seat. "I'd like to make it to the airport without having to explain to the British authorities why my son was brutally murdered."

"Unlike you, Mr. Thomas, I require him for certain activities," I reminded Jake's father. I jammed my knee against the back of Miller's seat. "You'll help me hide the body, right?"

"My job is to serve and protect you," he agreed. "No one told me I had to protect anyone other than you and your partner. I suppose helping you hide the evidence of murder fits my current job description."

"She's mean, son," Mr. Thomas, Deputy Chief of Staff of CARD, complained.

"Sorry, Dad. I like her just as she is. You're going to have to live with it. Now, why are we going back to the States? I thought we'd have more time here."

"Someone sold us out, and we've been tasked with finding them and dealing with them. Specifically, former Agent Johnson, now Agent Thomas, has been tasked with locating and eliminating them."

Jake straightened and twisted around to stare at his father, his expression turning frigid in its neutrality. "Explain."

"Someone in the system used Karma's phone to track her movements. The London shooting was an inside job. We're to hunt them down, and we're to make them disappear —permanently."

My eyes widened, and the memory of my kidnapper's single question slammed into me, and my breath left my lungs in a rush. "They asked me who had tipped me off—who had warned me Annabelle would be kidnapped."

Jake jerked in my direction. "Do you remember anything else?"

"I wanted to kill them for hurting you."

Will leaned between the front seats, stared me in the eyes, and said, "You did, and don't you doubt it for a second. Each and every one of those bastards deserved it, too. My only regret is the fact I didn't get to help."

Jake's mother crawled over her son to join his father in the back. "You'll have your chance. We have our orders, and we have been authorized to use lethal force using any means necessary. When we arrive in the States, we are scheduled for our briefing."

Sucking in a breath, Jake gaped at his mother. "*Our* briefing?"

Things weren't adding up, and I couldn't help but ask, "Aren't you supposed to be in Human Resources?"

"I'm a lot of things, Karma. Officially, I'm upper management in the FBI's Human Resources department. However, someone has to teach you the ropes. I was selected for the privilege. Of course, I may have threatened to start ripping off arms if I didn't have my way, but that's another matter entirely."

Someone else knew exactly what Jake's mother was, and I wondered who else knew I wasn't the well-adjusted, perfect princess my adoptive parents had worked so hard to raise.

Pauline drew a deep breath, held it, and let it out in a slow sigh. "They tried to kill you. They tried to kill my son, too. They'll try again. This time, however, we'll be ready for them. We have a license to kill, and we're going to put it to good use. We're to track down those responsible for the

Greenwich case, those involved in the Henry case, and those behind the London shooting, and we're to rid the Earth of them." Jake's mother smiled, and it was the most frightening expression I had ever seen on someone's face in my life.

I had no idea what was waiting for us in the United States, but I was certain of one thing: Jake's mother was a woman on a mission, and I had the feeling I was about to find out just how far a Fenerec would go to protect her puppy and pack.

License to Kill, the second book in the Balancing the Scales trilogy, is now available at all major retailers.

Looking for more in the Witch & Wolf World? The WATER WITCH Anthology offers a collection of short stories and novellas. If you prefer standalone novels, you may enjoy BENEATH A BLOOD MOON or SHADOWED FLAME.

Happy Reading!

Note: The series was initially planned to be a duet, but it was extended into a trilogy due to the author's inability to finish everything intended in the second book.

Afterword

I am often asked about how the Witch & Wolf world relates to our own. In many ways, the Earth from the Witch & Wolf novels is very much like our own. However, it is not Earth, not exactly.

While some of the events in the Witch & Wolf world overlap with our version of Earth, they are not the same. While certain events still happened, rather like fixed points in time from a certain time-traveling series, the specifics are often altered. The years and exact dates may not be the same. Some technologies have developed later—or sooner—than in our Earth.

Motivations and the execution of certain events, including terrorist attacks, have been changed. The inclusion of the supernatural would alter a great many things, including how wars are waged.

As such, there are discrepancies between the Witch & Wolf world and our Earth. No matter how hard the supernatural community tries to hide their presence, they have the power to change the world—and they do.

As always, all errors are my own, but some of those errors with history aren't actually errors at all—they are deliberate alterations to Earth's history to better fit with the inclusion of witches, werewolves, and the other supernatural.

Thanks for reading!

About R.J. Blain

Want to hear from the author when a new book releases? You can sign up at her website (thesneakykittycritic.com). Please note this newsletter is operated by the Furred & Frond Management. Expect to be sassed by a cat. (With guest features of other animals, including dogs.)

A complete list of books written by RJ and her various pen names is available at https://books2read.com/rl/The-Fantasy-Worlds-of-RJ-Blain.

RJ BLAIN suffers from a Moleskine journal obsession, a pen fixation, and a terrible tendency to pun without warning.

When she isn't playing pretend, she likes to think she's a cartographer and a sumi-e painter.

In her spare time, she daydreams about being a spy. Should that fail, her contingency plan involves tying her best of enemies to spinning wheels and quoting James Bond villains until she is satisfied.

RJ also writes as Susan Copperfield and Bernadette Franklin.

Visit RJ and her pets (the Management) at thesneakykittycrit
ic.com.

⁂

FOLLOW RJ & HER ALTER EGOS ON BOOKBUB:
RJ BLAIN
SUSAN COPPERFIELD
BERNADETTE FRANKLIN

Made in United States
Troutdale, OR
12/01/2023

15203718R00300